SINS

OF THE

FATHER

JASON MCDONALD

jason-mcdonald.com
Follow on X: JasonMcD_Writer

Good Twin Publishing
333 University Avenue
Suite 200
Sacramento, CA 95825

Good Twin Publishing and the Good Twin Publishing logo are registered trademarks of Good Twin Publishing LLC.

goodtwinpublishing.com
Follow on X: goodtwinpub

Paperback ISBN: 978-1-7378299-3-5
Hardcover ISBN: 978-1-7378299-4-2
eBook ISBN: 978-1-7378299-5-9

First edition November, 2025

Library of Congress Control Number: 2025933572

DEDICATION

For my loving and supportive wife and children, who keep the sparkle in my eyes flickering as they encourage my pursuits. Thank you from the bottom of my heart. I love you all.

ACKNOWLEDGMENTS

To write and publish a first novel and watch it find an audience around the globe and positive support is a miracle. To actually write a second book? A whole finger tapping exercise in self-critique and forever questioning whether it can live up to the hype and find its own success. Without support, it's a mountain to climb and potentially never reach the summit. With a cheering section?

You can conquer the world.

Sins of the Father is the sequel to my debut novel, *Pandemic-19*. Well over a year late to print, it was a labor of love to complete. I am a perfectionist when it comes to my writing, a good and bad trait for any writer. Countless drafts, tweaks, and letting it sit to come back with fresh eyes to ensure the story compliments the first book and continues the plot in a genuine and thoughtful way. There comes a time to let go, and let readers have a *sitting on the edge of your seat* ride with an original thriller.

Many thanks to those who inspired characters in this book. While the list is endless and many of my antagonists and protagonists are conglomerates of multiple people, a few are close to my heart. Different people sparked a thought and became the basis for individuals in this book. My dear friends, your decades of friendship warm my heart.

Without my magnificent wife, who is the glue to our family and just as strong a fighter as Julia, your support of this endeavor is priceless. My own wonder twins, who shine bright in my eyes and this world to show everyone what family is all about, whether you have a disability or not, inspire me every day. Down Syndrome does not define a person. It brightens the planet. Thank you all for being part of me.

Last, my wonderful editors. You keep my writing grounded and true. Without the honest feedback, positive and negative, I could never do this author stuff.

I hope you enjoy this novel. It was so much fun writing it.

Jason McDonald

SINS
OF THE
FATHER

CHAPTER 1

"Mommy? I can't feel Daddy anymore."

Julia sunk back in the seat of the airship, Emma's words cutting deep and setting a torrent of fire that caused tears to erupt. The last radio transmission, more than three hours ago, had painted a bleak canvas of Ryan Carmichael's health.

Can't seem to stop the bleeding. Just need a minute to rest. Get some sleep.

Going unconscious and no way to stanch the flow of blood that was drooling out of Ryan's wound, Julia saw the writing spray painted on the wall. She hoped, hell, she'd even tried to pray to whatever crap gods that were, in the off-chance they remotely valued life, they'd get off their royal asses and actually *do* something to save her husband's life. Ryan had just averted a disaster of biblical proportions in saving Emma and David along with every living soul from monsters that wanted to remake the planet. Delusional in their goal of using the kids to subjugate the world to their will with a forever vaccine, Ryan saved the last remnants of people, if only for a short period of time.

Not that he was against a vaccine.

He had taken his like a good little soldier countless times in service to country and civilian life, even for the last virus. Using Emma and David as tools to keep it going instead of finding a real cure for the whack jobs and Un-dead lurking in the shadows, that was a no-go he could not let happen. Subjugation to remain *normal* a few months versus what was right in getting a sure remedy to fend off the problem once and for all, people had decisions to make.

Stand and fight, let real scientists if any were left work a cure, or bow down and take it.

Freedom and choice still had a place against dictatorial tyranny.

With Ryan fading and looking to be permanently out of the game, it was up to Julia to keep her kids alive and secured away and not wind-up Guinea pigs. All the false gods had to do was act, fulfill all of the beliefs placed in their laps, and ensure Ryan didn't die. Show to everyone that blind allegiance and faith in higher powers wasn't a lie, a con to reap worship, and put their supposed love for all humankind before godlike indifference and thirst for blind obedience and misdirected loyalty.

Not too much to ask in sparing Ryan, the real savior of humanity.

David, sitting silently, head bowed, cried. A quiet act, meant to mask his own pain. As the man of the house title suddenly hanging over his head again if his dad died, as Ryan always pretended was a duty passed from father to son as the protector of the Carmichael name and family as oldest son, being the oldest son, David found a sliver of comfort. His father had taught him everything he knew, passed on lessons of life and when compassion was the weapon over continued violence. Even in Ryan's moments of super dad being a bad ass mother, like the time when the hick boys bullied Emma at the pizza place, Ryan showed that forgiveness meant something still. He whooped asses to the bone, and then bought the good ol' boys' beers when they apologized to Emma. That small gesture showed Ryan valued peace over hate.

Most people wouldn't have done that.

That example stuck with David, his father being just a man like every other dad. Fallible, human, principled to his beliefs, and doing anything and everything in his power for right and wrong. Perfection was a myth, and even though his dad tried to be the best and exhibit a model for David to emulate, the boy knew that you just did your best. Nothing was always the right answer. On occasion, a show of force was the choice, even if it cracked the façade of the person you worshipped. Not in a bad way, but shedding light on the mystery under the shell. Dad was his hero, faults and all. He hated to fight, but would do whatever to protect his babies.

Family and their small unit came first.

Emma stared out the large window of the airship, watching the clouds below as the craft kept above the fluffy layer to keep out of sight. She stood still, not a tear, not a sound, simply focused on the burgeoning blue of the morning light. She felt cold, weak, with the pit of her stomach sour. Any minute a froth of puke at the ready to hurl past her lips. She kept it at bay, curtailed the urge, and pushed her emotions away.

Think of Dad. Focus and help him get through this.

It was a tall order for an eight-year-old to do all by herself. Even if she could manage to miraculously have super powers to assist her father from afar, there was no way it would work. She *was* just a kid. Emma knew better, that even being just eight, she was older than her biological age. At least, she *felt* that way. Three years post-collapse of the world can cause you to grow up in a hurry, whether you want it to or are prepared for it to happen. Emma wasn't sure which was the right answer. All she knew, was she had to do something if she could manage it. As she was lost in her head, she heard a shoe scuff the floor behind, and turned to see.

"We've got to keep going," a voice interrupted from the doorway.

Julia pivoted, shook her head, and felt the anger rise. "No! We stick to the plan until we have proof."

"The mission was to get to the rendezvous point and wait. No radio transmissions since the last one, and that was weak at best he's alive. We can't compromise this airship and the people onboard on a hunch. You heard him. Bleeding out bad and losing consciousness. My orders from him were to keep you all safe at any cost. That's what I'm going to do," Marcus sighed.

Marcus' face, grim with sadness, showed a level of warmth she didn't expect. Julia knew he was right. As the one in charge of the expedition, and as she had learned was the former executive officer of an old navy aircraft carrier captain named John who was the leader of a ragtag group of survivors, the odds of her soldier boy living with the wound he described, slim to zero at best.

Glancing over, Julia frowned. "Your agreement or not, we stick to the plan and go there. Changing objectives, not an option."

"I won't jeopardize it. I'm sorry."

She huffed. "It's only been a few hours. Anything could be going on. He's stuck laying low so he has to be quiet. He's stopped bleeding and fixed himself up, and is resting to get his strength. It could be as simple as that. What's being around a little longer going to hurt?"

Marcus stared back, trying to show compassion at the situation, while exerting the authority he knew he had to press in order to keep everyone safe, and *alive*. "Julia, I get it. Really, I do. But, the mess left behind has stirred a hornet's nest of trouble we are in no position to fight. If we're found floating around up here and they happen to have a gunship or some ancient biplane with a gun on the front of it, we are goners. This beast isn't built to ward off bullets. We get hit, and it is game over for us. We start the death spiral as the air escapes and no telling if we manage to land, let alone survive. We have to get as far away as we can. I can't allow the risk."

Julia nodded. "I'd hoped you wouldn't say that. There are things you don't know or understand, but we *will* arrive on time and wait. There's more at stake than you could possibly know." With the last word, she pulled out the pistol Ryan had given her, and took command of the cockpit. *Her* mission remained the same.

Time to fulfill it.

CHAPTER 2

"How much is he worth?"

A low voice, its tone gravely and harsh, answered. "Enough to feed us for a year. Maybe longer if we negotiate it right."

Hesitation, he could hear it in the response, the first person replied seconds later. "Are you sure? You *know* what they'll do to him."

"Does it look like I care?"

"You should."

Anger this time. "I don't give a rat's ass. I never got *the shot* and am fine. They don't mess with me. We keep our distance and do our thing. That's all."

"You should have gotten the shot. Maybe you wouldn't be as mean as you are if you had."

Defiance? The voice hinted at it, though it could have been meant as a joke.

"Lambs like you and your mom got the shot. Did what you were told and huddled together hoping things would be fine. Lions like me? No one tells us what to do. We're warriors. Patriots that don't take crap from anyone."

"If you say so. But, you know that lions get hunted and killed, right?"

Ryan Carmichael caught the tail end of a conversation as he started to regain consciousness, his senses slowly providing coherence. A headache brewing in the frontal lobe felt like a sledgehammer was used to smack him silly. The pain in his shoulder hurt like a son of a bitch. He'd never get over how bad a gunshot wound felt. The nerves were on fire, but at the moment, none of his extremities moved. Feigning like he was still out of it, he listened, hoping he might get more information while his body regained itself.

If, it actually could.

One voice faced him. The older one by the slightly muffled sound, had his back to Ryan.

"He's not our problem. *You're* mine. Look at all of this stuff. He has to have done something really bad to have that kind of bounty on his head."

Ryan could tell the first voice, the one who was on the fence, was young. Sounded like a teenager. Girl, maybe sixteen if he opened his eyes to peek and verify. Seems someone thought they had the motherlode in their grasp.

Too bad they were wrong.

"We don't even know if it *is* him. You know the kind of things they do to survivors. He has to be one. Probably one of the resistance fighters we hear about. We can't just hand him over."

The older voice, now coming into focus, a man who sounded like he was mid-forty, spat a reply. "I don't care. I'm left taking care of you. We do what we have to do to survive. Thinking of others left us a long time ago."

"I can't. I won't. He's still a person. I remember the times before. We can't just stop being people."

The teen had humanity still, Ryan could tell.

The older man must have grabbed her hard by the sound of it. "Listen, you piece of garbage. I promised your mom I'd take care of you. But don't get it in your head that I won't sell you to those crazies for a toy if you go against me."

"Uncle Jim, don't. Please," the girl cried out.

"He's dead meat anyway. A bullet wound like that and he's a goner."

The girl seemed unsure. "He's still breathing, and not the *close to death* kind of breathing we've seen before. If we could get him out and lie him flat, we could tell. We have to try, don't we?"

The deep guttural laughter from Uncle Jim said otherwise.

"I'd listen to the girl," Ryan whispered, his eyes still closed. "She's more human that you."

Uncle Jim must have thought the girl said something as he soon punched her hard in the arm. "Don't ever disrespect me, Melissa!"

Melissa yelled out in pain. "I didn't say anything, honest."

"Leave the girl alone or I'll snip off your balls."

Uncle Jim put it together and turned. "Fuck you, Dead Meat."

Ryan opened his eyes. He was still inside the Humvee, the driver's side door three-quarters opened. The man called Uncle Jim, looking like a grizzled woodsman with gray strands streaking his brown beard and long hair tucked under a black and orange baseball hat, stood next to the door, an old hunting rifle aimed at Ryan.

Remington pump action .270 caliber for hunting deer. A classic.

The girl, sixteen on the dot and cute under all the dirt and grime, was terrified. He could tell by the expression on her face. A shower and change of clothes for the poor kid was long overdue. Ryan knew the comment about being sold scared her, and he knew she should be petrified. Young and able, she'd make someone a prize for whatever they wanted to do to her.

Ryan's smile hit a nerve.

"What the hell you smiling at? I'm the one with the gun," Uncle Jim barked.

Ryan took a deep breath. Held it in, and then exhaled. No coughing fit, so his lung was still inflated which meant the bullet missed.

A good sign.

Not getting a response, Uncle Jim tapped the driver's side window with the barrel. "I asked you a question, Boy."

Green eyes glared from behind Ryan's pain. "Did I studder? I believe I said leave the girl alone or I will snip off your balls and ram them down your throat."

Uncle Jim wasn't used to disrespect. "Tough words for a guy who has a gun on him and a bullet hole the size of Texas in his shoulder by the looks of all that blood," he spat back.

Ryan winked to Melissa. "Not the first time."

The young girl managed a shy smile. Humor was vacant being with her uncle.

"I'd say sorry if I cared. You gonna feed us for a long time. Dead or alive, don't matter," Uncle Jim grinned as he raised the rifle and began to bring the barrel down to point it at the side of Ryan's head.

Pffft. Pffft. Pffft.

Uncle Jim grimaced, the rifle barrel slowly coming down. Grabbing his stomach, he touched it, pulled his hand away to see the burgeoning blood, and fell backward to the ground. The rock his head swiped on the way to the dirt knocked him out cold, undeserved peace on his journey to Hell.

Ryan wasn't sure if he saw relief or a twinge of sadness in Melissa's eyes when she saw his pistol emerge from his right side and realized what was going to happen. She simply stepped out of the way and waited before her uncle fell. He reached out to her, hoping she would react. A swift kick of her well-worn combat boot to his head was her silent reply.

A raspy breath, blood spurted from the mouth, then Uncle Jim was gone.

"Not sure if I should say thank you or not. Even with as bad as he was, he kept me alive at least," Melissa shrugged.

Ryan coughed, and it hurt like hell. He had momentarily thought about not killing the bastard, make a bargain for Ryan's own life and safe passage to get on his way, until Uncle Jim went there with the selling the girl part.

There was no way in hell that was going to come as long as Ryan had breath to fight and his human side still intact.

He hoped that managed to stay around a bit.

Feeling a new wind catch his sails, which had to be adrenaline pumping profusely through his bloodstream from just having killed a degenerate and saving a young girl's life, Ryan smiled. Not a simple, sort of grin, but a face widening with rampant joy kind that let everyone know he was happy and alive.

"Mister, you're getting color back in your face."

Good news for him.

Grinning, but keeping the pistol ready in case his take on the girl was wrong, Ryan looked over his shoulder. "I've got enough food and weapons in here to keep you going for two years, or, you can come with me for a chance to live as normal as that is and with people who will protect you."

Melissa wasn't sure if she could believe it. "Real people? Like in a community?"

Ryan nodded. "Survivors like you and me. Fighting the good fight to bring us back from the brink of all of this crap. What do you say?"

She managed to get real color in her cheeks to show beneath the dirt. "I'd love that."

Ryan smiled. "Great. I better not die then. How are you with needle and thread?"

CHAPTER 3

"Take another step and I'll blow you to hell."

He couldn't help but chuckle.

"Something funny, Asshole?" The man emerged from the shadows and pumped a shell into the chamber, the shotgun ready to send lead slugs the intruder's way.

He felt the barrel slam into the small of his back. Hard. Pushed forward and then retreated, only to find its way back and jab him three or four more times. It hurt a bit, but at the same time it was about to get crazy and he enjoyed the moment while it lasted.

"That anyway to treat your best friend?" Ryan Carmichael shrugged, lowered his bandana, and turned to the right. Grinning from ear to ear he said, "Got any real coffee? I'm parched."

The shotgun lowered. The figure on the trigger end stepped back and placed the gun against the wall and smiled. "Ah damn, Man. It's good to see a real human face. Missed you, Buddy."

Ryan walked over and wrapped his arms around the larger-than-life mountain of a man. "Missed you too, Honcho."

Honcho Gutierrez picked Ryan up in a huge bear hug and squeezed. Ryan coughed as the air constricted in his lungs and he felt a twinge of pain from his shoulder wound. It felt great having that feeling again, the comfort of a dear friend. It had been too long and he could only imagine what the last years had been like for one of his oldest and dearest confidantes.

Placing Ryan down on the ground, tears formed at the corner of Honcho's eyes. "I never thought I'd see you again. But, then out of anyone who could survive this shithole existence, it would be a cockroach like you."

Ryan tried to contain a laugh at the statement, but couldn't hold it in. He let it out and it felt good. It had been a pretty shitty existence the last three years and he was lucky to still be alive given the crap he had been through in just the last month alone. He had found the rainbow and pot of gold at the end when Julia and the kids came back into his life. He just had to make sure the momentum kept sending luck his way.

"*You're* still alive," Ryan offered in return as a statement of fact.

Honcho gave him a sideways look, his right eyebrow raised. "Me? I'm out here in the middle of the damn Olympic National Forest. I wasn't right in the middle of everything when the planet went down the toilet."

Ryan nodded. The remote cabin was Honcho's second home away from Seattle, his piece of tranquility. When society started the downward trajectory with no point of return, Honcho packed up and left. More like a rustic shack from the outside looks, it was what lay beneath that would keep him alive for eternity. Built over the top of a decommissioned missile silo, one of the Cold War's most secret of secret facilities, below it was a bunker within a bunker. The two friends had spent years getting it back into shape, more for a fun place to spend time in the middle of nowhere than to house Honcho's side business dealing in secrets and information that were supposed to remain locked away.

"Got the scars to prove it."

"Prove what?" Honcho asked, lost on what his friend meant.

"My scars from being in Hell. Been a rough couple of years."

As the shock started to wear off seeing Ryan, Honcho's eyes got wide. "Wait. If you're here, what about Julia and the kiddos?"

Ryan sighed, hung his head low. Waited a minute to answer. "Emma turned into one of *Them* and ate David. It was horrible. The blood, guts strewn all over. It still haunts me."

"Ah shit, man," Honcho started, before something hard pressed into his back.

"Don't move."

Honcho raised his arms up and stood motionless. "I'm toast, aren't I?"

Ryan nodded. "Burnt to a crisp. We're taking everything."

Feeling he had nothing to lose, Honcho turned quickly and faced his enemy. "Can't take me out like this," he yelled and in one motion grabbed his adversary and pulling him close, took a knee. Staring into the eyes of his attacker, he said, "How are you doing, Little Buddy?"

David frowned. "Dad! He got me!"

"You let you guard down, Son."

"Not so fast," another voice rang out.

Honcho looked around and saw nothing. Letting David go, Honcho started to reach for the shotgun. Listening, he focused and heard another sound off in the woods. An inch away from having his gun in hand, the voice erupted from behind.

"Got you!" Emma howled, poking Honcho in the back with her finger.

Ryan's little ninjas made him proud.

Looking over his shoulder, his right eyebrow raised inquisitively, Honcho stared at Emma. "Who are you?"

"Uncle Hon," Emma pouted, thinking he didn't remember her. "Emma," she pointed at herself.

Smiling and turning to her, Honcho reached out and gave Emma a huge hug. "Hello, Beautiful. I knew it was you."

Ryan walked over and grabbed the shotgun to secure it. Eight-year-olds and unsecured guns didn't go well together.

Still bent down, Honcho glanced at Ryan. Three, instead of four. "I didn't expect you and then get surprised by the munchkin posse. Do I need to ask?" The concern in his voice was heartwarming during the end of the world.

Ryan recognized the look. "Julia's here, just watching the vehicle and our supplies. OK to drive on up and get it below and out of sight?"

Honcho nodded. "Sure. Of course. I'll get the door."

Being in the middle of nowhere in the forest was a refreshing break from reality. The quiet of the trees as wind blew the leaves and made a rhythmic sound soothed hardened souls. The smell of pine and nature all in one, wafting the nostrils with an aroma free of death and decay felt invigorating and sad all at once. It had been years since any of them had felt this way and now being in the moment was bizarre, and familiar. With the Humvee secured below, Honcho invited everyone inside. Rustic on the outside was an understatement. Once past the door the grandeur within felt like home.

Within the confines of all four walls, you'd have no idea you weren't actually inside a hermit house from the outside appearance. Leather couches and a recliner, big screen TV affixed to one wall and a DVD collection you could find anything to watch, glass coffee table lined with magazines, and a menagerie of art worth millions pilfered from the Seattle Museum. A decent kitchen for any medium-sized party. Add double pane windows to open for a cool breeze and enjoy a sunrise or sunset. It was suited for topside visitors.

Not like he had anyone show since death came knocking over three years ago.

David and Emma swarmed the DVD collection and began to root through to find something to watch. Not having entertainment for three years and an endless supply of new things to watch called out to them.

Finding an animated movie they hadn't seen before, David asked if they could watch it. "Uncle Honcho? Um, does your TV work?"

"We're out in the middle of nowhere with no electrical lines," Honcho called out over his shoulder as he moved around the kitchen. "We have our own sneaky supply. Go ahead."

Walking over to the refrigerator Honcho pulled out three bottles. Grabbing a bottle opener, he popped the tops and handed them around.

Ryan looked at the label. "Made with *Honcho Hops*?"

A sly grin. "Of course! Grow some myself and the rest I snagged from some of the craft breweries around. Stockpiled enough supplies to make my own homebrew."

"Well, it is cold and tastes good," Julia smiled as she reached over to clink Honcho's bottle.

"Thank you, Julia. At least *someone* appreciates my hard work."

"What?" Ryan shrugged as he took a long sip. "It was just a comment. Not a critique. It's really good stuff. I haven't had a decent beer in years."

Pointing to the fridge Honcho said, "More when you're ready." And, catching himself in thought, added, "Hey? Kids need anything?"

Julia shook her head. "No, they're good. Had some juice boxes on the way here. Don't want to aggravate the wee bladders if we can help it."

The grown-ups sat enjoying their beers as the children, led by David's prowess with all things tech, curled up on the couch with Pete the gray cat snuggled between him and Emma as they watched the movie. It had been ages since the three adults had seen one another, simply sitting and having a drink. After each's bottle ran dry, Honcho grabbed three more and passed them out. The dark cloud hung in the room and no one wanted to burst it, but Honcho was Honcho, and had to ask.

"So, what brings you four wicked travelers up my way?"

Ryan took a long sip, let it sit on his tongue, and swallowed before he answered. "We missed you."

Julia nearly spit out her beer. "Ryan!"

Glancing at her sideways, Ryan leaned in. "Well, we *did* miss you. But, as you might imagine, the world is kind of a bleak place and my dad tried to kill me so…" He whispered the last part to avoid young prying ears.

Honcho *did* spit out his beer. "Reg did what? I figured he would be dead by now. Wait, sorry for saying that."

Ryan held up his hand. "No apologies necessary. He should have been dead and maggot food. Seems he made a deal with the devil and my family was part of the price."

Julia, realizing that there was a deeper conversation coming, decided to excuse herself and occupy the kids to keep their focus on the movie. They had been through hell and more the last month on the run. Hearing the details again and pieces the parents had kept from them wasn't something David or Emma needed to imagine. Having a chance to just be kids snuggled on a comfortable couch engrossed in a cartoon movie was the best therapy. Besides, it had been too long since she had a chance to relax with them both without fear or worry waiting around the corner.

Sensing they were about to get into some serious shit, Honcho reached over to a cabinet on his right and pulled out pure liquid gold. Setting the bottle on the table in front of Ryan, he let the image sear into his old friend's eyes. Picking it up, Ryan scrutinized the label, turning it over and over as he read the words. Shock was an understatement. Snatching it back, Honcho poured two fingers into some glasses. The dark amber color glistened inside and the prominent legs screamed a worthy drink.

"I can guess how you stumbled upon it, but how did you get *this*?" Ryan said as he held the glass in his hand and swirled the vintage Scotch, the legs creeping down the sides.

Honcho winked. "I know a guy who knew a guy."

Ryan took a sip and let the vintage booze sit on his tongue, the taste pure and smoky without a hint of harshness. Holding it there, he tilted his head back and opened his throat, feeling the liquid slide down. It was in the top three of best Scotch he ever had.

"Good stuff, huh?" Honcho nodded.

Ryan sighed. "That, my friend, is delicious."

"It better be, for fifty grand."

It was good Ryan was between sips or he would have spit it out. "Fifty thousand a bottle?"

Honcho shook his head. "Fifty thousand a pour my dear compadre."

Ryan let the statement sink in as he took another sip. Finishing his glass, he waved it at Honcho who gleefully poured another two fingers. This one he let sit, let the drink breathe a bit. "Thanks, Buddy. I needed this. But seriously, where the hell did you get this fine and delectable nectar of the gods?"

The eyebrow raised ever so slightly, as if in slow motion to taunt Ryan, before Honcho answered. "One of my 'clients' was a connoisseur of fine Scottish single malts. A collection that almost rivaled the one that Brazilian guy had and sold off and The Scotch Whisky Experience in Edinburgh lets you tour. Or, at least, did. Hey, wonder if it's still there?"

Ryan knew the place well. Had been there for a Scotch tasting tour with Julia for their honeymoon. Located on the Royal Mile just down the cobblestone road from Edinburgh Castle, the collection Honcho mentioned was priceless. Over three thousand bottles of single malt Scotch, a variety that ran the gamut with some uber rare bottles, the oldest being a Buchanan's dating back to 1897. Just thinking about it made his mouth water.

"And, you happened to get it *how*?"

The devil's grin screamed five finger discount. "Well, he didn't make the cut when the world died and his collection was just sitting there. Couldn't let it be all alone, afraid and scared, could I?"

"No, I guess not," Ryan chuckled.

"Took that and a few other 'things' he wasn't going to miss. Someone might as well drink up and enjoy watching the world slowly die." Honcho said it with such sincerity Ryan almost bought the bullshit, but knew better.

"Better you than nobody," Ryan winked.

Feeling there was no better time than the moment at hand, Honcho nervously tapped the table. "So, your dad. Um, what the hell happened Ry?"

Ryan took a slow sip, and decided to start at the beginning.

Getting shoved out of the helicopter by his former mentor and friend Mark Simpson. Believing Julia and the kids were dead. Wandering around and encountering the first group of Brainers and getting shot. Three years trying to survive amid the death and decay of humanity he encountered with the Un-dead, Lurkers, Bolts, and other Brainers. Coming across David and then the survivors. Seeing Mark alive and trying to get David back. Meeting John and hatching rescue plans. Finding Emma and Julia and finally getting them only to lose his whole family again. The airship adventure to California. And the finale with finding out his father was not only alive, but connected with the brain trust and billionaire boys club in Mike Goldberg, Elliot Mann, John Beezer, Bob Gains, and his old friend, Mark.

Honcho sat without a word as Ryan told his tale. Sipping his Scotch in small dabbles, Honcho's eyes blinked rapidly during certain portions and slowly for others. He nodded occasionally, shook his head a few times, and grimaced. If anyone other than Ryan sat across from him and laid out a story like the one he was hearing, Honcho would chalk it up to too much liquor. A fanciful elocution to entertain party guests.

He knew better.

The last part was the hardest to hear. A life on the run with the kids in tow. Evading and dodging pursuit. Close calls. And, living day to day not knowing if tomorrow would come.

"I've got to ask what it is like, the world out there? Complete ghost towns or what?"

Ryan took a sip. Thought how to answer, and just let the words fall. "No real life in the country. Un-dead scavengers is all. Cities seems to be where anyone, good or bad, have migrated to, but those are decimated. Ruins and rubble. If there are any survivors, and from what I know it's sporadic at best, they're trying to stay a step ahead of the real threats in the Others, Mark and my dad's people. It's like Hell came topside and a new boss is in town."

Honcho teared up. For someone of his size and girth, all six feet five and who knew how many pounds, you wouldn't expect someone as intimidating looking as he did to look like he was going to cry. He kept it in, though he had to wipe the corners of his eyes to keep the water at bay.

"Damn Ry, you guys are lucky to be alive. That is some heavy stuff you just laid on me, Man."

Ryan tilted his drink for another draw. "Try living it. Our lives were turned upside down and it's not even over. They're looking for us and won't stop until they succeed or I stop them. It has to end."

Honcho took another sip and swallowed. Then, he decided what the hell and downed the last bit. Poured some more and topped Ryan off. Seeing Julia and the kids brought back memories, good memories he hadn't thought about for a long time. It warmed his spirit and cracked the exterior of the hardened man.

"So, why here? Me? You had no idea if I even made it. Unless you just figured you all would crash my place and run amuck in the deep dark wilderness," Honcho winked. He had a feeling he knew the answer, but needed to hear it.

Ryan had nothing to hide. Their friendship, built over decades of trust and loyalty, was always brutally honest. No matter what. The hard part was where to even begin with the details, the dark secrets and lies. The line where truth shattered into a million pieces and the lies surfaced as fact. The month on the run had given him plenty of time to ruminate on the information he knew, or thought he did.

Trying to parcel it all into coherent buckets was messy.

"If anyone made it, I figured you would. We built this place, not for this shithole planet we have now, but for something less sinister. As soon as reality started to stray and the whispers percolated, I knew you'd be here. I had to take a chance and hope you didn't end up someone's dinner."

Honcho smiled. His old friend knew him well.

Taking another sip, Ryan looked up and continued. "I heard a lot of crazy shit between my dad, Mark, and those rich bastards. On the surface, some of it makes sense. Other parts, I wonder if it's all part of the deception and sleight of hand to distract from the truth. I need to know what's real and what's absolute bullshit. Especially if I'm going to stop it."

Honcho nearly spit out his Scotch, which would have been a travesty given the amount of money it would have cost three years ago. "Dude, are you serious? Go underground. Go up North and find a nice forest to call home. Hell, stay here in the bunker and keep me company. But, try and stop them? Man, that's a death sentence waiting to happen."

The stone-cold eyes didn't need to say a word. He did anyway.

"Honcho, it's not that simple. They will *never* stop. They're gone, like crazy no rational brain pieces left gone. Emma and David are like evil madman crack to them. Those assholes will die trying to get my kids back in order to carry out their bonkers plans."

Honcho closed his eyes. Ryan was right. If half of what he said was true, and not that he didn't believe him, but if what the nut jobs said was real, then pursuit for eternity wouldn't be out of the question.

"What are you thinking?" The green of Ryan's eyes sought a response.

Honcho's eyes betrayed him. "I've got one nagging question I have to ask. Given all the shit that went down, you had them both. Could have popped a cap and been done with it. Why didn't you?" Honcho knew, but he wanted Ryan to say it.

Ryan sighed, knowing the truth. "I was ready to kill my dad, up close and make it personal for what he did to my babies. Could have gone back inside and done the deed and then blown the house up. I just couldn't do it. My kids were finding out the real truth about me, so how could I explain to them I outright killed their grandfather, even after what he did to them? Explosion seemed more in line with what I could live with. Mark? Had him in my sights. Figured I'd let him go all villain monologue to get the answers I needed. That was a cluster and nearly got me dead. I won't make either mistake again."

As he thought about it, really thought hard and dove into his mind, Ryan faced a reality he never imagined would crawl inside. The real truth, the one he figured was it, was more complex than what he told Honcho. The old soldier would have gotten all the intel he could, and then eliminate with extreme prejudice. The son and friend, tormented by the effects of the virus, grappled with his own humanity.

Or, what was *left* of it.

The demon lurking in his bowels, the one vying to be top dog but being repressed while he could still manage it, wanted its revenge. Yearned to kill his father and old friend.

Ryan knew it would happen.

The rational brain losing out to the beast. Unless he found a cure or could stave off the worst of what was growing within, it was a foregone conclusion. He had wanted to kill them both when he found Mark was still alive and then encountering his dad at the mansion. Exact justice for the torture they put Emma and David through for three long years. When push came to shove, his mind faltered on outright nailing dear old dad to the wall. Couldn't face letting the blade loose. Call it sentiment or love, he let emotions win. Mark was a different story. He was saving him for last. Had hoped to drain him of every ounce of information before bringing a gruesome death to Mark's front door. Ryan failed there too. Not from any emotion or hesitance. Leaving his father alive let Mark off the hook for a sliver of time. Ryan wouldn't fail the next time they all met.

No matter if it killed him, Ryan was resolute on making dear old Dad and Mark pay the price.

The wheels spinning furiously in his head, Honcho looked straight at Ryan. "I get some of that. But you dropped people getting Emma and Jules out. Emma saw *you* shiv fools. And from what you say it took to get up here, along the way you used the fifty-cal to dust some nasty hombres. Even had old David learn to mop up some of the psychos. Shit, the boy learned to shoot. Not much difference to me."

His friend made a point. Bad guys were bad guys. The world was a different place. To survive you killed. No questions asked. Ryan's children were getting a crash course in how to navigate an apocalypse Wild West style. Grandpa or an old friend were enemies.

Sentiment was a weakness now.

Ryan nodded. "You're right. A villain is a villain no matter if they're family or a friend. Hell, I'd have them off you in a heartbeat if I had to do it.

Probably Emma though. You'd never expect it."

Honcho stared. Then the eyebrow raised before he laughed. "That little princess *would* be the death of me."

"You know it."

"Listen Ry, whatever you guys need, you know I'm here for you. Those kids, Julia, they mean the world to me. You, not so much," Honcho said, the humor in his tone a nice touch for a really crappy situation.

"Love you too, Big Man," Ryan kissed back.

The old friends sat sipping the last of the Scotch, relishing in its refinements and waning refreshment until the last drips were consumed and only dry glasses left. No words, no looks beyond simple nods. Just quiet and serene. It felt good to be here. Be with his friend. Ryan couldn't help feeling like he had just put a huge bullseye on Honcho's back by invading his sanctuary. He knew that Honcho would go to the end of the Earth for him and the family. It was one of the traits Ryan felt so endearing and a bond that kept them glued together these many years.

Sitting back in his chair, Honcho tilted his head back, left it there for a few minutes, and then leaned close, elbows on the table. "Go over the last part for me again."

"Which part?" Ryan asked.

"The part with your dad at the end, before he shot you."

Shrugging his shoulders, Ryan went back over it. "Well, Mark was on one of those evil villain diatribes yapping away. Somehow, I missed seeing my dad in my scope. First shot, he must have slipped down and hid. He got out of the Humvee, goes around behind it, and shoots me. Not how I had planned for it to go down. So, I'm hit from his piss poor aim and he yells at me. Couldn't make it all out, but something along the lines of I ruined everything like always. He sacrificed everything and did things in order for me to live. Now, I should pay for his sins. It was so quick. I got up, dropped my load of C4, and ran. Blew the bag and got the hell out."

The eyebrow was deep in thought. "Any idea of what he meant?"

Ryan shook his head. "Not a clue. Only thing I can think of is it relates to whatever he did for this band of wackos. Part of the reason I'm here. To find out."

Pursed lips stared back. "So, the *real* reason you came all this way materializes. You need me to dig for information."

Bright green eyes, big with sadness, answered. "I don't know who my dad is Honcho. No clue what he was involved in. If I can piece together what is real and decipher the lies, maybe I can get my head around all of it and actually do something about it. Otherwise, I'm shooting blind. I need to know."

Truth and lies. A world Honcho knew too well. Fact and fiction depended on your interpretation. The right spin could be the difference between falling into the abyss or taking a foothold to be believed, even if it was the most ridiculous statement in the world.

Honcho winced, and then poured another round. Given the discussion and what was left to come out that Ryan had yet to share, it seemed appropriate.

"Thanks Honcho. You are the most gracious host."

Low grumbled response. "Don't share that with anyone."

CHAPTER 4

The old silo.

It wasn't just Honcho's private and secure lair to keep isolated from prying eyes and now the aftereffects of the virus, but its design and location served a more clandestine and, in many ways, subversive purpose.

Ryan had met Honcho during his first tour, Ryan a special ops grunt and the latter a young intelligence analyst. Their chance encounter, sparked over a failed recon mission where information collected proved worthless, turned fruitful when Honcho broke protocol and rank by stepping between an irate Ryan and the green lieutenant who provided the bad intel. Honcho, tasked with the more mundane radio channels to eavesdrop, caught wind of a peculiar conversation coded in ancient Persian, which Ryan's team heard the results of in the field, but had no context to decipher. Coming back empty handed, the lieutenant blew off a pissed Ryan. When confronted about the radio traffic that should have been a red flag to stand down from their mission, the lieutenant proceeded to lie. About to deck the superior officer since Ryan's team had come under unexpected resistance and fire, Honcho stopped Ryan and proceeded to drop the lieutenant himself in front of a two-star general. As the dust cleared and all facts came to light, Honcho spent a day in the brig for belting a superior and got transferred to Ryan's unit to support their field operations. The coded conversations when put into context proved beneficial and a follow-up mission retrieved valuable information that saved countless lives.

That volatile beginning began a decades old friendship cemented in trust and respect.

Years of intel work often in the dark recesses of data collection from illegal intrusions capturing state secrets and analyzing the results, Honcho finally moved onto greener pastures. In reality, he went polar opposite. Getting his teaching degree and Master's, he went on to be a special education high school teacher, and really great at it. A huge bear of a man with a soft touch who could make the worst lesson come alive. It was a new journey suited for him. But, when you are really good at something and have an innate ability to find the impossible, it's hard to completely leave the fold.

Honcho was too bright to let go.

Side government consulting for the harder intel projects proved lucrative, all to fuel and supplement his teaching career. Ryan faced a similar dilemma. The best of the best, he got roped into the occasional black ops *complete government deniability mission* to handle touchy situations. Until Julia came around, and then he made sure to severe his ties. The powers that be tried to entice and even threaten, which came to a halt when Ryan appeared from the shadows inside a career high-level official's secret vacation home and nearly handed the man his own balls.

Ryan was never bothered by the man again.

Honcho kept at it and built what was affectionately known as the Moose Mountain Lair, or Moose Lair for short, complete with inconspicuous solar, satellite receivers, and deep mountain reservoir water, all to continue his side hustle. A computer nerd's heaven with the amount of technology housed within the concrete walls deep inside, it rivaled most government facilities. Not in breadth of wall-to-wall server farms that ran computations and housed data.

No.

Honcho had the assets to build a complex infrastructure, but that would have been overkill. A few large mainframe servers bought at auction and repurposed suited his needs. They were relics, built to last a lifetime, but deemed too old and bulky. Not for him. Some new hardware, network cables, and cooling units and the old code used to run them that was written to never bug out, and Honcho had the backend to work his magic.

The front end was another story.

Solid PCs with enough RAM memory and multi-processors to run the space station kept Honcho's enterprise afloat. Huge monitors to multi-task expanded the desktops. He could run programs on each and keep an eye on the results. It was reminiscent of NASA's space command center, though for a much different viewing purpose to not keep a mission working, but to dig and extract information and data from the web and foreign networks. Custom programming to run it all, a favor from a friend on the fringes of the dark web, and Honcho ran intel from the comforts of his fortress of solitude, remotely from home in Seattle with the occasional trip to check in.

And, he still taught students during the day before the world crashed and burned.

A weird tone sounded and a table lamp flashed on and off, disturbing the tranquility of the cabin. Honcho looked at Ryan, his eyes steeped in fear. Quickly rising from his seat, Honcho motioned his friend towards the back.

Understanding the non-verbal communication, Ryan moved to the couch and tapped Julia. Pointing for her and the kids to follow, she scooped up the sleeping Pete while Ryan grabbed David and Emma by the hands and led them towards Honcho.

"All the way down," Honcho ordered as he pointed behind to a hidden doorway and stairs that led to the silo below.

Julia nodded and descended. David and Emma followed with Ryan a step behind. Honcho pulled the false wall back into place and secured the lock on the heavy door. Step after step they went further into the ground, the coolness of the concrete walls a refreshing break from the warmth above. Emerging out of the stairwell tunnel into a large open area, the Carmichael family gathered until Honcho appeared and shut and locked the last three-foot-thick metal and concrete door for the passage.

"Follow me please," Honcho smiled before he led everyone past an immense blast door into a dimly lit tunnel.

He made a right turn and flipped a switch, and standing outside of some room, directed everyone inside. It was a home away from home. Huge leather couches and chairs, multiple large screen televisions mounted to the wall, and every detail you could imagine from carpet to tables and bookcases to make the room not seem to be deep inside some bunker but as if it was inside a comfortable home designed for living. Julia took the kids and Pete to the couches and plopped them all down and then grabbed a remote and turned on the television before heading to the DVD case to find a suitable movie.

Ryan had been watching for a few seconds and when he turned, Honcho was nowhere to be seen. Stepping out the doorway he looked left and right down the empty corridor. Turning to check on Julia, he suddenly got picked up by his larger-than-life friend and moved out of the way. Following Honcho, Ryan was about to speak before Honcho held up some device in his hand, waved it over David, and then Emma.

Three quick beeps each.

"Dammit," Honcho frowned. Doing the same to Julia and then walking over to Ryan, he waved it up and down. Julia beeped. Ryan, nothing.

"What's going on, Honcho?"

Honcho set the device down on the short bookcase behind the couch. Leaning back to rest on it, arms crossed, he closed his eyes.

Ryan walked over and touched his arm. "What is it?"

Honcho opened his eyes and looked right at Ryan. "RF."

Julia looked at Ryan, the worry in her face showing she was scared. "What's an RF? Are we OK?"

The information clicked.

The look on Honcho's face was part disgust, part intrigue. "Didn't you check them out? Anything else you need to tell me?"

Directing his response to Julia, Ryan frowned, "RF. Radio frequency.

Based on what just happened, you and the kids have a tiny transmitter embedded in you. My guess now, it's how they tracked you guys back East. Short range, which is why they have not been able to find us since California."

David and Emma had been listening and not wanting them to hear anymore, Julia pulled out a DVD, popped it into the player and hit play. She then sat down and refocused their attention to an animated adventure story they hadn't seen since before the fall of society.

Ryan stood, his head aching at his failure. Not like he had the tools to scan them. The device was cheap and found at any big box tech store or the strip mall shacks that sold everything imaginable when it came to electronics. It never crossed his mind they were walking beacons sending signals to be caught.

Honcho grabbed Ryan by the arm. "Be back soon Jules. Man talk."

Ryan shrugged and waved to Julia. "Drinks in the fridge."

The big man led Ryan down the corridor and took a left at the first door. Opening it, he pushed Ryan in. The brightness from the computer screens lining the far wall didn't warrant an overhead light, but Honcho turned it on anyway and closed the door. Directing Ryan to the nearest chair, Honcho grabbed one, turned it around, and leaned on the backrest.

"Talk, Dude."

Ryan sighed. He had hoped to have *the conversation* later, when everyone had a chance to unwind and rest their weary bones.

Honcho tapped the back of the chair. "Seriously. We need to talk. The Ryan I know would never have let that one slip through."

Honcho was right. Ryan was slipping, his methodical acuity at preparedness to prevent a long list of things slowly eroding one by one.

Clearing his throat, Ryan dove right in. "I'm infected, or for lack of a better description, the virus has decided that I am lucky enough to start a descent into madness and end up a killer of killers."

Honcho laughed. "Seems that already happened my friend. Your kill count rivals the best of them."

Ryan shook his head. "No, not the good kind of killer. Without that maintenance shot to curb the virus, I *turn*. Become the worst of the worst monsters out there roaming around."

Silence. It must have lasted five minutes before Honcho said a word. "So, you not only came here to get information on how to stop what's going on topside, but leave your family in my care for when you bite the bullet, so to speak?"

"You could say that."

It was true. If he failed to stop Mark and his father, defeat the menace of nut jobs trying to eliminate society and bring about their own rise of a new order bent on obedience and control, he'd have to die before he hurt anyone who didn't deserve it. It was the long game all along, though Julia didn't know it.

"OK, we can go back to that insane concept in a minute. First, how did you not check them out? That's like ops 101 for you weirdos."

His eyes closed tight, Ryan answered. "I'm losing myself a bit at a time. My usual precautions, I miss some. Should have known, but really, how could I?"

Honcho reached over and smacked Ryan in the arm. "Dude, it's all right. I'm just messing with you. You wouldn't have a clue unless you were part of them or had the intel I have collected. You came to the right place my dear friend, and you know I will do everything I can to help. Even shoot you myself," he grinned. "You know I owe you at least one bullet for all these years putting up with your lame ass. Maybe even two."

Ryan managed a smile and a wink. "I'm so screwed Honcho. Help me. You're my only hope."

CHAPTER 5

"You couldn't manage to kill him and make sure he stayed that way?" Reg Carmichael yelled at Mark Simpson, the rage inside exploding as the words spewed out.

Mark Simpson took a step back and wiped the spit from his face. "He's always been quite resilient."

"What else don't I know about my boy? Anything pertinent to our current situation you want to share now?" The venom in Reg's voice meant business.

He pursed his lips, wondering where to even start. There was so much he could divulge, though most simply perpetuated the myth of Ryan "The Ghost" Carmichael. Mark's old friend was a legend in his own class.

Reg was growing impatient. "Tell me!"

Mark decided to take a seat. The metal leg of the chair screeched on the concrete floor, echoing in the small room. Leaning back, he began. "Your son is the best of the best. No one, and I mean no one, has ever been like him. He is tenacious, driven, and will stop at nothing to complete his mission. Morality and a conscious guide him, though now those are probably cracking under the strain of the virus. That makes him even deadlier than before. He is the nightmare you hope never shows up at the foot of your bed."

Reg looked incredulous. "Bullshit. Ryan? He doesn't have the balls on him."

Wide eyes stared across the table. "Was I the only person there when he sent two quick shots to kill our driver and gunner, and then proceeded to blow the road all to hell?"

"Luck," Reg shrugged.

Mark was growing irritated with Reg brushing off Ryan's skills. "Not luck. Focus. He once sat dug into the side of a mountain in Afghanistan waiting to scope a local warlord holed up in his fortress who had been kidnapping local girls and selling them off to insurgents for kid brides. Day after day peering through his scope, waiting, watching, morning and night. Never moved. Finally, the guy came back, but Ryan couldn't get the shot. Worked his way down the side of the mountain in the dead of night. Sneaks into the man's compound, and it's got like forty guards providing security. Goes into the bedroom, removes the guy's cock, and leaves it on display in the middle of the courtyard. No one sees him. Heads back up the mountain and waits until the guy is found. Then, proceeds to blow apart every man who came through the front gate with a long distant fifty-caliber head shot. Let's just say after that, not a single girl was taken. A ghost who could break into that place and kill? The legend was born."

Reg laughed. "We have the numbers and the resources. I'm not worried about him."

Mark slapped the table hard. "You should be pissing yourself! Ryan will do anything to finish his mission. And, this needs to sink into your brain. If he's not dead from you shooting him, then you've just pissed him off even more. He will come and if he does, he will wreak havoc like you have never seen. We created a monster inside of a monster. He won't stop until he kills all of us."

A smirk or a smile washed over the older man's face.

"Something funny, Reg?"

Now a full-blown grin. "Seems the boy has some of the old man in him after all."

Ever since Ryan rescued Julia and the kids, the hunt to retrieve their escaped possessions continued in force for Reg and Mark. To the younger man, a soldier turned scientist, getting the children back meant continuing his research for a vaccine to control the virus and his other pursuits. Move further up the rung to direct the orders versus receiving them and doling out the work. For Reg, it meant being the one in control, meeting out punishment for disobeying, and more than anything, exacting revenge on his oldest son.

Where he once had love for Ryan, Reg only had a festering hatred now, the seeds of it growing each day that Mark failed to find the son. Reg expected his capture within hours the last time he saw Ryan's face. While the father's aim wasn't quite what it used to be, he knew it was effective watching his son stagger away into the darkness. Wounded and blood flowing out the bullet hole with each pump of Ryan's racing heart and rising adrenaline, Reg assumed that an unconscious or mortally injured body would be found.

No such luck.

It was as if Ryan has disappeared into the ethos and his family with him. Hours turned to days, patrols up and down the Bay Area and beyond scouring for any sign. Days turned to weeks. Each returning group reported nothing of substance, except the occasional ghost story of a monster in the sky or UFO gleaming under the moonlight. The man had been on foot and ran away, his prized 1968 Mustang abandoned, and not a trace to be found. It was possible he tried to swim and succumbed to the ravages of the cold Bay ocean water. But, nothing surfaced or any remains discovered during daily searches.

Ryan's "Ghost" nickname was well earned.

The search area expanded every day. Further south in case he somehow circled around and headed that way and inching north through California, Oregon, and now into Washington. RF pings caught everything in its wake. The Un-dead, or what was left of the scavengers, were useless. Same for the crazy marathon runners and Generation Z flesh biters. The mercenaries remained valuable assets, if you managed to get someone in front of their leader without getting tortured and killed. Offering supplies and munitions to get them to assist on the search proved positive, if only to reduce sending out Reg's own people and lose them to carnage or capture.

Survivors were scattered all over and while they were great test subjects, it was only true if they were not privy to the transmitter in their blood. Word had spread over the years so any left to find were outcasts or loners. Ryan didn't have one, a result of the grand plan to initially use him as a lethal weapon to spearhead the rise of the new republic.

A shortsighted decision that now meant he was a grain of rice in an endless ocean trench with zero light to guide you.

When Ryan blew the mansion and the servers in it, he effectively sent Mark back to the beginning when he had been so close. The Stanford lab had not been operational yet and all of the research in the blown underground facility in Virginia turned to ash. Serum vials, blood, everything had been destroyed. Left with nothing tangible, the research team was forced to start over.

Square one again after three years of volatile and mind-numbing work was not what the Council wanted to hear.

While memories were left unaffected by the virus, no one could recreate the maintenance vaccine from thin air. They needed actual fluids to finish the work and absent live specimens, the hunt continued.

Back at home, Reg sat with a cold beer, feet up comfortably, looking out over the balcony of the penthouse. He needed the break from Mark or he swore he'd kill him for his failures. The view provided an excellent panorama of the decay and destruction the virus wrought, buildings imploded, piles of cars rusting along the freeways, the Un-dead wandering in search of scraps.

The scene made him smile.

The world was gone, not even a shell of its former self. The future was ripe for the rebirth, a rebuilding of society and order. The carnage and debris would be removed and town and cities rebuilt, all for the greater good. He couldn't help but feel happy at this moment knowing that even with his grandkids on the run, they would be found. It might take some time, but it was destiny. Nothing could stand in the way.

Not even his own son.

As he took another swig from his perch, Reg thought about Ryan. He knew he once loved his oldest child, recognized it from the memories that existed. *That* love had left a long time ago when the virus decided to kill his humanity and leave chaos in its wake. Only bitter disgust and hatred remained, ripe and fermenting a toxic juice from the last month after his boy emerged from the grave and dealt a death card against Reg's plans.

So close to triumph and in an instant, all gone.

Stepping into the foyer of Mike Goldberg's house and seeing the black silhouette would have scared any other man. Not Reg Carmichael. As soon as he took a step inside and closed the door, he *felt* the presence and wasn't afraid. There was something about it that he couldn't quite place, until the *voice* responded.

At that moment, the fire ignited and continued to burn hot and bright.

As the night wore on and he felt in power, he kept it in control. Seeing Ryan dressed up like some soldier brought an internal laughter he contained because it was so comical. His son *thinking* he could stop them?

Not a chance.

A fanciful attempt at bravery Reg thought, until seeing the determination in his boy's eyes and the vibrant color reflected in them. At that point he knew his son was something to recon with, but had no idea the depths of his resolve. Watching him kill one by one the billionaires with no remorse or sense it bothered him, just added wood to the pit inside Reg's stomach.

Hotter and hotter it burned until the sun was nothing in comparison.

When they got upstairs, he was sure Mark would soon be right behind, ready to end the growing nightmare of losing their captives. When that didn't materialize and he got a rifle butt to the back of the skull, only to wake up and find Julia, the kids, Ryan, and the Mustang gone, reality about his own failure soon fanned the heat.

Only Ryan's confirmed death would quench the flames.

The world needed order. It had gone centuries without it. Nations vying for dominance. Dictators forcing their rule, only to die in the end when the populace rebelled. Democracies failing to bring about change and a semblance of an inclusive society. At every turn, the world couldn't put the needs of the people over the selfishness of the individual.

The virus changed that.

Now the ruins were ripe for a rebirth. Eradicate the whines of the one and encompass the many to follow. The phoenix from the ashes to bring salvation. Certain liberties and choices would no longer exist.

It had to be that way to set the foundation.

No more ideology of "me me" and Constitutional protections. America had long ago abandoned any moral right to adhere to them. White privilege, constructed on Puritan teachings and racist demagoguery where one group profited off the backs of others, had no place in the new world. Everyone would be the same and expectations equal for all. Adhere and follow the path to assimilate.

Rebel, and die.

It was simple, really. Some would control but be bound by the principles of the whole. Reg couldn't help but laugh thinking about the billionaire boys thinking they would somehow be top dogs in the new regime. They were an end to a means, manipulated for their power, wealth, and influence. Once the real vaccine was in place, they would have been demoted to puppet roles, relegated to cheerleaders to support the cause. Get people onboard with the maintenance booster as the answer to all of the woes that befell the planet for the last three years. The failure of the previous vaccines and their uncontrollable side effects, being a miscalculated accident.

Even the mass refusal to get the vaccine from the loyal and the ignorant. Those bastards were wild cards. While they could avoid the shot and be the flag bearers of insanity, they still needed to be brought into the fold. The only way to assert total control was to get them onboard.

The problem was the messaging and the demi-gods of the cause thinking they were running the show.

A real cluster fuck was a better description.

The President had royally screwed that one up. Going off script to promote remedies and products as cures that funneled money to himself, family, and friends. He was looking at self-interest and his own misaligned dream of dictator in chief. The concoctions not only didn't work, but as the intermixing of drugs and chemicals traversed the bloodstream and one of the manufactured vaccines came to begin the new world emergence, the cocktail of crap created side effects that spiraled out of control.

Created the chaos that now roamed the lands.

Decades in the making, and then the plan fell apart. Human ego and distraction. Greed and apathy. The vaccines would have staved off everything, or most of it. But those damn followers and ignorant base of imbeciles who fueled and blindly walked behind an egotistical megalomanic who they could not completely control. Amplify that around the world where governments were a step behind and those puppet masters couldn't act fast enough to reign in their toys.

Eventually, everyone would be infected, vaccine or not. It was the odds.

David and Emma were supposed to right the ship.

Bring order back and rectify the human failings that created the mess. If only the original vaccines had worked. They wouldn't need his grandkids. And, Reg was fine with it.

No love lost for the little cretins.

In fact, he relished in their torment, knowing how much it had hurt Julia.

He would have found even more reasons to feel wonderful inside if he had known Ryan was alive missing them and *then* when he found out his precious babies were test subjects.

The smile wouldn't be able to be pried from Reg's face.

A knock at the door interrupted the daydreams of killing his son. No one should be disturbing him, and a rage began to circle and rise to the top. One more sip and Reg got up and opened the door.

"What the fuck do you want?" Reg sneered at the soldier standing in the hallway.

Head bowed, the man answered, "We got a ping, Sir. Faint, but it was caught in one of our flyovers."

"Where?"

Reddened eyes from lack of sleep peered up. "Washington state, Sir."

CHAPTER 6

Ryan sat with Honcho and spilled his guts, figuratively, but it felt like he was puking them out with each tidbit he shared.

Honcho listened, and made notes as Ryan talked. Occasionally he asked a question, but mostly scribbled in his notebook. When Ryan was finished, Honcho tapped the tabletop ten times, and then closed the book.

Looking up, he pursed his lips.

"The vaccines carried a tiny RF transmitter. Low frequency and band that if you happened to freak out the radio or cell phone, though they're on different bands, you'd just chalk it up to some weird interference. The 5G network was supposed to be the avenue to track everyone. Cell towers and wifi pinging your location into the master server farm data center. All of those wired cities? Free wifi service? A front to expand the outreach. It ties into what they told you. If you can track people, you can begin to exert the control you need. That beep topside? Catches the signal they send out periodically to track people down. Short distance, maybe a mile or two. My system caught it far away so I don't think they located them here. My guess is that's how they got Julia and the kids after you rescued them. The short-range ping."

Ryan felt the wind leave his lungs. If he had been on his game, innocent people wouldn't have died when John's people hid his family. Taking a breath in, Ryan managed to put a sentence together. "Why didn't I ping then? I got a vaccine."

Honcho stared, his eyebrow raised, deep in thought. He wasn't sure how to answer so he just let it out. "When everything died, I was left by myself with a lot of time on my hands. At the beginning, I poked around the deep dark recesses of intel and came across a lot of shit while power supplies and backup generators worked so I could download what I could. You, top of the list. Had hoped to figure out where you might end up secured away with Jules and the babies. Try and ping you when shit got better by piggy-backing

29

off the cell satellites. Well, guess what my digging in the dark weeds did? Surprise! You got the dose all right. But you got a different cocktail. Seems they hoped to turn you into one of those freaks and use your certain set of very specific skills to do their bidding. So, keeping the tracker out meant while they couldn't track you, neither could anyone else know Ghost was delivering death to their door."

"Goddamn motherfuckers!" Ryan yelled, hitting the table so hard it echoed in the room.

Honcho let it all sink in. It was difficult to take in he knew, being a Guinea pig for some mad scientists to control. But he also knew it came with a huge advantage. No tracker, no finding you. No finding you, leave death and destruction in your silent wake.

"Listen, Ryan, first thing is neutralizing the transmitters in Julia and the kids. They're good this far down, can't penetrate the rocky soil and the concrete is littered with copper to create a nice insulated net to keep any signals from penetrating anything here. A Faraday cage on steroids. Then, we figure out a plan, OK? We'll do this and do it together. Just like old times, right?"

Old times. Taking down bad guys and saving the world. A different time and place, but the same house cleaning effort, just with fewer resources, support, and weapons to deal death certificates. Ryan hoped he could last long enough to succeed.

Standing up from his chair, Ryan nodded. "You are one of my oldest and dearest friends, Honcho. Likely the only asshole one of them still alive too," he smiled before moving over to hug his friend. "Love you, Big Guy."

Honcho squeezed hard. "Love you too, you pain in my ass."

Before they returned to Julia and the kids, Honcho grabbed a black bag from one of the storage rooms littering the main floor of the bunker. With multiple levels, the top two floors were the primary areas used the most. The deeper recesses of the bunker were rarely visited, but contained supplies and an assortment of odds and ends that were useful only in an apocalypse.

And now was the perfect time to dust them off.

The two men walked into the room in time to see the end of the movie credits. Julia looked over her shoulder and frowned. Ryan had not realized they had been gone so long, so he mouthed a *sorry* to her. Honcho went to the short bookcase behind the couch and placed the black bag. Unzipping it, he fiddled with the back on a wand like device, popped three AA batteries in, and snapped the back on.

Hitting a switch, Honcho reached over the couch. "Which arm did they inject the vaccine?" he asked Julia.

Confused, she answered, "Uh, the left."

Nodding, Honcho said, "This is going to sting a bit," before he waved the device over Julia's arm and pressed a button.

A short whizzing sound emitted from it before it turned high pitched and Julia screamed out. "Ow, that hurt!"

Ryan motioned for Julia to keep it together. "Sweetheart, I'll tell you later. Right now, it's the kids turn."

Honcho asked about the kids and proceeded to perform the same task. A whiz, high pitched sound, shouts of ouch, and then he placed the device back in the bag. "All done. Ice cream for brave kids."

"Ice cream!" the kids yelled in unison.

Looking at Julia and then Ryan, Honcho offered, "Don't worry. It's not old. Make it fresh myself with powdered milk and fresh stuff when I milk the cows in the pasture and harvest some fruit."

Leading the kids to the small kitchenette, Honcho served up ice cream while Ryan sat on the couch. David decided on the fresh strawberry while Emma wanted chocolate. Sitting at the table, Honcho scooped it out and kept the kids in conversation while Ryan talked to Julia.

"What was that all about?" Julia asked, rubbing her sore arm.

"Short story. The vaccines contained tracking devices, which is how Mark found you back East. Seems all a part of the bigger plan. Really throws all that government conspiracy crap that the right wingnuts spouted off about into a whole different light. That device killed the signal so they can't find you anymore."

Shock stared back. "Are you serious? Tracking devices? That's so Orwellian. I wonder what else we thought were lies and crazy talk is actually true?"

The look on Ryan's face must have betrayed him.

"Something else to tell me, Husband?"

"Seems I didn't have one. Honcho caught wind of intel about me. They had me as part of the bigger plan scenario."

Julia wasn't sure how to respond. Asking meant opening a potential Pandora's Box. Ignoring it could potentially harm the kids. Sighing deep, she managed to get out, "What?"

Ryan leaned closer. "You know some of who I used to be long ago. The work I did for JSOC and SAC-SOG SMU. But, it goes a whole lot deeper and becomes a really surreal conversation you might not want to dive into at all."

"JSOC?" Julia's confused face asked.

Ryan sighed. It was a passing comment to her, light on details during their road trip north. "Joint Special Operations Command. CIA was the SAC-SOG part and SMU a reaper unit that never officially was closed. *Reaper* being the operative word since we didn't leave footprints on missions as you never saw us coming or going. Like death. We were the best of the best taken from all branches of the military and whittled down from there to even fewer."

"Give me the cliff notes version as it pertains to today. You can spill your sordid past later.”

The words hurt, but he understood. He had kept so much hidden and locked away. He couldn’t really be mad at her for feeling the way she did. Any sane person would say the same thing to him if they knew the whole story.

“College version then. Seems Mark and the powers that be gave me a funky cocktail for a vaccine, which is responsible for my growing personality and charm. They left out the tracker in anticipation of me turning into a psycho and utilize my past talent and expertise to reign in their enemies. No tracker. The new version of the Ghost could move freely in the shadows.”

Julia frowned. “I hate that nickname of yours.”

All he could do was shrug. “Didn’t give it to myself. I could lurk in the shadows and get things done quietly and expeditiously without being seen. It fit then and still does. Something to use to our advantage as long as we can. Before,” Ryan paused, sadness rimming his green eyes, “before I am not me anymore.”

She threw her arms around him, the sobs quiet and controlled. There was that inevitable scenario, his last curtain call in the future, and him not writing a sequel that painted a happy picture. No vaccine, no Ryan Carmichael.

At least, not the Ryan she knew and loved.

Wiping the tears away, Julia looked at Ryan. “We will find a way to keep you, well, you. No matter what or how, we’ll find a way. You can’t bail and leave me alone with those two crazy nuts.”

Ryan chuckled. “I hope so. Though a break from them wouldn’t hurt. They’ve been driving me wacko the last few weeks.”

Julia smacked Ryan’s arm. “You were gone three long years. So, no. You’ve had your break. I’m the one who needs it. They’re *insane*.”

The laughing felt good. His belly hurt thinking about his kids and the shenanigans over the last month on their road trip to the Northwest. Even the dismal predicament they were in didn’t keep Emma and David from being just kids. Silliness. Playing jokes, and the occasional tantrum from being crammed inside the Humvee showed they were still eight-year-olds.

If only crazy and able to still drive their parents nuts.

“They are little devils, aren’t they?” Ryan whispered. “We could just leave them with Uncle Honcho for a bit, let them make him go mad.”

Soft hands caressed his face. “If we did that, he’d never help us then, would he?” Julia frowned.

“True.”

“So, what do we do now?” Julia asked, her brown eyes staring deep into his.

Ryan leaned over and kissed her lips. “We find out what we need to know and get to work stopping this madness. Keep the kids safe and take the fight to Mark and my dad.”

"As long as you kill them for what they did to our babies. Those bastards wrecked what should have been formative years for our kids. Even in the apocalypse, they could have at least had other kids to play with and a semblance of a life. The four of us together at least. Make them pay for our lost time. You owe me that."

Ryan's devilish grin didn't need to say a word.

CHAPTER 7

Being around Honcho was a breath of fresh air.

Ryan's chance to feel a tiny sliver of normal, if that was even possible anymore, in what was left of the world. Conversation with anyone who knew the old him, the deadly professional, had been years ago, and he felt his exterior cracking and the old Ryan peeking out. The *in control and able to handle any situation*, Ryan "Ghost" Carmichael.

It felt damn good.

Julia tucked the kids into some beds after they said goodnight to Ryan and Honcho. David and Emma hadn't slept on real mattresses since they left the confines of Mark's control. It had been sleeping bags, the ground, or the back of the Humvee. Being atop a real mattress and tucked into soft sheets sent them to dreamland in minutes. Taking her leave, Julia joined Ryan and Honcho back in the main living area. The men were deep in talk, so she grabbed a drink from the fridge and took a seat.

"No, that's crap," Ryan replied to something Honcho had said.

"I'm serious. All true. The cables don't lie."

Julia looked around the table. "Anyone going to fill me in?"

Ryan tapped the table. "Honcho here was telling me about all of the diplomatic cables that went back and forth the last month before the world went off the deep end."

Taking a sip of her drink, Julia shrugged. "And?"

Honcho raised his hand. "Twenty-three cables between the White House and the U.K. Prime Minister. A project called Chrysalis. I am of the opinion that it relates to our current situation around the virus. Ryan has other ideas."

He closed his eyes, thought back decades to his service time. When you reached a certain level of effectiveness, you became privy to information at the highest classification when they expected you to carry out certain orders that fell into very gray areas.

"Project Chrysalis went dormant in the 90s. At least, the one I know about. It wasn't a vaccine or super solider project bent on world domination. That one was a secret NASA project meant to take people to the Moon for missions. 'Chrysalis' being the idea of transforming the Moon into a secret base of operations to run ops against the Russians and Chinese. It was too costly and not ideal from a logistical standpoint. At least, that is my official position on the matter."

Honcho shot Ryan a wicked raised eyebrow. "Official position? Spill it for her, secret agent man!"

Ryan had an answer, but it was so unbelievable to try and explain.

Julia poked his arm. "Talk, Husband."

He blew out some air, pursed his lips, and sighed. "The moon landing has always had its detractors. Filmed in the desert or some Hollywood studio. The American flag seemingly waving in a breeze when there is no oxygen in space. The truth is, man did and has, visited the Moon. And, even someone in this room," Ryan murmured under his breath.

Honcho's eyes were playfully huge. "What did you say at the end there?"

"Yeah, I missed that last part." Julia looked confused.

Ryan looked at them, his green eyes big and bright. "I might have said people have visited the Moon more recently and a really awesome person sitting at this table has seen it in person."

Shock was an understatement. Julia sat still, not sure if Ryan was telling one of his crazy stories or laying it on thick. She was beginning to hear tales from his past and Honcho knew most of his escapades. But this one was hard to swallow.

"You? Went to the Moon?"

Ryan nodded.

"*Right.* When? And, how?"

Secrets no longer held any meaning. The world wasn't the same place. Keeping it all locked tight within for no other reason than orders, duty, and non-disclosure by penalty of death didn't have the same sway today as it did a few years ago.

"Space is the last vestige of conquest. Old world ideals around colonialism if you will. There is no more land grab unless you count the poles, and those don't reap or didn't reap the same benefits as an unexplored body in space just waiting to be pillaged of its resources. The American Space Force, while comical when that red-headed moron stole the emblems and tried to chest puff his importance about creating it, was already a thing long ago. In fact, there is a base on the Moon. Been there since the late 70s."

"You are so full of shit, Ryan," Julia laughed before catching Honcho's face.

"No, he's right. I just can't believe they'd send him into space and then let this hot dog back on the planet."

Ryan smiled. "Ever the supportive friend, Honcho."

"You know it, Buddy."

Julia sat back in her chair. It was fiction, had to be some weird story between these two that was made up to get her. She had heard some really far out ones between Ryan and Honcho and this took the cake. She had never heard anything remotely close to a base on the Moon and a space army. It was the kind of made-up stuff some desperate storyteller would try to lay on a crowd to be the center of attention.

"You two almost had me," Julia smiled. "But that is the most out there crazy line of BS you guys have ever tried."

Honcho got up and left the room. Five minutes later he returned and plopped a huge binder in front of Julia. "Go ahead. Open it up."

Julia opened the cover and turned page after page. Twenty minutes later she quietly closed it. In disbelief at what she had just read, she motioned for Honcho to grab her a beer from the refrigerator and he obliged. Two gulps in she looked around the table, shook her head, and passed the binder back to Honcho.

"You two assholes are ridiculous," was all Julia could manage to say.

Ryan feigned the hurt. "What?"

Honcho too. "My poor self-esteem."

Two more swigs of beer and Julia couldn't help but laugh. "Besides the mystery of this place I had no idea about until driving up the dirt road, this is what you two did when Ryan visited?"

Ryan and Honcho both smiled.

Titling his glass back and letting it sit on his tongue, Ryan finally swallowed. "We've both led a pretty wild existence and it only seemed fitting to capture all of it and turn it into movie. BP thought we should so we all spent some time reminiscing about the old days and turned it into an action movie."

"Action movie? Aren't there national security laws or something you'd be breaking by divulging secrets like this? And BP, how'd you rope him into this scheme?"

Honcho cleared his throat. "We changed a bunch of the underlying details so we're or were, all good. Besides, it was BP's idea."

BP.

Ryan hadn't heard that name in a long time. One of the other musketeers and his longest known friend, BP was another spoke in the wheel of Ryan's world. While Ryan had gone the clandestine special operator path and Honcho the intelligence whiz route, BP was the smooth talker who could sell a car to a dead man. In the service if you needed something and couldn't get it, you talked to BP. A magician who could deliver the hardest request, he was an asset in a war zone when the comforts of home eluded. After the service, he managed an internship at a movie studio and with a deftness for conversation, managed over time to work his way up the ranks until he ran a production company for one of the biggest Hollywood players in the game.

The movie script wasn't far off from the truth. The last reported American on the Moon was in December, 1972. None since. No one seemed to have questioned why that was the case, a burning desire to be the first on it, and then all of a sudden, a stark departure from exploration of the Earth's only satellite and a resource of unfathomable magnitude.

Only tepid scientific experiments on various space stations.

That was the public perception. If you could keep an astronaut alive on a space station, you could send living pods to the Moon. Humans had been back, en masse, and its exploration provided advances to modern science. The discoveries unbelievable. Taking the past three plus years into context and the desire of madmen to control the planet, the reality wasn't that hard to figure out why it was kept such a dark secret.

The entire story, or at least, as much as Ryan could remember, was for a different time.

"Damn, I miss BP," Ryan sighed. "I hope the end wasn't too bad."

Honcho slapped Ryan across the back. "End?"

Ryan watched as Honcho reached over to the counter and grabbed a remote. Touching a few buttons, one of the large TV screens came to life with nothing but static. Hitting another button, two beeps followed by two more echoed from the surround sound before an image popped up on the screen.

"What the hell, Honcho?" an irritated voice replied before suddenly changing tone. "Ryan? Julia? Oh my god. You guys are alive!"

Ryan stared at the man lit up on the big screen. BP smiled, the joy on his face a sight to see. Ryan couldn't help but feel a tear drip from his left eye before wiping another away. All he could muster was, "How?"

BP waved behind him. A second later his son and daughter appeared. "Yo, kids. Uncle Ry is in the house!"

Julia waved. First seeing Honcho alive and now BP and his kids, she felt a small sliver of hope rise from her stomach. If good people had survived all this time, there was a chance life could emerge from the muck and decay and take a foothold again. A few minutes of conversation catching everyone up, and then BP's kids excused themselves as it was late.

"All right kids, grown up time," BP said to the group. "Time to get to business. Ry, we all thought you were dead!"

Ryan shrugged. "You know I'm like a cockroach. Can't kill me that easily."

Julia nodded. "Good or bad, we just *cannot* shake him."

"More like black mold. Slowly kills you from the inside is what he does," Honcho mumbled.

Ryan glared. "Wow. I can really feel all the love from you three."

BP laughed. "You know we love you, Bro."

Laugher erupted all around. After a few minutes, Ryan started from the beginning and filled BP in on the last three years like he had for Honcho. BP listened, nodded, shook his head, and spit out his water at the more incredible parts of Ryan's story. When he had finished, BP smacked the table.

"I'm sensing another script here boys," BP clapped with his hands. "Gold, pure gold."

"Not sure we could pull this one off now," Ryan offered. "The location costs alone and cast egos would make it a killer shoot."

"Literally, a killer shoot if Ryan has his way with his dad and Mark," Julia smirked.

BP's head shook from side to side. "I just can't believe your dad of all people. What the hell happened to him?"

Ryan took a deep breath. He had a month to think about it. No real answers came to mind, just the bits and pieces Reg had divulged. He hoped Honcho, with his vast network of resources to scour through thousands of petabytes of data, could offer up some clues.

Honcho decided to chime in. "That's one reason why they're here, BP. Use my tech to dig in the crap and find out some answers."

Lost in thought for a minute at seeing another old friend, a lightbulb clicked. "Hey BP," Ryan began. "I know we're in the middle of an apocalypse and all, but you still have that vast list of 'things' in case of, well you know, all of this?"

BP beamed. "You know it Ry!" And then catching the question asked, "Why, what's going on inside that head of yours?"

Ryan sat back in his chair, hands behind his head. "My Dad and Mark know I'm alive and Mark by now has filled my wonderful father in on my back history. Hopefully has them both shitting bricks thinking when a bullet will blow their brains out. They feel they have us on the run with nowhere to go and living day by day. What they don't know is I have my two best friends in the world helping me out."

Honcho smiled. He thought he knew where the conversation was about to go and liked it.

Continuing, Ryan closed his eyes. "If we can find out the truth, the real truth, then we can have an actual plan. There's a network of survivors out there ready to act. John and his people for one. If we have enough and can supply them with the necessary toys, and looking at you BP, the right props to confuse, I think we have a chance. Slim like five percent, but a chance."

Julia saw the sly grin and smacked Ryan. "What are our real chances you clown?"

Ryan leaned in. "Seriously? If I can keep my shit together and we get the intel and stuff I think we need, I'm confident at the ninety to ninety-five level. The five to ten percent left is where improvisation leaves me open. I know we can disrupt and even stop them, but not totally sure we can necessarily end it all. At least, until I know how deep and far it reaches."

Honcho and BP nodded in unison. Ryan was a super star at completing his missions and one focused operator when his facilities worked. Even if only half his engine was running, he was better than the top tier guys on their best days. With the right intel to show the way and whatever supplies and toys Ryan concocted up he might need that BP could scrounge up or send him in the right direction, Ryan's friends knew the three amigos working together again had a shot at success.

The band was back together.

"Hey, got to sign off. Late and need to conserve power my way. Been great everyone. Call me later." And then, BP was gone.

Ryan looked at Honcho and before he could even get out the sentence, Honcho raised his hand.

"DoD satellites are still working and so are the major cell carriers, though cell towers are pretty much useless. I hacked into the North American DoD sat overhead and got the beast to give me a private channel for sat phones. Use a USB cable from it and a program for video conferencing and there you go. When everything essentially died, I went through my phone book trying everyone I could before cell service got cut off. No one answered except BP. We've been video buddies ever since."

Honcho's abilities never ceased to amaze Ryan. The guy was a tech guru and brain trust. Having the satellites overhead was a treat as Ryan began to think how to use them to their advantage and expand the reach of the rag tag band of people connected to John. Ham radio kept people talking, but Ryan knew a more secure path kept out infiltrators who had a darker agenda. Secure sat phones meant private conversations and planning. He just had to link everyone together and get the whole thing working right.

That was going to take a whole lot of effort and ingenuity to work.

Julia tapped Ryan's shoulder. "Babe, it's late and I'm exhausted. Think I'm going to check on the wild ones and go to sleep. You two probably have a lot of catching up to do so I won't wait up. Good night, Honcho. And, thank you."

"Hey, for my three favorite people, anything. This bozo, meh."

She kissed Ryan on the cheek, and then Julia disappeared out the door.

Honcho motioned towards the black leather recliners. Stepping into the kitchen he grabbed some glasses and from the cupboard pulled out a bottle. Ryan was seated in the far chair facing his, so Honcho handed a glass, poured, and sat down. Smiling at his friend, Honcho shook his head to say to not even ask.

"Good stuff," Ryan coughed. Not from rough booze, but he'd opened a pretzel bag and got dry pieces stuck in his throat before taking a sip.

"My own homemade whisky. One of the craft brew guys had some barrels and ingredients so I brought them here and there you go. Seems he was looking to do some spirits and with things happening had full barrels screaming for attention. Then, made my own concoction that's aging away."

A better sip minus dry bits. "Not bad at all. A different flavor is floating around. What is it?"

"Sherry casks. Adds a reddish tint to it. Different for sure, but as it's aged it gets better."

Ryan felt an elephant in the room. When they showed up expectedly, he had hoped to find Honcho with Liz. When nothing was said immediately and things got crazy explaining the past three years, it slipped his mind. Now, with time to just talk, it seemed he should ask.

"Hey, Man, I wasn't not going to ask, but you know things got all crazy filling you in and all. What happened to Liz?"

Honcho sighed and flipped the recliner legs up. Taking a drink, he waited until it was gone. "She might be alive, or not. When everything happened, right before it got really bad, I came out here to get everything up and going for us and her parents. My bro was tasked with our parents back home to eventually get everyone all cozy here when we could manage it. Figured we had a bit for her to pack her folks up and me make this place cozy for the old people. Then the ferries stopped running and people either died or turned into walking human zombie robots. They got stuck at her dad's. A week, two went by before cell coverage crashed, and when I managed to finagle a working boat and get across the Sound, they were gone."

"Gone? As in not there or the other?"

"Just gone. Not even a note or anything. Place looked like a tornado went through. My guess, they either grabbed what they could and tried to get here or got corralled up. Though, she only knew of a cabin this way. Not the exact location. Been trying to find them ever since."

Ryan felt for his friend. The not knowing was the hardest part. Finality was better, because at least you had some closure one way or another. "Sorry, Honcho. I'm really sorry."

Honcho raised his glass. "No worries. I've had a long time to think about it. Wishful thinking I'll ever find them. Seattle is a dangerous place to be from the chatter I heard."

Ryan lifted his own glass. He'd lost his loved ones only to magically get them back. It didn't seem fair. He wasn't going to question the flip of the coin, just humbly rejoice inside he was fortunate while others still grieved. "To Liz."

Honcho clinked Ryan's glass. "To Liz."

CHAPTER 8

Sleep evaded him.

Much like it had the entire time on the road the last month. His shoulder ached something fierce and no amount of booze or less than potent pills could ease the pain. Throw in the nightmares and body tremors and Ryan was a huge mess.

Ever since being reunited with his family and being on the run, Ryan tried every trick in the book to hide his agony. The last thing he or they needed was for him to break down and lose it. Emma and David were scared of the boogeymen, Mark and their Papa coming to take them away. Julia, trying to keep herself together, he'd find occasionally sobbing, her worry at losing him forever at the forefront of her mind. She was tough and hard, but still fearful at what the future didn't let you peek under the wrapping paper. Add in seeing their father and husband writhing and sweating bullets from his own demons, and the Carmichaels were a hair short of becoming complete basket cases. Plus, spewing black blood didn't help Ryan not to appear as a monster for the kids.

Keeping that hidden was a precarious game of hide and seek.

Not every night was like this, as he had some restful ones where he could actually find some slumber and catch a few winks. Usually, it was due to complete exhaustion and his body and mind completely shut down.

Comatose was a better description.

On the nights his brain worked overtime, Ryan secluded himself off somewhere, more to hide his growing concern and uncontrolled body. The kids didn't need to see their father that way. And, hiding it from Julia kept her from nagging at him. Asking questions he knew no answers for, and worrying when her focus needed to be on the kids, over him. He'd had thirty days and nights to rummage through the cobwebs of his thoughts. Venture back to his childhood. Scour conversations. Remember a detail that seemed off.

Nothing leapt out.

Reg was a truck driver. That's all. Ryan had gone with him a few times on deliveries to the coast and Ft. Bragg. Pallets of goods for grocery stores and all-in-one places that had pharmacies too. No other stops on the way. So, if his dad was part of something back then, the son was oblivious to it.

Even Reg's military service was ordinary. At least, as far as Ryan knew from the pictures and stories. Helicopter crew chief for CH-53 helicopters, the big Sea Stallion birds for super heavy lifting. Stateside deep in the South. That's what Ryan had been told as a kid. The photos his father took sitting with the side door open as the beast flew around weren't of some war zone in Vietnam. Not that being there right in combat had a greater meaning than being on his own soil. Either could have led Reg to the path he was on now.

Ryan just had to find out the 5 Ws or some of them to start piecing the puzzle together.

He must have fallen asleep on the couch. When the tremors came and the convulsions, his body contorting into painful poses, Ryan nearly screamed out before catching himself. The last thing he needed was to wake the kids and have his terror reverberate off the concrete walls to echo down the hallway. Five minutes turned to ten, and ten to fifteen before it all stopped and he managed to curl into a ball. Probably not the best position to be in, but it felt appropriate as the tears formed and the salt fell down his cheeks.

Checking his watch, the time said six-thirty. Realizing the kids would be up in the not-too-distant future, he found a tin of delicious smelling coffee in the kitchen cupboard. Pouring some scoops into the basket of the coffee maker, Ryan found a mug and waited.

Time was his enemy and he knew it. If they were trying to track the Carmichaels and had made it this far north to scout, he hoped they hadn't caught his family's signal. Paranoia, or being prudent, he wasn't sure which one, Ryan needed a plan, a robust detailed and diagrammed outline for the just in case. He knew the silo in and out as much as he could remember. There was no way anyone could easily breach the main door above and the supply door where the Humvee was parked was blast proof too. Add the extra blast door they passed on the way in and the other in the garage area and they were sealed in tight like sardines that were still good years later.

No one was coming in the main routes.

The silo did have a hidden backdoor. A secret way in and out that wasn't on any architectural blueprints. Call it the escape hatch, it was the only other way in or out. It too had a multi-ton blast door between it and the silo so confidence was brimming full.

It was Ryan's way out for some recon missions to check the area.

The RF pinging made him nervous, scared even. He had to scout, get a lay of the land again if it meant making a stand. Julia wouldn't like the idea and the kids would protest, but he knew what he had to do. He was still a special ops veteran, had the blood of a soldier coursing his veins, even if older and with a leg in the grave. Being prepared was a natural extension of his mindset and this was no different than if he was still classified and doing government sanctioned or off the book missions. If anyone lurked within a few miles, he had to know.

It was the only way to protect everyone.

Getting out before the wild ones woke or even Julia to mount a protest, Ryan found Honcho already behind a console, typing away. The French press was half devoured, so he must have been at it for some time.

"Hey, Sleepy Head. Finally awake?" Honcho joked.

Ryan smiled. "Couldn't really sleep. Plus, all the virus effects on my body. Progressively getting worse, so I'm up. Got some things to do."

Honcho knew without a word about it spoken. "You know the way out. I'll keep them occupied until you get back. Need anything before you leave?"

A deep breath sigh. "Nah, I'm good. Just some recon to get reacquainted and fresh air. Anything I should pay special attention to or avoid?" Ryan knew Honcho was security minded, so knowing where to avoid traps and trip wires would keep things quiet.

"Ah, I see your eyes flickering. Everything is remote controlled now. No wires or devices above ground beyond hidden cameras. Didn't want Bambi accidently blowing up, you know?"

Ryan smiled. "Awesome. I like my feet right where they are." Turning to leave, he caught himself. "Find anything yet?"

Honcho pursed his lips. He flipped over a faded old black and white photocopy of an image of Reg standing in front of a CH-53, and threw it down in front of Ryan. The caption credit, from 1970 and a world away from the United States, simply added to the deception his dad created long ago.

"Shit."

"Go on your walkabout for a bit. We'll talk later."

Taking the cue, Ryan waved two fingers and was gone.

Gearing up took some time, but he wanted to be sure his ghillie suit, a body covering to attach branches and other forest fauna to help blend into his surroundings and stay hidden, was well adorned with the right camouflage. It meant venturing out the secret tunnel and exposure before he was ready, but Honcho had literally wired the place with full video and monitors near the blast door that gave a bird's eye view for a thousand meters any direction. Running outside and grabbing everything he could off the forest floor that was green, he hauled it back inside and got to work. Satisfied with his haul of foliage to conceal himself, Ryan suited up, checked his gear, and with his M4 set to kill, went for a walk.

Honcho's Moose Lair lay inside the Olympic National Forest and the park. At a lower elevation, it meant Ryan's destination would take some time to hike the mountain range. He wanted to get as high as possible to really get a view of their surroundings and with dense trees to maneuver, his work was cut out for him. This far out he didn't think he would see much, the cities and towns were far enough away and the range would inhibit some of his sightlines. If anything, Ryan figured to catch some fresh air, maybe catch any planes running reconnaissance, and begin taping together his action plans A to Z.

It was a little after nine in the morning by the time he reached the nearest summit. He had made some great time finding a deer path and taking it up the side to stop a few meters from the top. A quick water break and then he could lighten his load and rest a bit. He only needed his long-distance scope and binoculars, so leaving his pack close by meant he could move more easily through the trees and brush. He didn't think he would need it, but he grabbed the parabolic sound amplifier and hustled to the top. Prone facing east, Ryan put the earpiece in and took in the sounds of nature.

It was a military grade device capable of extended miles of crystal-clear sound recognition. Rustling brooks of water, deer and elk scampering through brush, even bears and mountain lions in the distance that he hoped to avoid. Peaceful was an understatement taking in nature.

Until the Hawkeye radar plane's twin propellers cut the serenity of the forest.

Dead was a better word for how still Ryan lay beneath his ghillie suit. A fire ant wouldn't get him to move. Lying motionless, he pulled the parabolic dish close and tilted his head to the right to catch the airplane, a newer E2D Navy carrier-based aircraft, its huge circular dish sitting atop its roof, bearing down on his location. With no carriers afloat that John knew of, he assumed it was out of Moffitt Field. As it grew close, he felt the hairs stand up and his stomach feel queasy.

It's only a recon, Ryan tried to assure himself.

Passing overhead it went a mile further north and then made a hard bank to the right. Taking his que, Ryan slithered back down the side of the mountain for added cover and wedged himself between a large boulder and tree. Fumbling with the radio dial, he turned the volume up and clicked the scan feature. He didn't think he could catch any secure plane channels even with his stolen equipment, but maybe luck would keep rolling sevens.

He didn't wait long to cash in.

"Base, this is Aerial Eight over Washington. Over."

"Aerial Eight, base acknowledged. Status report? Over." The familiar voice echoed in his earpiece.

"Base, negative confirmation on pings. Repeat, negative pings received. Orders? Over."

Reg Carmichael's voice, void of any emotion, beat inside Ryan's eardrum. "Keep looking. They're somewhere around there. He had a friend in Seattle so check the city. Find them now. Over and out."

Seattle was miles away and gave Ryan and company breathing room. If the RF trackers were generic, there was no way they could pinpoint the signal specifically to Julia and the kids. The trackers were disabled now, but if Reg's people had caught an earlier ping and managed to triangulate, then the net could close sooner than later. Honcho might know more, so getting back to find out seemed a better option than lounging atop a mountain for a fresh breeze.

As he was about to throw his pack back on, his earpiece caught a transmission when it started back to scan mode.

"Did you guys see that?" It was a hushed female voice, young by the sound of it.

A quiet reply. This voice deeper and male. "Yup. They got a bird looking for something or someone. Better tell King."

CHAPTER 9

"Where's Ryan, Honcho?"

Honcho was sipping coffee at the table in the kitchenette. It was still early so his hair was a mess and the circles beneath his eyes evident. "I know not of this Ryan of which you speak."

Julia sighed. "Come on. He didn't come to bed last night and now he's nowhere to be found. Where'd he go?"

A long sip of coffee, and then Honcho got up, poured her a cup with powdered vanilla creamer, and motioned for Julia to sit. "A walkabout."

"A walk a what?" She chugged down the coffee, and waited for an answer.

Honcho smiled. "You know? Like an Australian walk around the country. He couldn't sleep, so he decided on an early morning recon mission to scope things out."

She shook her head. "Still not sleeping. It's getting worse, Honcho."

Concerned eyes. "What's getting worse?"

Julia wasn't sure how to answer. "How deep did he get into the weeds on things and how the virus has affected him?"

He leaned back and crossed his arms. Then Honcho took a sip, thought about it, and spoke. "Besides the intel I picked up and what he said about a few things, I'm still a bit lost on the whole thing."

Shaking her mug for more coffee, Honcho obliged and then Julia set it down. "He's losing himself a bit every day. Decisions become a bit more rash, though rooted in a sort of brilliance I can only assume come from whatever training he had as a soldier. Something that a person might decide was too risky to do, Ryan finds a way to do it, and then succeed at it. At some point, whatever luck has gotten him this far might just run out."

Honcho reached over and took her hand. "Listen. I've known that asshole for a few decades and trust him with my life. Even if he went absolutely insane and wore his underwear on his head and ran around naked, though the image makes me want to throw up, I'd follow him to the end of the Earth. And guess what, we're already there."

She wasn't entirely sure how to take that statement. "Well, I hope he doesn't get to that point."

"No, I definitely don't want to see him with his cock flapping in the breeze."

Julia laughed, the picture front and center. "Let's make sure he doesn't."

Honcho saw something else in Julia's eyes. "There's something else, isn't there?"

She bit her lower lip. "You notice anything about Emma?"

He didn't quite catch the question. "Besides she's grown since I last saw her?"

"You were a teacher and dealt with special education children. Something not seem quite, *right?*"

He had noticed it, but chalked it up to Emma being a smart little girl and all the hard work Julia and Ryan put into her getting the therapies she needed. "Her speech is really coming along. But, I figured all the work you two put into it."

She shrugged. "No therapies for three years, Honcho."

The picture began to paint itself without the need to use the words. He saw the look on Julia's face. "You think the virus and vaccine did something to her?"

She nodded. "I haven't said anything to Ryan because him worrying more, well, who knows what it would do to his already fragile state. But there's something going on and I don't know if it's a good thing or a bad one. We need to find out."

"Mark didn't say anything about it?"

"No. He's hellbent on trying to create the control vaccine over everyone he barely spent any time around her beyond the pokes and prods."

The eyebrow raised. "What about David?"

A shrug. "He's always been a bright kid. I can't pinpoint anything specific. But, I see some stuff in him too. She's the one who is night and day from everything I know. Comparing her to friends and kids we know, or used to know, she's progressed in ways I couldn't imagine. And, done some things I'd almost say were extraordinary."

The words struck. "Like what exactly?"

Julia looked down, almost as if she didn't want to say. "The day Ryan found us at the research facility, Emma had drawn a picture days before of him coming to see her. It was eerie because it captured really close what happened that night."

Could be as simple as a girl missing her father and projecting to her current situation. Reading more without some science behind it was creeping down conspiracy road.

"OK, odd but not conclusive to anything. Not discounting the weird factor, but we'd need more to go on."

The virus and vaccines had done their damage. The ruins of the world outside of the silo, screamed it. If there was a positive to it, the ability to help a little girl with Down Syndrome overcome her disability, or at least keep up with it, then the science made her even more valuable.

As soon as that thought hit Honcho's mind, he cringed.

"Julia, if the virus and vaccine did something to Emma, then we have even more to worry about if they find out. Every parent with a kid who has a disability might do anything, and I mean anything, to give their own kid a fighting chance at a typical life. Emma becomes a walking target."

The realization wasn't lost on Julia. She had thought about it. Lost countless nights of sleep worrying if Mark ever found out and did even more harm to Emma. Both of her kids were pawns in a larger game, a sinister plot that madmen used to fuel their insanity. There was no way those bastards could win, at any cost.

"Do you think you can dig in your world and find out anything at all? I need to know."

Honcho smiled. "For her, I'd move the world. David too. You guys are all I have left. Ryan, dude can kick rocks," he winked.

"Thank you, Honcho. But please, do not say anything to Ryan. Let him focus on whatever crazy things he needs to do. He doesn't need more to cloud his brain."

"Promise. But, at some point if I find something out that is absolutely critical to what is going on, I have to tell him. He is the kind of guy who needs all the right intel to develop the right plan. Deal?"

Julia sighed. "Deal."

As the word left her lips, two sleepy bodies appeared through the door. Tussled hair, yawns, and pajama legs halfway up a leg, Emma and David went straight to the couch and curled up. Pete trotted in right behind. Grabbing the remote, Honcho turned on the television, flipped it to the DVD player, and cycled through until there was agreement between the siblings. Movie on and their attention directed at the screen, he went to the fridge and grabbed ingredients for breakfast.

"Omelets anyone?"

A round of yes' and in a moment, Honcho was hard at work to fill the bellies of the little beasts.

CHAPTER 10

"Next time you go off for a day hike, you might want to warn me ahead of time," Julia huffed as Ryan walked into the room.

The kids were eating a snack and playing a board game and managed a quick smile before focusing back on the board. Honcho was in the far recliner sipping coffee, staring at a tablet screen. He waved a hand and shot a glance before going back to whatever occupied his attention. Julia met Ryan at the door and whisked him outside.

"Listen, before you say anything, I'm sorry. I'm stressed and not seeing you there this morning made me feel alone again. But please, if you know you are going to be gone, just tell me."

Ryan kissed her forehead. "Of course. I hadn't planned on an early hike out, but I couldn't sleep and figured after the warning bells I'd get a step ahead of whatever is coming our way."

Julia saw the look in his eyes. "Tell me, Ryan."

"They had a radar plane looking for signal pings. Since Honcho disabled yours, they aren't catching anything. But, they also aren't going anywhere either. My dad had to remember Honcho lived in Seattle and sent the plane east of here. My guess, if they think you're here, they'll soon send people to really find out."

Fear stared at him and Julia swallowed before talking. "Are we safe here?"

Ryan smoothed her brown hair back from her eyes. "Down here, we are. Would take a direct missile hit three times over to get us. If they decided to siege, we could last years with all the MRE and other rations Honcho has stockpiled. Unless the kids keep growing and eating, then it's a few days."

A smile. "They are growing, aren't they?"

"Big as weeds. But there's something else and I need to talk to Honcho about it. There are people out there too. Caught a radio transmission. No idea who, but he might know. Could mean we have some allies to help out."

Julia moved out of the way. "Go on. Figure it out and make sure you make it for lunch with the kids."

"Roger that," Ryan smiled as he kissed her cheek and went to talk to Honcho.

The big man was so deep in thought he didn't see Ryan sitting across from him. When he realized it, he jumped as if he had seen a ghost.

"Jesus, Ryan. Don't creep up on someone like that. Bound to give me a heart attack."

A warm smile to ease the fright. "Sorry, Honcho. You looked so focused I figured I'd just watch like a creeper until you came back from the beyond."

A sigh. "I think you are the one who is from the great beyond my friend. Or, your dad. Not sure which at this point. Anyway, I'll fill you in."

The statement caught Ryan off guard. "OK. That seems cryptic. But first, a question for you."

"Shoot."

"I was up on the ridge taking a look and caught a big bird doing a signal search. Got a glimpse of their radio chatter and nothing else was pinging so they got sent off to the city to search. Figure my dad remembered you lived there so they're off hunting for you."

Honcho laughed. "Me? No. As far as anyone knows I'm worm food. Left a body in the house just in case someone came looking for me."

"Damn. Jokes on them then. I also caught a local transmission. Some people listening into the channel besides me. Mentioned someone called, King?"

Honcho's normal complexion turned a shade paler. "Did you say, King?"

"I did. Something wrong?"

A minute, maybe two passed. Eyes focused and lips tight. Then, Honcho finally spoke. "King controls all of King County. Nothing in or out without permission. All I've caught are radio chatter that paints a pretty dark picture. Not someone you want on your bad side."

Ryan let the words sink in. King could be anyone or anything. Someone looking out for their people or some really bad character on a power trip. If the group weren't Brainers, then there was a chance they were survivors simply trying to keep themselves alive. And if they were, then they could be assets for a fight or allies worth some negotiation.

"When you say dark, like what?"

Honcho stared into Ryan's eyes. "Like stringing up people who don't belong kind of crazy. Like I said, radio talk about what they've done to interlopers, so I don't have any real experience. Just that feeling in my stomach."

The world was dark, dank, and full of crazies who killed without a second thought. For three years Ryan dealt with people like that, Brainers fitting the bill. It wasn't until he came across John and his band of misfits that actual survivors fighting against evil existed. There were others fighting the good cause, but somewhere in the mix were those who only had self-interest.

Screw anyone not in your camp and anyone outside is a threat to reckon with and eliminate.

He knew the type, the mentality, kill or be killed. Not out of any hatred, but the innate desire to live and stay one step ahead of death. Outsiders weren't part of the clan.

Then, there were the ones who didn't fit at all. The assholes that somehow made it out alive. They had their brains intact. Could reason and feel. Just decided to take advantage of the situation and pretend to be the top dogs. This King could be anyone, fit into any category. Be the leader of the Northwest Brainers for all Ryan knew.

One way or another, he had to find out.

"I know that look Ry and it's not a pretty one," Honcho frowned. "Please tell me you aren't thinking what I know you are going to do really soon."

Ryan smiled. "Recon, my big brother from another mother. We need all the help we can get. And if we can potentially set a trap, I think we try and recruit more resources."

Honcho stood up. "You're not firing on all cylinders, Dude. What if you, well, you know? Decide to ventilate an entire town of people because they look at you funny? Whether they deserve it or not. Just saying."

An affirmative nod. "Point taken, Honcho. If I can keep the stress down, I can manage it. Like I said, recon first to see if it's even doable."

"I'm guessing alone?"

"This Ghost runs solo my friend. Someone needs to protect my valuables."

Honcho laughed. "I knew you'd stick me with those rotten kids."

CHAPTER 11

The radio chirped alive, interrupting his dreams. Glancing at the clock and seeing it was still dark, Reg hoped the disruption to his sleep was inconsequential. It had been weeks since he had needed to have someone killed for irritating him.

"What?" Reg barked into the receiver.

"Sir, we have confirmation on multiple signals. Hard to pinpoint, but we have them."

Sitting up, Reg asked, "Where?"

The solider didn't answer quick enough.

"I said where, Asshole?"

"Apologies, Sir. We have them in and around the Seattle area."

Reg wasn't sure what to feel or say. Not like he had feelings. Those left long ago. He was on or off. Anger or nothing. A weird dilemma, if he cared about it.

And, he didn't.

"Great," Reg muttered. "Get me flight ready. We're going hunting."

It had been a month since he last saw Ryan. Technically thirty-three days. For seven of them he required recuperation from blast injuries from all the flying debris Ryan's bomb blast sent in its wake. A slight concussion, scrapes and bruises, and a broken finger from hitting the pavement after being thrown twenty feet.

Seven long days to seethe.

The remaining days he spent ordering all available troops to scour the coast and inland searching for his son and family. Any potential hiding place from his memories of his boy and where he might slither off to and lick his own wounds.

Every recon came back with zero intel.

Sacramento was a bust. Pismo Beach nothing. Oakdale a ghost town.

Even the old family house, where Reg figured Ryan might go for sentimental reasons, even if it was nothing but a pile of rubble, proved uneventful without a trace. It was as if he simply vanished.

Like a ghost.

The remaining days were spent listening to the stories Mark told. They made Reg want to vomit. Mark painted Ryan as some super soldier, a man who could do and did the impossible. A shadow among shadows who disappeared with no evidence he was ever anywhere. The countless missions with lives saved. The hundreds of confirmed kills.

The ones that would never be acknowledged.

What drew particular interest for Reg was the story that came up often and was brushed off with uneasiness. He knew Ryan was a soldier, a mechanic was the official story, supposedly stationed overseas at some base working on tanks and trucks. On one R and R trip home, Ryan came back in a cast, his right pinky finger mangled. When asked, he gave curt responses. A tank track accident nearly severed off his finger. Doctors managed to re-attach and he'd be as good as new.

The facial cuts and bruises told a bit of a different story.

Ryan always diverted the talk. Turned the conversation around and onto a different subject. Mark told Reg why, and if he could feel any respect for anyone, there would be twenty gold bars for Ryan. But, he didn't have those human attributes anymore. Only growing rage festered for Ryan when Reg learned the truth.

Covert operation. Deep inside enemy territory. Ryan and Mark as a sniper and spotter team performing advanced recon for an upcoming mission. A perfect sniper's nest on a top floor of a blown-out building with an escape line to another building and the safety of a river extraction less than a klick away. They sat for a few days waiting and watching, their intended target a top general playing both sides of the war. The mission was to catch him in the act of meeting a local insurgent operative known to the CIA.

What they saw? Was much worse.

The general was executing civilians, who failed to deliver narcotics to their destinations within a specific window to avoid overhead satellites. The drugs fueled his own personal ambitions and power-hungry drive to be feared. Radio silence kept Ryan and Mark from reporting in, but with an open order to only eliminate active threats, the gray area was too wide to move forward. Day after day a local was used as a prop, a warning, for those who either disobeyed or didn't meet expectations. When innocent children became targets for the sex trade, Ryan pulled the trigger.

It proved fateful.

The general's brother didn't take kindly to the hit. The area swarmed with soldiers and choked off the escape route. Building by building and floor by floor the search for the shooter, inched closer to Ryan and Mark. The team split up, Mark managing to shimmy down an air duct and hide while Ryan got captured after a lengthy gun battle that saw the body count impressive for a single operator to do solo.

Ryan had killed two top generals, the sons of the leader of the region. The interrogation went sideways, and even though Ryan was beaten and tortured, his silence only made his situation worse. The father of the deceased decided to cut a finger off for each son and started with the pinky finger on Ryan's right hand. Using Ryan's own knife, the father began to cut it off before being interrupted.

His first mistake was leaving Ryan alone.

Comes back to beat Ryan more. Take another finger too. But the idea of denigrating the American operator was too much to pass up. Use it as propaganda to bolster his standing among insurgents.

That was his second mistake.

A man like Ryan was trained for death. Torture a walk in the park. A normal soldier would crumble under the beatings and mutilations. A special operator used it to his advantage and strengths.

In the five minutes being left alone, Ryan had cut his bindings using a small blade from the back of his BDU pants. No one had bothered to do a thorough search of his body.

That was the last mistake.

When his enemy decided that urinating on him was the path to humiliation, Ryan turned the tables. Cut the man's cock off and handed it to him. And to add to the legend of what would become, The Ghost, Ryan proceeded to kill every soldier in the building by slitting their throats and burning the place to the ground. Then like a giddy schoolboy, he skipped right out the front door.

No trace, nothing to directly tie Ryan to the massacre. For all anyone outside the bubble knew, the deaths were retribution by warring factions seeking to take control. Plant that thought of doubt, and let the rumors run amok. Per longstanding policy, the American government swept it all under the rug. Buried it deep to protect the CIA and their double-faced dealings with criminals.

Locals who found the carnage whispered a story of a ghost. A shadowy figure seen against the backdrop of the raging inferno skipping merrily away. The seed for the legend firmly planted, it kept growing and after Ryan's rehab stint stateside, continued for years to come.

Reg sat, the story feeling too surreal. Ryan as a real soldier seemed impractical. Being a trained killer and elite operative for the government a fantastical story. If true, his son was an enemy to reckon with, an adversary like no other.

It felt good to finally have a fight worth his attention.

"What part are you not getting through your head, Reg?" Mark's frustration starting to boil over.

Reg grinned, evil permeating the right corner of his mouth. "If what you say is true, that my boy is the baddest bad ass of them all, *and* he's on his way to turning into something with so much evil the devil is an altar boy compared to him, then I say we need him. And, we need him soon so we can control the monster inside. Imagine the things we can do with that kind of death dealing carnage maker on our side."

Mark for the first time was almost speechless. Rather than go down the rabbit hole, he left it. He didn't need to add to Ryan's mystique. Just find a way to kill the bastard and be done, regardless of what Reg wanted. If he could help it, it would be a death worse than any Ryan had delivered.

The thought burned in a smile that took hours to fade.

CHAPTER 12

"You get signal to Seattle, right?" Ryan asked as he added the last of his clips to his tac vest.

Honcho nodded. "Got a dish high up the mountain that can send and receive. You still sure about this?"

A whisp of air blew out. "As sure as I can be right now. Besides, if my dad and Mark are in Seattle, maybe I get a lucky shot or two," Ryan winked.

Julia wasn't impressed by the guy talk. "I still don't like it. What am I supposed to tell the kids?"

"I'll handle it. I won't be gone too long. A day, maybe two. In and out if I can help it." The smile said he was telling the truth, as hard as truth was to swallow.

"Fine," Julia shrugged. "Bring them something back at least."

"Will do."

Ryan found Emma and David sitting at the table, crayons blazing away at creativity from somewhere inside their memories. David had always been an artist, his skills even at an early age a marvel to see the final products. Emma had been learning to draw circles and lines, far behind her peers and brother. Looking over her shoulder, Ryan was amazed at the image staring up at him. A seascape, their last family venture to the coast. It was beyond the skills of an eight-year-old. Not a masterpiece of Van Gogh or Thibaut, but damn near close.

"My little artists hard at work I see," Ryan motioned as he took a seat and watched them work.

"Hi, Dad," David mumbled, barely looking up as he was deep into a dinosaur drawing of a T-Rex that was impressive.

Emma stopped and touched Ryan's face. "I need to draw you, Dad."

Ryan smiled. "I'd like that, Princess. You and your brother are getting really good at your drawings. Lucky Uncle Honcho stockpiled enough crayons and paper for eternity."

Two nods.

Leaning on the table, Ryan cleared his throat. "Hey guys, old Dad here needs to go on a little trip into Seattle."

David looked up, his eyes beginning to redden. "Seriously, Dad? Just stay here with us."

Emma turned her head to the left. "Bubba, Dad needs to go. He's got stuff to do. And he'll probably bring us some toys back!"

His smart little girl seemed to read his mind.

"What are we supposed to do with you gone?" David began to whine before catching himself. "I know, Dad. Take care of everyone and make sure Uncle Hon doesn't get into trouble."

His son still knew the drill which made Ryan happy. "Yes, David. Big man for Dad, right?"

David tried to snap his fingers and winked. "Got you covered, Dad."

Kissing them both before he left, Ryan placed a small box in front of each before leaving. "After I'm gone you can open them up. Not before, OK?"

"OK," echoed in unison.

Getting to Honcho's boat in Port Angeles meant travel along the 101 in fading daylight. According to Honcho, there was no life, good or bad along the way. Until you got to the heart of the city, and then avoiding everything was the way to stay alive. The boat was anchored at the Port Angeles Yacht Club, a fitting location given Honcho's loathe for the elite class.

The direct route meant certain death.

Two alternatives always worked, though took considerable time and energy. Backroads west of the airport and snaking to the coast to hike along the sands was the best option. Going as far as the Tumwater Creek to then hike hidden in the trees took you close to the docks. That took less time, but meant deeper into the hornet's nest and potential discovery if you played it wrong.

It was really a flip of the coin.

Ryan took option three. The airport might provide some intel, or at a minimum, an opportunity to see if it was still a viable place to land a plane. It meant more time outside of cover, but a chance to get information and see where it might take him. John was working on expanding the network of resistance survivors and had a few mechanics who might be able to revive some planes. Create their own transport to bring the fight to Mark and Reg.

Besides, it was on the way and he could skirt the city and still hit the beach and march right on in.

The small beat up four-cylinder pickup Honcho loaned Ryan was almost as quiet as a mouse and convenient for the trip. The paint job left a lot to be desired if that mattered much in the apocalypse. Not that the dark blue didn't help add to nighttime camouflage. The Aztec painting on the hood of the half-naked lady, bright and brilliant under the crescent moon, was something Ryan hoped went unnoticed. Honcho had at least replaced the glass pack exhaust to keep the noise level down.

When you come across an old low rider past its prime for free, you can't be too choosy in what you select.

Taking South Critchfield Road and coming up on the airfield, Ryan saw nothing but darkness. Flipping on his night vision, the runways were intact, a good sign, and relatively free of debris. Mental note made, he skirted the chain link fence to hook up with West 18th Street and then to South Milwaukee Drive. It ended at the Olympic Discovery Trail, but with some bolt cutters handy, he snipped the lock, moved the steel pipe from its hole, and then drove along the paved path to reconnect with South Milwaukee further down. He took it as far as he could before parking the truck in a grove of trees near the coast and proceeded on foot, using the tree cover to walk and enjoy the sounds of the water.

His peaceful walk didn't last long.

A hundred yards in, Ryan encountered a group of what had to be Brainers. At least, he thought that's what they were by the lack of children. Huddled around a campfire, sitting in chairs and the occasional laughter permeating the silence, five men and two women cajoled as if the world wasn't over.

It just didn't sit right.

Erasing the distance, Ryan found a place in the shadows to watch and listen. The conversation was mundane, the stories told bordering on boring, and the hint of what he could only describe as feeling secure permeating the group. He did catch the snippets of talk about their kills, but so nondescript in details it was a toss-up on whether they were really Brainers, or something else.

I don't have time to find out.

The thought brought more from the depths of his mind. He tried to shake them out, but they kept coming.

Just kill them and be done. They're talking about people they've killed. Erase them and move on.

Ryan tried to silence the voice. Wanted it to just go away. It was getting harder to shake it.

No, I can't kill innocent people.

He still had some control. Thought he did anyway.

No time for a pity party. Even if they're not Brainers, they could belong to the King. Honcho said King had outsiders dispatched with malice. Want to die before you find out who's responsible for this mess?

The voice was right. Kill or be killed.

Half an hour later, Ryan located Honcho's other borrowed possession. A small sailboat hysterically called the Sea Nympho. Anchor up, Ryan was finally at sea, the hours of travel ahead in the dark a worry for any debris or wrecks he might encounter, but a relief to be off land and less visible to hopefully make up some time.

The journey gave Ryan unbridled time to think, a luxury he hadn't really had since rescuing his family. On the boat listening to the water part and ripple by, Ryan felt at ease. Not a real sailor by any stretch, he had grown up around all kinds of boats. Sailing on Hobie Cats was the closest he came to an actual sailboat with real sails which for a kid, being able to navigate successfully was a massive win to remember for today. He wasn't going to try and make his first solo trek with a full-size boat using only sails, so the small outboard motor had to suffice. Besides, maneuverability just in case and consistent speed would make the trip smoother and quicker, at least he thought as much.

With time to kill and nothing to capture his attention on the way, his mind had hours to think and take in the sights.

His expectations for the world had a low bar. Having seen death and destruction from the east to the west, Ryan figured Seattle was as desolate and dreary as the rest of the country.

He was so wrong.

Coming into Elliot Bay, Seattle was awash in lights. Something he hadn't seen anywhere else. Not an entire city on the electrical grid kind of illumination.

No.

The Space Needle and Belltown were lit up like Christmas. Down by Pioneer Square, the sign beckoned, saying life was either carrying on like nothing ever went down, or was a trick to draw in unsuspecting travelers and then insert any horror movie death as a conclusion to their demise.

Flashbacks to better times.

If he wasn't seeing it with his own eyes there was no way to believe it. He had expected rubble and blackness and got a city pretending to be alive again. The shadows were supposed to be his friend and a lone light a beacon where he needed to go. This turned the plan upside down and sideways.

All he could do was roll with it.

Needing a safe place to park the boat, he found it at Smith Cove. Replete with more boats than you could imagine, he found an open slip and maneuvered the Sea Nympho into place. Secured to the dock, he had a long foot journey before he made the Elliott Bay Trail to then cautiously work his way into downtown.

"Rooster in the hen house."

The mic chirped in Ryan's ear. "Isn't it fox in the hen house?"

Ryan smiled. "Rooster. I'm on the prowl."

A sinister laugh. "Wife might have an issue with that, my friend. Take care. Call if you need your ass rescued. We'll ignore it."

"Thanks, Big Man. Keep the fort secure. Over and out."

Darkness still gave Ryan some cover, though with the morning sun coming he wasn't sure how long. Skirting the inner part of the city would take time and simply be like finding a needle in a haystack. He could scout around, but the clock was ticking, and time not a friend. The cautious operator would keep silent and, in the darkness, find a place to hole up and watch from above to see what transpired.

Ryan was feeling more offensive minded.

Cut the bullshit and go right to the source. It had so many negatives to it, but if it worked there were some advantages to dealing with it straight on. Not that he was planning on doing it right at this very moment.

His special ops brain was still firing a few cylinders.

He hadn't seen a soul around. They could be Brainers and if they were he was a goner. His plan, thought up in less than ten minutes when he saw all of the glaring city lights, was to find a quiet observation post and check things out.

Discreet.

A few blocks down past the railroad yard he found a Washington DMV building. Tall and deserted, he figured why the hell not, and proceeded to pry open a side door and secure it behind. Quickly moving from floor to floor to the roof access, he used his bolt cutters on the lock, and slowly pushed on the door to go outside. Scanning the rooftop, still under the cover of darkness, the building took up a whole block and had multiple places to hide and conceal. Huge HVAC units and solar panels offered multiple locations and gave him the run of the roof. Finding a spot with a perfect three-hundred-and-sixty-degree view, Ryan set his ruck aside, took out his binoculars, and dove into Peeping Tom mode.

The barricades and high fencing around the old arena caught his attention first. Scanning the grounds, he saw guards walking the interior perimeter. Focusing past it, Ryan pursed his lips as more came into view. The whole Seattle Center area seemed to be some kind of compound, broken up into separately fenced areas. From Queen Ann Avenue to 7th Avenue and between Mercer Street and Denny Way, multiple buildings, parks, and grassy areas were cordoned off. He couldn't tell the whole extent of it, but it seemed like a part of the city with importance.

And, that was where he needed to be to find King.

As morning came and sunlight filled the streets, Ryan saw life emerge, one body at a time. Slowly at first, but as the minutes ticked by, more people came from the shadows of buildings that still stood intact or from somewhere beneath the ruins of others. Normal looking, if normal meant anything in the current world. Relatively clean, engaging in conversations, and the occasional kid in tow.

He had to take a second look as what caught his eyes seemed unreal. A man and woman, walking casually, engrossed in some kind of intimate talk by the way they leaned in and listened to the other, carried paper coffee cups.

Coffee?

Backtracking their route, Ryan saw the line of people, single file, standing on the sidewalk outside a coffee shop. That's what the sign said anyway. A few people sat in what looked like old Adirondack chairs lined against the outside wall. Laughing, smiles, ordinary interactions you'd seen three years ago. All taking place after a massive virus took down the planet and society disappeared. Or, so he thought.

Surreal was an understatement.

Ryan sat down. He'd been here before, thinking life was starting back up only to find a bullet tearing through his shoulder. He should have seen it, but mere days after losing his family and all alone, the want of seeing and being around real people clogged his vision until it was too late. The severed heads were testament to the depravity he would come to know as Brainers.

Brainers didn't keep children around. That was confirmed not too long ago. Seeing miniature humans with adults was something survivors did, family or close ties. Maybe even taking on the responsibility and adopting when blood relations didn't exist. All of the images below were out of sorts, but in the same breath, if anyplace could revive humanity and get back to life, Ryan figured Seattle was the city.

Time for a walk.

He hadn't quite come equipped to blend in. Black BDUs and a spare urban pair to infiltrate the daylight were the clothing choices of this old special operator. Take off the overshirt and go incognito with an old Gogol Bordello concert t-shirt he borrowed from Honcho from when they played Bumbershoot years ago and Ryan got to witness their awesome stage show, and he might pass for a local.

Maybe.

Ditching his gear topside of the DMV building and taking only his Sig tucked in the back of his pants and a few extra magazines in case of a firefight, Ryan snuck out the backdoor into the daylight. The plan was on version twelve, ready to simply throw it all out and play the whole thing by ear. He had to be cool, but not too cool to draw attention. Observe and blend in. Gain intel and find answers. All alone in the middle of people who may know everyone and watch him with an evil eye if they thought he was an outsider.

Only time would tell.

Invigorated and feeling a bit alive, the fresh air was a treat. That's how he felt out in the open and not sulking in the shadows. People smiled as he passed, polite good mornings shared and reciprocated. Children playing with toy cars and throwing around balls.

Seattle looked like, Seattle.

The barriers and people strolling with guns, painted a different picture. Not overt, but subtle, an impressionist's view of the world. Three years ago, he would have figured liberal protest, a bit far to the left of left, that took over city blocks in anger over police brutality. It reminded him of the Capitol Hill takeover, though without the people living in tents. No one seemed upset or angry. Not a soul paid attention to the fencing or weapons. Everything seemed like it was just the way of life.

Normal.

When you jump into the lion's den, you better be prepared to face the beast. Or at least, partake in the culture and acclimate. The coffee shop beckoned, though without knowing what you had to exchange or pay with for a cup of Joe, getting in line was a bit risky. *What the hell*, Ryan thought, *I might as well make myself at home and meet the nice people.*

"Oh my. I forgot my wallet," Ryan smiled when he got to the front of the register.

Generation Z shook her head. No more than eighteen, hair dyed different shades and an eyebrow piercing with a smiley face button attached, the girl managed to smile back. "Like, I have not heard that one before. What can I get you, Love."

The Scottish accent threw him. But only for a moment. "Filter coffee. No room, Lassie," he answered in his best Scottish impersonation.

Her pale cheeks took on a red hue. Embarrassed? Flattered? It was hard to tell. "Long way from Skye, Mr. American?"

It took a second to register. "Aye. A few summers tucked away on a nice little croft overlooking the bay."

Handing Ryan his coffee, she touched his hand, caressed it for a split second, an implication of affection there. "Next one's on the house."

Green eyes glowing, Ryan winked, proceeded by a short bow of the head. "Until then, Love."

The encounter, if during any other time, would feel right. Flirtation was what people did. A simple word, touch, wink, nod, it all went down without a second thought. Three years ago, if he had walked in the door, the same scene might have played out. Likely would have, given his personable nature. *If,* he was single and in the market. *People person* was what Julia said. A natural personality of unknowing charm that drew people to it like flies.

Somehow though, it felt weird and absolutely *wrong*.

Besides the age difference, which in apocalyptic land you take what you can get in finding friends and companions, the cheeriness and everyday chit chat was out of place.

Or, seemed like it.

Ryan got in line for a coffee, a *real* coffee, something that he would have done the last time he was in Seattle visiting Honcho. Talking, laughing, people watching, would all have been expected and not given a second thought. Now, it was odd to feel warm and fuzzy when the world was different. Throw in the flirt and hand touching and it was like society had never fallen into chaos.

Polar opposite feelings washed him up and down.

Hot coffee in hand, Ryan left the shop, sipping as he walked, smiling between sips, vigilant eyes searching for intel and scraps of information. Most of the neighborhood stood, the occasional ruins of a building sporadic. Apartment balconies housed plants and other assorted treasures, the lower levels boarded up and secure looking doors guarding entrances. Businesses began to open. Bicycles passed and runners sped by.

It made little sense.

An air horn blew Ryan back to reality. Glancing around as inconspicuously as practical, a fish out of water since he had no idea what the blaring siren meant, he had no idea what to do. A hand suddenly grabbed him by the back of the t-shirt and pushed him along and through the open door of a building, which quickly slammed shut and the sound of locks engaging echoing behind. Standing in darkness with a stranger behind him, he began to turn around and then stopped as the hand released and a small light overhead turned on.

"Not from around here, are you?"

Ryan stared blankly as he turned to face the voice.

"Anyone who lives inside this protected space knows what the siren means. Anyone who is trying to attack knows it too. At least, the alive ones. So, you must be a survivor passing through or something else. Got a name?"

Ryan focused on the woman standing three feet away. Her blue eyes and short blond hair atop her tall stature made her presence intimidating, if you felt someone at your eye level a threat. "Ryan."

She motioned towards a stairwell and directed him to go up. A flight up, there was a heavy metal door already open and as he walked past, the woman closed it behind her and bolted it shut. Pointing to the next flight, Ryan got the idea. She secured the last door and walking around him, went to a small table near a window, and sat down.

"Come and sit. I think we have some great conversation ahead of us."

He hesitated for a second as he took in the apartment, and she must have realized it. Reaching in her jacket pocket, she pulled out a pistol and placed it in front of her.

"I insist."

Holding up his hands, Ryan smiled. "Yes, Ma'am," and then took the opposite chair.

"Ma'am? Jeez, you are making me feel really old. Usually, I get a nod, sometimes even an all right, but the formal response speaks volumes. Probably, just a nice polite man used to easing the tension in the room. Am I right?"

Ryan stared ahead, his eyes searching hers. "Maybe?" he managed to blurt out with a chuckle.

"I'm Mary Sorensen. I hope this is one of those nice to see you scenes and not one that gets ugly."

Hands in front of him on the table, Ryan tapped the old plastic tablecloth. "No, Mary, all good here."

Smiling, Mary leaned back. "Great. So, let's get some talk out of the way before the action starts."

"Action?" The confused look on his face said a lot.

"I think you'll be OK, Ryan."

CHAPTER 13

"Drink, Ryan?"

He waved her off. "Just had a great coffee so I'm good, thanks."

"Suit yourself," Mary replied and picking up the pistol, went to the refrigerator and pulled out a bottled water. Taking a few swigs, she replaced the cap and sat back down.

The siren blared again. Figuring why not, Ryan got up and looked out the third-floor balcony window. He couldn't see anything that warranted the alarm, but he had that gut feeling he'd know soon enough.

Given the metal doors and heavy deadbolts, it wasn't Santa with presents.

"What's going on, Mary?"

She tapped the table for him to sit. "We have a bit of time. Our early warning system gives us about fifteen minutes lead before *They* come."

Ryan pursed his lips. "They?"

Mary grinned. "The dead."

"Haven't seen any zombies myself." He figured he would let her explain. Dead today had different interpretations.

"Not movie zombie dead, dumbass. But all of those people who are dead inside. Lost all their humanity? You know the kind."

Ryan shrugged. "Depends on your definition of *dead*."

Mary put her elbows on the table and looked hard at Ryan. "Black BDU pants. Zip up black boots. The band t-shirt was a nice touch. The observant eye says former cop, militia dickhead, or spook. Though a dick wouldn't listen to that awesome band."

"Boo."

Laughter broke the moment. It could have gotten really tense, but Ryan's single word spoke volumes. She eased back in the chair, but kept the pistol close.

"Listen, Mary, no need for the gun, unless it makes you feel better. If I wanted you dead or was a threat, I'd be the only one sitting here right now."

Shaking her head in acknowledgement, she put the gun back in her pocket. "Can't be too careful nowadays. Too many infiltrators trying to breach our nice little slice of normal."

A playful wink. "True. Seems they have a bit of a tell though, right?"

A nod. "That they do."

Glancing at his watch and knowing minutes had passed, Ryan tapped it. "You were saying, my dear Mary?"

Getting back into it, Mary sighed. "Right. Sure. So, you stuck out a bit to someone who used to be, well, used to guys like you hanging around. Not the testosterone ball dragging kind, but the discreet, eyes flittering back and forth keeping a watchful gaze on any shit about to go down type."

Ryan shook his head from side to side. "Sort of a compliment, I think."

Three fingers up on her right hand. "It was, and probably the best you'll ever get from me. First, this is a survivor outpost. One of the bigger ones in the Northwest. Second, the dead are a mix of those crazies who try to eat you and then those assholes who just want to have fun and kill you. Third, you don't remember me, but I remember you. Had to be sure it was you, and the funny bone sarcasm screams, Ryan Carmichael."

He couldn't place the face or the name. He sat staring at her and just couldn't place it. "So, Mary, did we have some nasty thing in a demolished building and I forgot to call. If so, I'm sorry. Lost my phone, like everyone else."

Mary chuckled. "You wish you had. No, we met at Lab 33. I was Mark's lead researcher."

Ryan's body tensed, his neck muscles tightening, ready to strike. Anyone who had worked for Mark was someone who might still be a threat. Smile or witty statements didn't immediately make you a friendly. The new world held secrets, and keeping wary kept you alive. He tried to place the face and first name, but kept coming up empty. "So, what brings you here then?"

"Trying to stop Mark from killing us all."

Slight relaxation. "You have my undivided attention. Go on."

Mary Sorensen introduced herself and gave him the thirty-thousand-foot short answer. A doctor with quite a pedigree, Mark Simpson recruited her from the University of Washington School of Medicine for her work on virus analytic spread models. Working directly for Mark, she ran all tests and trials. Crunching data and statistics, Mary was part of the central team with all level access. As time wore on and it became apparent that Mark was losing touch with reality and his own humanity, she sought to warn her higher up contacts, only to have her concerns invalidated. As the last days marched forward and the real threats increasingly apparent, she grabbed all the research data and information she could and left.

"I remember you now. Brash and bold, telling it like it is. The truth, not the bullshit. Got you in some deep water."

Mary nodded. "No one wanted to believe what was unfolding right before their eyes. Our models began to predict a surge, not just the virus, but the aftereffects. The different groups that began to show up sporadically at first, walking flesh bags that were essentially brain dead. The psychos beginning to kill people and eat parts. Even the militia type douchebags who started to kill for sport. Tiny blips here and there across the country, but it began to paint a pretty dark picture. Look where we are now."

"Paradise," Ryan grinned. "An everyday vacation filled with fun."

Three rapid sirens blasts interrupted their conversation. Mary motioned for Ryan to follow her and led him to a bedroom, the window covered with tiny slits to view outside. Three stories up, they had a great view. Stepping up to take a look, he saw *Them*, hundreds of Bolts running down the middle of the streets. Occasionally one would veer off and ram right into a door, appearing to attempt a breach. Most held tight, and the Bolt simply hissed and went on. For those that didn't, they forced their way inside, emerging a few minutes later to rejoin the onslaught of the herd.

"Pretty insane, isn't it?" Mary whispered.

"What the hell?"

She tried to contain a laugh. "You haven't seen this before where you're from?"

Ryan focused, watching the rampaging mass of killer flesh march past. "Not like this. My guys and gals roamed about a dozen unless one of them called for reinforcements. A few more would come, but nothing at all like *this*."

"That's the shitty part. They're evolving."

Ryan stepped back, his mind racing and taking him to the Brainer camp he encountered a month ago. He had seen it firsthand in them. Even with the Lurkers and Bolts deciding to buddy up and be pals in the tunnels. Traveling north, he saw none of it. More from keeping way off the radar. This new development was bad.

End of the whole world kind of news.

"I've seen some of it. Not like this though. How long have they been marauding cheerleaders of death around these parts?"

Mary chuckled at the description. She needed the tension breaker. "It's been coming slowly, worse each time. Probably the last month or so they've been regular. Come from someplace they hide and try to pillage for people. We've been able to fight them off, but they get smarter each time. Testing our defenses, looking for weak spots. Last week a few managed to get through and it was pretty bad."

He'd seen their carnage plenty and didn't want to end up on the breakfast table this morning. "Are we safe?"

An affirmative nod. "Those doors below will hold. Even if they got through the front door, the others would keep them at bay. Unless they really want something or someone, they move on to easier pickings.”

If they knew how many of their own he had disposed of in creative ways, they might make him their number one most wanted.

“Awesome. How long do these raids of theirs last?” He was on a timeline, and if the raiding party lasted too long his return trip got extended.

Mary frowned. “Usually lasts a few hours and then they leave if they come up empty. Last time it took days to send them away.”

Ryan took it all in. He could handle a few hours. Days was not in the plan. If he had to stay put with Mary and kill some time, he needed intel on the King. Broaching the subject so early might show his cards. He thought about it, in the back of his mind, as Mary caught him up on how they knew each other and the history with Mark. As he watched the Bolts frantically search for fresh blood, it crept toward the surface. There was a grace and subtlety he needed to walk, just as a precaution against having walked into a Brainer camp that had evolved beyond imagination.

“You guys seem to have things pretty well in hand. The city looks almost the same as the last time I was here years ago. Minus the barricades, fences, and crazies running around. What’s the story there? I haven’t come across a city so *intact*, like Seattle, anywhere.”

Mary tapped the table as she looked at him. “Interesting question. When things went south and people were still milling around with all the upheaval over police and government, a few took charge to step up and basically bring people together who weren’t raging psychopaths. It hit hard here for sure, like a fog rolling in from the Sound. Knowing who was who and not wanting to kill you a battle for life at the start. This area ended up as a magnet for those trying to stay alive. Eventually things quieted down enough to push back and King was able to build what you see today. Oversees communities like this all over the place.”

The story made some sense. But there was something Mary didn’t say that kept Ryan’s radar up and fishing for information.

“Wow Mary, you all managed to do what a lot of cities couldn’t. Someone stepping front and center and taking the lead. This King sounds amazing.”

Mary nodded. “One in a billion. No one like the King. Keeps life going and the dead at bay.”

Every city he had seen from the East Coast all the way to the West had massive destruction. Many resembled Dresden from World War II, completely wiped off the face of the planet. Most were shells of their former grandeur with rubble and debris painting a dire picture. Ryan hadn’t seen a single city left this *pristine*.

There was more to it.

Feigning shock, Ryan said, “Seriously, is the rest of the area around here as ship shape? I can’t imagine the whack jobs didn’t try and raise this city and others to the ground." It opened the door. Just depended on if Mary walked through.

She took the bait. "Oh, King knew what was going down, so there was time to prepare for them to come for us. Push out and get rid of the ones who turned and brace for the ones who'd come along later."

That was what he was waiting to hear. Most everywhere else, the lunatics were imbedded in the community and destroyed it from within during the first few months as they ravaged and rampaged. This King was either an oracle who saw the future or had some advanced knowledge about what would or could happen and was able to eradicate the enemy. Build compounds and networks of communities and cities to seemingly thrive in the apocalypse.

His couldn't not say it. "Wow. Long live the King!"

Over the next few hours Mary and Ryan talked and observed the Bolts as they worked their way through and back out of the city. The teamwork was extraordinary. When a Bolt found a place that seemed an opportunity for penetration, a blood curdling howl erupted. Then a half dozen gathered in support to attempt a breach. They worked meticulously trying to remove or break down the defensive block, a door or boarded up window. When their efforts failed, they moved on to the next potential target. Watching the thinking behind the actions and cooperation among the group was fascinating and terrifying all in one. It was evolution at play and brewing a cocktail of intelligence beyond imagination.

Scary shit.

Between all the action on the streets, Mary fed him more information. It was either an instant trust from knowing him from before the chaos, or a deliberate ruse to deceive and feed him crap. Ryan wasn't sure which, but he took it all in to digest and catalog for later. Parts of it he knew from being privy to the details and conversations with Mark. Other pieces tied into what he learned scavenging the records. More from his brief conversations with Mitchell and John and putting two and two together. Where he had gaps in information, she fed the details with stories and data that made his skin crawl. Secret trials. Failed experiments. Unreported deaths in the tens of thousands across states that added up.

Beyond what the virus claimed in bodies in the beginning.

The rush to design a vaccine they could control killed countless test subjects. As Mary dove into the weeds of the discoveries, she made it clear that she wasn't a part of the decisions handed down. Mark compartmentalized his leadership team structure, where those loyal to the cause kept from those blind to the real work. She had only begun to realize the truth as chaos fired down and the window to escape narrowed. Day after day the data provided didn't add up as the models showed positive results and a predictability that from a researcher's mind, screamed fabricated. It was only after receiving a blind copy of an e-mail meant for someone else, the truth began to ooze through the cracks of lies. She grabbed everything she could, downloaded files onto a USB, and faked an illness to work from home.

Within an hour she was driving cross country to Seattle.

Ryan sat back at the table. He knew firsthand what he was told back in the Bay Area by his father, Mark, and the billionaire boys club. He wasn't going to share any of that juicy information if he could help it. Those conversations were his gauge against what Mary provided and he had learned. There were holes, inconsistencies, and connected dots. What was what as true versus bullshit was the land-mined road ahead.

"So, the control part of the vaccines. They tried to do that and it failed. What was the plan then?" Ryan knew, but had to dig inside the crap to find the gold nuggets of truth.

Mary pursed her lips, thinking what to say. "There was speculative research that some type of antibodies, RNA, rDNA and other pieces of the puzzle, might be able to be cloned and used to ward off the side effects. Not a permanent solution, but something like the flu shot you get every year. Variants change and morph, but a vaccine that stays on top of it and prevents you from feeling the bad stuff. Though no flu shots now!"

He chuckled at that revelation. "Maybe we're not rid of that quite yet."

"Well, it would take some serious work to find the right sequence and specimens to test. I came across horrific e-mails where the subjects died and they just dumped the bodies when the incinerators couldn't handle the load."

The San Francisquito Creek. He'd seen the body count in person.

Deciding to test the waters, Ryan waved his hand. "You're talking side effects, right? Would something like a vaccine prevent someone from turning into one of those monsters killing and pillaging? Or, is it more like keeping the status quo with all of us?"

Mary stared, searching Ryan's face. "What do you mean?"

He had to tread with care. "All of the dead out there. Would a shot bring them back or prevent people from becoming one of them?"

Wide eyes looked back at him. "Oh, I got it. Well, I'm pretty sure the virus once it gets a hold of you like that, you are long gone from becoming a productive member of society ever again. Keeping someone from joining them? As far as I know, anyone who was going to joined the other team a long time ago."

Not particularly positive news.

"Well, that doesn't sound very good. What do we do with all of the losers then?"

Mary shrugged. "Hunt them all down and eradicate them from the face of the Earth, I guess."

He clapped his hands together. "A new business venture. Charge by the creeper."

He must have hit a nerve because the response was short. "They were real people once."

Hearing the words loosened his guard. Just a bit. "Sorry, Mary. Sometimes this new existence makes me use a coping mechanism to deal with all the loss. Humor, my wall to hide behind."

Mary reached over and touched his hand. "I'm sorry too. Still can't believe all of this."

Taking a chance to check and see what was on the other side of the door, Ryan asked, "Say, what if there was a way to get a vaccine for people. How would you go about making it?"

Mary was quick to answer. "UW still has facilities that survived. I do a little bit of research in my old building."

The other cloud to pierce for an answer. "How do you manage that? I saw all of the lights working on my way here. Every power grid I know has been down for years."

Mary smiled. "You'd need to ask King. It just does."

He did need to meet King. How was the question. As he thought about it, Mary, who had been the one doing most of the talking and spilling of information, had a realization.

"Say, you never told me why you're here in the first place?"

With all of her stories and answering his questions, he hadn't divulged much of anything. Put up or shut up time.

Ryan sighed deep, trying to add a bit of sadness to fake his way out of this. "I lost my family and don't have anyone else. Hoped to find an old friend might still be alive and take me in. Saw all of the guns and fences here and figured a loner wasn't going to be very welcome. Stories about King and all I caught from some drifters along the way. Managed to sneak in and was trying to blend before you found me. Find my buddy and see if this was real or not."

Mary nodded. Absent family, if you could find a living friend you might just make it. "This friend have a name?"

He could lie, which was the better choice. Or, feed her a truth and see where it went. Honcho was known around town from his time bouncing at the clubs to add an air of legitimacy while he went to college. No job and rolling in dough from his side gig would bring questions. Have some fun splitting heads and making contacts with musicians was a way to keep under the radar.

"Honcho."

Mary's eyes brightened. "Oh, King *definitely* wants to meet you."

CHAPTER 14

Honcho enjoyed the company.

Three years flying solo with the only people to talk to pictures on the wall or BP over video left the spirit depleted. Having two rambunctious kids running around and an actual live adult a few feet away made him feel alive once more.

Not that it had been all doom and gloom dreary sequestered out in the wilderness.

For most of the time, he had Magnus. When hell began to eek its way out and overrun Seattle and he came to get the silo fully operational for Liz and the family, he brought their dog, Magnus. A little bit of this and that, he was the kind of sweet pup that was the best guard dog for any sound that lurked and a worthy bed warmer for cold nights. Honcho knew travel would be rough cramped into Liz's Jeep Wagoneer with her parents and all the crap they'd want to bring, so man and dog came out first.

The first year was great.

Even with Liz lost in the wind and hunting every clue to find her, Honcho and Magnus made the best of it. Hikes up the mountain to long for home across the Sound and nights curled up in the recliner watching old movies, the two enjoyed the time. One-sided conversations debating literature and music, it was just like at home. Magnus would bark and disagree occasionally, but mostly stare and then fall asleep when it got to be too much.

The second year was OK.

Magnus was getting on in years and things started to catch up. Hikes got shorter and more infrequent. Nights erratic with multiple potty breaks for an old bladder. And that was just Honcho keeping the poor dog awake. Having free reign wandering the underground facility, Magnus would sometimes get lost and not find his way back. Which meant Honcho had to search floor to floor until finding the pooch asleep on an old cot. That precipitated locking the lower-level doors to keep him contained to the upper levels.

Year three hit and age caught up. No more hikes, just walking around outside to sniff the woodland smells. The dog bladder couldn't hold anymore in the night, and he'd sleep right through.

Finally, three months before Ryan crashed the scene, Magnus went peacefully one night, asleep in Honcho's lap as they both snored away. It was crushing losing his best little friend and bond with Liz. Isolated and alone, when the Carmichael's arrived it raised him back up, and hearing everything they had been through, especially the children, burned his resolve to find answers and solutions.

He had to no matter the cost.

Trolling through the data dumps on his servers searching for any clues and multi-tasking talking to Julia, Honcho grew more concerned with the situation. A snippet here and there like a cracked egg shell meant nothing. Glued here and there with something Julia or Ryan mentioned began to build a profile. After six hours glued to the laptop screen, he finally called it a day.

"I'm done, people!" Honcho announced. "Who's game for some pizza!"

Julia shook her head. "Some good take out around here I guess?"

Honcho thumped his chest. "Me man. Me use brick pizza oven to cook."

She couldn't help but laugh. "Seriously? You have a pizza oven all the way out here?"

He nodded. "I sure do. Use it for pizza and making all my own pottery for cups and plates. Paper only lasts so long and dishes break, you know?"

"Ever the efficient one."

A sad look responded. "Topside was supposed to be our home away from home to ride out our years. Down here my secret lair to control what was left of the world."

Julia shuffled over and wrapped him in a huge hug, kissed his cheek. "I'm sorry, Honcho. I know you miss them. I do too."

The big man wiped away a tear. "Ooh, dirt in my eyes." Looking at Julia he smiled. "Having you all here helps. Though that man of yours I could do without," he winked.

Julia couldn't help but giggle. "He is something else. Grows on you after a few years though."

"He does. Like a fungus on your toe."

The brick oven was topside, but all the ingredients in the kitchenette, so Honcho went to work. David came over to help and Emma read a book to her mom, which was more storytelling from the pictures than the actual words. Ready to go, Honcho excused himself and took the pie upstairs to cook. Checking the cameras before leaving the last blast door, the all clear checked off and he went out, locking the door behind and closing the false wall. Gas on from one of the camouflaged industrial-sized propane tanks and in a few minutes the pizza was cooking away.

Sitting outside in his lawn chair, beer in hand, Honcho relaxed. Out in the forest, far from people, he felt secure and alone. The tree canopy gave shelter from above and in the right spots a clear view of beautiful blue skies. Sipping and enjoying as the birds flew overhead, it was peaceful.

The huge military transport low and loud overhead broke his serenity.

Bolting from his seat, Honcho ran through the cabin to the silo door and below, securing the exits as he descended each floor and into his main control room. Checking his monitors, he watched as the plane banked and turned towards Seattle. The warnings for the RF scan didn't scream this time, so he assumed that the destination was SeaTac.

"Ah shit," he howled out loud. "This isn't good."

Grabbing the radio from his belt, Honcho hit the button. Three short presses and then wait. A minute. Two. Then five.

No response.

Not wanting to break radio silence, he tried again. This time ten minutes passed. No voice or sound came.

"Come on, Ryan. Answer me dammit!" he yelled to himself.

Looking up at the monitors, he saw another plane captured by his surveillance cameras. Smaller, more discreet, likely a Gulfstream or corporate jet. It too banked and headed towards the city. As he watched, the hairs on his arms stood, the uneasy feeling something was coming sending fear down his spine. Hopping out of his seat he ran to the kitchenette to see Julia holding Emma in her arms. David was busy at play, but the scene was off.

Honcho cleared his throat. "Everything OK?"

Julia looked over; her eyes wide. "All of a sudden, she started crying. Saying something about Ryan I can't make out."

He motioned towards the ceiling and mouthed a warning.

"Seriously?"

Honcho nodded. "Caught two birds flying home."

Julia kissed Emma on the top of the head and took her over to the couch. "Here Sweetie, watch a cartoon while Uncle Hon and Momma talk about lunch."

Emma smiled. "OK, Mom." Then, without warning she asked, "Is Daddy going to be OK?"

Julia, caught off guard, nodded. "Daddy is a tough guy. He can handle anything."

The little girl frowned. "I hope so. It feels funny in my tummy. Daddy has to hide before the bad men find him."

Julia patted Emma's head and hurried over to Honcho.

"She like this often?" The concern in Honcho's voice showed.

Julia sighed. "More since Ryan showed back up in our lives. I don't want to call it premonitions, but it has been odd. Like, she feels him or when something happens. Progressively stronger over the last month."

"Our very own Ryan early warning system."

Julia shrugged. "Guess so. Something you spooks are used to I bet."

Honcho's eyebrow raised. "Spooks? No. I didn't get to go around all fancy pants playing spies or shivving people. Dirt and hiding in the shadows trying to stay alive was for those fools. At least for Ryan, that's how it was. Hot coffee and a computer screen in the safety of base was my luxury digs. But, I was shifty hiding my treats. James Bond like."

A warm smile. "I stand corrected."

Changing his tune, Honcho whispered. "Listen, we need to warn him about the party that's coming. He's not answering my call. Not sure what's up, but it's got me worried."

Panic washed over Julia. "What can we do?"

Honcho pursed his lips. "Not much unless I really break radio silence with a distress call. That might get answered, but also put him in a bind."

"Should we?"

He shrugged. "Tough call. He's been in worse spots. I'd hate to add to whatever fun he has found right now and rain on that parade."

Her tears materialized. She couldn't hold them back. "I'm scared Honcho. Are we always going to be on the run?"

The big man reached over and hugged her, the love of close friendship and comfort for him more than her. He was scared for his old friend, but didn't want to add to her misery. "Not if I can help. Honcho is going to make sure of it."

A dinger sounded.

"Oh crap! Pizza. I'll be back," Honcho said as he hurried out the door.

Julia looked over at the kids. David was still busy and Emma had fallen asleep. The last month had been hectic and Julia's nerves on fire trying to keep her head straight and follow Ryan's lead. She wasn't used to just blindly going along with anything, but he had made it clear that debate wasn't an option.

He was adamant about not arguing and wasting time.

It got heated a few times, more from her persistence in asking questions and his saying to just trust him on it. She hated it, loathed the gaps in information he left out, the unknown about the future. When they had downtime and a chance to talk late at night he did share, but she could see in his eyes there was more to everything and he was holding back.

Cracks emerged, but she wanted it all out before she lost *him* for good.

CHAPTER 15

As Emma lay quietly, eyes closed, she saw him.

Sitting at a table with a woman. Emma couldn't make out the conversation, but she *felt* Ryan's uneasiness, the need to hold back what he knew. Her dad sort of knew the woman, had met her a long time ago. He still wasn't sure about the information she shared, so he kept quiet.

As much as a sometimes chatty Ryan could.

If only the words appeared, Emma might know what to do. Being at Uncle Honcho's though, she knew she couldn't do much of anything. Telling her mom would only make it worse, or so Emma thought. Every time she got it wrong before, the mean people yelled at her. Screamed, pointed their fingers in her face. It was scary, even wetting herself a few times in the process, which made their anger worse.

Mom was different, she knew it. Dad too.

They loved her and Dad had come and saved them all. She knew the dangers he faced, saw it vividly in her mind. He was a hero, willing to die to save his family. The fear still viciously held its fingers in her brain, kept her from completely sharing her dreams.

She hated the feelings.

Even Uncle Honcho would do anything to protect her, David, and Mom. Dad, no way. That was a joke between old friends, though he said it, it wasn't true. She didn't know what they had been through, only snippets of sentences and images that flashed.

Scary pictures from long before she was born.

The first time it happened, when she was five and not long after the world stopped, left Emma speechless for a week. Her body felt different, her mind not her own. Thoughts came and went. They were prisoners on a ship, poked and prodded, sleep a rare time to curl up and cry.

Her Mom had begged and pleaded to be with her, to have time to keep

Emma's therapies on track.

Though, all led by her mother.

The man she knew as her dad's friend Mark allowed it, over the objections of the doctor who tormented her and David. Hypotonia was her enemy, the result of her Trisomy-21. Affected her speech, physical attributes, and ability to do regular things like her brother. Down Syndrome was a monster in many ways, keeping her body from being normal.

As time wore on, it all changed.

Therapies, once prevalent, no longer occurred as resources dwindled. Yet, Emma excelled in every way. Her physical limitations diminishing over time. Everything eventually catching the eye of the doctor. More tests, prods, needles the size of straws. Pain unlike anything, and he and his nurses relished in it. Comparing twins and their development took on a whole different light, and then the visions and dreams came. She locked them up tight and retreated, her only way of protecting those she loved. Until David became the target and she protected him. The nurse flung across the room when Emma willed it.

From then on, she was kept a secret, a pawn in some game she didn't understand.

Deciding to get up, Emma went over to where her mom and Uncle Honcho sat. She didn't want to do it, felt she had to say something. The feelings wouldn't go away.

"Mom, it's Dad. Something is weird." Tears began to fall down Emma's cheek as the words came out.

Julia pulled her in close, held her tight. "What's wrong, Sweetheart?"

"Daddy's in trouble."

Honcho looked over, confused. "Your Dad will be OK. He's just checking on stuff and will be back soon." Giving Emma a hug, he shooed her away to watch another video.

Julia glanced over at him, and seeing her wide eyes, Honcho caught the fear. There was more to what Emma said and it seemed he was in the dark.

"Jules, what's she talking about?"

Rather than give bits and pieces, Julia just spilled the secret. At least, what little she knew about it.

"Ever since she had the vaccine, the first one they gave us, Emma has been a bit different. Her speech improving astronomically beyond expected, physical abilities, academics too, but she seems to have some ability to *see* things."

All the color drained from Honcho's face.

"David too. The boy is brilliant. But she is off the charts in ways that she shouldn't be because of her Down Syndrome."

Honcho sat, his breathing deep and slow. Two minutes before he responded. "Are you saying the kids are doing that twin thing that happens, or going to a whole different level like oracle predicting the future kind of weird?"

Julia couldn't help but laugh. "Well, there is the *twin* thing going on. But beyond that, I'm really not all that sure. All I know is Emma *felt* Ryan each time he was near. Knew he was alive and coming for us. And ever since we have been in close proximity, she's been able to feel what he feels, see parts of his thoughts. She's been right every single time."

"Does Ryan know?"

She shook her head. "No. I think he suspects a few things, but I haven't said anything. He has enough on his plate with what is happening just to him that adding this on top of it? I don't know what that might trigger inside. We can't lose him. We need to find a cure that won't end up killing my children in the process."

Honcho sighed. Never a parent, he could only imagine the anguish inside Julia. He was part glad he and Liz chose not to have a family, part deflated he'd never know the bond. Wanting to do all in your power to help your kids and feeling helpless.

Tugging on his gray goatee, Honcho leaned in. "I'm guessing Mark knew all of this? Hence one of the big reasons he wants them back so bad?"

"Only some of it." Her voice cracked, betraying the part she left out.

Honcho grabbed Julia's arm. "Hey, it's me. Uncle Hon. We're all family here. If I'm going to be able to help fight this, you can't leave anything out."

"Somehow she hurt a nurse who was tormenting David."

The words didn't register right away. Then his mind went to Emma physically throwing an adult across the room, which was impossible. When it hit, his eyes sparkled with recognition and the nature of what Julia said slapped him across the face.

He had to ask. "Like, with her mind?"

Julia nodded.

Emma was the most valuable prize on the planet. If her disabilities were diminishing, parents the world over would want whatever lurked in her blood to help their kids. And, every freak and insane madman looking to rule what was left of society would want her locked up to do their bidding and control the world.

Honcho pushed his seat back and went to grab beers from the fridge. Popping the tops off two homemade lagers, he motioned for Julia to put a new movie on for Emma and David so they'd have to watch it from the start and give Honcho time. Emma had been trying to ear hustle and stared intently at him instead of her movie, creeping him out a bit because he felt she might be running through his mind opening doors that needed to stay shut. Smiling at him when the thought crossed, he pointed to his head. She shrugged and doubled winked, which made it worse. Taking her cue, she went to David and led him to the couch as Julia brought up Sponge Bob from the media player.

Half a bottle slugged down in seconds, Julia sat down at the table. Figuring it would be gone soon, Honcho leaned over and grabbed another bottle and popped the top. Placing it within reach, he sipped three times and set his own beer down.

"I know there is more to all of this and feel like a whole big chapter or nine are missing from the book. What aren't you *still* telling me?"

Julia tilted the bottle back and soon the rest was gone. "Honestly, I don't know. The whole time we were captives a lot of conversations floated around. Problem is, these weren't your normal chit chats. What was real and what was bullshit is hard to shovel. Mark and his people are insane. Like escaped from your worst horror movie asylum nuts. Deception and compartmentalizing information were all a part of his scheme. He trusted no one."

Honcho chugged the rest of his beer and instead of giving Julia the new one, slugged that one back in a few gulps. "Was there ever going to be a maintenance vaccine, or were Emma and David the ones he was going to use to control everyone?"

Julia got up and grabbed her own beer. Leaning against the countertop, she sipped as she talked. "Truth? Your guess is as good as mine. I always thought that was the case because that was all Mark talked about. But now, after talking to Ryan and seeing my children the way they are, what they are *becoming*, I have my doubts. All I know is they cannot have my babies, no matter what."

Honcho leaned over and clinked her glass. "No fucking way. No matter what."

CHAPTER 16

Reg Carmichael breathed in the air.

It had been ages since he had been in Seattle, the last time when he was a long hauler taking glass from California up into Canada. He stopped for a meal and a drop off of materials with one of the outposts for the cause. The breeze carried a wonderful freshness, none of the smog or stench most cities permeated. Even post-pandemic with all that died and rotted away, the ocean wind along the Sound brought trees smells and even water.

It put a pep in his step that had been hiding for a long time.

He stepped aside and let the crew unload the transport vehicles. Two Humvees for him and Mark to run command, a large troop truck, and some smaller SUVs found their way to the tarmac. As the soldiers geared up, Reg looked around the mostly empty airport. The majority of the aircraft at King County International, the home of the rich and decrepit who parked their private jets there for their own selfish importance, had flown to remote parts of the world attempting to evade the pandemic. What was left stayed locked in hangars or had been pilfered long ago for their metal and parts. Only skeletons remained.

"What a wonderful day to die!" Reg howled.

The commander of the protection detail approached. "Sorry, Sir?"

Reg grinned. "A whole lot of people are going to die today if I don't get what I want."

Not sure how to respond, the officer nodded. "Yes, Sir."

Mark Simpson exited the plane and headed towards his Humvee. Barely acknowledging Reg, he gave a wave and opened the door to hop in. The hunt for Ryan and his family had been going nowhere with resources scouring the country. The short transmission for RF signals meant nothing as there had been no subsequent pings. For all they knew, it was a blip or anyone who didn't know they had a tracker and had failed to cut it out. Reg immediately seeking to fly up and go on an expedition tied up men and their largest plane.

All for a whisp in the wind.

Ryan was the deadliest man on the planet. Reg's failure to recognize that was a mistake. And, Mark hoped, a fatal one for Ryan's father. The man was a menace, a zealot, a thorn in Mark's side. Reg craved the idea of killing his son if he didn't join the cause.

Not that Mark minded at all.

Ryan was a problem that needed to be eradicated. Reg's exuberant fascination with Ryan and going on goose chases without viable intel was not conducive to finishing Mark's research. Plus, Reg blew off the advice of treading with care when it came to Ryan.

The Ghost.

Mark knew what Ryan was capable of, had been at the man's side on numerous occasions when the soldier did the impossible. Understood that Ryan was a soldier who played by rules, but when they meant people got hurt, he made his own. That ability to turn off his conscious was his biggest asset.

Made Ryan an unstoppable foe if he was far into the process of turning.

For all Reg and Mark knew, it was a trap perpetrated by Ryan and his merry band of misfits. Likely a wrong lead that would come up empty. No matter what, Reg needed to be knocked down a few pegs. In charge or not, there was an order to things and as a former soldier, a way to go about the hunt. If Reg didn't start listening to advice, he was going to find himself on a pike dangling in the wind as a feast for the dead.

The knock on the window brought Mark back. Turning and rolling down the window enough to hear, it was hard to hide his disdain.

"First target?" Reg asked.

Mark smiled. "There's a group that controls Seattle and a bunch of the outlying areas. They might be open to some sharing of information."

Reg frowned. "What about his friend, Honcho?"

"I doubt he's there. But, I will send a team to check it out and report."

A nod. "OK. Make it quick. I want Ryan before me so I can watch his face as his wife dies slowly, an incentive to join before moving onto the kids if I have to do it."

Mark smacked the door. "Are you incapable of listening with that thick head of yours? Ryan won't be found unless he wants to be found. Turning or not, he's still the best."

Reg smiled. "I have a hunch. A feeling. My boy will slip up and then he's mine. You can have those horrible kids. Torture them all you want."

"Did you ever care about those kids?"

Reg looked up in thought. "Probably did. Even with these new emotions coming, I just don't care. They're obstacles and lab rats to me now, nothing more."

"Yes Sir," Mark replied, the defiant tone evident, and motioning to his driver, rolled the window all the way down as the vehicle left to rid the stench of Reg from his nostrils with fresh sea air blowing in the wind.

The sight shouldn't have been a surprise, but it pinged an old memory. Interstate 5 to Seattle was a sea of wreckage. Trucks with their trailers overturned, abandoned cars, and the remains of the dead littered the freeway. With the window down Mark could hear the crunch of bones below as the Humvee rolled over. When an obstacle got in the way, the troop transport with its massive three-inch thick steel bumper guard simply pushed the wreckage to the side. What should have been a short ride turned into an hour excursion.

Mark hated the wait.

He could see them along the top of the embankment, silhouettes trying to hide. They were obvious, their inability to stay perfectly still betraying their presence. A shuffle, an arm that moved, the light catching their camouflage just right.

A trained solider like him could tell the difference.

He counted at least thirty along the route before coming to the massive wall of trailers that blocked their path. Stopping fifty yards before it, Mark had the driver leave the vehicle running in case of a quick retreat. He didn't have any agreements this far north so playing it coy and faking his demeanor had to work. A firefight was not conducive to his mission.

At least, not right now.

Taking his binoculars, Mark scanned the fortification. Slits cut to look out from the trailers. Access points for foot traffic. It was really built to be an obstacle for vehicles versus to keep people out. That resonated.

He might be able to bargain after all.

Getting out of the Humvee alone, he had barely walked twenty yards before the first bullet exploded the concrete ten feet in front of him. Looking up, he walked another few yards before the next bullet hit five feet to the right. Unbuckling his belt and leg holster, he held it out. He took another step and continued until he found an old SUV and climbed on top.

No more shots rang out.

"Thank you for not shooting me," Mark yelled. "Is there someone in charge I can speak to about a matter that may be beneficial for both of us?"

He heard a banging sound ahead, movement. Then a face appeared atop the trailer, behind a turret-like structure. Short black hair, maybe late twenties. Rugged features belonging to someone who relished the outdoors. Then, from different sides behind rusting cars he caught the movement of shadows. Quick flashes of black, and then they were gone.

"I suggest you run like hell towards me before they get you," the black-haired man shouted.

Looking left he saw him, or *it*. Teeth bared, the dirty face almost unrecognizable among the debris. Hunched over attempting to hide, the killer was tracking his intended target. Not wanting to be his meal, Mark hit the receiver on his throat mike, barked a quick command to stand their ground, and then slid down the hood and ran. As he took off, the beast and another emerged from the shadows. The other one caught Mark off-guard as it was closer and if it angled right, he was a goner. Sliding over the hood of a Corvette, he heard the first shot ring out and saw the woman, lighter and faster than her partner, fall to the ground.

"Left and then up the ladder. You'll see it," a voiced yelled.

Ten feet left and ahead Mark saw it. Two rungs at a time before a hand reached down and pulled him up just as the ravager converged on his location. Another shot, this one too close and loud, echoed in his ear. As he turned, he saw the man fall to the ground, writhing from the bullet to his head, before others of his kind came out of nowhere and began to feast. The sound of flesh ripping from the body and the chomping of human muscle excited Mark to the point of arousal, not sexual in nature, as that emotion had long ago withered away. No, arousal of thought at what torment he could rain down on Ryan. He wondered what it would feel like to his nemesis as he was eaten alive.

Mark couldn't contain the grin.

The black-haired man flung Mark around. "Holster. Now."

Still gripped in his right hand, Mark handed it over. "Thank you," he replied.

"Huh? Oh, sure. Welcome."

The dark-haired man wasn't the only person. There must have been thirty people behind the barricade. As he looked down and around a few more popped into the open.

Ragtag was a compliment.

Clean and supplied with weapons immediately said organized, which to Mark meant a hierarchy and a leader. He already knew that, but seeing it in the flesh added to his inclination that working out a mutually beneficial agreement would get him his prizes.

If not, Mark knew he'd burn the whole camp to the ground.

"That happen often? The group eating their own like that?" To Mark, it seemed like an evolution of the hunters. Waste not.

The black-haired man nodded. "It does. More and more as we have cut off their food supply."

A wicked grin. "Nice to know."

The grin must have been too much as the man warily took a step back. "Know what?"

Sensing it. Mark shifted gears. "Oh, to be careful with those things. Don't want to end up on the dinner table, you know?"

"Yeah, sure."

The black-haired man pointed towards a ramp and directed Mark to follow it. Traversing the tops of trailers and finally descending to the freeway, he kept his eyes ahead with the occasional glance to the side. Gather intel and know your potential enemy was what you did. How many, armaments, how their defenses were constructed, it all added up to knowledge to potentially use later.

If you had to make a point.

A tap on the shoulder sent Mark towards a waiting open air jeep. "They'll take you to King."

Turning around, Mark motioned towards his belt.

The black-haired man smiled. "If you make it out, you get it back."

"Just don't lose it. Wouldn't want anything to happen to you." Mark's words bit hard, the emotionless statement's meaning understood.

The jeep weaved its way up the freeway through a path that only the driver seemed to know. Fast and furious, the vehicle leaned as the driver, a young stoner looking guy with an eyebrow ring, drove like it would roll at any moment. Past the stadium and ferries to the left, they finally exited the freeway and headed left into downtown.

Seattle didn't feel like a decaying pond of death.

The streets were relatively free of wrecks and garbage. Not a body or bones visible. It looked relatively the same as the last time he breezed through, though now it was more like a ghost town. He wondered where they were going, until he started to see life here and there and then the tall walls and barricades. As they got closer the reality began to sink in. People acting like it was three years ago. Laughing, eating, even what looked like shopping.

The sight made his skin crawl.

Nearing a manned barricade, Mark saw the Space Needle and he needed to choke down his growing anger. Life acting like nothing happened and three years a radar blip in time.

People thinking the Constitution and Bills of Rights were still intact and they had choices and could make their own decisions.

It was unnatural, a slap in the face of everything Mark's masters stood for and sought to implement. Subjugation to live, that was coming, and the image slowly helped to recede his wrath. Soon he thought to himself, soon enough they would all know the true meaning of obedience.

The barricade retracted and the jeep drove inside. Within the walls he was surprised to see tiny homes, those small prefab structures that had been popular on the cable shows, all lined up methodically and pristine. Passing what must have been the residents, he received the occasional wave or smile and he reciprocated.

It made him want to vomit.

Finally, the jeep parked outside the Needle and a guard motioned him out. Two more appeared and not wanting to keep his host waiting, Mark obliged. Directed through the lobby doors and to the elevator, another guard hit the button to ring it. Squawking and squealing of the lift echoed in his ears as it descended. Working electrical, he noted, along with all of the other tidbits he managed to witness, was cataloged for later. Pushed inside, the elevator quickly ascended up to the observation deck with the three-hundred-and-sixty-degree view, the anticipation exhilarating as things were about to get crazy.

As the elevator door opened, Mark was surprised again. He expected an empty room or at least, chaos of furnishings left from before the world turned. Instead, he found a neat and orderly what could only be construed as communication center. Desks and chairs lined along the floor to ceiling windows. Large monitors stood in the middle. Comfy couches and bean bags encompassed what appeared to be meeting or relaxation areas. It reminded Mark of a tech company trying to woo employees with fun perks.

The ping pong table cemented that thought.

He followed the guard through the labyrinth, catching the stares of the people watching his movements. A stranger in their midst. Once he passed, they went about their business. Eyes open, but not too focused. Ears perked, but not obvious. Floating around among the chatter he caught bits of conversations. Check-ins with outposts. Status updates on supplies. Movements of the psychos around the city and outlying areas.

Even eyes on his troops and their ride to Honcho's house.

His escort ended up on the west side of the deck where you could see Elliott Bay and the city below. Standing against the glass he saw a woman. Medium height, light brown hair. Thin, but muscular. As she turned, he produced a fake smile.

"Mark Simpson. Nice to make your acquaintance."

"Mark Simpson, huh?" King said his name without any emotion.

"Nice place you have here." Mark's attempt at pleasantries was comical.

She waved the guard away and pointed to a chair. "Why are you here?"

Taking his seat, Mark fidgeted until finding a comfortable position. "Sightseeing of course. Been a long time since I've been up this way so I'm visiting an old friend."

The lies smelled. Troops and the fly overs weren't vacation planning activities.

King frowned. "Cut the bullshit. You're wasting my time. Get to the point or go home."

Mark leaned back in his chair. The smug look said it all. "Home? I don't think so. I think I'll stick around. Need to talk to some people."

She walked over and stood a few feet from him. "Listen, this is my city and I say what goes on and what doesn't. You don't dictate to me. You want to offer something in return, I might listen. Otherwise, get the hell out."

Tapping his knee, he almost whispered it, trying to keep wandering ears from listening in. "I'm looking for a guy named Honcho. Need to pick his brain."

"Not a clue where anyone by that name is."

Her poker face wasn't the best, but he could tell she was telling the truth. "Sorry to hear. Really need to talk to him."

"Why?"

Mark motioned her closer. "I'm looking for my cousin, Ryan Carmichael and his family. They are in grave danger and I am trying to help."

His poker face was gone.

"From you, I'm guessing. Good luck. Lots of land up this way."

"Well, if they decided to venture up this way for say a holiday visit, where might someone go to avoid the spotlight or find resources to say, stay protected?"

King stepped back, leaning against the glass. "That seems like pretty important information. Valuable stuff even. You able to pay for it?"

Mark shook his head. "Are you able to live without your city?" He pointed to a Comanche helicopter coming in from the distance.

King nodded she understood. A sudden explosive flash and then the helicopter was gone. "I don't like threats. Come with me."

They walked over to the monitors and Liz pointed. As she did, Mark saw them. A hundred members of the ragtag band of Seattleites surrounding his plane from the safety of hidden locations. The shoulder-fired SAM missile aimed at his plane made a statement.

"Doesn't mean much. I can find another ride home."

The pistol that suddenly cocked next to his ear changed his mind.

"So, we can play who has the bigger one or work on a deal. I have the biggest right now if you really want to find this Ryan and his brood. Supplies and weapons to fend off undesirables like you. If you have aircraft to fly, you have access to what I want."

Mark laughed, maniacal and guttural, an almost prehistoric sound. It rose until the room was silent.

"We can deal. But if I don't get what I want, this whole place burns to the ground with everyone in it."

Sirens suddenly blared, interrupting Mark's threat. King threw him a look, so he followed to the large floor to ceiling windows. Standing beside King, he watched as he saw the scene unfold below. Survivors scurried inside of buildings, pulling doors behind. Previously opened gates closed and were barricaded. Shooters took up positions high atop scaffolding and from what he could see, the roofs of what remained standing of downtown.

He'd never witnessed an event before, but as the beasts came into view, a stampede of crazed lunatics seemingly appearing from thin air, Mark smiled. Not from a glee in what was about to transpire. He could care less if anyone lived or died. It had a broader meaning, and one that played well to get what he wanted.

The horde was evolving, their movements less frantic, more calculated. He saw it in their gait, the expressions that popped up here and there that he could actually see underneath all the grime. Cooperation, like raptors on the hunt. Even the bee mentality when the hybrid African kind decide to all hit a target and sting the poor bastard to death.

If King had to deal with intrusions like this and other threats, he still had the advantage.

CHAPTER 17

Reg Carmichael had his own agenda.

It aligned with the larger picture. If someone really sat and paid attention, it progressed the cause further than the mediocre short-range plan that drove the present. He had let Mark wander off and venture into the belly of the beast. The King ran Seattle and everything around. A merry band of survivors plucking away an existence a step ahead of poverty. He had heard the stories about what they did to interlopers and especially the mercenaries that roamed freely in search of blood sport. Heads on spikes at the borders of the King's empire. Bodies strung up for the meat eaters to dine.

If he didn't know any better, he would have thought the Seattle residents were of his mind.

Reg knew better. They weren't out conquering, on the offensive. They were passive, their efforts put towards making the world a more placid place to live. Mark felt different, so Reg let him take the ride and find out for himself. With luck, they would kill him and Reg would be done with the bastard.

The elder Carmichael was in search of a more expensive prize.

Naval Base Kitsap, on the west side of Bangor, Washington, was the home of the west coast fleet of Trident submarines. Bremerton across from Seattle and in the Sinclair Inlet had aircraft carriers, one of which he knew was operational, sans a working crew. While a carrier would be a great base of operations again, the sub base contained missiles. Securing that kind of firepower meant changes to the game.

With no working ferries to cross over to Bainbridge Island, the longer land access went through Tacoma and over the Tacoma Narrows Bridge. From there, hours of freeway driving on roads that remained littered with obstacles and roaming bands of psychos. It meant an overnight stay, but if the prize was found it would be worth its weight in gold.

Heading out, Reg checked in with the unit heading out to Honcho's house. Located in West Seattle, his home had a beautiful water view just above Beach Drive. Reg wondered how the teacher could afford such a nice house. Probably handed down from Liz's family who were life-long area residents.

"Alpha Team, report."

"This is Alpha Leader. We are approaching the residence now. Over."

Reg's impatience grew. "Can we make this quick?"

The earpiece's speaker hissed. "There's a weathered note on the door. Over."

"Well, can you read or not?" Reg spit as his anger grew at waiting for information.

"Says 'Went underground. If you're reading this, you're not dead.' Will look inside. Over."

The words didn't mean anything. And, meant too much. Code for someone important. Honcho could have gone anywhere. Based on the cryptic message, it sounded like he was alone or had been if whoever didn't find where he went. Weathered meant it had been up for ages and not recent for Ryan to discover. It also didn't mean Honcho was even alive. Three years trying to survive in fun land could have brought any number of demises for his son's old friend.

Reg waited for the team to finish their sweep of the house. A few minutes later and the earpiece chirped.

"Alpha Team Leader. Empty house sans an expired body. Pile of bones. No clothes. We did find some maps, but nothing circled or notated. Over."

The anger seethed. "Dammit! Dead end." Then, closing his eyes, a thought flew in. "Grab the maps and bring them. Might actually be something there."

"Roger, Sir. Over and out."

Reg squinted. Not from the sun shining overhead, which for Seattle some might call a sign from God. Though there was no God as far as he knew. Just a nice day to break up the clouds and rain. The team wouldn't take long to return and his detail was still loading up supplies. He could sit and wait impatiently or go for a stroll.

The stroll won.

Down the runway for a nice walk, a cool breeze blowing and the sun warm against his skin. Glorious was an understatement. Each step a moment for triumph. The cancer was in remission, his strength and resolve like never before. It felt good, the body whole again and the mind a rock of decision. The world was coming together as planned, the pieces moving around the chess board. There was still plenty to do in preparation of putting the new world order in position to govern, but as each component came online, the idea of failure reduced twenty-five percent.

A loud boom echoed. Towards the city, a fireball in the sky blossomed and smoke soon filled the air.

"Mark," Reg shuddered, his body building up the rage inside.

They owned the skies. An explosion in the air met something unsanctioned, and Mark skirting the chain of command. He thought he was in charge still. Reality sucked. The Council had said the two men needed to play nice and work together. A cooperative relationship until Mark was no longer an asset.

Reg felt otherwise and made sure Mark knew it.

Turning to walk to the plane, the glint caught his eye. It moved, and any stationary object would have been constant. This was on and off, as if whatever it was rocked back and forth. Focusing in its direction, cautious to be inconspicuous, Reg got hit with the big picture. Armed people with guns trained on his troops. He could barely see them, but knew better.

The camouflage was off for the surroundings.

Meeting the King was supposed to be cordial. He knew any traveler was suspect, armed soldiers flying on a large transport and then splitting off in different directions. Make nice and secure a deal.

Seems that might have gone down the toilet.

Figuring what the hell, Reg waved. No way anyone on the other end didn't know it was aimed in their direction. Acknowledging his predicament was showing his cards. He could have quietly let his men know. Dealt with the intrusion and shown who was boss. While it would have been a smile earner, a more casual approach for it might give him some points with the King. Get word back hiding their soldiers didn't faze him and maybe salvage whatever shit Mark had just dropped on top of everything.

That card might keep him flush with Aces.

CHAPTER 18

Ryan felt the unease.

Who wouldn't, given he was a stranger in a new place. Seattle felt like a dream, a mirage created from a sunbaked walk in the desert your body finally had enough of the heat and decided to make the most of it. Supposedly governed by some dictator who ruled with an iron and vicious fist.

At least, as the stories went.

Mary was quite the chatty companion as they walked from the secured apartment along a path littered with armed civilians hustling people to safety. The conversation bounced between the casual, the best places to eat in town that were in business, to the morbid, how King spiked the heads of those who threatened the community on pillars to warn anyone who might get the itch to repeat the process.

King did not discriminate.

Even the inhabitants faced the wrath if they fell out of line and didn't follow the rules. Stealing was strictly verboten. As a community built on sharing and similar to communism as everything went to the collective, taking more than your share or outright theft meant you died.

No ifs, ands, or buts.

As Mary explained, while it might be harsh and against every principle of being an American who held dearly to their rights, it simply didn't and couldn't work in what was now the remnants of society.

The whole was more important than the individual.

Ryan found that statement profound. If everyone had put their own self-interests last and the world first, it might still exist. At least, if the playing field had been equal. If what he had learned and was continuing to uncover was the real truth and not concocted by the minds of psychopaths to divert from their evil, then nothing anyone could have done mattered.

Evil was going to rise and take over.

Reaching the Space Needle, Ryan noticed the buzz of looks back and forth. Not directed towards him and no one paid him any mind. Two guards were deep in whispered talk. A few head nods towards the top of the Needle, and pointing in the direction of Tacoma. Whatever was going on it seemed it was distracting enough that even when he and Mary approached, the guards were oblivious to their presence.

"John, hey John," Mary interrupted. "Need to talk to King."

The guard named John, a perfect throwback to grunge with his blue plaid shirt, holey jeans, and lumberjack boots, turned. Maybe thirty and his shoulder-length brown hair whipping as he focused on Mary, smiled. "Hey Mary. A bit hectic around her right now. King has some VIP visitor upstairs so we're on a bit of a lockdown. The Skinny invasion hasn't helped."

Mary reciprocated the smile. "VIP, huh? We don't get many visitors these days beyond the weirdos or the trespassers. Any idea who?"

John shrugged. "Not really. Came into King County in a big plane. Soldiers of some kind. Some drove up here and the others went south."

Ryan's arm hairs stood. He knew.

Before Mary replied, Ryan touched her arm. She felt what was implied as she was thinking the same. John caught the movement, and for the first time looked at Ryan.

"Who's this?"

Mary motioned Ryan forward. "Sorry, John. I should have introduced my cousin, Ben."

John looked Ryan up and down. Saw the t-shirt and nodded. "Gogol Bordello. Awesome band, Man."

Ryan gave a thumbs up. "Bumbershoot years ago. Last time I got to see them live."

"Punk with an accordion. Got to love it."

Feeling he had made a new friend, Ryan jumped in. "Hey John, question for you."

"Shoot."

"The guy who is talking to King. An old dude or a less old dude?"

John frowned. "Why do you ask?"

Ryan had to play it cool. "Oh, you know. Some soldiers running around causing trouble and being outsiders, you always wonder if the old get dead or somehow keep surviving."

Head cocked to the side, John pursed his lips. "Yeah, Man. Like, can old dudes keep up and not get it from a Skinny? I hear ya."

Ryan loved the interpretation.

Thinking about it, John answered. "Well, he wasn't like an old, old dude. Like grandpa status. He was an old dude, but more old dude like you."

At least John was honest. Old to a younger guy like him was anyone over forty.

Ryan managed to laugh. "I'm vintage. Not yet a relic."

Mary nodded and so did John.

"Well, if King has a visitor I'll come back. Not important," she grinned before waving goodbye to John and grabbing Ryan by the arm, led him away. Hearing the familiar sound of the blades, Ryan glanced up to see the helicopter vanish in an explosion that rocked them to the core. Short range aircraft was a problem, and a helicopter offered landing on a dime to offload troops on the hunt.

Hurried steps and quickening the pace, Mary maneuvered them away from the Needle and back towards the apartment. She knew it and so did Ryan. The man had to be Mark.

Putting distance between him and potentially being seen or found was increasing the odds and the chance for everyone's survival.

Nearing the street, Ryan stopped at the corner. If Mark was searching for him or them, it meant he had a bead on possible locations. Ryan knew Mark would send troops to check on Honcho's house. Hopefully the dead body sent them packing. If anything had been left behind that might provide intel on other places to search, potential hideouts for Ryan and the family, then that required him getting back quick. He needed to ask Honcho about it.

"Listen Mary, if Mark's here then I've got to hide. Make myself transparent and slip away."

She had seen his stature change along the way and figured he was going to try and bail out. "Bad blood between you two? Me? I up and left. Pretty sure I have a target on my back, hence not wanting to see him and face the music. You worked for him. All chummy buddies back then. Something I need to know?"

He hadn't told her anything, simply implied they needed to leave based on her past with Mark. For all she knew, they could have parted on good terms. Keep it simple and lie like hell.

"When things got down to the end, I bailed. Self-preservation. Didn't bother to say goodbye. Not proud of it, so I'd just like to keep out of his way and not face any wrath if he's pissed still."

Mary stared, pursed lips, her eyes searching his. She sighed, shook her head from side to side, and nodded. "I get it. But, where will you go?"

Ryan hadn't told her about his family. Even if they had been chummy and avoided Mark and Ryan meeting King, trust was pure platinum. She didn't have that yet.

"Not sure. Maybe head East. Just get far enough and deep into oblivion to catch some air."

The statement caught her off guard. "East? Isn't that all desolation and a bunch of nothing?"

Ryan nodded. "It is. But, probably best for me to just find an old farm and plant some seeds. This all here, lots of people and society? I left that behind long ago."

The lie was good. He just hoped she believed it. There was a sliver of truth, a desire to be away from all the madness and have roots again. The city wasn't the place for the kids. Away from everything where they could hide and be safe was his wish.

Ryan just had to keep from making the turn.

CHAPTER 19

The blood from his mouth, black and thick with mucus, shot out.

There wasn't much to do but let it ride. Ryan was used to it, the episodes that previously freaked him out, now knowing what was coming. Hiding an episode from Julia and the kids had been an endeavor of the highest magnitude.

Excuse himself to go take a piss and run like hell to prevent them seeing the vomit spew like some horror movie monster.

Sitting on top of the roof gathering up his gear, it was hard to contain the emotions. He knew the catalyst that was responsible, the buildup of adrenaline and stress that gave way to the calm. His body could fight on if under fire and avoid the debilitating spectacle. It was the moments when his body chemistry began to come back to normal that it decided to body check him and throw his ass on the roller coaster of side effects that plagued his physical being.

Realizing Mark was close and a desire to bounce the confines of the city kept things stable until he had a chance to think. Then, all hell broke loose. He had hours to kill before he could get to the boat and sail under cover of darkness. With nowhere to really go and time to wait, his mind went to work relaxing as his body eased, and it all came crashing down.

After an hour this time around, writhing and contorting, blood trickling and oozing from his mouth and nose, it subsided. Ryan was left in pain, typical and just another thing to suck up and combat away. Hidden beneath one of the large HVAC units on the roof, he let his body ease and stretched a bit. Ten minutes later, and he was good to go.

Getting word to Honcho and Julia crossed Ryan's mind. Breaking radio silence wasn't an option. There was another way, analog tech that had gone the way of dinosaurs, the only issue in finding one that worked. Wracking his brain until it hurt, the thought smacked his frontal lobe.

"Maybe. Shot in the dark, but why the hell not?" Ryan mumbled as a plan materialized.

Cell phones and VOIP lines, those voice over IP desk sets for business, no longer worked. Same for most any phone line as companies moved to digital and fiber optic to bring more bandwidth and better services. Technology required power, and while it seemed King had a monopoly on the grid within the walls and some outlying areas, the junction boxes for the phone companies were dead.

No juice, no ring.

What might be working were old fax lines. The archaic boxes government utilized for sending information. Government was usually last to the party, relying on old and dated tech for years past their life expectancy because of reliability and the cost to upgrade their systems. Old phones lines still existed as a necessary back-up for emergencies and crisscrossed the country from east to west. Find a fax line, get a signal, and call home. Better yet, find an old analog line, tap the receiver then hang-up to clear the buzzing signal, and get into the dead zone of an open line. Ryan remembered those days of free calls.

Dial the hardened landline for the Moose Lair and hope Honcho picked up on the first ring.

It was all wishful thinking on Ryan's part. Finding an analog line still operating was a needle in a haystack. Technology ruled. Phone companies didn't want old hardware around to support. The lucrative money was in new tech and devices. Charge for the upgrades that government and taxpayers subsidized, and bleed customers for the use. Plus, keeping around all the seasoned support and staff meant salaries. Get rid of them and hire cheaper labor.

Win/win for telecom.

Regulations though required the old lines remain. Power goes and cell towers fail, then the country went silent. Couldn't have that. So, the old telephone poles and thick lines stuck around. A headache to maintain, but since all the new cables ran from pole to pole and through the same underground channels, there was money in it still and wasn't going to disappear. Unless the world fell apart and maintenance stopped.

The future was a bitch.

Collecting his gear and working backwards into the old DMV building, Ryan let the coming darkness hide his movements. He hated the waiting game, sitting to let the time pass until he could transform into a shadow and lurk amongst the blackness. Given Mark and his goons had landed in Seattle and a day cruise out of the question, he had little choice. Finding his way back inside earlier had been an option.

It just didn't work out that way.

Another Bolt intrusion had sounded the alarm as he left Mary. Not knowing how long he'd have to wait out this latest attack, Ryan decided to run. A cooler head should have prevailed, the one of a special operator who bided his time. The killer fighting its way out from the dark recesses of his gut felt different. Yin and yang a fight for supremacy.

Deadly Ryan won.

He managed to flee the onslaught by a block and sneak into the DMV. If he was trapped, so was Mark, and that meant Ryan could wait.

Formulate the next plan.

Now, wrapped in the dusk as the sun descended, Ryan frantically searched for a fax machine. He knew he wouldn't find an old rotary in the building by the looks of the newer desk phones and quick peeks in conference rooms. As he wandered, breaking radio silence began to gnaw at his brain. Shaking off the thought, he was about to give up when he found the prize.

A copy room tucked in the far corner of the third floor.

Walking in, Ryan turned on his flashlight, the red lens offering diluted illumination. Four steps ahead, and there it was, a once light gray beast of advanced communication, its exterior now browned from age. Feeling anticipation growing, he stepped over. It was hard to contain the jittery adrenaline building within. Grabbing the receiver, he placed it at his ear to hear the familiar buzz of a working line.

Ryan didn't have *that* kind of good luck.

Deafening silence roared back. In that moment he lost it, throwing the receiver handle into the wall to listen to it crack and break apart. Enraged, Ryan picked up the fax machine and hurled it out the open doorway.

He shouldn't have done it.

As it crashed and bounced off a desk and toppled a cubicle wall, Ryan heard *Them*. The high-pitched squeals of the death dealers. Turning his ear to listen, he caught the yells and swore he heard actual *words* among the howls. Not within the building, but from beyond the glass windows. Stepping out of the copy room and over to the windows, careful to put out his flashlight, he saw a group of Bolts in pursuit of someone below.

He couldn't make it all out, but whoever they were after was coming in his direction.

"Shit," Ryan mumbled.

The pendulum swung. Save a life or let nature take its course.

He had places to be and diverging from the path had all kinds of repercussions. Watch and let someone die. Step into the mayhem and expose his ass. Neither felt right.

No alarm had sounded this time. At least, not that he heard. Maybe this was a breach that had yet to be discovered. If the person running was the manual alarm, then their death meant countless others might perish if they didn't get to safety inside.

Choices.

Running to the right for a better angle, Ryan pulled his Sig from his thigh holster, adorned the silencer, and pulled the trigger.

Pffft. Pffft. Pffft. Pffft.

Four shots to blow the corners of the window and weaken its grip. When the last shot rang out, the Sig minus the silencer slid back in its place and the M4 came up. A sudden cracking sound, and the window leaned out and crashed to the street. Reaching the barrier between the floor and the open air with a certain death if he tripped and fell, Ryan aimed and fired.

The first Bolt went down, proceeded by the next and the next. One after another they fell, until he'd nailed at least ten before the rest got wise and looked up. Hidden in the darkness and the suppressed M4 not revealing itself, they searched the opening for any indication there was a warm body present. Sniffed the air like wild animals searching for a scent. Coming up empty, they retreated back to wherever they had come, leaving their prey to run off and hide.

Ryan had watched as the figure kept running and managed to get inside of *his* building. He wasn't sure how, but it complicated his life and plan of getting out of the city and back to the safety of the silo. Friend or foe, anyone was a potential enemy.

He'd unfortunately soon find out.

Huffing his way down the stairs, careful to keep ears listening and steps silent, Ryan quietly worked his way to the first floor. He had been quick, so whoever was below had not had an opportunity to work their way to the upper floors. Stopping at the door, he waited, counted to three, and carefully opened it. Taking a step back to cover himself, he hoped he didn't find himself on the end of a bullet.

Nothing.

Stepping out and to the side, door pushed closed, he titled his head. No sounds. Five steps left, careful to stay in the darkened shadows, Ryan panned the expanse with his rifle, the scope searching for a heat signature.

Not a trace.

Five more steps and a sudden sound. A soft squeak really, but the obvious drag of a tennis shoe on concrete. Focusing in on the direction, Ryan stepped over debris littering the floor and eyes locked, found the intruder huddled beneath a cubicle desk, sobs beginning to break the silence. Oblivious to Ryan's presence, the figure kept sobbing until the suppressor of Ryan's M4 tapped the forehead.

"I'd stop that if I were you," Ryan ordered, his tone direct, the volume barely over a whisper.

Looking up, the figure, a young girl, eighteen or nineteen, stared.

Ryan kept his aim. "Who are you?"

"Mary sent me. You can't leave."

Ryan chuckled. "Um, yes I can."

The girl shook her head. "No, you don't understand. You physically can't leave. Soldiers are coming this way from the south. Got a sighting of them and another helicopter. They'll see you."

"What's your name?"

The girl shrugged. "Doesn't matter."

Ryan sighed. "To me it does. Bolts nearly ate your ass before I liberated them from snacking on you. You call them Skinnys. I'd like to know who I saved."

Pursed lips, full and surprisingly painted in a shade of red lipstick, answered. "I'm Megan. Mary's my aunt."

Ryan lowered the M4. "Nice to meet you, Megan. I'm Ryan."

Megan huffed. "Sure, whatever. Look, I'm supposed to bring you back. Wait until the all clear from our scouts say the soldiers are gone."

"How far are they?"

Megan looked confused. "How far? What do you mean?"

Ryan put his thumb and pointer finger together. "This close, or *this* close."

Megan got the picture. "You've got maybe twenty minutes before they're at the front gate."

"Shit."

"Yup," Megan agreed. "Anyway, King wants to meet you. So, you don't have much choice."

Ryan laughed. He tried to contain it, but there was no reigning it in.

Megan looked confused again. "What's so funny?"

Gathering himself, Ryan smiled. "While I'd also like to meet your King, I'm a bit of a lone wolf. Taking orders from someone I don't know is not up my alley."

"You *really* don't get it. King's outside waiting for you."

That was a potential development that really put a wrench in Ryan's plan to immediately bug the hell out.

Megan got up and pushed her way past Ryan. "Come on. Let's go."

When she opened the door, all he could see was a sea of people, maybe fifty strong. Two vehicles, an old Jeep Wagoneer, and a newer heavy-duty truck were pulled up out front. As he watched on, the passenger side door of the Jeep opened, and a person hopped out.

"For fuck's sake," was all Ryan could say.

CHAPTER 20

"Well, this an interesting development."

Ryan stood just outside the doorway of the DMW, his eyes either playing tricks on him or things were screwed up more than he imagined.

The woman walked over, her sandy brown ponytail swaying with each step. She smiled, the warmth of it genuine, and moving around Megan, gave Ryan a huge hug.

"Glad you're not dead."

Feeling a bit awkward, Ryan hugged back. The hesitation was noticed.

"I'd ask you how you got here, but there's not a lot of time for that," Liz Gutierrez shrugged as she pulled back to give him a once over.

Ryan looked down. "*You're* King?"

Liz feigned hurt. "What? You don't think I could handle it?"

"No, no. You are one of the baddest bad asses I know. Petite firecracker that could bring down an elephant. I've seen you in action bouncing at the club. Just from the stories I've heard recently, King seems a bit out of character for you."

She wasn't sure how to take it. "Um, thanks," Liz replied.

Ryan sighed, and shook his head. "Sorry. It's been hell for me. Just, I heard some things that to be honest, were quite sadistic. That, usually in my experience, has some deranged psychotic of a middle-aged white guy as the dickhead. Not someone who is an old friend."

Liz laughed. "Well, I appreciate the thought. Short answer, some true and some of it's not. Mostly to scare away the crazies. I have a lot of people to protect. Have had to do some things that in a different world, wouldn't be acceptable. You know?"

He did.

Ryan remembered she had said something about time, and given the posse was coming, wanted to get to it. "What can I do for you?"

Liz pursed her lips, the muscles in her jaw clenched. "As much as we go way back with Honcho and being friends, I have my people to look out for first. When someone mentioned a newbie around, and me getting a visitor looking for you, I put two and two together. Not sure how you got here or why, but I can't do anything to protect you."

The words were sharp. Not meant to be that way, but they cut deep. She was right, in her own way. If Mark knew she was protecting him, he'd level the place.

Ryan nodded. "I guess if I was in your shoes, I'd be stuck in a pickle too."

Liz reached out and grabbed his hand. "What I can do is give you a head start. I was going to hand whoever over if it wasn't you and be done with it. I've got a deal that for the shit we're living now, was too hard to pass up. Helps a lot of people keep living. But, I can't do that to you."

"Thanks, Liz."

"Best I can do. Sorry it can't be more."

Ryan got it. Sighing deep, he had to ask. "Listen, Honcho. What happened to him?"

A tear began to roll down her check. "I don't know. He was getting things set up for us somewhere. A surprise, he said. Things went really bad after we got separated. Had no idea where to even begin looking for him since he was supposed come back to the house and then let me know where to go. Then, time just kept moving forward. I started this and it just grew. I hope he made it and is living or it was quick. The alternative as you know, isn't a life."

"No, it's not."

Still holding Ryan's hand, Liz squeezed hard. "What about you? Julia and the kids? Coming here? Why?"

He had cards to play, and a hand that a gambler would love if the stakes were high enough. Bluffing was what he did best. Truth could be a death sentence, as friend or foe, he had no way of knowing if Liz could be trusted. Call it paranoia or trepidation, Ryan had to tread the edge of a cliff.

"Was the visitor, Mark?"

Liz nodded.

"Well, he decided my life was expendable. Left me for dead right before all this lovely crap went epic. Took my wife and kids. Did horrible things to them. I managed to get them back, and then lost them when my dad shot me. Super long story. Came up here to rest the latest bullet hole."

The astonished look staring back meant Mark hadn't spilled any details. Maybe a good thing.

"Your dad? He's still alive? I figured the cancer would have taken him by now. If anyone was going to shoot their son, I would have put money on Honcho's dad pegging him."

There was no way to not laugh. Honcho and his dad had a complicated relationship. Though Mr. Gutierrez was not the gun toting crazy like Reg.

"No, my pops went psycho nuts like the others. Managed to get in remission somehow and keep evil leeching into what's left of this shithole world."

Liz gave him a half smile. "Sorry, Ryan. About Julia and the kids."

Thinking he'd throw a Hail Mary, Ryan chucked it. "What if Honcho was still alive?" As soon as the words left, he knew the answer.

"As much as I miss him, that life left a long time ago. Had to move on and survive. If he's alive, I hope he's OK and happy. Living as best as he can be in this life."

Ryan sighed. "To Honcho."

"To Honcho."

One of Liz's bodyguards tapped her shoulder, leaned in and whispered, and then stepped away. The grimace on her face painted a bleak picture.

"If you're going to get to wherever you need to be, you better go. I can give you an hour. Beyond that, it might draw suspicion. Mark figures my people will assist the search effort for you. This group is loyal to a fault and won't divulge who you are. The others follow orders, but I can't afford to share information."

Ryan nodded. "Understood."

Letting go of his hand, Liz gave him a long and loving hug. "I don't know why he's looking for you, but make sure you nail his ass to the wall for Julia and the kids."

"Top of my growing list along with dear old Dad."

Within ten seconds Liz was gone. Megan too, having spirited away during the brief reunion of old friends. He felt uneasy, the whole episode surreal, and suddenly blew chunks of black goo onto the sidewalk.

That, was a first.

Staring at the mess that had just erupted, Ryan realized his clock was ticking, the hour hand blazing towards the finish line when his total turn into a permanent death dealer would become final. He figured he still had some months if he was lucky, probably a few weeks at most if he was honest. Too much to do and too little time to do it all.

Liz didn't ask the hard questions. Maybe she either lied or Mark really kept her in the dark. She seemed surprised at what he did reveal and even about Honcho. She was right too. The world ended and you did what you had to do to survive and live. Even as close as they were geographically, with shit the way it was and how it all unfolded, Honcho and Liz were galaxies apart. Needles in a haystack with no way of getting to one another. Distance and death boundaries to reconciliation.

Or, was it?

Ryan closed his eyes. Honcho was resourceful. A man who thrived on information. He had a radio in the silo. Could have spent time searching the airwaves for Liz. Get bits and pieces and put some intel together. He had the stories about the person known as the King. Someone had to have been able to feed him something about who the person was, even if sketchy at best. Man or woman. The fact he didn't know that one important bit of intel stuck out. Honcho wasn't the type to miss anything.

He's one of my oldest friends and I trust him with my life. Ryan's inner monologue began to unwind. *How could he not know more about Liz being the King? He said he kept looking for her. All he had to do was get into Seattle and walk the streets. Hell, scope it out from the water. Was he that afraid of the stories he supposedly heard?*

As the thoughts percolated, Ryan came back to Earth. The countdown was on and minutes fading away. If he wanted to know, he had to get back to Honcho and find out.

Better get to it.

CHAPTER 21

Seeing Liz alive brought a mountain of questions. Honcho not knowing she was alive?

Even more.

As Ryan worked his way to the water to get back to the boat, his mind raced like wildfire consuming a dried forest, the tinderbox of his mind ablaze in thoughts. Getting barely an hour to vacate the city, much less now as he was on the move and had a late start to it, Ryan couldn't help but think his ticket was punched.

He swore he saw the Reaper reflected in a few windows.

Throwing up his middle finger to assert his station atop the food chain of the living, Ryan wasn't going to die anytime soon. No one, not Mark, not a Bolt, definitely not a Brainer, was going to take his ass out of the game. His own death would come on his terms, when he was ready, and not a second before he decided it.

Screw the universe.

With a muddled mind to wade through, Ryan watched the sun dip below the mountains and fade into oblivion. As darkness cast its shadow and he morphed into his old and familiar skin as a nightwalker, a twinge of excitement panged his body. Not the sexual kind, though he wouldn't mind a turn under the sheets to ease his tension and to feel the softness of a woman's touch. Being on the run wasn't very romantic and no time for it.

He *was* married, after all.

He knew what he felt was the nerve endings getting ready for the fight that was coming, and coming hard for the man known as, *The Ghost*.

Ever since the encounter with his dad and Mark, the revelations about what was happening to him plagued his mind. Ryan struggled with the inner voice he had trusted without question since his first days of combat. That monologue had kept his ass alive, centered and on task, both feet planted on the ground and not inside a body bag.

A little over a month ago, he wouldn't have questioned it. Now, as the familiar tone rang inside his ears, the pitch lower and more baritone in its delivery, it encouraged the fight, was a cheerleader for confrontation. When before it acted to level his own trepidation and support the right decisions, today and ever since it had thrown caution to the wind and simply said, *fuck it.*

Maybe it had always been that way. He just ignored the truth.

Pushed it all aside and figured he should do the right thing. Though what was right or wrong anymore was the flip of a coin. The new voice might be right and just long buried. His past decisions actually wrong, different outcomes the better end to a story.

Ryan shook his head, tried to drip the conflicting thoughts out his left ear, then the right. Strained to keep focused and alert as the darkness enveloped the night and he still had a few blocks to go before he could set eyes on the boat.

Checking his watch, he was at the half-hour mark. He had made progress, pretty good in fact, though under different circumstances caution meant taking a few hours to slink back. Given the impending posse on his ass, and the dismal head start, though a very appreciated one, Ryan sensed Mark getting close.

It was a feeling he couldn't shake.

Paranoia or stress the likely culprit, Ryan was feeling the hair tingling on his arms. He might be taking the road to insanity and a one-way ticket to the Devil being afraid of Ryan taking over Hell.

The signs were there.

Even the Reaper, as he passed the last set of windows before taking the path to the old boat, looked back at Ryan with fear in its eyes. He felt it too. And then, he wasn't sure what happened, but it felt like an internal switch clicked off. His humanity and want to be good vanished. All that was left was a raging desire to kill.

A fire that burned red hot like never before.

Two steps later he saw them, a six-man team silhouetted by the reflection of moonlight. Ryan could tell they were pros, the spacing, the non-verbal movements, the leader stopped with his fist closed and raised. Kneeling, the team was looking in the opposite direction of Ryan and had no clue of his presence. Exposed in the open now, the right choice was to step back to the cover of shadows and wait them out.

The dead switch inside said otherwise.

Pulling the strap for his M4's sling tight, he pushed the rifle so it went snug against his side. Grabbing the MP5 strapped to his chest to loosen it, Ryan got the barrel up and focused.

Thirty yards to targets.

Keeping them in his sights, he moved, methodical, each step quiet, yet deliberate. The team hadn't moved, as they were watching what Ryan discovered was a group of people huddled around a fifty-five-gallon drum with a warm fire burning in its bowels. The survivors were armed, probably a defensive posture guarding this part of the King's territory. Rumblings of chit chat floating across the cool air.

Twenty yards.

Still unseen, Ryan swept behind, hunched low, eyes never straying from the team. He tasted it, the salty wetness of sweat on his upper lip. Licked it away and savored the minerals as they hit his tastebuds. Clamored to keep the blood pumping in his veins from exploding with the desire to kill.

Ten yards.

Three steps and the MP5's strap was pulled back tight. Left hand to his breast and a quick yank.

The special operations blade came forward as Ryan's right hand grabbed the top of the last man's helmet. The sharp steel tip entered at the small indentation between the skull and back of the neck. Head pulled back, the blade slid quietly in and with a twist, the man was gone.

Pushed to the side, Ryan performed the same exercise with the next man.

Startled, the third soldier began to spin around. Head turning right, the blade sliced through his eyeball and out the left ear.

Three to go.

Wiped clean on his pant leg, Ryan replaced the knife and went for the Sig Sauer in his thigh holster. He knew it would make some noise even with the suppressor, but even in his madness, there was a method to his actions. Screwing the silencer on, he let it rip.

Pffft. Pffft.

Last man standing.

The team leader was now turned around, facing Ryan, the shock on his face comical. A former SEAL in his old life, the swiftness of someone taking down his entire team in seconds felt like a dream. Dropping his SCAR to the ground, he pushed the 7.62 mm assault rifle away and raised his arms.

The soldier knew he was done and there was no way out of this shit show.

"You must be, The Ghost."

Ryan nodded.

"Simpson said you were the best and to watch our six. Guess that was a waste."

"He knows better," Ryan smiled.

Glancing past, the soldier's momentary fidget caught Ryan's radar. The Sig touched the man's forehead and the brains blew out the back.

"Shit," Ryan mumbled, as the familiar sound of a missed sniper round blew by.

Rolling for cover, he caught the glint of the scope's lens. *Rookie move,* Ryan thought. *Sending a boy to do man's work.*

Sling release for the M4 yanked hard and the barrel coming up, Ryan peered through his scope. Reaching to it, he clicked the selector switch for heat signature reading.

Nothing.

Then, the slight orange hint of a finger radiating warmth. Ryan focused in, then a few degrees to his own left. Felt a slight breeze, adjusted his aim, and let a round loose.

Pffft.

The orange sliver dropped.

So much for getting some interrogating in before having to kill them all.

He could still get intel, though his bold move potentially limited its effectiveness in the short term. Long game, it might work out if he played it right. The odds weren't really saying to bet on Ryan Carmichael as he fell more and more into the abyss of lunatic killer. He only hoped he managed to stay sane enough to make the kills that mattered.

Pilfering through the bodies of the dead soldiers, the crew around the fire stood clueless, a bottle of something tasty being passed around and probably wickedly horrible by the coughing fits after each sip. Ryan didn't find anything useful. Not that he expected to find a map with a huge X or a document with the evil plan typed on it. The team wasn't as rookie as he thought. The only valuable asset he wanted was a radio to listen in on conversations. He took one, and piling the bodies atop one another, pushed a few grenades beneath for good measure.

Fishing line hooked to one depressed trigger.

Reeling the line out, Ryan crept away down the side of the trail. When he guessed he was far enough away, he yanked the line and ran. Ten seconds was all he had, and by the time the blast blew the men to mangled hamburger meat, he was close to a football field away. Not a bad sprint for an old guy.

Anyone hearing or seeing the explosion would focus there.

Earpiece in, Ryan listened. Expected immediate chatter. Still on the run, it was maybe a minute before he caught anyone. Almost to the boat now as he had been on a marathon run, he waited for it, and the words came.

There was no mistaking the voice.

"Goddammit! Can someone tell me what happened?"

No one answered Mark Simpson.

Agitated, Mark roared again across the coms. "Someone better answer or I swear I will put a bullet in each and every one of you."

Static.

"Sir, we were a few blocks away and just got here. Charlie is down. Repeat, Charlie Team is down. Over."

Mark didn't seem to understand. "Down?"

Bravo leader replied. "K.I.A., Sir. All of them."

"How?" was all Mark could ask.

Thirty seconds of silence. "Looks like grenades. Nothing but hamburger meat left of them. Out."

Ten minutes of back and forth gave Ryan time to board the boat and cast off. Let the current push him far enough out before engaging the engine. Bow aimed toward Bainbridge Island to get far enough away before heading northwest back to Port Angeles. As the distance grew and downtown Seattle faded into the night, the radio barked once more.

"Base, Alpha Leader. We got a boat heading across the water. Can't make anyone out, but it's moving. Could be a ghost boat or someone leaving. Need assistance. Over."

"We'll get a bird in the air. Drone is ten minutes out. Over and out."

Ryan couldn't help feel the game was about to get messy.

CHAPTER 22

Emma shot up, the screams bringing even Honcho into the room.

Julia was holding her tight, trying to comfort her daughter as the waves of tears and crying rolled over her body like a tsunami.

"What happened?" Honcho asked, his large frame now bent on one knee.

Fear shone in Julia's eyes. "Nightmare. She says the bad men are after Ryan."

Honcho didn't quite catch the perspiration beading on Julia's forehead. When he did, he realized she didn't think it was just a young girl's imagination feeding ghoulish thoughts in the unconscious mind.

Seeing the initial perplexed look, Julia followed up. "Their connection. She senses when things are tweaking him."

Emma pulled her head from her mom's chest. "Daddy's in trouble. He needs me."

Trying to contain the sobs that kept coming and now the furrowed brow of David, Julia had her hands full with the kids and with figuring out how to explain it all to Honcho.

David, deep in thought, got up from his bed and over to his sister. "He needs us, Emma. Twin super powers, right?"

Emma managed to laugh. "Twin power, Bubba."

Ten minutes of comfort and then the Carmichael children were back asleep. Emma curled up next to David now, finding comfort in being close to her brother. Julia pulled the door almost closed to leave just a small opening for Pete to scamper out if he needed to use the litter box.

Heading back to the living area, Honcho already had drinks ready, as he assumed it was needed after the episode with Emma. Handing over the wine glass, Julia took it, gulped two sips and shook her glass to get topped off.

"Thanks," Julia smiled.

Honcho slugged back some vino, and decided to dive in. "What the hell is going on, Julia? I can't know what to do if I don't know what all we're up against."

Another long sip before Julia curled up in one of the leather recliners. "Ever since Mark and his demented scientists started in on my babies, things have just been, well, I'm not sure how to really say it, but the two of them have been in tune. Not just each other, but Emma and Ryan. It's like there is a link tying all three of them together. Emma more so than David. But, it's there."

"You mentioned a bond."

Julia shook her head. "Not just a bond. Emma *feels* Ryan when he's close. Or, in range is probably better. Though the distance she can peg grows further. Wasn't there until the first time he showed up, and then ever since it's unbreakable. David senses his sister and the thoughts. So, while he doesn't feel Ryan, he feels her."

Honcho moved from the small table to the recliner next to Julia. Poured some more wine in her glass, and downed the rest from the bottle. He felt there was more, and if she wasn't going to be totally upfront, he was going to push buttons.

"We have got to cut through the crap Julia. I know there's more to this. The freaky telepathy twin stuff is one thing, but the Ryan connection is a whole different black box you're keeping pretty closed off. Spill it."

Julia took a sip, was just about to say something, and then the lights began to flicker. Honcho put a finger to his lips, and grabbed her by the hand. Leading her back to the kid's room, he leaned in close and whispered.

"Lock the door and do not open it unless I radio you. Take the back door down to the lower level and lock it behind you. Follow the yellow line to the stop sign. Immediate right and down the corridor. Black door. Stay there. If you don't hear from me in an hour, wait until morning and then take the stairs topside. There's a secure hatch hidden by a fake tree stump. Watch the monitor and then bug out. The silo blows if I don't hit the off button for the kill switch."

Julia felt her energy leave. Life on the run didn't allow for any peace. "What is it?"

Honcho kissed her forehead. "Got intruders who tripped a camera above ground. Hope it's not trick or treaters."

She managed a slight chuckle, and as Honcho pushed her inside and past the doorway, Julia swore she saw his eyebrow raised, a thought rolling around in his head. It meant something else *he* wasn't telling her, but by the time she realized it, the door was shut and sealed tight. Wait and see was all Julia could do in the moment.

She hoped she saw Honcho, and her Ryan, again.

CHAPTER 23

Honcho didn't like lying to his best friend's wife.

It wasn't a total lie, just not the full spectrum of transparency he wished he could reciprocate when he had the expectation from her. When the warning lights flicked, it was true there was someone who tripped a camera and caused the alarm system to react.

The who was the lie.

At least, someone that at this stage of the game was off limits until Ryan returned. He had said as much to Honcho. Keep Julia close, and watch her like a hyena waiting to devour a wounded animal.

Honcho felt dirty having to hide the truth, but Ryan was his oldest friend and the one with one foot in the grave. He was in charge, until the time came when a bullet to the brain relieved him of command.

Heading to the topside door, Honcho checked the cameras to be absolutely sure, and seeing the familiar face staring at him through the hidden camera in the fake toaster, he laughed, and then cranked the handle to open up.

"About time your lame ass got here."

A hug greeted Honcho. "You know, it does take some time to get here from Sacramento to make sure no one knows I was coming," BP grinned.

Honcho held him tight. "I still don't know why you live in that god forsaken town."

BP shrugged. "Better than L.A. with all the wackos running around. At least in Sac, I know the area. Can stay hidden away. Plus, it will always be home."

Leading BP down the first flight, Honcho asked, "So, how *did* you get here so fast?"

BP sighed and wiped his forehead. "One of our last movie shoots was out of the Bay. War picture. Used some miniature scale subs for part of it. Had one parked on the Sacramento River near our local studio. Got a small team of stragglers who managed to stay alive, so we use the sub to find people, and keep it afloat. Took it for a ride and dirt biked from the coast to here."

The eyebrow lifted. "All by yourself?"

BP grinned. "You think I'm crazy? No. I brought some friends along. They're camped at the coast keeping the sub secure. Don't want anyone taking my prop. Might need it for a future pic, ya know?"

Honcho nodded. "What about the kids? They cool with you leaving like that?"

The pause to respond spoke volumes. "No, but for Uncle Ry and the kids, they understand. I filled them in on some of the more PG details. They want everyone safe as much as we both do."

The deception was sinking more and turning into quicksand.

The larger-than-life man sighed, his heart and mind shrouded in doubt. When Honcho contacted BP without telling Ryan and asked for help, which was a huge ask for anyone to make given the circumstances the world decided to heap on who remained, the old friend in BP didn't hesitate. Ryan was their brother, through thick and thin. While neither man had the harsh tours like Ryan, they still served in the same deadly combat zones under fire from the occasional RPG or suicide bomber looking for his virgins that would never come.

You didn't need to take a bullet or give one to be bonded for life.

While Ryan was the shadow man of the trio, the giver of death for those that deserved their glorious path to Hell, their old military skills complimented one another. Honcho had kept them all informed on the latest intel so they could do their jobs and stay alive another day. BP had worked his charming personality and got Ryan the occasional treat in a weapon that was hard to come by and let him stay a ghost without betraying an American kill shot. For Honcho, BP kept his ears open and got tidbits from his clandestine outings into towns and villages trading what the locales thought were black market American goods, but were actually chipped for GPS and exchanged to track insurgents.

Ryan?

He reaped the benefit of his friends' work. What he brought was a sense of unity and protection under dire conditions. He kept them all safe, doing what he did best, making the world at the time a slightly better shithole taking out bad guys one at a time. BP and Honcho knew they could sleep at night knowing their best friend crept in the pitch black to let society keep moving towards democracy.

It was their turn to return the favor.

A world away and decades in the past, they were still brothers to the end. No one in the trio thought twice about stepping up and risking their life for one of the others. It wasn't just an outdated code among former soldiers. It was brotherhood, friendship, and real love that men weren't afraid to share or declare.

BP scratched his head. "So, are we really going to do this?"

Honcho shook his head. "As much as I don't like it, we are. Not a lot of choices right now."

He understood. "Guess so," BP agreed. Then pointing, he motioned below. "Well then, you going to invite me into the lair or not?"

<h1 style="text-align:center">CHAPTER 24</h1>

Ryan didn't want to ditch the boat.

Getting pegged by the drone wasn't high on the list. Sending the sailboat in the opposite direction, south towards West Seattle, making it look like it was abandoned and simply being carried by the current and breeze, that might give him breathing room.

If only for a minute or two.

He knew if he was caught on the video feed, his ass was a goner. Even if it didn't have a missile attached to it, if it found him there was no way to hide or evade for long before support personnel came to capture him. It would circle and circle from a watchful distance, outside of gun range. Being on foot on Bainbridge was a last resort. No intel and no transportation meant he was just waiting for a cavalcade of problems to rain down from above.

The drone was just the start.

Alone and in territory he had no clue what lurked around, Ryan couldn't languish and take his time. With Mark and the goons close to his trail, the daring move was to hightail it as fast as he could back to Honcho's silo. The smart money was wait them out, but that meant finding a place to hunker down and sit patiently, and then move on.

It was also a losing choice given the metamorphosis that was increasingly transforming Ryan into a cold-blooded killer.

He was a ticking clock, the second hand spinning wildly around the face as the minutes sped towards the hour. His complete demise to step into the abyss was a guess when it would come. All Ryan knew was he had a deck to play still and a winning hand if he could use his poker face.

It was all a gamble, but one that might tip the cards his way.

Ashore and on the hunt, Ryan found what he required, though the going would be tough. The old girl's bicycle had flat tires and was a smaller frame, not exactly the right size for his height. He could manage the tires with the pump in his ruck. He learned the last bike trek going to the airport looking for the ultralight that a tire pump might come in handy in the future.

Knees to his chin trying to pedal? Not much to do about that.

He had too many miles to travel, and since he didn't have a racing bike built for speed, the kid bike was the best he had going for him. Air for the tires, an old energy bar for stamina, and a swig of water. Presto.

Time to go.

Riding in the dark along a lonely and desolate road didn't provide for much entertainment to pass the time. Debris and wildlife that with no human invaders allowed for a return to people-free times, kept Ryan focused and awake. Hitting a hidden pile of junk or a moose that decided to walk across the road as he trudged along at a decent speed wasn't his idea of meeting his end in a crash. Head split open or worse, knocked unconscious only to wake up to being a feast for some carnivore.

No way he wanted to see that happen.

Methodical and consistent, keeping in the middle of the road was the idea. Mile after mile he went. Nothing of interest. Not a peep of sound. Boring and soul crushing in fact.

Then, the radio came to life and it all ended.

"We're almost to Kitsap. Status report?"

Ryan knew the voice. Wanted to rip the man's spine out and let a hyena skull fuck the remains.

"Can you give me a status report or not?" Reg Carmichael hissed.

The other voice answered. Mark.

"Contact with the King. An agreement is in place to assist. Lost a team to an explosion. Not sure if they screwed the pooch or something else. Over."

Reg's tone hit through the roof. "Are you telling me an entire team of your ex-specialists got burned? No fucking way! Are you sure this King didn't do it?"

"Like I said. We have an agreement. She knows the consequences. Over."

Ryan listened to the back and forth, and the news nearly made him crash. Reg and his team were to the west heading to Kitsap's sub yard. Ryan knew it, had been there many times. Deployed a few times out of it too. He didn't have a direct path there, but if he hit Poulsbo and went south, he'd get there. A gamble, sure. What he decided to do when he got there needed to get worked out.

Kill or be killed.

Ryan reached the outskirts of the base under cover of darkness with time to spare. Based on the chit chat between his dad and Mark, Reg was waiting until the morning and daylight to search the base. That meant Ryan had a few hours before sunrise to get into position and scout. The bike trek went fairly quick once he got into a groove. The distance wasn't bad either, though his knees ached a bit and he had to stretch a good fifteen minutes to feel like he was ready for what was about to come.

Ditching the bike, Ryan went across an abandoned farm that butted up against the base and once he got to the fence, used his cutters to make a hole. With a forest of trees to conceal him, he walked until he got to where he hit another fence, cut it, and was staring at an open field with tiny bunkers and roads.

Missile storage, he said to himself.

Taking a knee, he pulled his ruck off and opened the top to get his field binoculars. Caps off, he panned the area.

The specs didn't see a thing.

Not surprising, he thought. The above ground bunker openings offered some concealment from his location. Keeping low he moved to the left, being sure to stay far enough back he could lay low and blend in if required. Thirty yards left he spotted them, tucked against the wall of one of the far bunkers. Focusing in, he didn't see any guard patrols. An odd development, but if his father was as confident a dick as Ryan figured he was, Reg probably believed no one would try and attack.

Stupid mistake.

Taking only the essentials and angling between the bunkers, his goggles down and night vision selected, Ryan stepped one foot after another, his pace deliberate and the MP5 scanning the terrain. Nine-millimeter rounds and the suppressor of the HK would keep the noise level to a minimum.

Until, it was too late.

A twelve-man team spread out with Reg in tow, made thirteen enemy combatants. The first to go was a soldier on watch. Head shot and he slumped down. Then in order, Ryan went one by one, until the first half dozen were removed from circulation. Easy enough to do as they were in their sleeping bags.

The next group he found around the other side.

Circling back to attack from the west this time, Ryan pegged the soldier on watch with his blade. *Pffft, pffft, pffft* went the next three from his MP5. Stepping closer, Ryan saw Reg, his back turned, gazing at the stars. No more than twenty yards. With two unfriendlies unaccounted for and his trigger finger itching for a kill, he thought about it, before letting go.

Wait. His time is coming.

As the last word flashed across eyes, one of the last two members of the team appeared, running from the right. The other came running from where Ryan had massacred the first team. Coming into view, the soldier was about to yell out when he stopped and instead, raised his rifle to take aim.

Pffft. Pffft.

The running soldier crashed into Reg, knocking him right off his feet. The other who was slow to aim fell to the ground, twitched, and then stopped.

"What the hell, Dubrowski!" Reg screamed, unaware of the man's plight.

"Watch where you're going!"

Pissed and laying with two hundred pounds of dead weight atop him, Reg moved to push the man off. Then, feeling the lack of movement, the light bulb clicked. Looking up, the rage that had been suppressed began to boil over. The face staring down had an irritating smirk from ear to ear.

"Hi, Dad."

Reg spat in Ryan's direction. "Won't you *die* already?"

CHAPTER 25

Decisions have consequences.

Sometimes, the bite you in the ass kind for making bad ones, and Ryan knew it.

It was the outcome from your actions that actually meant something. Eliminating the soldiers was a no brainer. Less people to try and put a bullet in him. On the plus side too, he now had transportation to make the trip back to Honcho's sooner than anticipated.

Not killing Reg?

Well, that was the razor's edge Ryan was standing on, waiting for the blade to cut deep.

Keeping his father alive could prove invaluable, or be the worst decision Ryan ever made. Seeing Reg floated so many scenarios through Ryan's brain his head hurt like a son of a bitch. Immediately off him with a bullet, but that was too gracious for what the bastard did to Emma and David. Blade to the back of the skull and slowly push it in, then watch him writhe in agony as life left the building. Have some fun with a field interrogation and torture the fuck out of dear old dad. That one had some appeasement to the rage within. A slow and methodical extraction of intel as body parts got severed and skin sliced off?

Ryan really wanted that ending.

The rational thinker that still had some sway had other ideas.

He kicked his dad in the ribs to get his attention. "I'd say I missed you, Dad, and I guess I did back in the Bay. A reprieve for you of sorts. I *am* going to kill you. The method and way it *happens*, all up to Papa for what you put my babies through."

Glaring up at his son, Reg seethed with anger. "Fuck you, Ryan! You still think you have say or control over any of this? The wheels are in motion. Not a damn thing you can do about it."

Pffft.

The graze in the same spot he had shot before back at the mansion started to bleed.

"You fucking asshole!" Reg shouted.

As the last word came out, the sole of Ryan's boot came down hard on the side of Reg's head, knocking him out cold.

There was some time before dawn, and Ryan had to get to work. He collected all the gear from the dead and tossed it in the back of one of the SUVs. The other one he pulled the plug wires, cut them up, and chucked in every direction. For good measure, just in case someone was crafty, he rammed a blade through the radiator thirty-nine times. He wasn't sure why that number, but for some reason it felt appropriate.

With Reg secured in the front passenger's seat, seatbelt pulled tight and the zip ties on his hands yanked so hard they were cutting into the skin, Ryan ran rope around his dad too to keep him from trying to escape.

"Not going anywhere, you worthless piece of garbage," Ryan muttered to himself.

The bodies he momentarily thought about burning or even hiding, but it passed. Animals needed to eat too. So, Ryan left them exposed to the elements, and hoped the feast was plentiful.

Packed up and daylight peeking over to the east, Ryan cranked the key and drove through the base to get to Trident Avenue and out the front gate. Taking a left on WA-3, he headed north to the crossing at Port Gamble where the 104 hooked up with the 101. The distance was short, but it was the unexpected and any blockages beyond Poulsbo that worried him.

Satellite radio was long gone and so were terrestrial stations. Figuring what the hell, he selected the CD player and was surprised to hear some decent tunes. Not exactly his cup of tea since he was an old school punk kind of guy and 80s New Waver. Throw in some classic hip hop from back in the day with pounding trunk bass to vibrate the mirror, and Ryan was good to go. Finding country tunes made his skin crawl, but as he sorted through the disks, he found some twang he could tap his foot to as a former drummer.

The music as much as he wanted to hate it, made Ryan break a smile.

Watching the sun come up and passing along at a decent pace as the road was fairly clear, the trip took no time at all. Looking over, he must have really knocked Reg out, as the old man didn't move an inch. The peacefulness was relaxing, as if his dad was awake the conversation was sure to get messy and a hard right to the jaw to knock him back out was waiting in the wings.

Reg could have been faking, though the breathing seemed to indicate otherwise. Not that Ryan hadn't faked it once or twice. Stuck in a rough situation and needing to throw your enemy off their game. Done it to Julia and the kids as a game around the old house. Pretend to be out cold no matter what they did to him, and then spring to action with tickles or the dreaded kissy monster. That was fun. Doing it to those looking to kill him?

A survival practice that training ingrained into your body to keep you alive.

That's when the old photo of Reg during Vietnam and some of what Honcho had found began to formulate a picture for Ryan. Reaching across the seat, he backhanded his dad in the side of the face.

"Wake up."

Reg's head snapped to the right from the blow. "Motherfu-" he got out before Ryan smacked him again.

Ryan sighed. "I got the same damn training, Dad. Don't try any of that shit with me."

Shaking the blow off, Reg turned. "Not sure what you mean, Son."

"Got some friends in low places. You didn't serve stateside. Saw your old bird on one of your 'missions' with a caption to it. What's the real story? And don't lie, I've got more intel to dispel your bullshit."

The old man laughed. The kind that wasn't meant to be funny. "How did your 'friend' manage to get a hold of *that*? Was supposed to be locked up tighter than a virgin in Utah."

Ryan shook his head. "Must you be vulgar?"

Reg shrugged. "I can be any way I want to be, Son."

Another backhand.

"All right! Stop it already!"

Satisfied, Ryan jumped in. "What agency did you really serve?"

Reg sat quietly this time, seconds turning into a few minutes before he responded. "You'd never have heard of them. Didn't officially exist. We were called Omega. Part of the highest echelons of government doing the dirty deeds required."

That revelation made Ryan's stomach sour.

"I told you some of what we did back at that loser's mansion. Why did you need to kill him anyway? He *was* going to talk."

Diversion 101. Get your adversary to discuss something else and transfer focus of the conversation.

"You, Dad. Don't try and psych me. Same training, though mine was newer and more complex than yours."

Reg nodded. "Don't get your thong all twisted."

Ryan smacked his dad again. "*I* take them off women. Go commando when the briefs aren't protecting Mr. Happy. *Focus*. Make me angry and well, good ol' Reg doesn't get to breathe much more."

The scowl returned. "What makes you so high and mighty, Son? Mark told me some tales of your escapades. Seems the apple didn't fall too far from the prized tree."

This time, Ryan made his point.

"Motherfucker, you shit sucking bastard!" Reg screamed as just the tip of

Ryan's blade sunk into the meaty part of Reg's thigh.

Ryan twisted a bit, then retracted the Ka-Bar and wiped in on Reg's pantleg.

"All right already. Goddammit. I'll talk."

"Thank you, Dad."

Reg sat in the passenger's seat, sweat beading on his forehead. Ryan wasn't sure if it was the lack of breeze with the windows up, or his father feeling something about the crap he had done during his service time. Ryan doubted Reg felt anything at all, given the even tone and lack of inflection during any part of the story. The words flowed like a river, even and at a steady pace. Not a hint of regret, not even a shred of remorse. Though Ryan swore he caught a few times the presence of a smile during some of the gorier details.

Pride even.

As his father droned on, the details making even a hardened warrior like Ryan uncomfortable, he felt a moment of exhilaration, a twinge of *jealousy*, maybe? Reg had done some deeds that bordered on an immediate trip to Hell to be bent over and ravaged by demons. A few were more in line with getting the same kind of results Ryan would have performed. The old man had done some crazy shit and saved some people and maybe even the world at some point in service to his country. It was the evil that came out that left nothing to the imagination.

Ryan knew the psychopath led the wolf.

Clandestine missions around North Vietnam. Incursions into Cambodia and Laos. Treks infiltrating North Korea too.

The ones across the Iron Curtain took Ryan by surprise. He figured Reg was isolated to the war effort in Vietnam. There was no way to know why it diverged fronts. A war zone and then the Soviet bloc. His dad was sparse on the decisions there, but as the details came forth, Ryan caught the snippets Reg couldn't hide. He had been doing a fairly good job sticking to the stories, but as he talked, he soon failed to keep it all contained.

That's when the intel leaked, and Ryan would have pissed his pants, if he wasn't keeping a stone-cold straight face.

The Berlin Wall came down in 1989. Before Ryan finished high school. The Soviet Union couldn't contain Communism, as the people rebelled from a lack of everyday essentials. Resources fueled the fight against the West's aggressive drive to match missiles. The competition drove the Soviets to the brink of ruin from spending to stay a player in the global game. So, as what happens in all societies when the people are fed up with the disparity and cruelty of a regime, they rise up. With it, the Wall came tumbling down and capitalism rose from the ash.

That was what the history books *decided* to tell.

The truth was, like everything leeching to the surface nowadays, a bitter and ruthless twist of events that was far from what was best for the world. The Berlin Wall being sledgehammered down in pieces and showcased on the nightly news for the planet to witness, was in fact, according to Reg Carmichael, a deliberate act meant to sow discontent.

Ryan wasn't sure he had heard that right.

When Reg kept talking, it began to take shape into a ball created with lies that hid the reality of decisions made decades before the Wall crumbled down.

According to Reg, Vietnam was a cover war meant to expand the military and get them in fighting shape for a potential war with the Soviet Union. Strengthen the military technological advancements through increased spending on black projects and allow for government to then sell a confrontation to the people.

When it became clear Vietnam was not going away, and the build up to space began to envision a Moon base, The United States refocused its attention to NASA. Not that Vietnam and the Soviets played any lesser of a role. In fact, Omega, as Ryan was finding out, was just a player in the hierarchy of the evil organization.

The Order was the master behind it all.

A secret cabal that in the States Omega did the dirty work, in the Soviet Union something Ryan couldn't even pronounce correctly, and in China a word if asked to spell it, would fail miserably in the translation. When the global The Order sects began to infect government and took absolute root into every nook possible, the focus of their cause began to take shape. They eventually needed a catalyst to spark their plans into action on a grander scale, and the fall of the Wall was one that cemented the rise of The Order, and they never looked back.

Drop the Wall to foster hope, and then bring the hammer to destroy it.

With the Berlin Wall down and the Soviets not a perceived threat anymore, the spread of The Order and its mission proliferated. War depleted life and allowed for more to be born. The cycle of time over and over. Millions die and millions are born. Keeps the population under control.

No large-scale wars, and the people breed like rabid rabbits.

The Order was, order. Total control and obedience. Around since the beginning of time and in one form or another, though splintered and fractured, they were Knights Templar and in fact, many other community organizations or societies with ties to presidents and world leaders. Some well-known, others so secretive uttering their names brought death. Centuries and distance kept them isolated, until the world became the gem of manifest destiny and explorers raped and pillaged the unfortunate. It was then through all of the ship voyages and trade that the foundation of what would become The Order began to build its foundation. As modern life turned the corner, they were set on their mission.

It was only a matter of when they flipped the switch.

And, as Ryan soon found out, through their blunder with the virus and subsequent thirst to right their wrong using his kids as the solution to their problems, they wouldn't stop searching for the young Carmichaels.

Ever.

CHAPTER 26

Honcho secured BP away in the bunker.

Then, with some time to formulate, he began to work. The plan was to sit and wait for Ryan to return, and then spring the reunion.

Not the best thought out plan in the world. Honcho was winging it and as he had been deep into the digital files since Ryan left, they needed all the help they could get.

As soon as Ryan showed up on his doorstep and spilled his guts, Honcho was working *his* plan. Finding out his best friend was eventually going to go vegetable brain and psychopathic killing machine, Honcho knew protecting Emma and David was priority one. Julia was an outlier according to Ryan, and it could have been the degradation of his brain talking gibberish. If it *was* true, then making sure the children were in the hands of people who would die to ensure their safety a must.

Honcho knew he'd take one for them. BP too.

Distance and a world gone apocalyptic meant Honcho was on his own. Until he called BP back the night Ryan arrived. Filling BP in and struggling on how to keep everyone safe, BP said it would take some time to get up north, but he'd leave the following morning to help extract the Carmichaels and get them hidden away. The expanse of forest would have been ideal if the pinging and flights weren't overhead. BP, ever the man of a thousand resources, had just the place no one would ever find them.

Locked lips on location in case Honcho got compromised.

Taking his cue, Honcho went to fetch Julia and the kids. He hoped she hadn't spooked and bailed. Thankfully, she was sitting next to Emma while David played with Pete.

"You all ready to come back up?"

Julia frowned. "What happened?"

Honcho smiled. "Get the occasional bear that decides they want better digs come winter time. Hibernate in style. So, they come and check out my place. Had one that tripped the porch security. The bear spray sent the big guy packing."

David was the first to show his dismay. "A real live bear? And, we missed it?"

Emma was a bit more practical. "Bubba, better to miss it than be eaten!"

Honcho had to laugh, a hearty deep belly giggle that echoed in the room. "Eat you two? Not enough meat on your bones. Now a big bear like me? Me and that bear would have a real good wrestling match to watch!"

Julia just shook her head. Laughter and silliness were hard to come by in the new world. Fear and being on the run constantly watching over your shoulder didn't leave a lot of time for fun.

"Come on, you trespassers. I'm sensing we need to fill our bellies with some food!"

Honcho hustled back to the living area and started to whip up a meal. He needed to keep occupied. They hadn't heard from Ryan since he pinged them when he got to Seattle. It had been a day already and though Honcho knew radio silence was required, getting a status report to know his buddy was still alive kept eating at Honcho's gut.

"What's on your mind, Honcho?"

He sighed, and Julia could tell from the look on his face.

"I'm worried too," she whispered so the kids didn't hear.

Honcho turned, his lips pursed. "I have known that fool for decades. Been part of some of his exploits sitting in the back of the room cheering him on. That man is nearly indestructible, I tell you. And, staying off the radio to keep chatter from getting triangulated is standard operating procedure. But damn, I'm getting really antsy waiting around. This all is different than a war zone. He's flying blind. At least, war you have intel and a team to watch your six."

Julia wrapped an arm around Honcho. "I'm scared too. A little over a month ago, I thought he was dead. Then, this mysterious black clad shadow shows up dead of night, like a ghost, and it's Ryan. Alive. Then, I find all these things out about my husband I never knew and throw in what is happening to him? I'm overwhelmed. I can't lose him again."

Honcho touched her hand. "The man is a cockroach. I've tried to shake him for years. No way that guy is going to die. Not yet at least."

Julia smiled. "At least, he's *our* cockroach."

A boot scuff interrupted the conversation.

"Who's a cockroach?"

Emma and David turned. "Daddy!"

Running over to Ryan, they wrapped their arms around his waist and hugged tight.

Ryan grinned, patting them both on the back. "Missed you guys. Were you good while I was gone?"

Emma looked up. "I was. Bubba wouldn't let me watch a show."

Trying to defend himself, David offered a poor excuse. "I told her *after* we watched my show she could."

Julia shrugged. "Nothing changes."

Honcho caught a whiff of it, subtle, but it was there. Finishing up with the breakfast, omelets with fresh veggies and homemade cheese and some fresh baked bread for toast, he motioned for the kids and Julia to grab seats and put plates down for them.

"Eat people. Let me help your dad store his stuff and then he can eat with you all."

Not wanting to argue as he had just walked in the door, Julia agreed. "Sit kids. Dad will be back in *five* minutes."

Ryan heard the urgent request, and obliged. "Five minutes. Maybe three."

Honcho followed him down the corridor, far enough out of reach of prying ears, before saying a word. Touching Ryan's shoulder, he dove in. "*What* happened?"

Ryan laughed. "That obvious? I thought I kept it pretty tight."

"You did. But, I *know* you. Been brothers for a long time and through some serious shit. Something is up. Spill."

Ryan needed to tell him about Liz. That development was not something he could keep quiet, not without guilt. Honcho deserved to know his wife was still alive. Right now, there were other pressing matters. He could ramble on about it, or just show Honcho. Pointing down the corridor to follow, Ryan walked the length, headed towards the far stairwell and went below. Honcho began to get nervous, before Ryan took a left, went all the way down, and then a right. Gesturing at the closed door, he shrugged.

"Didn't know what else to do." Ryan reached for the doorknob, and pushed it wide open.

Honcho's dark complexion turned white. "No fuckin' way."

Chained to a chair by the far wall, Reg Carmichael glared from behind cold, dead eyes.

CHAPTER 27

"Did you scan him?".

Ryan grinned from ear to ear. "No."

Honcho slapped his forehead. "Did we not just go through this?"

Trying to contain his laughter, Ryan held out his hand. "Decided to cut the damn thing out instead. Though you might want to have a looksee."

The pallor was fading, and color filtering back to Honcho's face.

Ryan leaned in. "Don't worry. It's not active. Just figured for all the pain my old man has caused, he deserved a bit of payback."

Honcho caught the tone, almost a sense of pride, and quickly blew it off. Come back to *that* later. "At least the brain is firing on a few cylinders."

"Yup."

Turning his back to Reg and pulling Ryan close, Honcho whispered. "But why here? Of all places? If they somehow track him, we're stuck."

Ryan nodded. "I figured it was the best place to interrogate him. Quiet down in the depths protected from prying signals above and close to your toolbox of goodies."

It made a bit of sense. No outside scan was getting in.

"OK. But then what?"

Ryan shrugged. "Once I get what I need, I kill him."

The words bit hard. Nonchalant, no emotion. As if Ryan was simply throwing away a dirty napkin. His face was like stone, flat, but the eyes burned bright with hatred, a fire Honcho had never seen in his old friend.

"Ry, I'm beginning to feel like you're losing it. Just the blunt truth."

A sigh, and Ryan nodded. "I felt a switch turn off out there. I'm still hanging on with the real me, but things are progressing down the path to Hell. I feel it."

At least he was being honest.

Grabbing Ryan's shoulder, Honcho asked, "So, what do we do?"

Ryan tapped his friend's hand. "We get to work."

Reg sitting in the Moose Lair brought a whole new dimension to the storm Honcho knew was brewing and waiting to spew forth like a hurricane. Figuring what the hell, he just let it out.

"We got a visitor. Maybe he can help."

Ryan looked up, not sure what to say.

"It's BP. I called the cavalry. We need it."

Leaving Reg to ferment a bit in the dark, Honcho led Ryan to BP. The walk was quiet, the only sound the echo of boots on the concrete floor. Julia would begin to wonder what was taking so long and the questions begin to pile up. The less she asked, the better things would be, Ryan hoped. Dropping BP into the mix would ward off some discussion, and hopefully divert attention to what was going to transpire in the bowels of the silo later.

Knocking first, Honcho turned the knob. "You up?"

A rumble of movement, a squeak of shoes, and then BP was there. "Ready and waiting for the fun to begin!"

Pushing the door wide open, BP was at first surprised to see Ryan, then it faded and he wrapped him in a hug. "Ry! Good to see you, Brother!"

Ryan reciprocated, relishing in the warmth of love from BP, but feeling inside it chipping away from his own feelings. Not because he didn't, but the virus planting a foot and not letting go. "Good to see you too. Julia and the kiddos are waiting upstairs eating breakfast. Had a diversion to share with Honcho, and I'll fill you in later. But now, need to hustle before they all get antsy and ask a shitload of questions why we've been gone so long."

BP nodded. "All good, Brother. Let's get our grub on!"

The men hurried to the living area of the old silo and walked in to find Julia laughing and David jumping up and down. He was telling some sort of story that from the sound of it, was funny. Emma sat staring at her brother, trying hard not to crack. Her statue didn't last long, as she burst and the chuckles ran out like a broken faucet. Suddenly realizing BP was with Ryan and Honcho, Julia pursed her lips, and tapped the table.

"All right, Mr. Monkey Pants. Finish your food."

David protested. "Ah, Mom! It's funny!"

Julia smiled. "Yes, Son, it is. But, time to finish up. Plus, we've got a visitor."

The kids turned and saw BP, their faces lighting up. "Uncle BP!"

"Hey, you rotten little weirdos."

The joking was a welcome addition to the growing feeling of claustrophobia inside the silo. The kids hadn't seen daylight in a few days, and getting some fresh air would be a welcomed relief.

Taking seats around the table, Honcho plated food and handed it out to Ryan and BP. Taking his own, he found an opening and dove in. Forgetting the coffee, he got back up and brought the carafe and some mugs over, poured some sweet nectar of caffeine around for the adults, and settled back. A round of thanks greeted his gesture.

The conversations that came didn't involve anything related to their current situation. It was catch up time all around. BP filled everyone in on his last three years and how his kids were keeping busy. Elle was heading up the young adult brigade overseeing the relocation of stragglers brought into the local survivor organization once they were vetted. LP, as her brother was called, helped acclimate the young teenagers. It was a family affair, as everyone found out. With all of BP's connections, at least the ones still alive and not turned into marauders on the hunt, survivors were getting connected to groups and making some headway at a decent chance for life.

It had been word of mouth, growing more each year once the dust settled. As time blew by, and routes up and down the coast became clear for passage around Brainer encampments and known Lurker and Bolt dens, a bit of headway developed. It was still piecemeal, but by BP's count, the good numbered in the thousands.

Small, but with each day grew and gave someone on the brink of death a fighting chance.

Honcho talked about his adventures living in relative isolation and trips into towns for supplies. The encounters with people were nearly non-existent this far out. He had met some, loners mostly, a few banded together. More of his meetings were the avoidance of Brainer scouts and from what he observed, King loyalists. He did dive into the goldmine of finds with all of the booty he collected to make his homemade goodies. Those stories brought smiles and nods all around the table. Even Emma and David managed to appreciate the spoils brought back. No DVDs to watch if Uncle Honcho hadn't been pirating, as he said, in stolen stuff that really wasn't stealing when the world ended.

Ryan avoided talking about his own years alone. He didn't like rehashing the past and really didn't have any positive experiences to share. Those three years were death waiting to suck him in, until David fell into his lap and the wheels began to turn. That day set off events that for better or worse, sealed Ryan's fate.

Instead, he and Julia told stories of their time trekking north. Camping by the ocean and watching the night sky. Fishing rivers and lakes for food. Their stealthy sneaks into places to snag food and treats. Wild gardens picked clean of fresh produce. They tried to keep it light and positive for the sake of the kids. The horrors encountered and escapes from death's door being pursued didn't need to be relived.

Breakfast time extended to almost two hours, and knowing time was an enemy, Ryan pulled Julia aside. He had to tread lightly and keep everything vague, with enough substance to deter her from asking any deep questions, but having the right meat on the bones to feed her curiosity.

Telling her his dad was below? Not a chance.

"So, I didn't know BP was coming, but it actually helps us out. Another brain to help figure out this mess and if necessary, a gun to ward off the nuts."

Julia caught the sarcasm, as BP was not the gun-toting type. Honcho much either. Ryan was the bullets blazing one, though if it came down to it, BP and Honcho would go all three amigos in a hail of gunfire.

"The more the merrier."

Ryan smiled. "A regular party in here."

Julia hugged him. "I know you have 'boy stuff' to do. I understand. Just, don't be gone long. The kids miss their dad."

A soft kiss on the lips. "Got it, Chief. We will keep the video game time down to a minimum." Turning to leave, Ryan called to the kids. "Hey, you monkeys! Be ready by lunchtime. Picnic under the trees."

BP and Honcho were already below. Chairs flipped around, they sat quietly looking at Reg. Not a word, not a sound. Just piercing eyes working the old man over. Reg, for all his bravado, seemed at ease, maybe a little off, but gave back brown eyes that if they fired missiles, everyone in the room would be dead.

Seeing Ryan appear, Reg snarled. "About damn time the Golden Boy makes an appearance."

Ten paces without a blink. Reaching Reg, Ryan reared back and slammed his fist into his father. "Shut up."

Licking the blood from his lips, Reg grinned. "That's my boy! Turn, turn, turn!"

BP wasn't clued in on the intel. "What's he talking about?"

Another fist, this time into the chest. Reg huffed for air, and coughed.

Honcho took it. "Seems Ry here is going to go all demon on us shortly and wind up a psychotic killing machine. The virus has put him on the road to crazy town."

Turning to Ryan, BP's face lost color.

Ryan shrugged. "Seems I am the poster boy for the baddest of the bad. Soon to be the nightmare of everyone's dreams."

Reg spit. The blood, a bit thick and dark, hit the wall and oozed down.

"Can we stop it?" BP asked.

Ryan started to speak, before Honcho cut him off.

"We will do everything we can to prevent it. One reason old Reg is here."

Motioning for his friends to move back, Ryan knelt. "Listen, I *am* going to kill you. No way out of it. Like I told you before, the method and how long it takes, is all up to you."

BP cleared his throat. "Hey Ry, I don't know about all of this. Murder and all?"

Ryan pulled out his Ka-Bar and twirled it for Reg to see. "My dad thought nothing of letting my babies be tortured for some sick and twisted ideology. Three years! Murder? What about all of the people who have died for some idiotic scheme at controlling the world? It's justice for the dead billions left to rot and us barely able to survive. If you can't stomach it, get out."

Harsh and direct. BP saw it in his friend. "Listen, I got your back Ry. It's just, can't we use him to bargain or something?"

Honcho nodded. "I'm with BP a bit on this. I know what he did to Emma and David, and you know those brats mean the world to me. I have no problem putting Reg here in a world of hurt so he pisses blood and shits out his intestines. But, he has some use as leverage if we can manage to do it."

"Pussies," Reg bellowed. "Not men enough? Balls all shriveled up?"

"Fuck this," Honcho sighed, before knocking Reg out cold.

CHAPTER 28

"Do we have a status or what?"

Mark Simpson's irritation at his team leader began to boil. Reg Carmichael had missed his status update and every subsequent radio call. Both teams accompanying him too. Hostile terrain and unknowns meant calls might be missed.

Mark knew that.

As the hours stretched without a word, and knowing Reg was halfcocked on a mission only he was privy to all the details, Mark began to wonder. Reg was a loose cannon, and his actions since they lost Ryan a spiral into a black hole. Going off on a tangent without notifying anyone was a bad sign if he chose to chase shadows. They were supposed to be aligned with the same goal. Find the children and Ryan.

Anything else that got in the way or diverged from the mission was unacceptable.

"Sir, we found bodies. Over."

Mark let the statement sink in. Bodies meant anyone, though the inflection on the radio said it was their men. He hoped Reg was one of them, just to be done once and for all with the asshole.

"Carmichael one of them?"

The team leader answered. "No, Sir. Over."

The information just made Mark more pissed off. "*Any* intel on where he is?"

"None, Sir. There are tire tracks leading away, but nothing beyond that. Took one of the SUVs. We tried to ping it, but found the wiring harness down the road. Do we continue searching? Over."

Mark grimaced. Either Reg decided to go off on his own and killed his men, or someone decided to decimate an entire two teams of special operators and kidnap the old man. No one had the skills to do that.

Except?

The flash thought sent Mark over the edge. "Find me Reg Carmichael, and his son!"

"Yes, Sir. Rotors up in five on the bird. Drones in fifteen. Over and out," the team leader answered, and then was gone.

Mark sat back in his seat, the uncomfortable stench of loss wafting his nostrils. Not from losing Reg. That man gone would be a celebration. No, the loss of Ryan weighed on his mind, his ability to be a ghost moving in and out of thin air with ease to strike and then disappear.

The man was a cockroach.

Reg and his men should have captured Ryan. Or at least, killed the thorn. Two groups of former SEALS and Delta Force, the second best of the best behind Ryan, should have given up a better fight. Reg's protection detail was hand-picked. Their annihilation and losing their leader a statement. If they couldn't put up a fight, what chance was there of winning?

As Mark let the anger seethe, he tried to focus on the bright side. If Reg was in the possession of Ryan, which wasn't a sure thing, then there were a few advantages. One, it kept Reg out of Mark's hair. He could move forward and command as he saw fit. Two, it meant focusing on finding the children. If Ryan was around, they were close by. And then there was golden number three.

Time to unleash the Devil's dogs.

CHAPTER 29

"Mom? Daddy is *different*."

Julia smiled. "Your father is quite the weird one for sure."

Emma frowned. "No. Something is wrong. I can feel it."

Her daughter had shown signs of a connection with her father when he was close. The pictures at the underground facility proved that. Even some of what Emma had said since being back with her dad showed a bond that was growing each day.

The depths of it a whole unknown.

"What do you mean, Pumpkin?"

Emma sat, her head bowed, trying to find the words. Two minutes passed, and then she blurted out, "He's angry at Papa. Papa keeps saying things about Bubba and me, and Daddy is mad."

This was the first time Emma had mentioned Reg. Never over the last month had she said a peep. It coming now, Julia chalked it up to all of the commotion with BP being here and Ryan back. "It's OK. You probably feel Daddy being hurt by what Papa said back at the mansion."

Emma vigorously shook her head. "No, Mommy. Daddy is hitting him and Papa won't tell Daddy what he wants to know."

Julia sat back against the couch. David was playing with Pete in the other room. Her palms started to sweat, and she felt queasy. Whatever effect the vaccine had on her, Emma was evolving.

Into what, was the billion-dollar question.

"Hey, Daddy is fine. Just a bad thought. Let's finish watching our movie, and then you can help me with lunch. OK?"

Emma nodded and gave her best thumbs up. "OK."

As she settled back into the couch, Emma snuggled up next to her, Honcho burst in.

"Hey, Julia. Got a sec?"

Worried, she patted Emma and whispered, "I'll be back. Don't fast forward without me."

Emma nodded with a smile, then was back to watching her show.

Following Honcho out the door, Julia saw the look in his eyes. "What's going on?"

Reaching for her arm, he pulled her further down the corridor, past where David played with Pete. "Listen, we have some problems and I'm not sure what to do."

Thinking about what Emma had brought up, Julia asked, "It's Ryan, right?"

Not that far of a stretch to guess.

Honcho shook his head. "No. I've been eyes deep sorting through intel buried deeper than the Mariana Trench. Some stuff is popping up here and there. Didn't make any sense, until one piece seemed to bring it together."

Julia tilted her head. "What is it?"

"Did Mark mention anything, anything at all, about something called Aurora?"

Julia shook her head. "Not that I recall."

Honcho drew a deep breath. "Maybe a word in passing, phrase even, like Aurora Moon?"

Another shake no.

"Dammit," Honcho sighed.

"Why?"

Honcho sighed. "We might have a problem."

Leaning back against the wall, the cold concrete sapping her heat, Julia began to feel sick. "What is Aurora or Aurora Moon?"

Grabbing her hand, Honcho led Julia to the war room, his monitor heaven with screens full of data and words that began to run together as she felt the vomit forming in her gut. Pointing to the middle screen, enlarged and prominent, was a photo of Ryan.

"Seems our guy has been their toy since day 1."

Staring at the photo, and then the caption, Julia leaned over to the trash can and let the chunks flow.

Ryan Carmichael. Test subject Alpha for Aurora trials. Aurora Moon viral source.

Wiping the vomit on her sleeve, Julia stood up. "What does it mean?"

Honcho pointed to the far monitor on the right. "They wanted an army of psycho killers. You wouldn't know the trial tests as they came before you were born. When we were in elementary school, they did fluoride treatments. Under the guise of promoting healthy teeth. Millions of us across the country. That was partly true. The other part was an underlying additive, a hypothesis. For some it worked to justify the equation. The majority it didn't affect. Ryan was the supply of whatever he's infected with, something that pre-dates all this chaos. Been brewing inside him for decades until they decided the time was right to unleash it."

Julia felt her lungs constrict, and the air no longer able to breathe through her nostrils. Her head got woozy, and within seconds, she passed out cold. Catching a handful of sweater to keep her from smashing her head on the concrete floor, Honcho moved Julia to one of the bunks down the corridor, and five minutes later, she twitched, and then groggily opened her eyes.

"Welcome back, Stranger."

Julia tried to shake the cobwebs out. "What, what happened?"

Honcho's eyebrow raised, and the ever-jovial friend gave it to her. "You're kind of a wuss. Can't take any kind of bad news."

Raising up on an elbow, she took a breath in, and held it. "No, there's more to it."

Honcho's eyebrow raised up.

Julia frowned. "No, not preggo. Lack of sunshine, stress, and something else I'm not sure about."

Julia tried to get up until Honcho held out his hand.

"Listen, I'd lay back down if I were you. What I told you is part of what I found. The other, is more devastating."

Figuring she better listen, Julia rested back on the pillow. "Just hit me with it."

There was no great way to say it, so Honcho simply blurted it out. "Emma and David. Ryan was the carrier and first super dude in the arsenal they were waiting to transform. Others, where it managed to take a hold, the back-up infantry in support of Ryan and the cause. Weaker, but still harvestable subjects. As we know now, that group is a bit vintage, age-wise. Still relevant if they've managed to survive cut off from us. Bodies of twenty-year-olds. Maybe thirty if I've been generous having seen Ryan's ass these past years. The kids, well, the future army of the crazy sons of bitches."

The air left again, and Julia started to hyper-ventilate. Trying to bring the calm, she took slow breaths, held them, and then exhaled.

Continuing on, as he knew she needed to know, Honcho let loose with intel meant more for a dark thriller movie than real life.

Skipping ahead, as the beginnings were a long story, Honcho cut to the chase. When Mark pushed Ryan out of the helicopter and kidnapped the children, it was meant to eliminate the most virulent seed of the virus.

At least, for Mark.

If he controlled the blood supply, it gave him leverage within the organization. In the larger picture, the cabal of whackos wanted Ryan as the elite assassin and to bring about an army of them to keep order. Get out of line or do not adhere to the cause, you die. Emma and David were carriers, weaker given their age, but as they got older, the hope was they brought the fire rain of death. Getting rid of Ryan pushed the timeline back considerably, but did not completely bring the progress to a halt.

What it did do was encumber the vaccine serum Emma and David were meant to be as the Guinea pigs for the world. Two trials for different outcomes. The stress of it all on the children brought failed results.

That aspect was a disturbing fact.

Letting people descend into madness with no ability to control was not part of the plan. Get the serum and force reliance on it, and order would come. The crazies were a lost cause, no way to bring them back once the brain was shot to hell. Survivors could be contained, and the threat of turning into a psychotic killer enough leverage to leash people under the group's rule.

The information hung in the air like a cloud of methane gas expelled from a herd of cows. Heavy, smelling of something beyond sinister and worse if it managed to take effect, the idea that her children were the source of something meant to harm humanity made Julia's skin crawl. Emma was sweet, a gentle soul who loved everyone. Her disabilities made her a joy and real person, free of the baggage most people carried. David was like his father, bright, inventive, a lover of animals, and a jokester who loved to tell wild stories.

Just like Ryan.

Hearing that her precious babies were meant for some madman's plan on world domination and that they were on the same path as Ryan towards completely losing their humanity, cut Julia's heart in half.

There was no way in hell that was ever going to happen.

"You bozos weren't joking about the Moon, were you? Anything in all of that crap on how to stop all of it?"

The huge sigh didn't alleviate Julia's worries.

"You ever see a real photo of the dark side of the Moon? No. All doctored for a purpose. There's a reason why. As far as I know, the Moonies as part of Project Aurora are still there unless something happened. A small contingent of soldiers on a Moon base biding their time before being called to action. If they have a shuttle, well then, I don't want to think what happens. Hope they starved to death being cut off for three years with no ground supplies."

Julia coughed, trying to keep vomit from escaping at the thought. When she swallowed and took a breath, she asked, "So, what do we do?"

Honcho finally spoke. "There might be something, but you are not going to like it."

CHAPTER 30

"I will not allow it."

Honcho tried to pat Julia's hand, but she was not having it.

"It's insane first. Second, it separates us again. We just got Ryan back. He's already got problems. What if that affects him even worse and he really spirals? What then?"

She was right. Ryan didn't even know they were having this conversation. Soon enough, he would.

"Look," Honcho began, "it's not ideal. I get it. But, there's some things in motion that, well, better to have the kids far away than around even the protection of this place."

Julia stared at him, searched his eyes, and they didn't lie.

"My God, you have him, don't you?"

Honcho looked shocked. "I know not of this person you speak about at all."

She smacked his arm. "Cut the crap. You have Mark."

He lowered his head. "No, not him."

Confused, Julia searched for an answer, and it hit. "You have got to be kidding me. Reg?"

Honcho nodded.

"Where is that piece of shit?"

He held up a hand. "Secured away. Listen, a whole lot of things just all of a sudden got dropped like an atom bomb. No one has even processed it all yet. Ryan doesn't even know what I just told you. So, we have to tread lightly on it. Have a conversation and a plan on how to move forward. BP can take you and the little weirdos and hide you among his glorious band of survivors. Offer an army up of people who will protect you. Here? They're going to be scouring the entire area looking for Reg. They somehow find this place, which I doubt, it's a fucking siege. Kids get no daylight or fresh air. Ever."

While he had a point, Julia preferred the safety of millions of tons of concrete and rebar reinforced walls and blast doors than being out in the world exposed without Ryan.

"It's all a gamble."

He had to laugh. "True. But, if we have the cards and the hand, we win. Bluff is even better."

She caught the word, the intrigue forming a question. "Then, what *do* we do?"

Honcho waved her off. Everyone taking part and not having to rehash or debate over and over was the better option. So, sending her back to Emma, Honcho left and went to talk to Ryan. BP was sitting in a chair outside the door, reading a book he must have grabbed out of one of the numerous piles littering the lower level. Taking a peek at the title, Honcho chuckled. A history book covering the politics of the Richard Nixon era seemed like a lost cause to read.

Seeing Honcho, BP shrugged. "Quality father and son time."

Honcho shook his head. "Things are getting messy, old friend."

BP tried to contain a laugh. "You think? Reg here? They have got to be looking for him."

A deep sigh, and BP caught the unspoken words.

"Ah, shit. What now?"

Honcho could only say, "Got to get the kids out and soon."

BP nodded. Sooner than later had been discussed. He figured a few days.

"While you've been babysitting, I sifted through some really bad intel. Then, had to spill the bullet points to Julia."

BP braced for the news.

Honcho, his energy spent, grabbed a chair and sat. "You know all the fluoride treatments back in school?"

"I do."

"Well, our buddy in there was the seed of some really sinister shit. The best test subject results it seems. Passed that DNA down to the kids. They're not just valuable for this maintenance shot crap, but as the new army to march on the planet and subject people to a regime like never before."

BP coughed, the words in his throat caught by the dryness developing in his throat. "Wait? You mean there's more to all this shit than what we've known?"

Honcho nodded. "So much more I had to stop reading it all."

"So, Ryan? Mark tried to kill him. Reg too. If he's an asset, why do that?"

The short answer. "Mark has his own play at work. Get rid of Ryan and have possession of Emma and David, he controls the narrative. I don't think Reg missed from being a crap shot. I think it was on purpose. Wound Ryan, and take back what Mark tried to destroy."

"But, Reg? The venom he has for Ry. It's wicked, Man."

Honcho figured some was a ploy to throw Ryan off. Some a real hatred from Reg towards his son from what the virus had destroyed in the loving father. In the bigger plan, Ryan was a treasure, the Holy Grail that was meant to feed the rebirth of society under a cruel new order where disobedience meant death.

Ryan being the Grim Reaper to sow his sickle with vengeance.

"There is so much intel my head hurts. The problem is, sorting and sifting through what's real, and what is a breakdown that became the ramblings of lunatics. It's a sordid mess. Truth buried in lies. I'd take looking for a needle in a haystack over this. At least then, I know what to expect."

BP didn't need to hear everything to know what was at stake. The look in Honcho's eyes and the tone inflected in his voice betrayed the dire situation staring at them all from behind the barrel of a gun. He'd heard bits and pieces, rumors mostly over the years, as he brought in stragglers and got briefed. People who had heard from someone who knew a guy and even the rare tidbit from someone who claimed to have been an unknowing participant in the show. Honcho had the goodies, the deep state material that wasn't supposed to see the light of day. Putting two and two together wasn't necessarily adding up to four.

But, it was damn close.

BP pointed at the door. "So, what comes next?"

Honcho's eyebrow raised. "We get Reg to talk before Ryan kills him."

CHAPTER 31

"Go to Hell, Son."

Ryan, calm as a windless lake without a ripple in sight, pushed the blade tip into Reg's crotch. Just the tip, enough to make his father grimace with pain.

"That's my Boy!" Reg screamed out. "I can see the hatred in your eyes. As it feeds, little by little you turn into me!"

Honcho and BP watched from the back of the room. Ryan didn't even turn when they walked in, and Reg was so focused on his own rage, their presence went unnoticed.

Ryan shook his head. "That's where you're wrong, Dad. I will never be you. You tried to kill me, your oldest son. You let your grandkids, who you used to love, be used for a sadistic cause. Torturing them like nothing. Me killing you? Nothing more than justice."

Reg bellowed so loud it reverberated off the concrete walls. The wails of a lunatic in the asylum finding humor in using his own feces as paint.

Honcho braved to interrupt the great family catching up conversation. "Ry, hey, do you have a minute?"

Without even turning around, Ryan waved a finger. "Sure thing."

BP slid to the corner. Grabbed Ryan's Sig from its holster and sat with the pistol across his lap.

"What? Plan on shooting me, BP? I thought we were cooler than that, Slime."

Hearing the old nickname pissed BP off. "Reg, given what you've done to my god kids, if Ry doesn't put one in your skull, I'll gladly put a hole in it. Shut up and don't talk. Just stay really quiet. Or, I just might say screw it and pop your ass enough to not bleed out, but make it hurt, really, really bad."

Ryan was caught off-guard by BP and what came out of his mouth. It was damn funny and trying to not laugh was difficult. Ryan knew if BP said it, even with his disdain for guns, he meant it.

"Same goes for me, Reg. You're on borrowed time. You choose how you go out. Nice and easy, or burned at the stake. Doesn't matter to me which way." Honcho threw Reg a middle finger, a classic Honcho move when someone was a complete ass.

Ryan walked to BP, leaning in. "You good, Bro?"

BP smiled. "Never better. Go talk. I got this."

Closing the door and locking it just in case, Honcho motioned for Ryan to follow. Twenty yards down the corridor, he turned and pointed to a chair. "Sit."

Ryan stared at it, and instead leaned against the wall.

"OK, stand if you must. So, I'll just jump in. Since you've been playing tag with dear old dad, I've been eyeballs deep in shit. It took some time, but the bits and pieces over the last days has decided to paint an abstract like I've never seen before. Like, colors thrown against the canvas hoping to stick, and what runs makes a scene. Crazy shit. Anyway, short version, Julia and the kids need to get out and away from here like pronto."

Ryan cocked his head. "This is one of the safest places they could be. Why bail on it?"

Honcho cleared his throat. "So many reasons. Here goes nothing. The kids are carriers for some wicked experiments and you are the poster child for being the bringer of death, started from way back in the day. You, Daddy, are the seed. The kids are the next generation. They need doctors, and probably sooner than later to figure out how to contain it inside them. Then, in your various ghost haunting adventures, did you ever come across Project Aurora?"

Ryan stiffened, stood stone-faced. "Your security clearance means I can neither confirm nor deny."

"You ass," Honcho replied as Ryan began to laugh.

Nodding, Ryan tapped the wall. "You know of the Moon detachment of soldiers looking after the old base. They're dead now, given supplies haven't exactly been delivered in over three years."

Honcho's eyebrow began to lift.

Ryan hadn't caught Honcho's meaning before, and then it hit. "What do you mean experiments on me?"

There was no way to easily break it. "Remember fluoride treatments in school?"

"Yup."

"Well, all a cover for creating some type of future super solider. You my friend, were the best test tube baby. Others, the Moon men, like bastard half-siblings from a crack whore."

"And, my kids?"

Honcho reached out, but Ryan pushed his hand away.

"Spill, Honcho."

Clearing his throat, Honcho let it all out, everything he had discovered, the bits that made no sense, and the conclusions that when he was finished, made even a hardened soldier like Ryan's skin crawl.

"No way."

CHAPTER 32

"Come on kids. Grab your stuff. Make sure you have everything you need."

Procrastination and blatant disobedience didn't help.

Ryan helped Emma with her bag. David was still playing with his toys and ignoring the orders. Smoothing her hair from her face, Ryan bent down and kissed Emma's cheek. "It's just until I can meet up with you. Uncle BP will be taking you on a cool submarine ride and make sure you, Bubba, and Mom are OK. Deal?"

Emma looked at him, her eyes watery, but not ready for a full-blown cry. "Deal, Daddy. But, who will protect you?"

A legitimate question.

He pointed. "Uncle Honcho has my back."

Emma frowned. "That's only two of you, Daddy."

Ryan grabbed her hands in his. "You are my Princess, you know that? And, you're one of the bravest kids I know. Daddy will be fine. Been in worse situations than this. Besides, I have a secret weapon."

Confused, Emma touched his cheek. "What, Daddy?"

"You and your brother."

Giggling, Emma shot back, "Daddy, that's two secret weapons!"

Ryan nodded. "It is. But, they don't know that, do they?"

Finished and ready, he handed off her bag to BP and went to where David sat with his action figures. "Come on, Son. You need to finish packing."

David shot Ryan a look. "Why?"

Taking a breath, realizing the disrespect was his son's way of navigating through an information dump full of holes the boy didn't understand, Ryan sat on the floor. "Listen, Buddy. I don't' like it either. But, there's some really bad stuff coming. I need you as far away as possible and safe. With people who can help protect you. Dad's a one-man army. I'm super, but not that good.”

David shook his head. “Dad, you *are* super. But, what if I never see you again? I just got you back.”

Ryan saw the water flow, and then the tears blew up. His boy was right. Gone three long years. Reunited a month ago. Now, looking to separate with the humongous possibility of never seeing his children again. The thought weighed heavy, but he had to push it aside. Ryan was the best, and he knew it. Not in a cocky way, but in confidence proved time after time. This show though, was more than he had ever encountered and the odds in his favor slim to none. He might wreck some havoc, eliminate some players, but if it was as secretive and vast as Reg made it seem, Ryan could only do so much. He had to have help.

“Son, it’s going to be OK. I won’t lie and can’t make any promises. But you know me. No matter what, one way or another, I will do anything and everything I can to get back to you, Emma, and Mom. OK?”

David wiped away his tears. “I know Dad. I just wish I could help.”

Ryan leaned over and kissed his son’s forehead. “You can. Protect Mom and Emma. Uncle BP too. Got it?”

David nodded. “Got it.”

“Good, now pack up and get ready to go.”

Getting up, Ryan saw Julia out of the corner of his eye. She hadn’t spoken a word to him since the plan was shared.

Not one.

He knew she was pissed, angry, and had a right to be if he was in her shoes. She thought the bunker was the safest place on Earth too. He tried to smooth it over, explain what was coming ahead, and the potential if they were discovered, the silo becoming their tomb. At least on the surface, there was running room to hide. Walking over to her, he touched her arm.

“How long do I get the silent treatment?”

Julia shrugged.

“I know being apart doesn’t seem to make sense. In the scheme of all that Honcho found out and what may happen, me being away and the kids getting to a doctor that might be able to help, that seems logical to my tiny teeny brain.”

Julia held up her fingers, thumb and pointer barely apart. “This tiny teeny?”

Ryan snorted. Julia managed to laugh and give him a hug.

“Ryan, I know all of it. Doesn’t mean I agree. Not totally, anyway. You held back things from me and finally came clean. Guess I need to too.”

Surprised, Ryan grabbed her by the arm and led her out the door. BP, seeing the gesture, called out, “I got it.”

Staring into her brown eyes, Ryan asked, “Tell me what?”

Julia just went for it. “Emma and David, as you may or may not know given your own issues, are, well, *different.*"

Ryan's head began to think back to Mount Diablo, and he nodded. "I've thought a few things, yes."

"Well, what you don't know is that your children seem to possess some skills that no human except a super hero, can do."

"What do you mean?"

Julia slid to the side along the wall to give her some space. "No easy way to say it. Emma can do things with her mind. David, well he gets the occasional super strength. Those two are unique in ways no living person has ever seen. We've had to hide it, from Mark, and others. If they found out, we could be talking dissection of our babies kind of evil."

The wind left his lungs. If it was true, his kids had an even bigger target on their backs and a worth that had no quantifiable measure. Madmen would stop at nothing to possess them. Honcho was right.

Gathering himself, Ryan let it go. "Well, this would have been nice to *know* earlier."

She shot him a look. "Really? Like you've been upfront with everything."

She was right, but he had his reasons.

"Intel gets shared when there is a reason to share it. Sometimes, the dots don't all line up and you wait to have a definitive picture."

Julia huffed. "Well, how was I supposed to tell you our kids are mutants?"

Ryan pointed at himself. "I'm a mutant it seems. Really easy to just say it and let me figure out what the hell to do to protect them while I still have the capacity to think straight."

He was right. Though she hated to admit it, and wouldn't to him. Not right now at least.

"OK. So, what do we do then?"

Ryan raised his hands. "Even more reason to get them to a doc to see what is going on. Though if they are turning into supers, it might help me. Transforming into villains like me, well, that would be an evil that reigns for an eternity. You better be nice to us," he winked.

"Asshole."

"Love you too."

With Reg secured below and not going anywhere, and the kids safely tucked inside the emptied Humvee to make more room and BP manning the fifty-cal, Honcho rode shotgun, an M4 across his lap. Julia sat holding Pete's carrier, a barrier to keep the kids from arguing in the cramped vehicle. Ryan rolled out of the underground garage, secured the door, and crept down the dirt road towards the highway. Honcho had a portable scanner between them, pinging for any radar or transmission signals that might come from above. All clear for a few miles, they hit the highway, went left, and headed towards the coast.

The fresh air felt great. Windows down since the ride didn't have bulletproof doors and a slight breeze blowing through as the Humvee sailed along the highway. The tree canopy above offering a hint of cover while the shadows of the early morning trek assisted in some invisibility from above. Emma and David played on their devices, headphones plugged in to keep the adult conversations out. BP occasionally blurting out from above catching a glimpse of a moose or dear across the lake. Julia trying to console Pete who was unhappy at being cooped up in the cat carrier.

Uneventful, which was a good thing.

"Should we have left him like that?" Honcho leaned over and whispered to keep the kids from hearing him.

Ryan kept his eyes on the road. "He lost the right to any dignity when he hurt my kids."

Honcho nodded. "I get it. But, where is the line drawn?"

As far as Ryan was concerned, there was no longer a line.

"No, seriously Ry. If we become *Them*, we're no better in the end."

Ryan shot over a look, and refocused on the asphalt. "I'm becoming one of *Them*. So, in my mind, they reap what they sow."

Honcho was all for giving it to Reg after what Ryan and Julia had shared. Damn, the bastard deserved to suffer for what he'd done. His end being a justified close to an evil man. The problem for Honcho was the *how* Ryan had left him. There were boundaries in war. You just didn't do certain things if you were civilized.

Ryan chucked that sentiment out the window.

"But seriously, a knife ready to chop *it* off if he moves? That's a bit extreme, even for the devil inside of you."

If Ryan cared, Honcho had a point. But, Ryan didn't. His point was to his dear old dad. You want to keep something precious to you?

Don't fuckin' move a muscle.

"Guess we'll find out," was as good an answer as Ryan was willing to give.

All Honcho could do was sigh in response.

Ryan caught the glint in the side mirror. The sun was coming up from the east, they were heading west, but the lake offered rays of light to cascade down and illuminate objects. The Humvee hidden by the tree canopy was protected some. A boat lurking out on the water was not.

"We've got company," Ryan pointed.

Honcho looked, and reaching behind to tap BP's leg, motioned for Ryan to stop.

"Why?"

A finger aimed straight ahead as they rounded the bend in the road made the Humvee lurch to a stop.

"Shit."

Honcho got out and walked towards the blockade before Ryan could stop him. A bullet blew a cloud of road five feet in front of him.

BP barked through the headset. "Want me to light 'em up?"

Ryan grabbed his binoculars and scanned the group. They weren't soldiers, and by the looks, didn't appear to be Brainers. As he focused in, he saw one of the King's men he recognized from below the Space Needle standing on the door jamb of a truck.

Decision time.

"No, not just yet. But, fire a warning shot at the boat."

Flipping the fifty-cal to the right, BP let loose with a quick burst at the approaching boat. As the water spray erupted and soaked the bow, the boat stopped dead.

"Thanks."

"No problem, Ry," BP chuckled.

Turning to Julia, Ryan touched her leg. Nodding the unspoken, she bowed back, pulled her pistol out, and set Pete down on the floor.

Stepping out himself with his M4 in hand, Ryan walked to Honcho. The big man was still standing in the same spot. Touching his elbow, Ryan asked, "Why did you get out?"

Eyes forward, Honcho whispered, "One of those guys is a former student of mine. Figured I'd use that card."

Made sense.

"Drop the gun," a voice yelled from the blockade.

Ryan shook his head, no.

Another bullet rang out, this time in Ryan's direction.

Stepping forward, Ryan shook his head again.

This time, the bullet sprayed his feet with shards of blacktop.

Suddenly, another voice rang out. "Mr. H, is that you?"

Honcho nodded and yelled. "In the flesh, Jeff. Can you please tell whomever is shooting at us to stop before my very good friend here tells our buddy back there with the really big gun to kill every one of you before you can blink?"

Emerging from behind the truck hood, Honcho's former student Jeff appeared. "Hey, stop firing at them. That's Mr. H. He's all good."

"Thank you, Jeff," Honcho yelled back.

Pointing to his people, Jeff motioned to Honcho. "Mr. H., this is *King* country. You shouldn't be here without an escort."

Honcho shook his head. "Free country as long as I'm still standing. I'll go where I want."

Turning his back to the group, Ryan stood close to Honcho. "So, seems I really should have said this a lot sooner. I met the King."

Honcho's eyes widened. "And, you're still alive to tell me?"

An affirmative nod. "I am. A real tough son of a bitch. King is Liz."

He wasn't quite sure he heard it right. Put his finger to his ear to clean it out. "You said Liz is the King?"

Ryan smiled. "Sorry. Things got crazy with my dad and everything and we didn't have a chance to really talk." He had wanted to, to pry and find out why Honcho *didn't* know, but circumstances messed it up.

Honcho shook his head. "That's something you could have taken a minute to share with me."

He was right. Dead on in fact. Ryan wasn't running on all cylinders, and his focus and mind competing forces for him to grasp and hold tight before he lost the *him* inside.

"I'm sorry, Bro. I am not *me* and I feel I'm losing a bit of myself every day."

Honcho poked Ryan in the chest. "It's OK. At least, she's alive."

Ryan could hear the sadness in his friend's voice. Honcho had lost his wife at the beginning, hoping she was alive and they could be reunited. Then, finding out she actually was, had been so close, and he never knew.

Seemed genuine enough.

"Look, my boo hoo can wait. We have bigger problems right now."

Ryan put out his hand, and Honcho took it. "Still brothers?" Ryan asked.

Honcho gripped back. "Can't seem to shake you, so I guess I'm stuck."

Jeff and a contingent of armed men and women stood behind Ryan. As he flipped around, he saw no one over thirty. Twenty-two probably a generous assumption. Their eyes said at least they were battled hardened, the last three years probably fighting off Brainers and the Un-dead. Cold and steely, focused and searching for any movements in the tree line. Any other time Ryan would love to chat. Right now, he wasn't in the mood.

Honcho stepped a few feet closer.

"Mr. H. Good to see you made it!"

Honcho smiled. "End of the world take me out? Not a chance in Hell."

Jeff grinned and nodded. "For sure." Looking at Ryan, Jeff waved his gun. "Um, Mr. H., if he's who I think, he needs to hand them over."

Ryan began to step, before Honcho's arm blocked him. "Jeff, not a chance. My friend here is what you might call a professional. The only reason all of you are not dead is because I *know* you."

Jeff tightened his stature. His crew fidgeted, thinking about what to do next, before one loner in the bunch decided to raise his rifle and try to pull the trigger. The moment his finger twitched, Ryan's blade sailed across the distance and went out the back of his throat.

The other rifles started up, before Jeff yelled out, "Stop it. Dumb ass Brian got what he deserved."

Glancing around, the rifles went back down. Still fidgety, but it was clear Jeff was in charge of them.

"Thank you, Jeff. I really do not want to have to do that to anyone else," Ryan smiled as he walked over to Brian's dead body, pulled out the knife, and wiped it clean on the man's jacket.

Fearing the situation might explode if the crew had more time to think, Honcho shrugged. "What's going on, Jeff?"

Jeff, lips pursed, pointed. "He wants the children."

Ryan started to move and Honcho motioned no with his head before looking back at Jeff.

"Who?"

Jeff giggled like a little kid. "Some guy. Worked a side deal with my crew."

Honcho's head fell to his chest. Deep breath in, held it, and then exhaled. Raising his eyes, the eyebrow ready to strike a pose, he let it fly. "No."

He played his card. Time to see what it did.

"What do you mean, no?" Jeff looked confused.

Honcho shook his finger. "These people are under my protection. Not going anywhere, no way, no how."

Jeff, puzzled at the statement, pulled a radio from his belt. Clicked the button and said something into it. A minute later, he got a response. His face still confused, he shrugged. "Doesn't seem to matter. If you refuse, we kill you."

Honcho motioned Ryan over, kept his voice to a whisper. "We can hand them over peacefully and figure out what to do to get them back. Or, we risk a firefight and the kids get caught up in it. Either way, it's a bit of a lose lose for us. Only one option, Bro."

Ryan took a deep breath. Honcho was right. There was fighting to the end, or looking to fight another day. They were outgunned with nowhere to go. He hated making the tough choice, but he saw no other way around it.

"BP, you got that."

"Loud and clear."

Ryan looked up at Honcho, and saw the tears in his friend's eyes. "I wish there was another way."

Honcho nodded. "Me too."

Ryan went left and Honcho, still turned around, went to his left towards the water. BP lit the morning up, the fifty-caliber machine gun roaring to life. As he panned from left to right, the shells pinging off the top of the Humvee, Ryan came to a knee, aimed, and started to fire as some of the group fled to the trees. Honcho hit the dirt and flipping the barrel up, took care of the stragglers heading to his right. In less than a minute, the bulk of it was done.

Standing up and moving quickly, Ryan converged on the blockade of trucks. Around the backside, he put down two people trying to take cover. Honcho, all the way to the right and advancing past, looked down his scope and fired down the road. Jeff stumbled, took three steps, and collapsed to the ground. Still moving, Honcho fired another shot, and the body lay still.

Making his way to Honcho, Ryan rested his head on his friend's chest. "Sorry, Big Man. I wish we didn't have to, but there is too much at stake. No one gets my kids."

Honcho nodded. "No worries, Ry. I have your back. Always. Besides," he offered up, "Jeff was the biggest pain in my ass there ever was."

Ryan started to laugh, and Honcho burst out too. The lighthearted moment meant to ease the tension from the bloodbath that just occurred, felt good. Death was never fun to hand out. When it meant something bigger, keeping Emma and David safe, there was no looking back.

Be killed, or kill. Not much of a decision to keep yourself on two feet.

BP interrupted. "Got more company fellas."

Turning and sprinting back, Ryan and Honcho saw the boat pulled to shore and a dozen people hopping off.

"Want me to set a fire?" BP's words rang in Ryan's ear.

Focused and moving swiftly across the highway, Ryan waved Honcho to the left and he took the right. "No, we may have a need for the boat. Just watch our Six."

"Gottcha."

Honcho and Ryan moved as one. Each man taking a side, never allowing for any crossfire. The big man had been a soldier, trained in firearms and how to fight, but as an analyst, he was more comfortable behind a desk than in the thick of gunpowder smoke. Ryan was the expert, the man who never missed a shot. To Honcho's credit, all their times out on the paintball field paid off.

The guy was a natural special operator with the grace of a ballerina, even at six feet five inches and a mountain of a man.

As the last of their enemy went down for the count, Ryan put an end to it. Waving off Honcho, the two men met up and Ryan extended his hand. "Not too shabby there. If I didn't know you, I might go as far as to think you had been a special operator in a former life."

The compliment was appreciated. "No, just a great teacher who can be deadly playing paintball. Transferable skills."

"Sorry I got you into this mess. I know you are not a gung-ho gun nut. Hate the damn things even. But, I appreciate you dusting off the rust and going commando with me to protect my family. You too BP," Ryan added as he hit the throat mike.

BP pinged in. "What now, Hombres?"

Ryan pointed towards the Humvee. "We have enemies all around. Jeff radioed so someone knows we were out this way. Time to set a diversion."

CHAPTER 33

"This is crazy, Ryan. Even for you."

Maybe, Ryan thought to himself. At least it offered them a bit of a buffer and at the same time, gave some leverage for negotiations.

"It might be crazy. But, you have to think of it this way. Jeff worked a deal behind Liz's back. She won't like that and be pissed. She had me dead to rights if she wanted, but she let me go. Gave me cover to escape. She has more to gain helping than letting Mark and his puppets turn what's left of this world into a hell that won't end. I use *you know who* as leverage while you all get the kids to the sub and out of here. Gives us a chance. Slim, but a chance."

That wasn't even the crazy part.

Ryan was going to go back to the naval base and blow it to kingdom come. The diversion of all diversions to draw Mark's troops out. Then, deplete the detachment that accompanied his movements for a meeting with Liz. Put him in the crosshairs and at a disadvantage.

Honcho and BP didn't like it. At all. Julia was dead set against it.

"We can help," Emma suddenly offered.

David nodded. "We're Carmichaels. We support each other no matter what."

"Plus," Emma began, "have you told Daddy yet? You know, about our super powers," Emma tried to whisper as she put her finger to her lips.

Ryan straightened up. "What was that, Pumpkin?"

Julia got up and stood behind the children. She had hoped to never say a word, that the previous events were somehow sparked by whatever was going on inside her kids and would just go away. Each day came, and her fears grew as more materialized that seemed odd and normally could be dismissed. Added up, there was no way to keep discounting them as aberrations to just vanish.

"Well, there's no way to sugar coat it. You know a bit, but not the whole of it. Emma exhibits some type of mind powers. David, well, can you show Dad?"

The devilish grin said yes.

Walking over to the Humvee, David touched the bumper, and taking it with both hands, proceeded to lift it up. A few inches only, but enough to display a strength no adult man possessed.

"Pretty cool, huh, Dad?"

Honcho, who had been sipping on a bottle of water, spit it out. "Super David!"

BP just threw up his hands. "No way, Little Dude."

Ryan sighed. He had seen the transformation in others. Like the Brainers back east drinking the Regenetics brew. They didn't turn into super human monsters, just had some of their humanity, the darker part coupled with fun and laughter, roll back into their beings. But, and he knew the evolution was on overdrive, that if that happened to them, what could happen to two kids experimented on over and over for the devil's work?

Honcho cleared his throat. "So, since we're all playing Truth or Dare here, I might as well put my hat in the ring."

Ryan glared.

"I knew about some of this Ry. Julia asked to keep it a bit hushed. Then, I came across intel that blew even me away. You the seed, the kids the next generation. Seems evolution is moving at lightspeed."

Ryan, eyes closed, sifted through Honcho's previous dump of information back at the silo. Seeing now his kids having strange powers. As he worked the revelation, the planner within hurriedly scribbling notes, he looked up at Emma.

"Hey, Princess. Want to show me what you can do?"

Emma shrunk a bit, embarrassed. Julia coaxed her on from behind, and smiling, Emma closed her eyes, focused, and opened them up. Her ice blue eyes were wide, her face emotionless. As Ryan watched, he heard it. Thinking Honcho was screwing around, he turned, only to find Honcho just as surprised. The water bottle he had been drinking from, now on the ground, was suddenly collapsing in on itself.

As she watched, Emma took her right hand, and with a flick, she swiped left and the bottle hurtled through the air. Beaming with excitement, she ran over to Ryan and gave him a hug. "Proud of me, Daddy?"

Smiling down at her, Ryan leaned and kissed her forehead. "You are my special little girl."

David was next, and Ryan gripped them both close. Letting go, he bent down and touched their hands. They felt normal, warm to the touch, soft skin. Deep inside, he *felt* it. A sudden electrical signal that sparked from their hands and went through him. His own body felt on fire now, not hot and uncomfortable, but rapidly changing in a way that made him want to pass out.

Ryan's eyes got foggy, his brain hurt, and a second later he was gone. When he awoke, he was in the back of the Humvee, and Honcho was at the wheel. Julia was laughing at something he had said, and BP chuckled from above.

Leaning forward, Ryan tapped Julia's shoulder. "How long was I out?"

Without turning, she answered, "A few hours."

Noticing the darkness outside and the direction they were headed, he figured something else had happened.

"Group decision made I see."

Honcho took it. "Yup, my compadre."

"Anyone going to tell me?"

Julia finally changed positions. "You passed out. Then, a helicopter decided to make an appearance. We had to back into the forest and wait it out until they left. Jeff's radio call likely has the path to the coast crawling looking for us. Getting to the sub safely a no-go. We got back on the road and now we are executing what is now known as 'Plan Super Friends', courtesy of your boy back there."

Ryan wasn't sure how to take that bit of news.

He slunk back in the seat, brooding like a school kid, not sure what to think. He hated not being the plan maker since he was the one who always did them. He was the robot, the man who killed and slept like a rock. Involving the kids in it was not what he had thought, and definitely not the kind of uneasiness his deteriorating mind needed right now.

The former soldier sat, taking in the images that passed his eyes. Wished he could be fishing on the lake. Camping at a remote spot in the forest, fire going with some food cooking in a pot, sitting sipping a beer as he watched the kids play. Smiling and laughing at some ridiculous story Julia shared.

Anything to take his mind away from the thoughts lurking inside.

He wasn't sure what had happened. Didn't know if it was all a dream or real. He got snippets, pieces really, of Emma and David doing superhuman things. Partial words from Honcho and Julia trying to explain it. Feeling proud of his children for their abilities.

Then, the spark of energy before his lights went out.

Ryan knew he could ask. Just spit out the questions and get some answers. Part of him didn't want validation. The other, which was uncharacteristic of him, was afraid to know. His mind was slowly becoming a mess of mush with coherence of thought a feeble attempt.

Not that he was going completely crazy.

Just, he knew his reality sometimes bled with the weird visions in his own head. Movies that told a story different than what he knew to be true. Or, at least what he perceived as truth.

As he had found out over the last three years, and more so over the last month and change, real and false, true or not, was all a matter of opinion in some ways. Facts were gray, and as Ryan was beginning to see firsthand, even his own recollection and memories were not what they seemed. He might have been dreaming about the kids.

Whatever was real or true today, could wait.

CHAPTER 34

"This is the 'knock my socks off' plan you all cobbled together?"

Honcho stared at Julia, who looked over at BP, who turned his gaze towards Emma and David.

"Seriously? Have you all gone insane?"

The lack of an immediate response was not the best approach. Seeing Ryan agitated and his eyes afire, no one wanted to answer. Honcho though, took one for the team. He just hoped his friend realized the benefit.

"Listen, Buddy. We didn't say it was the best laid out plan. But, give it some credit. It does rip the socks right off whether you like it or not."

That part was true. Though Ryan felt it was more like ripping a bandage off a still festering wound that had stuck to the cotton pad and hurt like hell coming off.

They had annihilated an entire team of Liz's people and were looking to blame Mark's soldiers for it. Grasping at the hope that she believed it, or really believed Honcho telling her.

Up the ante on the game.

None of it mattered. Her people were gone. Blown to pieces by the fifty-cal and Ryan and Honcho going commando on them. Laying blame on Mark and his people was the chess piece to play. He had no loyalties. No compunction to honor a deal. If Ryan or Honcho could convince Liz at that truth, then the children had a chance.

"Listen Ry. We use our *secured away friend* as a bargaining chip. If we can lure Mark into a trap, then we all win."

Honcho had a point. It was what Ryan had planned to do, though solo.

Even if it was a thousand to one odds, more like a billion Liz would buy it, Mark had to go. A two-headed snake could still strike if one face got chopped off. Better to control the field on their terms than let the opposition run the pitch.

"I'm still not all that convinced this is the answer to our problems," Ryan shrugged. "It puts all of our eggs in one basket. I prefer we split up."

Julia wasn't sold either. Though, she got more details when Ryan was lost in his coma in the backseat. "We keep the kids hidden with your contact. Let her run some blood and see what she can do to help us out. You deal with Mark and the Menace."

To Ryan, this was winging it to the extreme, throwing everything together to execute in hours vs. days. While he had no problem executing a plan under those circumstances, he preferred the tactician's approach. Plan until your fingers bleed and with enough contingencies and backups to ensure success that your eyes hurt from the intense focus.

"Look Ry," BP chimed up. "I'm not so totally onboard either. I think there's too much risk. But," he managed with a weak smile, "I think it's a play to make. We need as many in our corner as we can get."

Ryan frowned and the tension in his body couldn't contain it any longer. "Am I the only one who thinks Liz won't welcome all of us in after we blew away a whole crew of her people?"

David waved his hand. "She doesn't know that."

Ryan didn't like his children as co-conspirators to a crazy discussion.

Feeling he needed to get his demons in order and understand the here and now, Ryan jumped in with both feet. "So, getting back to our current predicament, let me bullet point my understanding of what is proposed. We snatch up dear old dad and use him as leverage to lure Mark in. The twin terrors get shuffled off to safety for some pokes and prods of their blood to help out Mary. Hopefully get the good side ahead of the game and on the way to a win over the virus. We rally the troops and hope, no, throw a Hail Mary pass, that Liz will be onboard and decide to help us out. That sum it up?"

"Pretty much spot on," BP answered.

The eyebrow spoke. "Got to work all the details, but it's what we got."

Julia was last. Ryan saw her hesitation, but it passed. "Seems if we can get support and make a stand, we might be able to end being constantly on the run and fearing for our lives."

Ryan wasn't so sure about any of it. Spending more time with Reg and relying on an uncertain alliance with Liz he felt was out of reach put a pit deep in his stomach. Reeling Mark into a trap he didn't mind at all. In fact, being in control of the planning gave him a sense of satisfaction if it went his way. The kids stuck in the city if it got surrounded put people at risk, people who might do anything to up their chances at survival. That included Mary. Julia offered a response to that part.

"Look, if this Mary crosses us, I'll personally put one in her head."

Honcho threw up his hand. "Estranged wife or not, I'll do the same to Liz. Kids and the world come first."

BP had been silent, brooding in his own head space. He nodded. "Anyone doesn't join and fight alongside us, I'll kill 'em. The world has to get back to something positive."

Seemed they were all in some agreement.

Glancing around, Ryan felt the twinge he had missed for a long time. "You two guys are my rocks. We've been to hell and back, figuratively, and literally, in some cases. Without your help, I don't know how I can do this alone and protect my babies and Jules. I can't thank you enough."

BP nodded once to acknowledge. "Just make sure I get back to my own brood."

Honcho smacked Ryan's back. "We succeed, you owe me the best single malt in the world. Better track it down, my friend. BP and I will enjoy its fine legs as you watch and cry not getting any."

Ryan managed a chuckle. "I know a guy who knows a guy. But, he might be dead, so you'll need to bear with me a bit."

Julia sat in silence, watching the comradery and friendship. She had no one except her kids. Ryan was slowly losing it and his being around gradually creeping away bit by bit as time moved along. Her relationships all dead or lost because of the virus and ensuing apocalypse. Longing for just a simple brunch to be around another mom who understood life, someone who lived in a world of disabilities and managing a child's needs, the tears welled and dripped. Realizing it, Julia wiped them away.

For another time.

CHAPTER 35

Emma knew.

She could see it in all of their faces. Nothing overt, just the tiny fractions of a crinkle of the skin when eyes seemed to avert looking at her.

Not that anyone was treating her any differently than before.

She simply felt the heaviness in the air. David did too. Their twin connection, the mystery of a bond that science was hard-pressed to understand or explain, shot their thoughts across the bridge of their mind reading and she read his words.

He frowned, and Emma understood.

The adults had been hushed and huddled. Dad a focus of a conversation they weren't privy to, his eyes speaking, yet no sound. Something was up and she figured she knew what it was all about. David's thoughts betrayed the thinking too. Dad had been *strange* lately. Nothing that was far outside of normal. A hesitation here. A momentary glance where his vibrant green eyes seemed clouded.

The dark blood he tried to hide.

While Dad was an expert at keeping things hidden, the trickle of blood from his nose, a small droplet here and there he immediately wiped away, was no secret.

At least, she and David knew.

Mom? She seemed oblivious to it.

The acrid smell of it caught Emma's nose. Metal, with a hint of vomit. David had said so in private. Unless you were a shark, you would miss it. They could smell blood in the water from miles away, an itty-bitty microscopic sample drawing them to prey. For some reason, maybe it was the twin thing or possibly, as the two had discussed quietly while alone, it was a result of what was happening to *them*.

Sitting back in Uncle Honcho's underground hideout, the twins found time to talk openly as the adults scrambled around the facility. David had caught a snippet of a sentence mentioning Papa being there. Hushed voices had failed to hide the name.

"They're trying to protect us," David offered, though he knew there was more to it.

"We're eight, Bubba," Emma countered. "Old enough to know the truth."

She was right, sort of. Eight was a great age and their ninth birthday was coming up soon. At the ripe age of nine, the old people should realize the kids were practically adults and deserved to be in on whatever plan was being concocted.

David sighed. "Close to old enough. Maybe our birthday will let the cat out."

Emma wasn't the best at understanding her brother trying to use adult terms. The confused look on her face along with the shrug told him.

"Sorry. When we make nine, I think they might tell us more."

Emma smiled. "Got it, Bubba."

As they spoke, low and in quiet voices to not let anyone overhear if an adult happened to suddenly burst in the room, the lights flickered twice, and then cut out. The only illumination coming from the backup lights above the doorway. Grabbing each other's hand, the twins sat silently, and when the lights failed to come back on, they quickly moved to the far back of the room near the door that went to a maintenance corridor and access to more secure areas of Uncle Honcho's lair.

A beam of light brushed past the front, followed by loud footsteps that turned out to be Uncle Honcho. They could see the sweat on his forehead and rapid breathing, though the unguarded grin and eyebrow helped erase their growing fears.

"Everything OK, Uncle Hon?" David whispered.

Honcho nodded. "Sorry for the scare. I had to divert some power and the old wires didn't like it."

Emma caught the half-truth.

Seeing the look on her face, Honcho pursed his lips. "OK, not totally true. I did have to divert some juice for something, and it blew a fuse. Trying to fast charge a quiet ride we need to transport some supplies with us."

Emma shook her head, and decided to go for it. "Supplies and Papa?"

The question caught Honcho off-guard. "Who?"

David pushed. "We know Papa is here. Cut the crap and tell us."

The eyebrow raised, and they could see Uncle Honcho wasn't liking the sudden urge to step into adult stuff.

Emma got up and walked over. "Uncle Hon, we know. The walls catch stuff sometimes."

She was right, and it sucked.

"It's not my place to say anything, Kids. But, since we're all on team Carmichael here and the more you know the better you understand and follow *orders*," he emphasized, "your dad brought your grandfather back here. Now, we're going to trade him for some protection and time to help us figure this whole mess out. Got it?"

Two heads bobbed in agreement.

"Good," Honcho pointed towards them both. "I need your help gathering up supplies for the trip. So, secure Pete and come with me."

The trio passed Ryan in the hallway as he hurried by, a short nod to acknowledge them, but his face void of emotion. Scurrying quickly past them, he disappeared from view only to then find Julia turning the corner ahead.

"Any success?" she asked.

"No."

Irritated, not at him, but the situation, she ventured a request. "Mind if I try?"

Ryan shrugged. "At this point, I don't really care."

"Good," Julia motioned behind her. "Take me there."

Reg was still sitting in the same chair. The booby traps disengaged, he sat slumped forward, his bindings pulled tight to keep him from falling over. Eyes closed, they opened slowly at the sound of the opening door. The blood from his previous interrogation now dried at the corner of his mouth, he managed a sinister smile at seeing Julia.

"Tough girl deciding to pay a visit to her dear old father-in-law?"

Three fast steps and the fist unleashed. Connecting hard, square against his face, Julia's momentum carried forward and through, sending Reg crashing backward. Tucking chin to chest, the maneuver kept his head from whipping back against the concrete floor and an inevitable concussion. Surprised at the show of force, he didn't move for a minute, maybe two.

"Go fuck yourself, Reg."

The laughter from behind couldn't stay contained. At first low and trying to hide it, Ryan finally let it out and the sound echoed off the walls. "That's one reason why I married you."

Glancing over her shoulder, Julia winked, then focused back on her prey.

Reg spit out some blood in her direction, and when he did, she gave him a swift and purposeful kick in the ribs.

"Any more quips you need to get off your chest?"

Reg snarled, "You'll pay for this, Jules."

Another deliberate foot, this time at Reg's bad left hip.

Kneeling, Julia tapped his leg. "My husband can call me that. My friends can too. Never, ever, call me Jules. You don't deserve the privilege."

Cold eyes caught hers, devoid of any emotion beyond hate and anger.

"I'm going to enjoy killing you slowly, Bitch. No one else, just me."

Adjusting her footing, Ryan was caught by surprise at Julia's next move.

A lightning-fast right hand connected with the side of Reg's nose. The crack of the cartilage reverberated in the quiet. A stream of red erupted, sending a plume of spray out that misted in the still air until slowly eroding away.

"Reason Two."

Julia blew Ryan a kiss.

Reg didn't move. He sighed, closed his eyes, and shook his head. The audacity of his daughter-in-law was incredulous, to think she had any control. Striking him while bound, a puss move by someone trying to exert their dominance when in reality, a fair fight would eat them alive. Even in his seventies and cancer in remission, he was a lean mean ass kicking machine.

"Take off the restraints and try that, *Jules*," Reg mocked.

A fist came down on his sternum, releasing the air from his lungs.

Reg huffed, trying to catch his wind. She was tough, or attempting to portray herself in that light. He knew she was a runner and had been in law enforcement before the kids. Not a street cop, but dealing with ex-cons looking to avoid a final strike that would send them to prison indefinitely to rot away. He'd heard stories about her exploits, the foot chases through meth houses and rough and tumble wrestling getting someone cuffed and prone. Took no shit back then, though he had sorely figured motherhood had made her soft.

Seemed to still have a bit of the Type A rummaging around inside.

"I've got time, Reg. Do you?"

Reg turned to his left, the Devil's eyes replacing his own. Julia knew there was little to no hope at redemption for him. All she wanted was a slight reprieve from the cockiness to get what she wanted.

Smiling, Reg motioned towards his son. "I sure do. Not so sure about *Him*."

Another quick blow to the sternum, a creak responding to the closed fist.

"Keep acting like an asshole and what Ryan would do to you is nothing like a momma bear protecting her cubs."

Reg actually believed her.

Ryan was enjoying the scene and not being the one dealing the pain. Seeing his wife like this brought him a sense of pride as a former soldier. A take no shit and give it right back mentality when faced with an aggressor. While feeling the pride felt awesome, he also felt a pang of guilt for her even having to exert herself like this.

It meant he had failed.

"Enough Jules," Ryan whispered as he touched her shoulder.

Pushing his hand away, she didn't even look back. "Not even remotely close to it."

Ryan walked over and grabbing Reg under the arms, hoisted his body up and let the chair crash down from the weight of his mass secured to it. Leaning in, Ryan whispered something, and for the first time, Julia saw fear in the old man's eyes. She thought emotion had left the building, so this was a new chapter she might be able to work.

"Hey Babe, since I'm the one all geared up, could you maybe go and grab a few drinks? If we're going to be at this, we probably need some hydration. And oh, maybe a few snacks?"

Julia pursed her lips. "Fine."

She had barely left the room when Ryan took his knife and cut Reg loose. His hands were still zip-tied behind so he couldn't use them. Grabbing the back of his dad's shirt, Ryan pulled him up and around. Pushing hard, with Reg at first resisting moving, Ryan shoved hard towards the rear door of the room. Reg took a step, tried to duck, and the blow from behind jolted him to attention.

"Fuck with me, Dad, and I will outright kill you. Slow and over days. You won't know pain like the way I bring it. Cooperate and I promise your death will be quick. Yes, or no?"

"Lead the way, Sonny Boy."

CHAPTER 36

She felt it immediately.

A coldness deep within that sucked the life nearly out of her.

Catching herself with an arm against her brother, who had been carrying a box of MREs to eat while on the road, Emma stumbled. It sent David forward, nearly losing the contents. Immediately, he set it down and turned.

"I felt it too," David whispered.

Emma's eyes, usually bright blue, were dull and red. "Dad's gone. He took Papa."

That part David hadn't felt or knew. She was the one with the psychic touch. He had the strength and speed. Hearing the words from his sister, he sighed and pulled her into a hug. "Dad knows what he's doing, Em."

Her brother never called her that.

"I know," Emma managed to reply. "It's just, just," she stammered, trying to find the right words. "Dad's different. I *feel* it. He's trying to protect us. I just don't know if it's the right way to do it."

David hugged her tight and then let her go. Taking her hand gently, he squeezed. "Dad hasn't let us down yet, has he? He's like a real-life superman from the bits of stories he's told us. Even with whatever is happening to him he's doing what he feels is right for us. We have to support that."

"You know, Mom isn't going to like it."

A reassuring grip. "Not at all, but we've got to help Dad the best we can. Right?"

Emma nodded. "Yup."

David let go and picked the box up like nothing happened. Continuing on, he made his way to the upper level where Uncle Honcho was busy sorting stuff into bins. Emma veered off in the direction of the kitchen. She felt Mom had gone there, and hoping she was right, was going to run some interference for Dad.

"Hey, Big Man," Uncle Honcho greeted. "Just put it down there," he pointed.

David set the box down and turned to leave before Uncle Honcho called out.

"Hey? Where are you going so fast?"

David stopped, tried to think of a quick answer, and spun around. "Got more stuff to bring up."

Uncle Honcho sensed something off, but figured it was just a feeling. "Ah, right. Listen, how much more is there?"

Fast catalog of items. "Probably another three boxes of food. Then, water jugs."

Uncle Honcho ran the numbers. "OK. Put the boxes next to the other one. I've got to grab some things and will be back."

Not wanting Uncle Honcho to accidentally run into Dad, David bought some time. "Uncle Hon?"

The eyebrow raised. "Yes?"

David jumped right in. "You've known my dad for like, ever, right?"

The brow inched higher. "I have."

"So, like, he's told us some of the stuff he used to do when you guys were soldiers. Always the PG versions. Is Dad really as good as I think he is?"

Uncle Honcho let the brow relax.

"I mean, Dad is like the best of the best times one hundred, right?"

He wasn't sure exactly how to answer. Honcho had known Ryan for eons. Been privy to some serious shit. In total dark on others. It was a complicated question with a bunch of different ways to explain. Some PG, others bordering on a triple X rating. The boy was getting old enough to hear the truth, though it wasn't Honcho's place to break the virginity of his ears when it came to the exploits of one Ryan Carmichael.

"Fuck it," Uncle Honcho whispered under his breath.

"What?"

Uncle Honcho shook his head. "Nothing. Take a seat."

David walked back and sat on one of the storage containers Uncle Honcho had packed. Arms folded across his chest, the boy waited.

"So, you've asked me something that never in a million years I thought I would ever be in a position to have to answer. That's really your dad's job. But, given his modesty at his adventures and his humble nature, he'd only give you part of the story. I'm going to tell you something that you can never repeat, not even to Emma. If you do, break the soldier's trust I'm about to tell you, it's the brig for you. Understand?"

David didn't know what a brig was, but nodded.

Uncle Honcho grabbed a chair and pulled it over, flipped it around so he could rest his arms on the seat back. Head moving back and forth for a minute, lips out like a puffer fish deep in thought, he sighed twice, then focused on David.

"So?" David began.

Uncle Honcho raised his hand. "Your dad I've known for more than thirty years. He's like a brother to me. The way you feel about Emma? That's the same for me and your father. He puts others first before himself, no matter what it might do to him. He didn't start out to be a superman. It fell in his lap and the pieces just kept adding up until the myth of the man was his life."

David didn't understand, and Uncle Honcho saw the confusion.

"OK, let me just dive into it. Your dad didn't really want to be a soldier. But, there were things he was really good at that someone saw in him that could be used to help a lot of people. Your father can encounter a situation, and see it from every angle to find a solution. His methods might seem crazy and insane, but they work. When coming up against an enemy, that is one of his greatest assets."

"What do you mean, Uncle Hon?"

Grabbing a cold drink from the cooler, Uncle Honcho tossed it over. "Well, soldiers, the really great ones, all study the teachings of other great ones. That way when they encounter bad guys, they know how to win because they know a million different ways to do it."

"OK," David offered, still confused.

"Your dad knows all those answers, and knows that someone knows he knows all of them. So, your dad uses that to his advantage. He makes them think he is going to respond according to one way, and completely confuses them by doing something different they would never expect."

"Like?"

Uncle Honcho knew he had to tread carefully, but the truth sometimes was the best way to quench a young boy's curiosity. "There are soldiers who save the world one mission at a time. Heroes you never know their names. Your dad is one of those special people. Except, he thinks about the mission, *and* what happens next. See, you can accomplish your objective, like kill the bad guy, but inevitably, it pisses someone off and they come back trying to be worse than the other guy. That's why your dad always, and I mean always, sent a message to the next bad guy that what just happened was nothing compared to what would sneak in their door if they decided to fight back."

"How?"

Trying to not freak the boy out was the hard part of the conversation.

"Well, what would you do if someone tried to hurt Emma?"

David didn't expect to be asked a question. "Um, well, I'd protect her."

Uncle Honcho raised his eyebrow. "How'd you that?"

"I would stop them. Punch them if I had to and tell an adult."

"So, squeal on the bully and give him a bloody nose or black eye?" Uncle Honcho asked, more of a statement than anything.

"Yup."

Uncle Honcho grabbed a drink for himself, popped the top, and downed it quick. Refreshed, he continued. "Your response addresses that moment. But you know, bullies usually don't stop. You do that, and they come back worse. Or, they have friends that can make life difficult for you."

David thought about it. "I guess you're right."

"See, bullies run in numbers. Take one out and another steps up. Unless, you make an example of the first bully. See, your dad takes on the bully, and what he does scares the other bullies into not ever wanting to have your dad pay them a visit."

Too vague for a kid to comprehend.

The devil was in the details. So, Uncle Honcho pulled one out of the bag, from deep and dark in the past. "There was a terrorist who decided that stealing children was a huge money-making business. The who and where, not important. He had thousands of followers and a network that spanned the globe. Protected by dictatorship governments that relied on his support for their regimes. They provide the security from prosecution, he gives them the funds they need to rule. Ransom at its worst."

A nod.

"Well, trafficking in children and insane ideologies that run counter to modern society, makes that guy a really bad man. The dude didn't like it when someone didn't pay up. He made an example of a group of village children, and made the list."

"List?"

"Governments don't like terrorists who kill kids. He got marked for death. See where I'm going?"

David was beginning to get the picture.

"Problem is, you nail his butt to the wall, his lieutenant steps up and takes over. Kill him, and the next guy does. Well, that's the case if you just go in and shoot or blow the nasty sucker to pieces. Subtle is more discreet. The big guy is standing in front of his followers and suddenly spouting off on death to America and all that crap, and the lights go out. Next thing you know, he's standing there, but his head's gone when the lights come back up. Body upright, but like a headless horseman. Days later, his lieutenant chokes to death. A week goes by, and the new turd in control turns blue in front of everyone and expands until he pops. Literally. At that point, stories and rumors have gone around. Call it a curse, voodoo, Allah mad you're corrupting the Koran, whatever you want, but people tie it to something evil and decide on self-preservation. Give up their wicked ways to live."

"How'd they die?"

Uncle Honcho smirked. "See, that's the tricky part. All public deaths. A ghost is the only one who could do it. Your dad, he's that ghost. In fact, that was his nickname way back when. He went and did stuff that even the best could not. Still can."

David frowned. "You didn't answer my question."

"Ah. Well, to be the best, you need patience. Move an inch over a day. Be an expert at camouflage."

David knew that one. Hide and seek with Dad was a lost effort in trying to find him.

"The leader? Wire slipped over his neck from above and then yanked hard. Head came clean off. Lieutenant choked on an expanding pill that blocked his airway, then disintegrated. Placed there in his meal. The exploding guy? Super bad allergic reaction from a jellyfish coupled with some air pumped into his body from a CO_2 cartridge jabbed into his butt from behind."

The boy cringed. The images flashed across his eyes, the pictures of each kill hard to forget.

Honcho thought he probably shouldn't have gone there, but the boy asked. And, in the spirit of total transparency for a kid who was coming of age whether he liked it or not, the more David knew about his own father, the better at understanding that war and death were missions to save the world. Today, the here and now, was a battle that Ryan waged steeped in a father's love that meant more than politics or good vs. evil.

Ryan made the calls on his own this time around.

"Dad is a bad ass."

Uncle Honcho threw up the hush sign. "Language, Mi Amigo. Still got some rules to follow, Bud."

David nodded.

Checking his watch, Uncle Honcho realized the time. "Hey, where's Emma?"

He had been so engrossed in talking to Uncle Honcho and trying to run interference to give Dad time to escape he had failed to feel what else happened. Seeing the boy's face turn ash white, Uncle Honcho reached out to try and catch him, before David caught himself with a hand on the wall.

"What is it, David?"

He wasn't sure how to explain it. David simply grabbed Uncle Honcho's hand and led him to more questions than he knew the answers.

CHAPTER 37

Emma knew as soon as she left, it was a mistake.

She didn't know she was going to do it. Then, the compulsive decision happened. Not telling her brother what the plan was let the guilt begin to eat away at her decision-making process.

She was going to wait five minutes after David left. Go see her mom for a few, intent on just wasting time until she thought Dad had a good enough head start. Then, go find her brother and Uncle Honcho. Pretend and act like it was a surprise Dad had left with Papa.

Emma barely made it to three before the choice was made and she quickly gathered supplies into a backpack and left through the secret emergency exit.

Senses guided her along the way. She had never been to the bunker before and barely knew her way around the areas Uncle Honcho allowed them to explore. Somehow, her brain played an image in her mind to follow, and she just walked and navigated through doors and hallways until reaching a staircase. Squinting under the light of the dim bulb, she saw a fresh blood smear, figured it was Papa's, and ascended the steps until reaching a closed door. Five twists of the wheel and it opened to another hallway.

Twenty feet left and another staircase.

Fifty steps up, a short break to rest, and then another door. Three turns this time. Then, pulling it closed tight, Emma looked to find a small hatch to the immediate left. Pulling hard, it didn't budge. Another yank, and it flew up, nearly hitting her in the face. Climbing inside, she pulled it closed, and crawled until reaching another hatch. A soft push and the light nearly blinded her.

"Guess I'm here," Emma said under her breath.

Crawling all the way out, she saw that it was invisible to anyone who might stumble upon it. Two large boulders partially blocked the entrance, or exit as she soon found out. As soon as she cleared the tunnel, the door quietly closed and she saw she couldn't tell it was even there. The camouflage protecting its identity made it appear as a rock. She'd heard Uncle Honcho mention a fake tree stump was the only hidden entrance. This was one-way only.

Seems there were more ways in and out.

Getting all the way to her feet, she sighed, and took a breath. The fresh air was wonderful. The sun that peeked through the overgrowth of trees refreshing to the skin. Stepping all the way out into the open, Emma smiled. She hadn't seen the sun or nature in a few days. Feeling the cool breeze of the wind on her face, she touched her cheek, took one look back, and then was on her way.

Dad was the woodsman of the family. The guy who took them camping and knew everything there was to know about the wilderness and nature. He was a great teacher, taking the time to show David and Emma all the things he had learned from Papa. She absorbed, practiced, failed miserably a ton, then succeeded and soon was in her own right a small survivalist.

Just like her Bubba.

That was always with Dad or Mom close by in case she required help. She was on her own now, having decided that leaving Bubba back to deal with Uncle Honcho and soon Mom was the better choice. He could run some interference for her, but he'd be mad.

Pissed off really.

A bad word she knew she shouldn't think or use, though with nine coming up around the corner and the world completely different, maybe graduating to grown-up words would be OK. She'd heard Bubba use it once, under his breath. Probably going to be used a bunch since she knew he would not like feeling used for her plan.

She'd left him out of it, so the wrath was to be expected.

Glancing around, Emma sought a sign of which way Dad decided to travel. She'd learned he was careful with his tracks, acting more like a cat stalking prey undetected than some half-hearted hunter feeling superior to animals. It had been his job, profession, more like his *being*, a skill at moving silently and unseen that from what he had told the kids on a few bedtime stories over the last weeks, a valuable asset that kept him alive.

On more than one *against the odds* occasions.

From what Dad had said, though the details were always super PG with a pinch of salty language, the skill at being hidden in the shadows was easy. Making sure you left no sign of your presence, automatic.

Staying invisible, the hard part.

A trained eye could see the smallest detail left altered. Observe the slight indentation in the earth that a foot had passed by, a brushed leaf or limb askew an indication of a passerby. That was why the best of the best, like Dad, threw deception into the mix. Multiple potential paths for someone to follow. Circling around to throw off the trail. Purposeful footprints that directed the wrong way. All to make the hunter second-guess the real journey of the prey.

Dad's problem now was he had taught his tricks to his own children.

Emma took a deep breath, closed her eyes, and thought about something Dad has said once before on a camping trip. Something about if you're lost, how to find your way to safety. She didn't know which way was North, having come out of the underground bunker blind to her orientation. She knew Dad was heading east to Seattle.

The sun always rises in the east, Pumpkin.

Looking up, she saw the light to her left. Caught the center of her universe burning bright. "Dad's going that way," Emma whispered.

Knowing the general direction, she had a path forward. Being the right one, another story. That's when she *felt it* first. A shudder through her bones. Then, when attempting to shake it off, she *saw* it. To anyone else, they wouldn't know what it was or give it a second thought. To a Carmichael who had heard Dad's stories and played the tracking game, *wilderness hide and seek*, that's what he called it, you couldn't help but not see the sign.

A small puddle of water, no bigger than the size of a dime.

Spit, Emma knew. Meant to dry up and be forgotten. Had to be Papa's since Dad knew the consequences. It provided a clue and line to navigate as long as she kept her wits and eyes focused.

The forest was a dangerous place.

An hour in, traversing rocks, through brush and branches, even up the side of the mountain with a few breaks for her legs to rest, Emma spotted them. About a hundred yards ahead, descending through a swath of green she wouldn't have caught because of Dad's camo shirt and pants hiding his shape. The sudden flick of a branch hit her vision, and staring down, saw Papa getting a swift rifle butt to the back.

Hope Dad doesn't kill him too soon.

Emma had distance to make up if she wanted to keep them in sight. Down Syndrome wasn't the greatest disability to have when endurance was required. Even though she was as athletic as she could be, playing soccer before the fall of humanity and in the bunker hallways with David, running, and even swimming lately, there were still limitations. Hypotonia sucked, made your muscles need to work extra hard since they were laxer than a typical kid. She knew it was stupid trying to track them down and going on this insane mission to protect her father. They were strong adults.

She was a kid who had to fight her whole life for everything.

Somewhere deep inside, possibly the self-deprecation or the virus screwing with her brain, Emma felt *powerful*. A battle of good vs. evil playing games. Pity at being different from others came from long-held thoughts fought viciously to defeat a new feeling growing with each passing minute.

I can do this.

Emma knew the virus brewing in her blood had begun to change her. Had slowly come to terms with the idea. Watched as it morphed and transformed pieces of her bit by bit. She got less tired as the day wore on where before she was toast by dinnertime. Could run with Bubba in stride the first fifty yards and then taper off to be right behind. Physical acuity for kids with Down Syndrome like her was not a card that let you compete with the rest of the world. As the days and months turned to years since the fall of people, and the virus plagued her body, she couldn't help feel like she was turning into something strange. DS was part of her.

Not, what *defined* her.

Now, as she felt stronger and more resilient, and realized that whatever the virus and shots had done turning a little girl with a disability into more than just a side note, Emma's confidence exploded.

I am doing this.

As the inner monologue wrapped up the sentence, Emma looked up and with a huff, realized in her back and forth, had lost sight of Dad. Not a trace she could see from her current location. Hurrying the pace up, she whipped along the narrow animal path, careful to not trip on any rocks. The hundred yards turned to fifty, then thirty.

She sensed it and stopped cold.

Still as a board, Emma knelt down below the limbs for cover and scurried to the left. A pile of leaves covered the ground and quickly, she covered herself, leaving a small window for air and an eyeball to see out.

"The paranoia is cute," Papa chuckled.

Emma held still.

"Shut up, Dad."

More laughter.

"Someone was following us. I felt it. Better to be safe than dead," Ryan hissed.

Emma could see Papa, his eyes swollen and dried blood below his nose. Even all beat up, the coldness of his eyes and the sharpness of his words betrayed his hatred.

"Hopefully they kill you and leave me alone. Got to get those rotten brats of yours for the cause."

For the first time, Emma felt anger. Not that she had never been mad before because she did have a brother after all. This was something new to her current predicament, or the last three years really. With all that had happened, she had always kept herself contained. Rage, if it was there and really it wasn't, bottled up and locked tight.

This time, it spewed.

Fast as lightning, Emma burst out of her hiding place. Pulling the small knife she brought for protection from its sheath, she lunged at her surprised grandfather, who, caught completely blindsided by her sudden appearance, recoiled in fear. The blade came forward, inching its way at his gut.

Ryan thought about letting his baby girl exact her wrath on her tormenter. Stepping in the way, he caught her arm and with his free hand, pushed Papa to the ground. Stripping the knife away and pulling her in, Ryan kissed her forehead.

"My precious little ninja."

Embarrassed at losing control at trying to kill her grandfather, Emma could only say, "Level 11, Dad."

Ryan laughed. "I would say you've graduated a few levels, Pumpkin. Had no idea you were hiding there and the quick surprise attack at Papa? If I wasn't me, he'd be dead. Maybe I should have let you."

Emma managed a smile, and a wink at her seething Papa laying on the ground. "Thanks for not letting me, Dad. I'd say you deserve the honor."

Papa fumed. "You rotten little piece of sh-" he got out before Emma ran over and with all her strength, punched him right in the nose.

The sound of creaking cartilage echoed.

Ryan reached out and pulled her back. Bent low into her ear. "Nice one," he whispered.

"Thanks, Dad."

Papa couldn't touch his face with his hands zip-tied behind him. All he could do was bitch and whine about the pain.

"Got your ass kicked by my girl."

Papa's eyes narrowed. The darkness igniting a glow. "Take off my bindings and see how that little bitch does."

Ryan motioned to Emma, and she understood. Walked over and kicked her grandfather right in the man parts.

"Tied up or not, you can't hurt me anymore. You're my bitch now," Emma managed to get out, though not really sure what the bad word meant. It just seemed to elicit the right feeling as Papa slunk back and kept his mouth shut.

"Language, Princess."

"Sorry, Dad."

Ryan sighed, as what was supposed to be a two-man journey to Seattle now had a third wheel not exactly practiced in the art of survival and potential gunfights. The bravery was to be commended and warmed his heart seeing the fire in her spirit. She wasn't a warrior though, and given he knew she snuck out on her own as David was nowhere to be seen, or *felt*, Emma was going solo.

"You shouldn't be here."

Emma's eyes lowered. "I know. It's just, just, I *felt* you needed my help."

"Felt?"

"Um, yup."

Ryan blew out a big stream of air. "Care to say more on that subject?"

She paused, and then shrugged. "A feeling."

"Not good enough."

"Well," Emma began, "you need my help. Something bad is coming and you can't do it alone."

He had felt it too. A tiny sliver poking the skin that hurt, but you couldn't get out with your fingernail. Tweezers would work, but none were around when he decided to go on the one-way trek. Left alone, it would fester and turn into a lingering infection that an antibiotic might need to curtail.

Maybe Emma was the tweezers he failed to see he just had to bring along.

Reaching out and picking her up in his arms for a hug, Ryan kissed her cheek.

"Got a plan?"

CHAPTER 38

"Where is she?"

The frantic tone and animated body language required an immediate response.

Crickets.

Honcho shrugged. Not the best answer to a mother desperately in search of her kid, but at the moment all he had to offer. BP started to speak, but he had been occupied with other tasks and oblivious to the events. He decided he'd let Honcho bear the brunt of mama bear's wrath. David sat quietly, trying to shrink into oblivion and stay unseen. He knew it was his fault, should have felt it sooner, his failure at protecting his sister from herself and her one-girl army seeking to rectify the murky future that they all saw coming a potential death sentence for his twin.

"She went after Dad and Papa."

The statement startled Julia. "What did you just say?"

David raised his eyes. "Emma went to find Dad and Papa. Dad needs help and she figured she could protect him."

Julia's skin turned ashen at the words. Glaring at Honcho and BP, she focused her wrath inward, and moved towards her son. "How did you know your Papa was here?"

David could lie, or tell the truth. Either was not quite the whole story. Clearing his throat, humming and rocking to find the right way to say it, he threw it out there. "Emma felt him."

Honcho took a deep breath. The boy didn't rat him out.

"Emma felt what?"

Looking at his mom, David's feet swung back and forth, more a soothing action in the moment. Pointing to his head, he let it go. "Emma felt Papa's presence. You know she has that institution thing."

"Intuition," BP chimed in.

David smiled. "Right. Intuition."

Julia sighed. "David, cut the crap."

Jolting upright in the chair at being dressed down by his mom, David shook his head. "OK, OK. Emma felt something. About Papa and with Dad. So, we decided we'd occupy Uncle Honcho to give Dad time to get away. Emma was supposed to stick with me. I had no clue she was going to go after them."

Looking at Honcho, Julia pointed to her watch. "How much time are we talking here?"

Honcho thought, and stuck up a finger.

"An hour?"

Nodding at Julia, he frowned. "At least. The boy here talked my ear off. Didn't realize Emma was gone until it was too late."

Julia stepped back and sunk into the recliner. The wind was gone from her sails. Her baby girl was gone, with no idea if she would manage to find her father or even make it outside on her own. Emma was tough for a child with Down Syndrome, a fighter in life who could hold her own in a wrestling match with David. The wilderness and wild animals with killers hunting for her? The girl was not her father.

Julia hoped she was wrong on that one.

BP coughed to get everyone's attention. "Hey, we know which way Ryan's going. He's the least of our worries as we can figure that one out. Emma if she gets lost, is another problem. I say we focus on her."

"No shit," Julia barked. Realizing her response, she quickly apologized.

BP waved her off. "You have every right to be pissed. Ryan can take care of himself. It's only an hour, so it narrows our search grid." Looking at Honcho, BP focused on the wall map of the surrounding area. "Thoughts?"

Honcho nodded. "She couldn't have gotten all too far. Pretty sure we can track her. I say we focus here," he tapped, "and circle out. This ridge will keep her contained to the northern side."

David decided to jump into it. "There's something different about Dad. Emma felt it and I believe her. He's not the same. But, we trust him. If he decided to take Papa and leave us in the dark, he did it to protect us. We have to trust he knows what he's doing."

Honcho hung his head, and Julia caught the subtle display.

"What is it, Honcho?"

He took a deep breath, figured coming clean would stoke the already burning fire, but not much choice to keep secrets anymore. "The boy and girl are right. Ryan's oozing black blood. We all know that's a bad sign."

Julia chucked a bottle at him.

When it hit, Honcho knew he shared a bit too much in front of the boy. "Sorry. He needs to know about his dad. We're in a different world and the more David is told, the better he can protect himself and be a part of this ragtag bunch of losers if he has to step up and do something to save us."

Julia knew he was right. Still, she didn't relish her son losing all his innocence.

David was at her side, stroking her hand. "Mom, I'm not a real kid anymore, not with all that's happened. Uncle Hon is right. There might come a time I have to be an adult and if I don't know, I might make the wrong decision."

Touching his cheek, the tears fell. "So much like your dad. Even with the world gone to dark, still looking at what you can do to help."

"As long as he doesn't get a big head like Ry, the boy will be alright," Honcho winked.

Laughter erupted at the sudden levity. They all needed it and the momentary digression from the chaos lurking around the corner. Emma was alone, and with knowledge about Ryan's condition out of the bag, she was the priority. If Ryan was fading into what was inevitable for his future, at least Emma could be saved. Protect her, save the world.

He, could manage on his own.

BP, quiet for most of the conversation, had snuck out without anyone knowing. Returning suddenly, geared up and an M4 strapped across his chest, he snapped his fingers. "Let's go people! Time's wasting here."

Any other situation and Julia would not want David out in the open. He was still a target and staying hidden the best option. They needed all eyes and hands on this, so loosening her mama bear instincts and trusting David was becoming more like his dad and could add value versus be a liability, she nodded and he ran out the door.

Honcho grabbed her arm. "You sure Jules?"

Shaking her head, she tried to keep the tears at bay. "I'm not. I'd prefer he stay, but if we don't make it back, then he's alone. At least we can keep eyes on him."

She was right.

"OK, but if we're going to do this rescue mission looking for a tiny needle in a forest, we'll need comms. David good at being quiet on the radio game?"

Julia smirked. "Rayan taught him all the secret operator tricks on radio silence."

"Good. Let's find that rotten girl and get back before dark."

CHAPTER 39

Ryan wasn't sure.

Emma's plan was more of a hope and a prayer.

She seemed to have thought it through and the details as much outlined as could be given the lack of knowledge on what they faced ahead.

He was proud, and hesitant. So, he took the hope and chucked the prayer, all to Emma's dismay. When Ryan explained it back to her, the icy demeanor his daughter had erected began to thaw. She began to warm to it, even if she liked her plan better.

"You think it can work?"

Ryan nodded. "I think it can."

Emma smiled, gave him a hug, and then headed off for a bush wee.

Reg had been secured snugly tied to a tree a dozen yards away to keep his ears from knowing what Ryan and Emma brewed up. It ate at his bones, not being free and having to have his granddaughter dictate his future. He loathed the little miscreant, wished death on her when her value was depleted. While he knew at some point in life he had loved her, that sentiment was long gone.

Only hatred remained.

As she walked by, Emma managed a smile, and seeing his eyes ablaze in a darkness that she knew was aimed at her, she simply slapped his forehead. "How does it feel to be my bitch?"

The curse word caught him, and then he laughed. Even with a disability and what people perceived as a personality full of happy, he saw the strength in her and twinge of badass bubbling to the top. She was evolving, her disability no longer defining the person inside.

The future was no longer set in stone.

"Oh, sorry. Can't spit anything funny with your mouth taped shut," Emma winked. Bending a bit, she stared into Reg's eyes. "You think I'm nothing, just a piece of garbage because I have Down Syndrome. Well, Papa, the poop is you and your friends. I'm coming for all of you, and there's nothing you can do to stop me. And," she whispered, her face suddenly full of a hate he had never seen, "Bubba will make you suffer for what you have done to us. I promise that. Dad might let you live a bit. Pissed off super twins are definitely going to kill you."

Reg's laughter faded. He felt Emma's wrath and knew she was *different*. Could see her disability fading away. The physical aspects present as she couldn't change her appearance. Somehow, the parts that most people attributed to a person with Down Syndrome, the happy-go-lucky attitude, the constant cheeriness, even the lack of hate that usually was closed off. He saw she was a raging pre-teen like any other, her emotions front and center. He felt her words, the spite in each syllable, and knew what she told him, she *meant*.

"Go fu-" Reg started to spew from behind his covered mouth, before the fist pounded his face.

"Language, Papa. Don't ever speak to me like that again. I *will* kill you."

Staring at her, visibly shaken and for the first time afraid of a child, he shook with fear. Reg wasn't sure what was happening to him, and he didn't like it. His granddaughter, normally the sweetest thing on the planet, suddenly had an edge, an aura around her that was polar opposite of the prejudices people had about Down Syndrome. This girl was hard.

Just like her father.

Ryan witnessed the exchange from afar. He couldn't hear a sound or word of what transpired. What graced his eyeballs was his dad chuckling, Emma leaning in, Reg mysteriously going silent, and then the terror on his face. Throw on top of it Emma's solid punch, and shit was going down.

A warm fuzz enveloped his gut and the grin of pride radiated like the sun.

When she returned, Ryan thought about asking outright. Decided to see if Emma was going to tell him. A minute turned to two, and then five became ten. The growing *anxiety*, was that it? Maybe impatience was a better description. Definitely the elephant in the room kept smacking his head with a desire to want to know what the hell happened.

"Hey Pumpkin, everything OK with you?"

Emma, who had been sitting and eating a protein bar, glanced over, smiled, and shook her head. "Yup."

Ryan knew it was bullshit.

Trying a different approach, he decided to be direct. "I know something is going on. I saw you punch your grandfather."

She paused mid-bite. Thought about it, and answered. "Nope."

The double wink, because she couldn't do just one eye, made Ryan spit out the sip of water he had just inhaled. They both started to laugh, and she moved over and gave him a huge hug.

"Can't fool you, Dad."

"Not a chance," Ryan said quietly in her ear.

She kissed his cheek, then went back to her bar.

He waited for her to talk, and when she didn't, he motioned to her.

Catching the gesture, Emma shrugged. "Not much to say, Dad. Just let Papa know he's not running the show. I am." Looking up, she added, "Oh, and Bubba too. I told him Bubba was his worst nightmare." She left the last part vague.

Ryan took it in. He knew she was skating a real truthful answer. "That all?"

Emma smirked. "Yup."

He could press, be forceful, even pull the dad card. Choosing battles with her and keeping his daughter at least giving him some information rather than going radio silent the better choice.

"OK."

She side-eyed her dad, not out of anger, but an attempt at being funny. Catching it, Ryan gave it right back.

"Love you, Dad."

"Love you too, Ice Pick."

Hearing her dad use his personal nickname for her made Emma burst out laughing. He gave it to her when she was born because of her steely ice blue eyes. As she got older, it fit, more because when she gave a particular look, the icy blue stare was something you might get from a mob boss or some crazy lunatic who was as calm as could be, but in a second would liberate you with a blaze of bullets or a slip knot around your neck.

Getting back to their current predicament and reality, Ryan pointed to the trail they were taking, and hoisting himself up to throw on his ruck sack and grabbing his M4, went to get *his* dad. Emma finished her bar, packed the wrapper in her own backpack, and followed. Standing behind, she watched as her dad untied the bindings keeping Papa strapped to the tree and yanked him to his feet.

"March."

Reg, without any disagreement, walked to the trail and soon disappeared with Ryan right behind.

"Come on, Slow Poke."

Emma smiled, and soon joined the adults on their trek to Seattle.

CHAPTER 40

Mark pictured Reg dead.

His bullet riddled body obliterated by 5.56 NATO rounds. The only way for a positive ID done using a DNA sample.

The wicked grin must have been obvious, as Mark's second in command felt the need to ask. "Must be about Mr. Carmichael, the senior, Sir?"

Mark laughed, nodded, and shrugged. "Can't help it. Been waiting a long time to lose that asshole."

"Yes, Sir."

Focusing around to the current task, Mark pointed at the map. The area to cover was extensive, the paths in and out few. With a wide expanse of wilderness and only so many roads to travel, there were only so many places off the grid to hide. A daring hike through the thick woods to blend into the forest or traversing on foot black pavement littered with debris and obstacles when the path forward was blocked. Either provided potential avenues for capture.

If, they could narrow the grid.

"Focus your attention here and here," Mark emphasized with his finger. "Given the location of the attack at the base, there's only so many places they could scamper off to hide. We know the SUV, so find it."

A nod, and then his second was gone.

If Reg was really dead, though the prospect of it seemed remote since his body wasn't found among the carnage at the base, Mark would have to notify Diablo. Why the asshat insisted on being referred to as that, Mark could only assume the nickname made the annoying mosquito feel powerful. He wasn't, just a messenger boy trying to assert some kind of status among real men. As the errand boy for the leaders of the movement, Diablo had a semblance of protection and threw the fact around like a frisbee.

Keep up the annoying act and Mark wouldn't hesitate to shoot him dead.

Reg *did* have status. Was in fact part of the larger picture and had been since the 60's. Mark was a key player too. Though, he didn't come into the picture until much later. The whole flower power movement and protest rich decade, with the world trying to rise from the chaos still of World War II and for the U.S., Korea and then Vietnam, the time was ripe for believers to be recruited into the fold. The seeds planted decades and centuries before, adding to the flock meant moving forward with a plan envisioned long ago to right wrongs and enforce on the world a single rule.

The late 80's was Mark's introduction.

College, ROTC, and then straight into the service, he was a man for country and honor. Save the world and all that crap. Until, he saw the effects of the Gulf War, the lies perpetrated from governments on either side. Each felt they were in the right. Call it manifest destiny, regional power struggles, whatever disillusioned ideology you felt the most descriptive placeholder for what it really was, man's obsession with power and rule.

However you skinned it, it was millennia of tribal warfare, religious persecution, race wars, even simple bully chest-pumping, and the basic desire to be the only top dog. His eyes saw it through multiple deployments. The bright light of clarity coming from the mixture of NATO alliances and individuals who whispered from the shadows until he eventually stepped into the dark.

All to find a glowing and radiant answer to the world's chaos.

The Order provided the scope of what had to be done. The long-term vision for the planet. The sense of obedience and rule that the world desperately required as it descended further into ruin. It wasn't about playing God or even as some might believe a desire to run a dictatorship over humanity. The tenets were beyond basic.

Preserve life for those who put the whole before the one.

There was more to it. He wasn't ignorant of those facts. A governing structure and commandments that must be followed. Obey and life was an oyster, the shiny pearl inside your wealth. Fall out of line or resist, and face dire consequences.

The whole before the one.

That mantra, which was recited by a plethora of other groups and the fanatical cults that degraded the true mission of life, was key to the survival of the human race. Life had regressed to greed and selfish accruements of *possessions* that in the scheme of the greater good, didn't mean shit. People were failing their communities, even their own families and friends. How many parents used technology to watch and raise their children? Why was dinnertime no longer an event to sit and share the day, but devices and television to distract from actually having a conversation? Discrimination of skin color ravaged the U.S. and many parts of the world. Who was to blame for it all?

That last question, steeped in so many potential answers.

"Where are you, Ryan Carmichael? I know you're here. Come out and play," Mark sighed, the corner of his mouth turning up as the frustration rose.

Without a pause, his prayer, not to some false god but the infinite expanse of the cosmos, was answered.

"Sir?" the second in command interrupted.

"What?" Mark barked, annoyed at being disturbed.

"We got a hit."

The sentence lacked details, and that made the anger brew. "Like to add some intel *facts* to that?"

The second cringed from the rebuke, then spoke. "Sorry, Sir. Overwatch has vehicles on the move. Left the compound and headed north up the 99. Veered off to surface streets towards the Sound."

Details.

"Keep eyes on them. They might be meeting our friends. I want a report every fifteen. Understood?"

"Yes, Sir."

Mark stepped back from the map. The news might be nothing, just a normal hunt for supplies. Walled off like they were, the King's people still had to go in search of food and materials to keep their little community thriving among the decay. When he had met the King, Mark realized she was cunning and difficult to read. A stone-faced leader who kept her intentions tight to the chest.

Besides blowing up his helicopter.

Their agreement hung by a thread. Ryan might have a better hand to play with her. Mark doubted it. On the run, only so much he could do on his own, it would have to be a straight flush to get King to betray her people and set them up for death, knowing if Mark caught wind, he'd send her home to oblivion. The world was different and loyalties and needs hard to comprehend. Everyone who wasn't loyal to the cause was in it for themselves. Trust eroded. Insight valuable. Partners loose collectives that burned you at the first chance to get what they want.

He'd soon find out.

Calling after his second, Mark motioned to the SUVs. "Gear up. We're going for a ride."

Obedience nowadays was paramount to success. It came in many forms and was procured in a multitude of ways. Some, to say it mildly, were not the most Geneva Convention supporting or human rights accepted that the world had a few years ago. Today, you either gave it freely under false pretenses to stay alive, or it was not even a second thought.

The cause was life. Rebel against it, and die.

Mark didn't particularly care how he got it. As long as it existed and could be controlled with the outcome for noncompliance loud and clear, he kept trucking along with two goals in mind. First, get the Carmichael children and use their essence to save the planet from itself. There was no other alternative to save humanity.

Second, dissect Ryan Carmichael until nothing was left of the man.

The last image made Mark smile. Ryan, his former friend and confidante, was nothing but a knife twisting in Mark's side, preventing him from achieving the greatness he deserved. Where once a brotherly bond existed, first as a superior and then into a friendship that had saved the world on more than one occasion from the wicked frolicking ways of true madmen, that sentiment of love was long retired. All that remained was a sour taste of vomit that no liquid could dispel, no medicine that would make it simply vanish. Ryan was a disease like cancer. It started small until consuming the body piece by piece until death was inevitable.

He was Mark's tumor and had to be irradiated.

CHAPTER 41

If only the hike through the forest brought peace and tranquility.

That, would be welcome.

A nice trek through the woods, sightseeing, breathing in fresh mountain air and relishing in the great outdoors. Spotting a wild animal and watching from afar as they drank from a stream. Catching a glimpse of some critter scurrying to safety only to stop and make a stand to protect its brood before deciding the giants were formidable foes. Conversation filled with laughs and giggles from old camping stories and tall tales.

This bleak walk amongst the foliage brought a cloud of despair.

Emma coming along for the ride was a wrench in the wheel. Ryan had his hands full with his own father and out here having to be dad to his daughter diverted his attention in ways that affected his mind.

Dual personalities and keeping them separate to protect her.

Ryan had to be the loving father she knew, the protector and parent who made sure she was living life to the fullest. Encourage her to keep hiking onward when she seemed scared or hesitant. Force her to stop and rest when she kept her pain or breathlessness to herself and needed to rest before she passed out from exhaustion. Be the solid rock Emma required to make it beyond this hell hole of life.

He then had to mask his other self, the one she didn't know.

Being dad was opposite of the cold-blooded killer lurking deep within his bowels. He had graduated to that persona and knew it. Where once there was a line he would never cross, a black and white decision tree to his actions, the present was a place where pulling the trigger or slicing a jugular didn't even elicit a second thought.

The color gray had so many fascinating shades.

Keeping his new being hidden from her contradictory to being just dad. Reg being along didn't help at all. The snarky comments, attempts at reminiscing about the glorious old days, and penchant for diatribes with Ryan in the crosshairs meant most of the walk had Reg's mouth gagged to keep him from speaking or spitting Ryan's way. When he started to cough from lack of oxygen, Ryan's would pull down the restraint and let Reg breathe for as long as he kept his cool.

It never lasted more than a few hundred yards.

To keep the journey as pleasant as practical between Reg's venomous words and required breaks for Emma's young legs, Ryan told her stories. Some from his own childhood when his dad was not the monster today limping along in front of them. Others from before she was born and it was just him and Julia. The more relevant enveloping the magical day her and David graced the world.

Ryan preferred those to anything else.

To him, it was the exact moment his life truly had purpose. Before, he was part of a machine, a necessary wheel that kept the world crawling towards peace when evil decided to rain down on the parade. Even retired from active duty long before he met Julia, his consulting and occasional trips into the abyss to handle the most delicate missions' others failed to accomplish, it was rote muscle memory. Honor kept him attached.

Fatherhood severed the bond.

Not that he still didn't honor the code or believe in the fight. He did with all his heart. Transforming into a dad responsible for not one but two precious lives meant nothing else in the world mattered more than his children. As he began to realize, honor was ingrained in those who felt they had to step forward and do. A soldier believed in the rhetoric and truth of preserving freedom for all.

Kids provided the reason for living and protecting everything at any cost.

"You doing OK there, Princess?" Ryan whispered.

Emma gave him the side-eye. "Yup."

He couldn't help laughing at the gesture.

"Something wrong?" she asked, knowing her attempt at playfulness had brought out the sillies in her dad.

"Totally fine," he side-eyed back.

She began to giggle softly until it reverberated ahead. Reg caught the commotion, glared over his shoulder, and shrugged.

"That's what I'm saying." Ryan poked her in the ribs and it tickled.

"Dad, stop it!" Emma bellowed. "Leave me alone."

Ryan winked. "Can't do it. Dad Code says if you avoid talking it requires a tickle to loosen the tongue."

Emma poked back. "Then, the finger of death for you!"

He sidestepped, swiped with his right hand, and came around to face her. Fingers pointing, he pulled the triggers. Emma erupted in a fit, the feeling of her dad's phalanges poking her ribs excruciatingly ticklish even with her shirt blocking them. She couldn't help it, the giggles and roiling body shakes no match for Ryan. A lighthearted moment to kick reality out the door and enjoy some fun.

Fingers holstered, Ryan bowed. "Never mess with Darth Daddy."

Emma curtseyed. "Yes, my Master."

"Should of used my lightsaber," he grumbled, having been caught up and forgetting his alter ego didn't carry a blaster.

The cough interrupted the tranquil bonding experience.

"Mmm mmm, hmm hmm," Reg mumbled through his gag.

Ryan shook his head. "Figures."

Stepping over a log to his dad, Ryan saw it coming over the ridge. Far enough away, they were hidden by the trees. All he could tell was that it was some type of flying glider with a seat. Three seconds later as it panned to his left, he realized it was a civilian model. Snatching his binoculars, he focused, shook his head, and replaced the specs.

"What is it, Dad?"

Ryan sighed. "Someone trying to live another day, and failed."

Emma watched as the glider dipped, caught the top of a tree, and veered straight down. The sudden descent must have caused a fuel issue as it sputtered, the rotor stopped spinning, and it careened to a stop wedged twenty feet up. The weight held maybe a minute before the branch snapped and the craft landed upside down on the dirt.

"Stay here," Ryan ordered before running over to Reg, pushing him down, and hogtying his legs to the zip ties behind his back.

"OK," was all Emma could manage to get out before her dad sprinted away.

He saw it through the lenses. It wasn't a soldier, no weapon or uniform. The girl, the one from the city, was in the pilot's seat. Slumped over, Ryan saw the large red stain on her shirt. He knew who did it, the question was why. If they were looking for him and had some agreement with Mark, the King's people should have been off limits.

Unless, circumstances changed.

Reaching the wreck, Ryan cut the harness and pulled her out. The shot was on target, she didn't know what hit her and was gone before the thought even registered she was shot. *Why is she out here?* he thought. Made no sense unless she was looking for him because to her knowledge, he was nowhere to be found. Maybe she figured he'd see and flag her down or was off on some other adventure. It didn't matter now.

Until her death grip loosened and her hand unfurled.

"What the hell?"

Taking the scrap of paper, he read the note. Pursed his lips, frowned, sighed twice, and shook his head. The future was never a dull moment. If true, the game was changing the rules and throwing them out the window.

While he knew to expect the unexpected and never to throw himself totally behind a plan or anyone is the post-apocalyptic shithole that was running the show, some things you could count on. He just never in a million years could imagine that this intel was true.

A complication of a magnitude he never anticipated.

CHAPTER 42

"Can we find them or not?" Julia screamed.

Honcho looked at BP, who glanced back. "We have a general idea of which way they are headed. Beyond that, it's a guess to know the exact route."

Her fist slammed the table. "Not good enough! We came up completely empty the first time out. My baby is out there, maybe alone, with an insane lunatic and his assholes trying to find her. My husband has his father on some nature hike, enjoying some family time. Their paths might not even cross if he had a big head start."

David started to speak, before Julia shut him down.

"What were *you* thinking? Did it ever occur to you that your guys' plan to help your dad would backfire? Your sister took off. She is not like us in being able to survive out there alone."

He waved her off, defiant. "Emma is strong, Mom. She might not be totally like us, but she is the strongest one of us that I know."

The words cut sharp.

BP saw the anger coming to a head, and not wanting the boy to get the brunt of it, took it on. "Julia, it's not his fault. It's ours. Mine. Honcho's. Even yours."

She looked over, confusion and rage all in one. "What?"

Honcho walked over to David, and touching his shoulder, motioned him to the kitchen area.

BP pointed to a chair. "Sit. Please."

She glared, and taking a breath, pulled it out and flopped down.

"Listen, all of us know Ryan to the core. Honcho for decades, me all my life. Don't take it out on David. We should have known what Ry would do knowing what the plan concocted by us with him out cold entailed. He might be *retired*, but he's still the same man who has saved the world so many times by the seat of his pants I've lost count."

Julia, arms crossed, managed, "So?"

BP sighed. "You know he's stubborn. We know he takes everything on himself to protect those he loves. If he dies in the process, well then, he's tried. He doesn't like to lose. Determined to finish the mission type of guy. He's done things you cannot fathom, and probably never want to know about so you can sleep at night. That was the old Ryan yes, but it still lurks deep inside the man. The father will protect his babies. The husband sacrifice himself for you. The friend entrust us with your safety knowing we'd take bullets to keep you all safe. Whatever he's thinking, he's got a plan he believes will work. We should have kept better eyes on him knowing he would do whatever he had to do to insulate us from the chaos out there."

BP was right.

Julia hated that he was, but it was all true. Her Ryan was a rock, a man who put others before his needs, even when he was beyond exhausted and could barely take a step. The nights Emma's sleep apnea kept her waking and Julia had work the next day, he'd sleep on the floor to help his daughter go back to sleep. His schedule was more forgiving to tiredness and aching bones. The parents who didn't feel Emma should be mainstreamed in general ed and whispered their displeasure. Julia hated confrontation, preferring a gentler approach. He'd take it full on and offer up public embarrassment to highlight their discrimination and be the bad guy so she could remain the neutral mom. Even his stubbornness, which she hated and he simply said was him not letting others run him over, was one of the things she secretly loved about him.

He stood up for what was right, no matter the cost to him.

She should have realized the second he said he'd watch Reg what his true intentions were moving forward. Reg was a liability. If he was as important as he claimed to be, his people would use everything to find him. Get him far away and use him to protect Emma and David from Mark, and she couldn't be mad at Ryan for that.

"But Emma," she began before BP interjected.

"That girl is like her father in so many ways. David? He's Ryan junior. She's a more advanced copy of her dad. In many ways, a better version that he's always strived to be himself."

"But, he *is* a good man."

BP nodded. "Oh, I know. You have to realize though that he's done things no man should ever have to do. In the past, and now the future with Reg. Ry loved that man. Reg was his idol. To have your own father try to take and kill your babies? Jeez, I can't picture that crap movie. I couldn't do it, but Ry has no choice."

Julia was confused. "What do you mean?"

"Reg. Can you begin to wonder what is running through Ryan's mind knowing he's going to kill his own dad? That's a foregone conclusion. Reg is dead meat. Toast. He hurt Emma and David. You don't do that and expect to live if you don't want Ghost to wax your ass. You too. That boy was a shadow before you came around. Saw the light burn bright when he met you. I know you've had your ups and downs like everybody, but he loves you more than anything. Except the kids. You're second in line to them."

Julia laughed. "Oh, I know that. Same for him. My babies come before either of us."

BP smiled. "So, you see? He's doing what he thinks is right, no matter the cost to him. He never thinks he'll fail. And honestly, the guy is batting a thousand lifetime so far."

She wished she knew her husband inside and out. The deeper parts he still kept locked tight. She got snippets from him over the last month and a bigger image of what he'd done and seen in his past life. Even Honcho spilling some of it since their time in apocalypse bunker land. The problem was, that was the old Ryan who wasn't affected by the virus.

The current version was losing his sanity one day at a time.

Looking towards the kitchen, Julia shrugged. "What do we do?"

BP got up and knelt, his hand wrapping hers. "We find Emma. She can't have gone too far. Let Ryan go and do his thing. We have to protect the kids and make sure the world keeps rolling along."

Julia nodded. "Let's find my girl."

CHAPTER 43

Darkness crept in as the sun lowered itself to sleep.

They had made decent time, but with night about to drop, shelter from the elements and prying eyes meant hunkering down until the morning. Fortunately, Honcho and Ryan had hiked the area over the years and there were a few hidden gems to keep them safe and secure.

Directing them off the path, Ryan pushed Reg toward the right and a cluster of trees. Head grabbed and thrust low, Reg knelt under a branch and found himself suddenly inside a cave. The passage was a bit narrow, then opened up into a large chamber. It appeared it had been used before, a ring of fire rocks, soot on the ceiling, even makeshift cots made of wood and held together with some type of binding.

"Homey," Reg muttered as Ryan slid the gag off.

Emma kicked her grandfather in the shin. "Be nice!"

Reg grumbled something about being sorry, the inflection showing he didn't mean it, and took a plop down on one of the cots.

Ryan smiled and winked, and pointed Emma to a stack of wood. She grabbed a pile and threw it inside the ring.

"Thanks, Princess."

"Got it, Dad."

A few minutes later, and Ryan had a warm fire brewing. The flames flashing off the cave walls offering a dance that Emma enjoyed as she sipped on her water and ate a protein bar. Reg, hands free to eat, chewed on his, never taking his eyes off her. The eyes, dark and red, had a burning hate behind them that made Emma uncomfortable. She could be scared, or face the demon.

"It's not polite to stare."

"Piss off."

Her water canister hit its mark.

"What the fu-" Reg bellowed as the pain set in before he saw Ryan stand up, and the words cut off.

Walking over, Ryan grabbed her water, and returned it. "Nice shot."

"Thank you. Rude again, Papa, and I'll keep at it," Emma smiled.

Reg decided to choose his battles carefully from now on. Digressing away from what just happened, he decided to broach the elephant in the room. "Didn't plan on her coming along, did you?"

Ryan shook his head.

"Shame if something happens to her."

He began to say something but Emma's glare stopped him cold.

"Papa. I told you before what I'd do to you. I can't imagine what my daddy will do to anyone who tries to hurt me."

Ryan shot an eye over. "What am I missing, Ice Pick?"

Emma liked being addressed with her special nickname, especially with Papa in the hot seat. "I told Papa I'd kill him. Probably take me some time since I'm not a pro like you. Likely hurt a whole lot as many times as I'd purposefully mess up."

If Julia was here, Ryan would never hear the end of it.

Ryan couldn't help laughing at his little girl. She was becoming quite the person, confidant and defiant. Good traits he hoped weren't turning her into him. Pointing his knife at his dad, the apple piece atop it, Ryan winked. "That's my little girl. Proud of her."

Reg winced. "You both know the end of what happens. Why fight it? I have an army at my disposal who will never, ever stop. You are a small bunch of what? Handful of amateurs with one self-proclaimed bad ass leading the lunatics? Not a chance in hell you win this one."

Ryan looked at Emma who was beginning to stand, and she plopped back in her seat.

"Dad? You still have no idea who I am, do you? I figured old Marky would have spilled the beans."

Reg's eyes narrowed. "I'm supposed to be scared of some stories, Boy?"

Ryan patted his knee. "Stories? I have the highest count of confirmed sniper kills. The unofficial record for most enemy combatants eliminated by a special operator. Longest sniper shot ever, though that one can never see the light of day so the Canadian gets the high-five for the record. I've done things to keep this country safe and the world sleeping tight that you can't imagine. Reduced whole armies' ball-less by myself or with just a partner in tow. I can take your so-called troops out without them knowing what hit them. Eliminate your besties in a blink. You should be afraid. Not the other way around."

Reg snickered. "I've killed whole enemy bases and never though twice."

The image wasn't registering in the old man. So, Ryan lit the fuse. "What was your best friend's name? Red Fred? How did he die again?"

The forgotten name hit a chord. "Why?"

Stoking the fire, Ryan wasn't sure if that was the right move. "He moved to the private sector after you guys served together, right? Plane went down over Africa somewhere while on a trip to fund some energy projects and a terrorist group found him?"

Those details had not been shared beyond a need to know.

Anger seethed within. "No one knew it was a terrorist group. Official account was he died in the crash."

"Tsk tsk, Pops. He was selling innocent people out for a dime. His death was, let's say, gratifying. He asked for you, begged for me not to do it. Right won over wrong."

Reg lunged forward and Ryan caught him with a left to the side of the head. Father went down hard in front of the son, yet, while the blow ached like a son of a bitch, Reg slowly rose to his feet.

The old man wasn't about to take anything from his boy.

"I'd be careful if I were you, Son," Reg snarled.

Thinking a moment, the sarcasm reeked. "I could let old Ice Pick take a crack at you. Make it more fair for ya."

Reg spit to clear the blood from his mouth. "That little piece of garbage will get hers for her disrespect. Trust me. Right now, it's you and me."

Emma stood, and Ryan started to motion for her to sit, before letting the cards go where they may.

"The only garbage is you, Papa. I know I'm different. Can't do all the things that typical people can do. Even have trouble with easy things. But, I know my limitations and work hard each day to try to overcome them. I might one day, or never. I recognize that. You? You think you're a god. As Dad says, all gods fall because they forget who put them in power."

Reg laughed. The hand to mouth kind to try and stop from spitting out phlegm. "God? No little one. I'm bigger than that."

Emma closed her eyes and shook her head. "As my dad says, the room is getting so thick I can't stand up. Not enough head space for diluted people."

Ryan smiled. "Delusional, Pumpkin. That's the word you're looking for."

"Thanks, Dad."

Focusing back his rage, Reg let it go. "You're still garbage, girl. The muck on the bottom of a shoe that sticks."

Nodding, Emma felt the tear, and willed it away. "Lots of people feel that way about me, I know. But, guess what? My kind aren't going anywhere. Given what's inside me, I bet we'll be the top dogs soon. And Papa, people like you who think that they're better than people like me are the ones who are dog crap 'cause we're coming for you, and you don't stand a chance."

He had never heard her talk in such a forceful tone. Confident, with an air of superiority. So outside the spectrum for his little girl. Ryan felt a twinge of pride for her sticking up for herself and others. For putting her grandfather in his place. Whether it echoed in his deranged head, Ryan didn't venture to make any odds.

"Big words for someone who isn't even a whole person."

Ryan saw the tears she was attempting to hold at bay leak. Ever the protector, he took her arm, gently turned her around, patted her shoulder, and gave her a gentle push.

She immediately understood. "Thank you, Dad," Emma whispered as she sauntered off.

Reg must have known what was coming as he braced for it. Attempted to prepare a defense for the onslaught that was sure to come raining down. A father's rage for his precious daughter is like a nuclear bomb. You hear it coming, see the mushroom cloud, and can do little for the cloud that radiates the falling dust.

Ryan didn't make a sound.

Didn't blink either. His hatred for his own father belittling Emma, reducing her to nothing, was more than Ryan could take, let alone allow to go unpunished. Before the world was lost to the virus and its apocalyptic ruins, he might have retained a clearer head. Reasoned that violence wasn't the answer. Hell, even a few months ago he might have responded differently, with an ounce of civility and understanding that those ravaged by the virus had lost their humanity and everything that made them actual people.

Not today.

The blow found its mark. A fake right to the face opened Reg up as he made a vain effort to avert his face from a sure connection, leaving his ribs exposed. The left fist connected with the solar plexus, forcing Reg to gasp for air, then crumble to the ground. He started to hyperventilate, unable to breathe, the lack of oxygen sending his brain to sleepy town.

"Damn," Ryan murmured to himself, "didn't expect that."

With Reg out, Ryan had time to console Emma. He zip-tied Reg behind his back again and secured some 750 paracord around his feet to keep him from getting up. For good measure, a strand with no slack to connect the ties and feet so he couldn't manage to stand up.

Glancing around, Ryan didn't see Emma. Figuring she was near the cave entrance, he went to her, only to find the faint moon staring coldly at his face.

"Shit."

CHAPTER 44

The word shouldn't have fazed her.

Emma was used to the discrimination, the hateful people who felt she and others with disabilities should be relegated to the shadows. A life of interactions with idiots that thought they could worm their way into daylight and simply say whatever they wanted without repercussions. Those imbeciles she'd gotten used to during her short time on Earth. Hearing it from her beloved Papa?

A different stab to her delicate heart.

Papa was family, someone who was supposed to love with no conditions. Her only living grandparent that she knew of and one who before the world came tumbling down into chaos, an idol who said he cherished her as his oldest granddaughter.

Different times.

Listening to the denigration hit to the core. Emma had to leave, get some fresh air. Dad would put Papa in his place, she knew it. Probably give him a beating, or worse. She didn't really care. He deserved whatever Dad dished out. For what he allowed to happen to her and Bubba, and trying to kill Dad, Papa's fate was sealed one way or another.

Dad was going to use the old guy for something, and then kill him.

Thinking about the exchange, the whole bit, Emma found herself shocked, even scared, as she ran the last days over and over in her head. She was only eight, soon to find nine if she survived a few more months. Words and actions not normally part of who she was were coming to light.

Threatening Papa?

That was a new one. Coarse and direct language, forceful and showing strength, were not the attributes of a young girl of eight who also had Down Syndrome. They were more aligned with a disgruntled teenager bucking the parental units and authority figures. Emma knew deep down she was changing, evolving into what, she had no clue. The deep connection with Dad, *feeling* his presence, even knowing some of his thoughts, was more like her twin vibe with Bubba. Ever since the underground facility, the bond with Dad had grown. It also seemed to propel her growth in other areas that normally, would be trying to catch up with typical peers.

She knew ever since she got the vaccine, her body was doing all sorts of weird things. Her severe hypotonia, a big impediment to keeping up with literally everyone, was now a slowly fading memory. There were still bouts of fatigue for sure, though fewer and far between as she was forced to get stronger being on the run. Speech and language, excelled beyond even her imagination. Former friends at her current age with DS wouldn't be as proficient, if they were still alive.

Emma was off the proverbial charts.

Mom had worked super hard during their imprisonment to work with her, so a lot was due to the constant repetition. Lessons, reading with Bubba, even the finagled videos Mom somehow managed to procure. All of it helping Emma excel in a way that before the pandemic, were far-off dreams. Formal therapies out the window meant Mom had been winging it to see profound success. A young girl's body not meant to be doing what it was, all due to what coursed through her veins.

The virus was working a secret angle, and she was the prized test subject.

The rambling brain and distorted thoughts got Emma's feet moving and attention diverted and before she knew it, she was beyond the cave entrance and deep in the trees. Desperately looking around to catch her bearings, she didn't recognize any landmarks in the darkness, the only light the dim radiance of the moon.

"Oh, no."

She tried to feel Dad, and for the first time since their reunion, couldn't place his whereabouts. It was like the connection got lost and required some type of reboot. How to flip the switch?

No clue.

Even her link with Bubba seemed offline. Usually, she was cabled into his conscious, able to send thoughts and he could reply back. That twin thing was remarkable. Standing in the dark forest, afraid and unsure of what to do, she really needed her brother's help. He had protected her for so long after Dad *died*. Kept doing so when Dad's ghost materialized and saved them, though to a lesser extent since Dad told Bubba to try and be a kid again. As her fear built a wall brick by brick into a cage that caused her body to suddenly convulse, the want to scream out for help precariously on the tip of her tongue, Emma froze.

The sound of the breaking twig echoed.

The air caught it, straight ahead about seventy-five feet, give or take. Silence, and then a soft crunch of rocks underfoot. Hidden by the trees, the intruder stayed invisible. Another twig, soft and almost undetectable, broke to her left. This one only thirty feet. She was still, unwavering and partially blocked by a large stump. Gaining her strength, Emma slowly crouched until the former tree concealed her. One knee on the ground, she felt the pressure of the rocks digging in.

So, she bit her tongue to mask the pain from blurting out.

Closer the enemy came, though she had no knowledge if it was a person or wild animal. It could be raccoons on the hunt. Some wildlife using the dark to search for food.

Bears, or worse.

Huddled and wishing to remain unseen, Emma listened for any telltale sign of what lurked. No rustle of low-lying limbs, so it had to be smaller than a moose. Soft treading, so unlikely a bear. Purposeful steps, so it could only be…and then it hit her.

Emma, with all of her senses on blast, should have known. The sudden confrontation shocked her to the core. Face to face now, the breath hot and rapid, caused her to wipe the moisture away.

Wrong move.

The shape pounced and knocked her over, feet atop her chest, and then the licks began.

"What are you doing out here, puppy dog?" Emma managed to whisper.

The dog, as she saw in the faint light, was a black lab. Its collar frayed and worn, but the tag still there, duct tape preventing any noise against the ring holding it in place. A bit on the lean side, but not enough to say it was undernourished. The dog lapped her up, probably eager for the companionship if it had been all alone.

It wasn't.

Emma felt the presence, realized the two different sounds she heard was not the dog, but the canine and something, or someone, else. A hand suddenly gripped her shoulder tight. Then, the sting of something smelly got placed over her nose, and soon her eyes grew heavy and closed. Grasping deep to stay awake as sleep crept over her, Emma felt the fear. Tried to win the war, but failed.

In a swift moment, the happiness of dreams overtook her consciousness.

CHAPTER 45

Vapors from a fragrant hot chocolate enveloped Emma's nostrils.

She cracked an eye, searching her surroundings. Candlelight filled a small portion of a dark space. She couldn't tell much, worn wooden floor, a musty smell of the blanket she was on, and the sound of humming coming from behind her.

What was that song?

Familiar, yet she couldn't place it, not exactly word for word. An old tune Mom played on the TV when she was little?

That was it!

Emma remembered now. One of her old speech therapists recommended a video channel full of songs and books to help Emma learn words and sounds. Not just kiddie ones, but all sorts of songs that got reimagined to be more kid-friendly with videos. Mom would put it on, Emma would sit with Bubba and sing along, trying her best to pronounce and put letters to words.

Hard work, but little by little it paid off.

Squinting eye still panning for intel, Emma caught sight of someone, a shape really, huddled over what had to be a stove. Steam bellowed up from below and floated away, an odd sight to see against the shadows from the candlelight. The figure must have felt Emma stirring, as without missing a beat from swirling the spoon, it spoke.

"Awake now, are we?"

Emma didn't respond.

The voice, a woman's, attempted again. "It's OK. I'm not going to hurt you."

Emma raised herself up on an elbow. "That remains to be seen."

The voice chuckled. Old and raspy, with a cough and hacking before settling back down. "You're a funny one."

"A regular comedian on the circuit."

The attempt at humor elicited another round of coughing, a fit really, and a minute later was back to normal.

"Seems to be true. Would you like some hot cocoa?"

Emma, still on one elbow, sat upright and flipped her feet over the side of what she realized was an old cot. "Depends."

Another coughing spell.

"Depends on what, Little One?"

Emma's brain raced for a reply, something witty, yet definitive enough to show she wasn't scared. "Depends on who you are and why you took me? I don't like being kidnapped and am not scared to kick your butt if you try something funny."

The woman nearly fell over laughing. "Strong spirit, I like that. Not to worry, you're not going to be hurt."

"Then, why am I here?" Blunt, and to the point.

Emma couldn't see the woman's face as she was focused on the pot of hot chocolate. Until, she laughed, muttered something under her breath, and turned. Pushing a century by the number of wrinkles, the weathered face appeared kind, a warm smile gracing her lips. Bright white hair devoid of any gray, it hung below her shoulders, and looked shiny. The bright blue eyes, almost like Emma's, stared back.

"A good question. I happened upon you in the dark, alone and seeming to be lost. Figured you needed a place to be safe since the crazies wander about."

The words hung in the air.

"You've seen them?"

A chuckle. "I have. Not many nowadays, but on the occasion, they get lost and wander these parts."

"They're pretty scary."

The old woman smiled. "They can be, if you let them. Most people try to stay away and avoid them. Know where they are and keep away, far away. People have tended to gather together so they can fight them off if they have to do it. Cities are mostly where they go. Not stay way out here, except me. I like my alone time."

Emma still had the faint smell in her nose. Realized that her head was still groggy. Had to have been some kind of sleep medicine she figured. If the woman was on the up and up, why drug her?

The little girl had to play it carefully to find out.

The old woman continued her questions. "How'd you come to be out here?"

Emma yawned, a fake attempt, and decided to fish. "My head's fuzzy a bit."

A quizzical glance, before what seemed like a legitimate offer. "Oh, sorry for that. Didn't want you screaming out and attracting any of the weird ones.

Used a home remedy to calm you down. Must have put you out."

Emma could go in any direction with a response. Keep lying and possibly incur the wrath of the old woman, or skirt the truth enough and get back to Dad.

"I was with my dad and I went out to pee and got lost. We're just trying to live like everyone else. Keep away from people. Never know who they are now."

The old woman stirred some more, and satisfied, walked over and sat. "I've been living in these woods for a long time. Trying to live too, as you say."

As the last word left the old woman's lips, the black lab Emma remembered jumped up from behind and put its head in her lap.

"Old Betty seems to like you."

Emma petted the dog, who rolled over to expose her belly. It had been a long time since she had the pleasure of a dog's company, the last being before Logan and Luka passed away. "Hi, Betty," Emma smiled, scratching Betty's stomach.

"She likes it, right here," the old woman gestured.

Emma rubbed the spot, and Betty wiggled with joy under the affection. The old dog was a nice distraction from the real world, something to relish in, if only for a short time. It almost relieved Emma of the hole left when her dogs died, even though that was before the fall of civilization and so much had transpired since.

Time soothes old wounds, sometimes.

Emma sighed, and the old woman caught it.

"Something wrong, Child?"

Emma paused, collected her thoughts, and chose her words carefully to hide her sadness. She didn't know the woman or her intentions, and feeding her information could be deadly. "I just miss dogs. You don't find many of them around. Either they died, or got eaten. The ones you see are afraid or mean."

A witchy laugh, high pitched, and a snort. "Too true! Though my guess, if you work on them long enough, they just want to be pets again."

Emma shook her head in agreement.

"So, forgive my manners. I got all caught up with making hot cocoa and Old Betty here. My name is Doris. What's yours?"

Emma froze, keeping her fear hidden. Sharing her real name could prove dangerous, and if she didn't pull off the lie, Doris would see it. Smiling, her blue eyes bright under the brilliant candlelight from the small table next to her, Emma managed her story. "I'm Jennifer, but everyone calls me Jenny."

The old woman tilted her head, and Emma wasn't sure the lie was bought. She could only hope she sold it. Doris grinned, and Emma knew.

"Nice to meet you, Jenny."

CHAPTER 46

The drilling inside Ryan's head would not cease.

His brain ached from stress and fear for Emma. She could be anywhere, lost and afraid if she got turned around from going too far out, though he knew she was capable of keeping her head on straight.

For an eight-year-old with a disability, she was a smart little girl.

He wished she hadn't tagged along. It was what it was and he had to deal with the predicament. Going back with her would have ended his mission. Julia would have made sure he didn't leave. Deservedly, of course. Honcho and BP, devoted friends and protectors, would have nailed Ryan's ass to the wall. Ensured he couldn't wiggle a finger without their knowledge.

Moving forward took on the extra baggage.

Priority objective was finding Emma. Reg wasn't going anywhere passed out and hog-tied to a huge rock. He could move, just a bit. There wasn't any worry about escape. Where the girl vanished to was a mystery. Ryan figured, and he probably shouldn't have, that she'd stay close. The fight with his dad likely forced her outside for some silence and not hearing the brawl going down.

If he was her age, he knew he would do the exact same.

Though, not leave without saying a word. He'd stick close. Maybe she stepped out to clear her head or keep her ears free from the fight. Needed to pee and walked away. He wasn't sure how long it was, a minute, more, the last time he caught her in the corner of his eye.

Ryan couldn't nail it down.

If it was a pee, Emma should be within ear shot. The trees near the cave entrance afforded privacy and proximity. Same with a number two if she felt the need, and given her digestive issues, that was a possibility to throw in the ring. Either scenario, she had to be around.

"Emma? Emma?" Ryan shouted out, faint to keep his voice down, loud enough so she could hear.

Ears perked, he listened, and waited.

Not getting a response, he tried again, and waited. A minute, two passed, went to five and he felt panic brewing inside his belly.

"Emma?"

A lone chirp way off was the only reply.

Flipping his night vision goggles on, Ryan panned the forest floor. Searched for some tracks. Coming up empty, he switched settings, sifting through until he got a contrast in the dirt about twenty feet out. Hurrying over, he followed the steps as they worked towards the trees and disappeared. Bending to a knee, he pushed a limb aside and focused. The trail went another ten feet, veered left, and headed diagonally at a huge boulder. From there, as he kept the line in his goggles, she stopped fifty feet in a small clearing and must have been staring up at the moon behind him.

"Taking in the sights," Ryan whispered to himself.

From that point, she ventured to his right and ended up in the trees and an old stump. From the rustled leaves, he could tell she took a knee as her weight pushed an ident into the moist night soil beneath some rocks.

That's when he saw the paw marks.

"Oh, fuck no," he mouthed, until repeating it and hearing the words echo in his ears.

Fearing the worst, he descended on the spot, and soon realized another set of prints came from the side. Small, different ground pressure.

A woman.

Taking a closer look, the indentations got deeper, the paw prints alongside. Putting it together, the picture formed. Someone with what had to be a dog found Emma, and by the evidence he could extrapolate from years of tracking expertise, carried her off.

Things suddenly got more complicated.

CHAPTER 47

Honcho stayed behind with David this time.

The boy couldn't go off in the deep dark wilderness and help find his sister, no matter how much he pleaded.

With the first trek coming up empty and a need to regroup, time was ticking with darkness taking the mountain. BP led the way with Julia right behind. While it was more practical for Honcho to go since it was "his" mountain and forest, the logistics of getting his large frame quietly sneaking through the trees at night, not the best option. At six-feet, five inches, he provided too big a target to easily hide himself if the situation presented, even in the dark.

Besides, with radio headsets and body cameras attached to Julia and BP, Honcho could keep the boy occupied, feed directions, and watch his security monitors for any signs of life.

"OK, my guess is they went due east along this path until you hit the stream. Radio in when you are there," Honcho ordered.

Julia answered. "Yes, Sir."

Sensing the sarcasm, Honcho sheepishly apologized. "Sorry, wasn't meant to bark that."

"No worries. Just let us know if you hear or see anything and we have to go a different path."

"Ten-four. Honcho out."

BP, listening to the exchange, had to laugh. "He's worried too, Julia," he whispered over his hand blocking sound to the open mic. "He's gruff, but means well."

She knew it. The man, as large as his intimidating demeanor was, had the heart of a teddy bear. How else could someone who looked so formidable because of his stature be a gentle special education teacher with a heart of gold? Honcho was the best anyone could ask for in an educator for their child, a rock of stone you didn't want to mess with at a club when he ran security, and as a best friend who would die to protect those he loved.

Honcho was just what Ryan needed in his time of distress as the virus plagued his soul.

A half hour passed by uneventful. BP trudging a path for Julia to follow and Honcho chattering over the secured channel with tidbits of intel unfolding during his deep dive information work. The occasional e-mail between government agencies discussing protocols around addressing the pandemic. Video recordings between lead researchers caught surreptitiously and buried beneath layers of passcodes that outlined the issues faced as the virus took over and ran roughshod over containment. If these had ever seen daylight, the public would have known a glimmer of truth.

Though the lies perpetuated shadowed fact versus fiction.

Ten minutes of silence, unusual for Honcho, followed a sudden chirp in BP and Julia's ears.

"We've got a huge problem," Honcho sighed.

BP jumped on it. "Spill."

Julia heard Honcho clear his throat, a slight huff of air, and then her world devolved.

"One of my last arrays of cameras caught sight of Ryan."

Her throat dry, Julia barely got it out. "Was Emma with him?"

Only the night bugs responded.

"Honcho?"

He wasn't sure how to answer. He simply said, "No."

She felt the wind leave her lungs, perspiration bead across her forehead. A hand reached out to catch Julia as she fell forward, and the light in her eyes faded.

"Right. Got it. Thanks Honcho," BP sighed.

The fog in her brain still stinging, Julia caught the tail end of BP's conversation with Honcho. Shaking her head to loosen the cobwebs, she looked around, saw she was flat on the ground with a small towel under her neck, BP pacing a few feet away.

"What happened?" Julia managed to whisper.

BP turned to face her, his face grim. "You passed out."

Not the first time, and as she was beginning to realize, it would not be the last. BP looked concerned and she could see he wanted to ask. While she appreciated it, it wasn't the time nor place to get into her issues.

Raising up on an elbow, Julia rolled to the side and hopped to her feet. "What about Emma?"

"Not with Ryan, but seems she might have been."

The words sliced deep.

Julia felt her knees begin to buckle before realizing it, and then caught herself and kept her balance. "So, he *did* have her?"

"Honcho thinks so. Based on Ryan's reaction and what looked like footprints he must have seen. Ryan was freaking out, so the assumption is she was with him, something happened, and then she was gone."

She took a deep breath, held it, and let the pain go. "Gone?"

The cold night air stung.

BP wasn't the type to sugarcoat bad news. "As best as Honcho can focus in, there's footprints that appear Emma's size. Then, animal prints. Honcho doesn't think wild, but like a dog because then there were a set of adult shoes, and Emma's shoes are gone. Like, she got carried off."

Not what Julia wanted to hear.

"Listen," BP cautioned, "it doesn't mean *They* got her. Could be some survivor hiding out came across her and took her in."

The info could absorb any which way. The fact Honcho said Ryan was freaking out, a guy who was always calm and cool, spoke volumes. If he was only tracking her, how did he know she had left the bunker? Maybe he found her, decided not to bring her back and she tagged along, only to get lost somehow. Ryan was meticulous, methodical, yet with his brain and body suffering repercussions from the virus and concoctions forced through his veins, his mind might be slipping more and more as the days came.

"What are the odds someone nice got my girl? We don't seem to have that kind of luck."

BP, lips pursed, held Julia's hand. "I won't lie. We don't know. Emma is a smart little girl. Even with her Down Syndrome, she's morphed beyond it in ways we never could have imagined. There's a spark in that kid we are just beginning to see, so have some faith. Not the 'god almighty' crap kind. Religion is gone and all we have left is to believe in ourselves. Trust her, and in Ryan. If anyone can find her, that bloodhound will."

"Like a cockroach hunting for food."

BP laughed. "Like a *never will die* cockroach."

CHAPTER 48

Emma, or Jenny as she was pretending to be, kept a vibrant smile.

She hated to *fake it*, as Mom and Dad liked to say. However, keeping up an appearance that she didn't feel scared or knew something was amiss played into the game she had to play.

Act like the girl with a disability and disarm her captor with a happy face.

Downplaying her physical capabilities and burgeoning intellect was a hard thing to swallow. Emma had worked hard to grow as a person and show people that a disability was never defining, just a stray line that affected many, but never let the canvas dry because the picture was always being painted. Even though she knew she was an outlier, someone who was blessed with a gift most never received because of the way the virus and vaccines seemed to *change* her, she believed in her heart that the reason was different.

I'm who I am and what I'm becoming because of Mom, Dad, and Bubba.

They believed in her, supported her on the good days and bad. Made sure she got the best care when it was available. Advocated and pressed for her rights when it came to education. Even when the world ended, Mom kept at it to ensure her therapies continued, though from a mother's love and repeated encouragement as the sole provider because there were no medical professionals around. Just Mom leading the charge the best she knew. Bubba fostered a buddy system during the dark days, acting as a typical peer to show her the way. Without their undying support and sometimes harsh words when she crawled into a shell and they brought her out of it, Emma wasn't sure she'd be where she was without them.

Throw in Dad over just the last month alone.

Knowing he was alive brewed a fire inside Emma like never before to see her grow and accel beyond expectations. His proud face was the one thing she had missed the most during the years he was *dead*. The minute she felt his presence, realized he was actually breathing air and not fish food and bones on the ocean floor, Emma's achievements catapulted through the stratosphere.

Not that Dad alone brought the most recent sparks out of her.

Letting him take all the credit for it would be wrong, and unjust. Emma knew what Mom and Bubba contributed and could never fail to acknowledge them. Through the hell that Uncle Mark and Papa brought on her, unknowingly in many aspects who did what since Papa was supposed to be dead, her brother and Mom kept Emma constantly on her toes.

Dad just somehow worked the father-daughter connection right.

Back to the present, Doris moved quietly around the cabin, shuffling really, in a vain attempt to somehow force quiet to make Emma fall asleep. The hour late, Emma wasn't sure how long she'd been there, she could tell the old woman was tired. A battle of wills maybe on who would succumb first to the inside of their eyelids.

"Rest, Child," Doris offered with a warm smile. "Morning is around the corner and a new day awaits."

"We get to find my dad then?"

Doris' smile twinged, enough that Emma knew that wasn't going to happen.

"It's a large mountain, Jenny. No idea how long you wandered along. Could be anywhere."

The vague response wasn't comforting to Emma.

"I know he's looking for me. We can find a nice place to sit and enjoy nature until he comes."

The smile faded. "Something could have happened to him. Best to stay put and wait for help."

Help? The word sent a shudder down Emma's spine. She kept the fear to herself, hid it enough that she passed it off as feeling cold.

"Ooh, getting cold."

Doris stared, her eyes locked on Emma, seeming to gauge the veracity of truth to what the girl said. Seconds turned to minutes before she walked over and tossed Emma a blanket. "Go to sleep."

The tone hinted at the anger in the old woman. Emma felt she pulled off the lie, that the change in demeanor was Doris being exhausted from the trek back with Emma out like a sack of potatoes over the shoulder. Smiling as best as she could pull out of her trick book to hide the growing fear, Emma nodded, threw the blanket over, and pretended to go to sleep.

Eyes shut, breathing becoming shallow as she faked dreamland, Emma waited. She didn't know how long it was, couldn't tell the time involved as it was hard to do when you didn't have a watch or clock to check. Only her mind wandering to try to and grasp at the minutes as they turned to an hour or more?

She heard a faint voice, not Doris', and focused her ears to catch the conversation. Had to be a radio, as the tinny sound of a speaker occasionally delivered a weird sound.

"Bring her in. They're looking for some kid. Might be her, might not be her. If she is, great. If not, then let's see what she's worth to the dad to get her back."

Emma's blood froze. Being used as some kind of bargaining chip wasn't a great place for her to be in. She knew if she got turned over to what had to be the *Them* in the sentence, she was toast.

Burnt crispy toast.

Doris whispered back. "I can't bring her by myself. That's a problem trying to explain it if she's conscious and fights back, or a sack of sand to have to cart her down to the highway to knock her out again."

Knock out? That's what the funny feeling in her head was before.

The voice on the radio answered. "Look, we'll send someone then. Be there by sunrise. Keep her contained at all costs. Understand?"

Doris replied. "Yes."

"Over and out," the voice ended.

The old woman sighed, her head hung low as she contemplated the plan and how to go about delivering Emma. Glancing at Old Betty, Doris caught the head tilt of the dog staring behind the chair, and as the chair swiveled to the right, the sharp blow caught the temple hard, and Doris slumped to the left, blood trickling from a cut down the side of her head.

Old Betty whimpered, fear reflecting in the old dog's eyes as she expected the same for her. Instead, she found a warm smile and gripping hug as tears soaked her coat.

"I'm sorry, Betty. I'd never hurt you. I wish you understood why I did it. I can't let them get me."

Old Betty, cocked her head as if she was thinking about Emma's explanation. Satisfied with her deliberation, she licked the young girl's cheek.

"Thank you, Betty."

The unexpected attack came with no further planning except to flee. Emma didn't want to leave Betty with a dead body and no one to care for her. Seeing that Doris was still breathing made the decision to leave the dog easier. Besides, Emma was going to have a hard enough time herself trying to escape. Being responsible for a dog while on the run would only complicate matters.

One more huge hug and a kiss on the head of Old Betty, and then Emma scurried out the cabin door into the blackness.

She had caught the time on the clock and knew she had only a few hours to either find Dad or put as much distance between the cabin and her coming pursuers. Turned around without a clue as to direction, Emma looked up to find the Moon. Seeing it behind her, she knew to get back to Dad, she had to go right.

She remembered Dad talking about that during one of their camping trips. That meant going behind the cabin, veer right, and off into the dark. Try to stay on a line and somehow not get lost or worse, eaten. One foot planted and the other stepping to the side, Emma hustled off, pushing a branch out of the way and forcing herself to keep a quick pace to get as far away as possible.

On any other day, Emma knew she would enjoy a night walk in the forest. Absorb the coolness of the night, the sounds of the critters, even the smells that wafted her nostrils. Take her time to relish in the experience and stash the memories away for a later time to dream.

Not tonight.

Doris could come to at any time. Her anger at being hit and knocked out a rage to brew out of control. The old woman knew the mountain, the trails in the forest. Probably could sense a presence in her backyard and use Old Betty to track.

Emma was running blind.

Besides being a stranger to the land, she was a child, and critical to her predicament, she had Down Syndrome. Though her disabilities still existed to varying degrees, there was no erasing her DNA, some affecting her less than others. Plus, for some cosmic or alien reason, the virus and vaccines coursing through her veins had decided to compel a physiological and intellectual transformation that defied known science.

She was an oddity and miracle that in her heart, knew would change the world.

Sucking up the fear of being captured and used as an experiment plugged into drip lines to extract her essence, Emma pushed on. While her hypotonia was a constant battle of wills to get the body to do what the mind commanded, Emma felt her body and muscles respond in a way that never occurred in the past. Not so significant where she was running marathons or breaking records for the hundred-meter dash, but enough to keep momentum cruising along and fatigue buried deep.

Maybe it was adrenaline. Or, the desire to live.

She didn't really know. She was just a kid, trying to navigate the former world blown into oblivion and the new one rising from the ash ruled by an evil she couldn't comprehend.

Emma knew she was *different*. Felt a strangeness that couldn't be placed into a bucket to understand. Aware of her limitations due to her disabilities, yet cognizant enough to recognize the advances morphing her being that somehow and someway reduced her Down Syndrome into not something to belittle as *manageable*, but transformative and life altering enough that for any scientist and researcher, deserved qualified study.

Parents would want the juice for their own beloved children.

Being the Guinea pig or lab rat as she had been for three years didn't appeal at all in viewing her future. While assisting any way she could for friends and others who were in her same shoes was a no-brainer, it could only happen on her terms. Not as a prisoner locked away for the whims of crazed and delusional madmen.

Or, the modern-day madwomen.

As confidence and courage intensified, Emma moved as fast as her legs allowed. Not a full run, as in the dark that was a dangerous activity that could send her tripping over an unseen rock or tumbling down the side of the mountain to sure death. She didn't need to end up dying from a freak accident. Taking her time to prevent winding her lungs, though diligent in keeping moving along to put distance between the cabin and Doris, Emma felt something inside.

Pride?

She wasn't sure what it was or what it meant. Pride or a sense of accomplishment at being able to protect herself and not rely on Bubba, Mom, or even Dad to be her protectors? The question pecked at her conscious, drawing attention away from her mission and focus to get to safety. Except, where safety exactly resided was anyone's guess. Coming to a fork in the trail, the sudden emergence of dawn peeking light over her shoulder, the open terrain, still pockmarked with a grove of trees offering shade and protection, the sudden sight nearly made her trip over her shoes.

Emma smiled.

CHAPTER 49

The energetic smile quickly faded away.

When the forest floor suddenly moved and rose up to reveal a half dozen camouflaged men, Emma's heart sunk into the recesses of her chest. Stopped dead in her tracks, motionless to appear invisible, she watched in horror as the men, facing away from her location, pointed towards the trees a hundred feet ahead. Barely thirty feet in front of her, all she could do was stand still and hope they moved and gave her time to escape.

Wishful thinking on her part.

Maybe it was her breathing, a gasp of air evacuating her lungs that divulged her presence. All she knew was that within a second or two one of the camo helmets, the furthest in the back, turned to show a face painted to blend in with the foliage. A grin the size of Texas washed over it.

A millisecond passed, then the toothy grin soon gone.

Replaced by a spray of red mist and flying enamel, the soldier collapsed. His body weight hit the ground, breaking the former silence of the early morning, which caused a few other soldiers to turn their heads to see what interrupted the stillness, only to fall one by one. Blood caught the wind, and as the rising sun caught the particles, the air turned into a bright red hue that on any other occasion, Emma would gladly stay and watch. Fear gripping her body tight but not enough to keep her glued to the dirt, Emma started to pivot when the last soldier fell.

"Emma!"

She stopped cold.

Frantically scanning her surroundings, she didn't see a living soul.

"Get down!"

Dropping flat, she felt the gust of air pass as she hit the ground and rolling to her side, caught the soldier she missed catch one to the chest, absorb the round with his protective vest, before taking two definitive bullseyes that ended his life as they passed through the crack in his armor plate. The first weakened it. The second in the same spot cracked it.

The third dead on and to his heart.

Seeing the radiance of his eyes that had been locked on her fade out, Emma saw the life leave and vanish. She couldn't help feel a twinge of sadness, a snippet of pain at what he must have felt as one moment he's alive and the next no longer.

It quickly passed.

Staying down, she waited until she heard the soft footsteps next to her head.

"Hey, Pumpkin."

"Hi, Dad."

Reaching down, Ryan took her outstretched hand and pulled her up. Kneeling, he gripped her tight, the hug like a vise. Emma felt wetness on her cheek, knew it was silent tears, and as much as she tried to prevent it, the valve broke and she cried.

"It's okay, Pumpkin," Ryan comforted as he stroked her back. "Dad's here and you're safe."

She sniffed the snot back, decided she just had to blow, and turning her head, let loose. A weak stream flopped out. Wiping her nose with her sleeve, Emma kept her head against her dad, relishing in the warmth of his skin and the love she felt knowing he was there. Deciding to break the happy reunion, she pulled back and grabbed his head in her hands.

"Thank you, Dad. It was scary being gone."

Ryan wiped the tears away. Staring coldly at his beautiful daughter, a scolding deserved for wandering off, but given she just watched her father blow the brains out of a half dozen men, a softer touch might be a better approach. Eradicating the Un-dead was one thing. People who still were human to a degree was a different story.

The line for him was vanishing each day.

"I bet. So, tell me, what happened? One minute you're there and then next you're gone."

Emma was honest to the bone. Lying not her nature. How to convey her capture, not the easiest thing to share.

He saw the struggle, smiled to erase the frown she witnessed plastered on his face, and hugged her again before pulling back to look into her eyes. "It's okay."

She sighed, and then let it flow.

Five minutes later, her tears resided, Emma saw the wheels spinning in her dad. She'd just told him about Doris and the radio conversation. Why he was thinking hard she wasn't sure. The bad men on the way he had just annihilated so the threat was gone.

"What is it, Dad?"

He frowned, momentarily closed his eyes, before sighing heavily, "These guys aren't the ones you think they are," he corrected, having seen the quizzical expression on her face when he shook his head as she talked about the radio chat.

"What do you mean?"

"I tracked these guys from the south. They'd been hiking the woods searching for us. The people on the radio have to be different. To get here in the timeframe you mentioned, they would come from the highway north of here and then come south. We got between the two, and the other is still out there."

Emma froze.

She had believed she was safe, that Dad had stopped the threat. Hearing more were coming, her fear simply released a torrent she couldn't stop.

Ryan pulled her close, whispered in her ear, trying to give comfort and convey the seriousness of the situation. They needed to be quiet and vigilant. Crying didn't' help and travelled the air to prying ears. Their best bet was to immediately vacate the area and get to hiding.

Hopefully Reg was still out cold.

"Come on. I need my best girl to buckle up and go ghost," Ryan directed.

Emma nodded, knowing now what "ghost" meant and a sliver of her dad's history as the silent assassin.

Father and daughter trekked back to the seclusion of the cave. Its proposed security a genie's wish. Ryan knew it offered some defense if required and safety if they could ride out their pursuers. Keeping Emma in front and prodding her with directions, he prayed that they had enough of a head start to cover ground and get hidden without being spotted.

The hurried walk and whispered conversation kept them engaged. Ryan threw in some jokes to make Emma chuckle, silly ones to evoke the humor for her. The occasional tap to point a direction, they made their destination in record time, which surprised Ryan given he knew how tired she must be after her late-night escapade.

"You holding up, Pumpkin?"

She nodded.

Taking her hand, Ryan bent down, kept his voice low. "Listen, don't let Papa get to you, OK? I'll keep him gagged and still to make sure we can ride this out. Work for you?"

Emma smiled. "Got it, Dad."

Letting go, Ryan stepped around and slowly crept inside the darkened opening. Hitting the switch on his rifle, the flashlight illuminated the interior and still on the ground, he saw Reg, fast asleep. Reaching into the leg pocket of his pants, Ryan pulled out a bandana, crept the distance to where Reg slumbered, and quickly wrapped the cloth over his dad's mouth and secured it.

Reg didn't budge.

Ryan checked the old man's pulse, felt blood pulsing through the neck vein, and propped open an eyelid. Alive, but still unconscious. Leaving Reg, Ryan left to get Emma, who had sequestered herself in a small opening just inside the entryway to keep hidden. Motioning with his hand to keep quiet, she walked in and sat down, far away from her grandfather. She hated what he had become and being too close anymore made her skin crawl.

"Hungry?" Ryan whispered.

Emma shook her head no.

Ryan nodded, then took up post near the cave entrance. Even though it offered a concealed entrance unless you were standing right in front of the hole in the rock, the last thing they needed was anyone happening on it.

A firefight inside wasn't the best option to keep Emma safe.

Ryan sat, quietly, his M4 across his lap as he relaxed on a boulder. If you could call it relaxation with all the pent-up emotions flooding his body. Anger at even having to confront what was coming soon. Hate for his father and Mark for putting his children in harm's way and not taking their defeat like men. Sadness for Emma and David being forced at such a young age to live on the run, a normal childhood vanished forever. Grief for not being able to protect them in the beginning and feeling like a failure for not being able to let them be kids without a care in the world.

Burning rage for whomever sat atop the pyramid that sent the world to shit and sought to use Ryan's children for their madness.

He could feel the venom coursing through his blood. The power of the intense wrath that enveloped his being. The devil at the top would die, Ryan knew it. He'd never stop looking or searching for the asshole. Even if it meant Ryan's own death, the head of the snake had to go. Otherwise, the minions would keep looking for Emma and David, turning over every stone to find them. Ryan could do his best to ghost his babies, yet he knew in the end there were too many people they might encounter that had ulterior motives.

Trust was paper thin. People did things to survive.

Taking stock of the situation, Ryan felt alone. Even with Julia, Honcho, and BP on his side, they weren't headed towards crazy town and the eventual turn into the bad ass mother Ryan knew was around the corner. Each day he experienced a fraction of loss, a sliver of his soul and mind leaving the train station and headed off to oblivion. The rational thinker, the compassionate husband and father, the stone-cold executioner who succeeded on every mission, was slowly withering away. The Devil was a boy scout compared to what Ryan saw in his mind.

When it spawned, Ryan would be the worst killer there ever was.

No sympathy. No love. No feelings of any kind. A machine that ached to inflict pain and death without consequence.

Ryan just knew.

A morbid vision to fathom, he realized. He'd been around the block too many times to discount what percolated below his skin. As the days progressed, and the virus and its cocktail of drugs they'd put into his system fought for control, Ryan couldn't help wonder what it would be like, if he'd even be cognizant of the change and the switch decided to stay flipped on.

One minute, Ryan. The next, a monster bent on total devastation.

He hoped it transpired quick and away from his loved ones. That he'd have plenty of heads-up to possibly say his goodbyes and get as far away as possible. He'd thought about simply letting go and getting a bullet to the brain to make sure it ended. To not let evil win and be used as a pawn. The truth to his decision was selfish, a divergence from the soldier mentality he had grown up and dedicated his life to upholding and protecting its fundamental foundations.

He was simply afraid to die.

Even, if it meant he was a killing machine. A robot without remorse. Worse, a father who would kill his own children as an end to a means.

The thought sent a frozen chill down his spine.

There was no way he could ever do that deed. Brain turned to mush and his emotions withered to dust, Ryan believed in his heart he could never hurt his own flesh and blood. His own dad?

Fuck yes.

But, not his babies. Julia might be a tougher call, yet deep down that seemed a far-off scenario some primal piece of his gray matter could still control and subvert. He still had some nagging questions around her, but given everything if he had to vacate the premises, Julia was safe. He could kill everyone else, but those three were sacred and off-limits.

Honcho and BP would be tough to counter the gnawing bite to eradicate those fools.

Ryan laughed at that thought. His best buds in the world through thick and thin all these years. If any part of Ryan managed to live, he would spare his friends.

The rest of the world? Watch out.

Deep breath in, Ryan trying to harness his calm, and then shit hit. Fifty yards out, barely perceptible, his periphery caught the glint. Just a tiny sliver of light, but he knew what it was without a doubt. The scope glass wasn't aimed at him, but panning off to his right. Taking the cue, Ryan remained motionless. Blend into his surroundings and keep his eyes focused.

The last thing he wanted was a bullet to the brain.

Emma must have felt his body tense. She moved further into the recesses of the cave, a place to hide in the darkness and go invisible her next task. Ryan caught her shoe scuff on the dirt floor, not anything that was loud or would betray their location.

Just a momentary blip and then nothing.

He knew she was seeking cover and proud she didn't have to be told. She was growing up, becoming something he didn't have the words to describe. He *felt* her without seeing her. Her presence exuding an aura that burned bright and for some other-worldly reason, he sensed below the skin. It was creepy and fascinating all at once. She had talked about the bond with him, how she had known he was alive before seeing him face to face that fateful night he just happened to find her room in the underground facility. She believed it was no accident, that he was drawn to her too and it was meant to be, the cosmos reuniting father and daughter.

She was probably right.

Her and her brother, as twins, shared a bond that normal siblings didn't possess. Dump atop the heap the virus and the vaccines with their concoctions of chemicals, pinch some familial blood and genes to the mix, and there was colloquial evidence to suggest something extraordinary brewed within the Carmichaels. The kids had been Guinea pigs and Ryan, unbeknownst to him, he'd lived a lifetime of experiments he'd been clueless about until the news Honcho uncovered dropped a bomb of clarity in his lap.

The three shared a bond that defied logic and rational science.

Julia, even though as mom supplied half their DNA, wasn't connected in the same capacity as father and kids. She was a bit envious when it materialized and the nature of it came to light. She saw it first as a loss, and as time progressed, understood it was more curse than blessing. Emma felt her father, could read him, and as he slipped slowly away from beloved father and role model into the mold of whatever was to come, Julia could only imagine the pain Emma felt knowing Daddy was soon to be no more.

The tears for her daughter always secreted away.

For David, Ryan was a god. Father and son like their own set of twins, David being a mini version of his dad. Ryan held a pedestal spot that David worshipped, and Ryan knew it was torture for the son to see glimpses of his dad begin to crumble. The son felt it too, the bond with his dad. Not like Emma's, since hers for some reason was stronger. But he still had it, in its own manifestation.

Losing the man who had taught David all he knew and loved him to death was crushing the young boy's soul day by day.

As he sat still and vigilant, Ryan yearned for the day he woke up and realized it had all been a horrible dream.

No chance in hell he was right on that one.

CHAPTER 50

The bullet would have been on target.

Finger near the trigger, Ryan's M4 ached to let the 5.56mm shell loose to splatter a brain out the back of a skull. Rifles loved to send bullets down the length of their barrels, to find success for the reason they were designed in the first place.

He was glad he didn't jump the gun.

"Dammit," Ryan huffed under his breath.

Emma caught the word. "Who is it, Daddy?"

He could ignore their appearance, let them wander off in their search, or suck it up. Tough decision on the fence.

"Mommy."

Emma didn't respond.

Looking back, Ryan saw his daughter's pursed lips and wondered what she was thinking in the moment. He didn't have to wait long.

"We *could* just let them go away."

He wished he could do that and go on with his mission. He knew if he did, the crap he'd get if something happened to Emma, Julia would pull the trigger early on him.

Or, slip his jugular.

"No, Pumpkin. You left and worried your mom. I didn't take you back because we were already pretty far out. You need to go with her. Safer that way."

Emma frowned. "You *need* my help, Daddy."

Ryan managed to produce a quiet laugh and grin. "My little soldier girl. I'd hate to meet you in battle."

"You'd be toast, Daddy."

"I sure would be, Princess."

The pause in tension was soon interrupted. A low hum off to the left sounded an alarm in his brain, and Ryan, realizing what it was, finally clicked on his mic. "BP?"

A pissed off voice whispered a response. "Dude? What the fuck?"

Ryan laid it out. "Your scope gave you away to me. You might have company on your ass. Book it straight ahead. You'll see me."

BP clicked his mic. "Gotcha. Just cover my six."

"Always, Bro."

BP rose up with Julia right behind. Ryan saw the perplexed expression on her face. BP pivoted to simply tap her shoulder and moving, pushed her forward. She didn't need words to covey the meaning of his rough action. A full run as she dodged the trees, BP followed. Ryan stepped out for them to see, and as they closed the distance, he heard the hum again.

Drone.

Raising his M4 and peering through the canopy of cover the trees offered, Ryan drew the crosshairs of his scope on it. The belly camera was panned behind it as it approached overhead. The last highly modified version by the looks of it, he waved BP and Julia inside the cave and considered his options before he huffed.

Fuck it.

Dropping the mag from his M4 and clearing the chamber, Ryan yanked another magazine out from the side of his vest. Popping it in and racking a round, he focused his aim, let his breath out, and fired a shot.

The explosive round found the belly of the beast and in an instant, the drone caught fire and blew.

Stepping inside the cave, Ryan found Julia wrapping Emma in a huge hug and BP staring coldly back. Stepping a few feet forward, he shook his head.

"Dick move, Dude."

There wasn't much to counter the assessment.

"I didn't plan on her tagging along."

BP shoved the barrel of his rifle into Ryan's chest. "That one, sure. But taking off with Reg and not saying shit? We're supposed to be a team here. Going all solo death dealer not what we talked about."

Ryan bowed his head. "You're right. Did Honcho say anything?"

BP glanced over his shoulder before answering his friend. "I got the gist of it. Neither of us told Julia though."

"Thanks, Bro."

BP laughed. "Don't thank me yet. You're fucked."

"That pissed at me?"

BP stepped aside. "Your enemies have nothing on a wife as raging as yours right now."

Ryan nodded. "Hope she forgives me."

Emma was whispering, too low for him to hear. Julia was gesturing, her hands conveying how much trouble the girl was in. Seeing Ryan appear, they both turned, one smiling while the other gave him the stare of death.

He didn't like seeing Emma's eye daggers.

Confused at first, Ryan soon understood why Emma was the one with the death glare. She was getting chewed out for leaving the silo in the first place and being told she was lucky her dad found her. Emma tried to explain, and Julia kept at it, placing blame on her daughter and defending Ryan. Feeling sympathy for Emma, he knelt and took his daughter's hand.

"Listen, your mom is right, sort of. But," he said as he looked at Julia, "it's my fault. I should have taken you right back to your mom. My mission, my situation to handle. Can't have your mom worried sick about you. Me? I go missing, and Mom throws a party. You, the world ends," he winked.

Julia smacked his arm. "You're not getting off easy if you think that little speech helps. You should have brought her right back. Immediately."

Ryan nodded, more to acknowledge she had a point than agreed with her. He did what he knew was right, and would do it again in a heartbeat.

"Maybe I should have right away. If I did, you all would have kept me there. I have a mission to perform, and don't have time to debate it."

The words cut deep.

BP interjected before Julia ripped Ryan a new asshole. "Last I thought, we were a team. While you're the badass super solider, that doesn't put you above us. You should have turned your ass around and brought Emma back, if only to keep Julia from freaking out and worrying about her."

Ryan didn't feel like getting bogged down in a blame game. He knew BP was running some interference between Julia and Ryan. Taking the lead to bitch out his old friend so Julia wouldn't have to do it. BP had the insider information on the situation, knew Ryan's dilemma, and was playing best friend to the hilt.

Emma didn't wait too long to burst the bubble.

"It's not Daddy's fault. I left on my own, didn't want to go back, and stayed to help him because there are things you don't know. I feel it inside my tummy. Daddy needs my help and I won't go back."

Julia frowned, hesitated on what to say. Ryan started to speak, and Emma cut him off.

"Daddy's changing, Mom. He didn't want to tell you because he knew it meant he's losing himself and the bad thing is growing bigger. I can help him, but only if I'm close. Too far away, and I can't *feel* him." The kid was honest and couldn't lie if her life depended on it.

Julia felt her knees buckle.

Ryan saw it, and before Emma decided to totally ruin the reunion, he motioned Julia and BP over.

"Dude," BP began, and seeing Ryan's eyes, stopped.

Ryan sighed, and just put it out there. "We have bigger problems right now. Liz sent a message with one of her people. Girl got shot before she could deliver it. I don't know if it was meant for me or Honcho given the nature of the information, but our situation got five shades blacker. Part of the reason I couldn't take Emma back."

The cryptic explanation wasn't coming across, and Julia let him know. "Specifics maybe?"

Ryan shrugged. "If it was meant for me, they only had a general direction I went, so it was a needle in a haystack to even deliver it to me. If it was for Honcho, well then, it means he was not totally truthful about knowing his old wifey was alive."

BP pursed his lips. "Shit."

Ryan sighed. "So, that left me in a bit of a quandary. Take Emma back and leave her potentially exposed to capture or something else, or keep her close and figure out what the hell is going on."

Julia grabbed Ryan's arm. "What did the note say?"

He paused, before letting it out. "Mark's bringing out the big guns. Someway, somehow, those soldiers from the Moon survived and are on their way."

Julia's face lost the little color her pale complexion had to offer.

Compartmentalizing everything to keep it short, Ryan elaborated. "Long story, no time to tell it. Based on Liz's note, Mark is bringing them back to go on the hunt. She was warning either me or Honcho. As you might imagine, trust is in short supply these days, even with a brother from another mother."

Julia glanced towards BP. Ryan shook his head. "Never in a million years. Our bond is unbreakable."

BP caught the meaning and nodded. "We're solid as a rock."

"But, what if it was meant for Honcho? David's back there. Even if he lied about Liz, that doesn't mean he's not on our side."

Ryan shrugged. "True. It does leave a few things unanswered. There could be a legit reason he's hiding the Liz connection. Or, it's something worse."

BP tapped Ryan's arm. "That note say anything else?"

Ryan shrugged. "Just that demons would soon rain from the sky and to watch the old 'back' is about all it said."

Julia's bowed her head, the eyes shut tight. A minute, two passed. Her eyelids parted and saw pain sprayed across BP's face.

BP rubbed his head. "If what Ryan says is coming, it's bad."

Ryan let out a huge breath of air. "I'm *so* glad it's not one of my delusions."

Julia glared. "Say what?"

Ryan coughed, realizing he had said it out loud. "The door between reality and my imagination has been open a bit lately. What's true to my past and what's a figment of an overzealous creativity for movie scripts has been bleeding together. This being real, while *not great*, at least means I haven't gone completely bonkers yet."

BP could only shake his head. Ryan was digging a deep, dark hole.

Looking over at Emma, who was humming to herself and focused on her papa who was still out cold, Julia grabbed Ryan's arm.

So tight, it hurt.

"If it's true, how do we protect them?" Her brown eyes reflected the terror she felt to her core.

Ryan managed to smile. Probably shouldn't have, though it made him feel better. BP saw it, shook his head to dissuade what he knew was brewing in his old friend, and then decided to stay silent.

Let Ryan do Ryan the best he knew how.

Smile growing huge, Ryan said something that parted the darkness, if only for a moment. "I trained those fuckers and know how they think. They're my bitches, because this old dog didn't share all his tricks."

Julia felt her fear slowly starting to thaw.

CHAPTER 51

David felt the twinge in his stomach.

Emma was safe, but something was off. He focused his mind, searched for the twin channel they used to telepath communication, and waited for the ring to pick up on the other end.

It took a while, but the receiver picked up.

Are you OK?

I'm fine, Bubba. Mommy and Uncle BP are here too.

David breathed a sigh of relief. At least they were with her.

What about Dad?

Dad's here too, and Papa.

Everyone all together, great. I felt something, and know that there's something wrong. What is it?

Emma wasn't sure what to say, but knew she could never lie to her brother.

Come on Emma, tell me.

Dad says some bad men are coming for us. You, me, and him. From the Moon.

David started to laugh before the feeling hit his brain.

For real?

Yes, for real. There's more to it. He's been talking to Mom and Uncle BP. Says the message he got he's not sure if it was meant for him or Uncle Honcho, so he can't be sure if Uncle Hon can be trusted.

That wasn't a revelation David expected.

Are you sure about that?

I'm sure that's what Dad is telling them. At least, from what I can overhear.

Why would Dad not trust Uncle Hon?

Doesn't matter, Bubba. You need to find out and let me know.

CHAPTER 52

Honcho caught the blip on the screen.

He knew what it was, just had prayed to the gods of old goth music it wasn't ever going to happen in his lifetime.

A short one he'd once figured given the craziness he'd lived post-service, then imagined growing old teaching and retiring before keeling over, though he knew deep down it would end up back to square one if it came to it. Watching the trajectory, the program calculated the path and flashed a destination.

King County International.

"Shit," Honcho spat out, the realization of what was coming sending shivers down his spine.

Being in the intel capture business, especially the covert, beyond super-secret designations of the compartmentalized kind relegated for one or two sets of eyes, meant you saw a lot of information pass through your hands.

Not figuratively touched by his overly large fingers.

The modern age was all digital. Files and data, e-mails, and bits and bytes. Nothing physical, unless you actually required a printed copy. Most everything got scanned and digitized, so the electronic transfer of information was so much easier than the old days of basement file cabinets and rummaging through the drawers.

In many ways, scarier how easy you could access all the crap.

The Moon base intel Honcho knew from a variety of clandestine sources. Mostly, from his oldest friend, Ryan. Both had been active service when Ryan made his first trip and Honcho was still the unit's intel analyst. While the details then weren't shared beyond a superior's statement that "Ryan's going to the Moon to train some people" and any dissemination outside the unit was immediate grounds for a lifetime spent at a black site being tortured, Ryan spilled a few snippets on his return.

The rest, over time, came from back channels of intel crossing Honcho's screens and beers with Ryan when he could discuss without fear of reprisals. Especially, after the encounter when Ryan appeared from the dark at a high-ranking official's home wanting to remove the man's nut sack for threatening Ryan's family when Ryan decided to retire. More Moon trips were out of the question as the baton there had been passed along.

You don't mess with a ghost like Ryan.

Seeing the blip and knowing what it represented, and who was likely taking the scenic trip back to Earth, Honcho shuddered with fear. If Mark was calling in these guns, then the future wasn't going to be a great place to exist if Ryan and the team didn't defeat the evil coming back to town.

Damn fuckers didn't die up there.

Thinking of the kids, Honcho knew protecting them was priority over all else, even his own life. A no-brainer he knew and something that was beyond being said aloud. Even though he and Liz had decided long ago to not have kids, a decision rooted in a desire to not bring little ones into what they saw as a degrading social pool of septic proportions, Emma and David were loved as if they were his flesh and blood.

Besides, as it seemed to be revealed over the last days, they were destined to save the world.

Honcho needed to get word to Ryan immediately and prevent him from walking into a death trap. Going radio silent ignoring all their calls to answer, Honcho hoped getting this critical snippet of intel would kick Ryan in the ass and get him to respond.

Clicking the mic, Honcho was direct. "Bravo One, the boys are coming back to town, over." He knew Ryan would understand his old call sign, and even on a secure channel, Honcho had to be discreet.

Silence.

"Repeat, old friends are coming for a party. Time to get out the decorations for a homecoming, over."

It was like time stood still as each second and minute passed.

Fearing the worst, Honcho clicked over a channel to the one set for BP. "Prickle Pants, you there, over?"

Nothing but static.

"Can I get a status check, over? Got some information pressing I need to share."

Honcho didn't expect the voice that answered on the other radio. The one collecting dust for three years he kept charged and at the ready.

"Hey, Mountain Man. Long time, no see."

The anger within raged a burning fire so bright he had to throw water on it to remain cool.

He picked up the radio and clicked. "Now you decide to let me know you're alive?"

A brief pause.

"I know you know now I'm alive and kicking. Your best friend probably conveyed that to you. We caught word you were seen together, so I'm not going to dwell on my reasons for keeping quiet. I sent a message out hoping he'd get it, but haven't heard back from my source. He get it?"

Honcho didn't know what Liz meant. "What's the message and I'll ask."

Liz was direct. "Your old boss sent word he's upping his game. Some crazy talk about calling in resources from above to find the kids and relieve your friend of his life."

Waiting a minute to let her sweat, Honcho replied. "Thank you for the information. It will be taken under advisement."

"Listen, for what it's worth, I tried to find you. Sent out people for months when it all quieted down. Things went haywire when we left the house and had to go underground to stay alive as it was a horror movie times a million in the beginning. Then, as time passed and I had people to care for, it just got easier to think you were dead. I was wrong."

He let it sink in, the attempt at some type of apology.

"I still miss and love you. Hope you and your friend can do something about this nightmare. If I can help, please let me know."

Honcho finally clicked the mic. "Is that a half-assed apology I hear?"

Liz laughed through the speaker. "As close as you are going to get from me."

Taking her at her word, though trust from three years was long overdue, he decided to throw caution to the storm.

"I've got a plan, but can really use some help."

CHAPTER 53

Ryan wasn't sure he had any faith in what he heard.

When he decided to answer Honcho, and felt his old friend was still on team Ryan and not a new adversary, the brief conversation didn't appease the uneasiness coursing through Ryan's bloodstream.

Honcho kept it short with enough to back it up that on the face, it might work, but in the scheme of the shit show coming ahead, not enough meat on the bones to pull it off.

As Honcho put it, the fight coming had two outcomes. One, Ryan would come out on top somehow given his penchant for out of the box success that drove his storied career. The second, team Ryan failed miserably and the world would implode, though without the children to guide its demise.

Neither seemed appealing given the finer details chalked on the board.

To succeed, Ryan had to go it alone with Reg still in tow, though Liz would assist in recovery and broker the arrangement with Mark. Her people would convene on the airport immediately and blow the shuttle from the sky as it approached. End the threat from above and deal with the repercussions as they unfolded. Get Ryan close enough to barter Reg's life with Mark, and then let the sleight of hand of The Ghost wreak havoc.

The failure part entailed letting the shuttle somehow evade the onslaught of surface to air missiles Liz had acquired and the menace able to land. With Mark pissed at the attempted assassination of his assets, he'd rain hell down on Seattle like a torrential firestorm. At that point, it was either hand Ryan over or fight, and even though the smart move was giving him up, a life of servitude to evil didn't sit well with Liz. It was time to fight back for keeps.

Everyone knew that was a lost cause given the cabal's resources.

Still, if the head was cut off, and who possessed it no one knew, there was a marginal chance to throw chaos to The Order and have a fighting chance to end the insanity once and for all.

Wishful thinking, but faith in winning was a powerful tool.

BP and Julia weren't excited to see Ryan vanish into the woods, and Emma was borderline defiant in trying to tag along until Ryan pulled her aside for a quiet chat. She cried, hit him in the arm, apologized, and hit him again before hugging her dad tight and kissing his bent forehead. Whatever he said resonated with her, and obedience to his words put the young girl back under the watchful eyes of her mom.

"I still don't like it," Julia whispered to BP as they walked back to the bunker.

BP nodded. "Me either. Keeping the kids isolated and safe is our best bet at this juncture with the latest bad news. Ryan knows what he's doing, even if his brain is fighting itself. If he fails, the kids are locked away tight. We have that going for us at least."

The last word barely had left BP's lips before they heard the crack in the air and glanced up to see a bright flash of light and knew it was the shuttle bringing death from above.

So much for a stress-free walk back to David.

CHAPTER 54

He was a mile out, maybe more, when the gunfire erupted.

In the cool air of the Olympic National Forest, sound traveled unencumbered.

The hair on his arms stood up, the skin cold to the touch. Reg grinned behind his gag, and Ryan took the butt of his M4 and slammed it into his father's back.

Hard.

Reg stumbled to a knee, snarled something that was incomprehensible, before getting back up and continuing to walk. Ryan though about putting a bullet into his dad and retracing his steps to confront the bullets. He knew by the time he managed to get there he'd be too late. Reaching for his mic, he clicked once and waited for a response.

Nothing.

Breaking protocol to keep the line free of communication until BP brought the group back to the silo, Ryan hit it again and said a single word.

"Tango."

The code word wasn't obvious to everyone. In radio parlance, or the accepted NATO words utilized to convey the Roman alphabet, it was *T*. For BP, it had meaning.

Tango was a euphemism for an enemy.

Ryan waited for a response. Got nothing, and feared the worst. A quick assessment of options flashed across his eyes. He immediately checked off the ones that wouldn't work. Debated the potentials in lightning speed before throwing away. Focused on the three that spoke to him.

Chose the one that was ridiculous and sure death.

Holding his M4 across his chest, Ryan unscrewed the suppressor. Raising the barrel high, he pulled the trigger and let a three-shot burst fly.

Back to his chest, the suppressor replaced, Ryan clicked the mic again.

"Sierra Tango."

He hoped BP got the message. If not, then the outburst of bullets hopefully caught the attention of what Ryan knew deep down were his own pursuers. Maybe, just maybe, the idiotic gesture worked the magic he planned it to unleash.

It was foolish, sure to fail miserably, and in the larger scheme of the crap storm blowing by, his own death sentence. Not that he cared much anymore. Life was finite, his time on Earth predetermined by the cosmos. Ryan knew in his core that if he didn't go balls to the wall, throw caution to the wind and instead played the tepid game, his expectancy was definitely short-lived. For too long he over-thought his actions, worked all angles to find solutions, and chose the sure percentages for the winning outcome.

Sometimes, he had learned in just the last month, you just go for it.

Go offensive instead of defensive, push your enemies with the absurd to throw them into a tizzy and make them second-guess. Smack them across the face with a soft right and then uppercut with a south paw fist for the count.

If what he figured happened to BP, Julia, and Emma, then they got caught. The bastards Emma mentioned caught up. Laying a trap was the best option to draw them in and get his family and friend back. As he was securing Reg to a tree, the mic chirped.

Unexpected.

"Negate Sierra Tango. Tango Delta."

Ryan breathed in, and held it.

"We're Foxtrot. Stick to Mike, out."

The arm hairs relaxed. "Roger, and out." A momentary smirk washed over Ryan's mouth before retreating into oblivion.

Hearing the code, foreign to anyone but lifelong friends, kept the coronary from killing Ryan on the spot and instead, added a hip to his hop to get back on track. *Sierra Tango* meant sniper trap. If BP could manage, get the enemy to walk into a trap. *Tango Delta* that the threat was eliminated. *Foxtrot*, they were fine. *Mike*, the mission had to go on.

He only wished now he hadn't fired those shots.

CHAPTER 55

"Good Boy."

BP wanted to rip the man's throat out for the sarcastic tone.

Julia held Emma close, a barrier to keep unwanted hands from touching the girl. The first one that tried to snatch Emma away got a surprise knife jab that left a superficial cut. As the soldier reacted and attempted to punch Julia in the face for her transgression, Emma glared, her bright blue eyes radiating a hate that caught the man completely off-guard.

As his head began to hurt from Emma's gaze, he cowardly retreated to safety.

"That damn girl is possessed," the soldier spat to his CO. "Can we kill the man and woman and torture that little shit?"

The CO of the unit shook his head. "Orders are they come along for the ride. Leave the girl and her mother alone."

The soldier, nursing his wound and wrapping it with gauze, spit a loogy in Emma's direction. "Seems too much trouble."

Before the phlegm hit the ground, the soldier grabbed his head, screamed, and as Emma pointed directly at him, fell to the ground.

Dead.

"You were warned, Asshole," the CO shrugged, putting it together.

Motioning to his second in command, the CO pointed at the dead body, and taking the hint, the second nodded and took over. A few words to his team, and the dead man was stripped of his viable gear before being rolled down the side of the path and left for foragers to feast.

The CO walked over to Emma, hunched behind her mother. Hand outstretched, he wiggled his fingers, and Julia slapped the blade on top. Bending down, he forced a smile that looked like he was trying to crap his pants instead of pretend to be nice.

"Little Girl, no one here is going to hurt you. So please, can you not kill any more of my men? I would appreciate it. If you do, I won't hesitate to blow your mom up into tiny bits. Can we agree to be nice to each other?" the CO asked.

Emma pointed to the dead man and winked.

Lips pursed, the CO tapped the handle of his Beretta with his palm.

BP, seeing the soldier contemplate killing the girl for being disrespectful with her sarcastic non-verbal response, diverted attention from her to him. "Dickhead! I did my part. What now?" BP hollered at the top of his lungs.

The CO shrugged. "I'll take you to my boss. He's anxious for a reunion."

BP knew it wasn't going to be a hug and handshake kind of meeting. He was expendable, and was only making the trip back to Mark for his evil pleasure. BP had no value beyond being one of Ryan's best friends, a potential bargaining piece. If Mark was smart, and he knew BP from the old days, torturing BP for intel wouldn't work beyond satisfying Mark's own devilish satiations. BP would never break. Ryan was his brother in more ways besides blood, and Julia and the kids a second family.

The repercussions from Ryan?

Mark should be keenly aware of his old friend's burgeoning wrath.

Rough hands grabbing him by the arms, BP winced from the pain being jerked upright with his hands bound behind. It had been decades since the last time he was in a similar position and a world away. He never figured he'd find it in America, home of the free and land of the brave. Back then, it was Ryan who rescued him from a local supply deal gone bad meant to feed their forward base.

BP had faith he'd see his old friend dragging him to safety again.

When a soldier attempted to manhandle Emma away from Julia, BP wrestled free and stormed forward. Body situated for a tackle without the use of his arms, he put his shoulder low and head up, caught the man just right above the belt to drive him straight into the ground and land with a loud grunt. Julia pulled Emma away, aware of what was about to happen, but thankful for BP's protection.

The beating lasted a minute, probably more.

Rolling to his side, blood oozing from his swelling nose, BP caught their eyes. Even as his body wretched with pain from heads to toe, a flicker of humor flashed as he wagged his tongue and grinned. Mother and daughter couldn't help but laugh.

"What the hell is it?" the CO barked at Julia.

Arms crossed, her brown eyes seething with anger, she flicked a finger. "You made my husband's list for *that*."

Raising his arm up to slap her, the CO hesitated when he felt *it*.

Reaching up to his chest he pressed his hand against his left breast, pulled it away, and saw the blood. Even with his plate carrier on, it was no match for the powerful round that penetrated the ceramic and disintegrated his heart.

Three beats, five beats, and with nothing left of the critical muscle, he slumped to the ground as the last images to burn into his brain was seeing what remained of his men die.

CHAPTER 56

"You some hard people to find."

Julia caught the slight accent. Threw a reflexive arm around Emma.

BP, nursing his wounds from the vicious beatdown, managed to sit up and scoot over to a tree to lean his back against and observe what was suddenly unfolding before him.

The owner of the voice emerged from the shadows, his face coming into view. Pushing fifty, the gray around the ears falling to his collar, BP saw the prominent scar across the cheek, and immediately felt his chest tighten.

"Hola, Señora, and you, my special Señorita," the man greeted as his men descended on the carnage and fanned out, taking defensive positions as one stepped to BP to gauge his injuries.

"Who are you?" Julia sneered.

Catching his initial rude introduction, the man bowed slightly and straightened up. "My apologies. I should have continued myself before all of *this*," he motioned around to his people.

"That would have been polite," Emma stared.

"Yes, you are right, Señorita."

"My name is Emma."

The man laughed, and nodding his head, focused on the girl. "Emma it is."

"Thank you."

Stepping closer to mom and daughter, Julia pushed Emma behind, before the man realized the momma bear was protecting her cub, and he stopped.

Smiling, the man touched his chest. "I am Hector Reynosa Miguel San Carlos."

Julia shrugged.

Seeing her lackadaisical response, San Carlos' head bobbed back and forth as he thought, before something caught his attention and he regrouped. "Ah, you have not heard of me?"

Julia shrugged again.

"I see. Not a worry. That will all become clear soon, very soon."

The man that had been cleaning up BP gave a thumbs up, and retreated behind San Carlos. BP, still seated, licked his lips and motioned with his head to his restraints.

"Sorry, my friend, you are a loose candle."

"Loose cannon," BP corrected.

San Carlos nodded. "Cannon, yes."

BP frowned, rested back against the tree, and crossed his legs. "Might as well get comfy then."

San Carlos shook his head. "No, Amigo, we have somewhere to be."

Waving his hand in a circle, San Carlos' men maneuvered backwards, with two taking post with Emma and Julia to hustle them away. Another gently helped BP to his feet and pointed. BP didn't need the encouragement of a new beating, so he followed the rest.

Glancing around, San Carlos pursed his lips and huffed. "Didn't have to go this way, my old friend. You just needed to step aside." Turning away, he vanished into the trees.

The trek through the forest took an hour. With the occasional stop for Emma to sit and take a break, it was rather boring and uneventful as far as how things seemed to materialize for the three of them lately. No one was tortured, hit, or really even talked to as they made their way. San Carlos' men were vigilant in their actions, keeping eyes and ears perked along the path for potential ambushes or enemy combatants.

The only roadblocks the occasional wildlife that crossed their journey and lingered before moving on.

San Carlos though, he was quite the chatty Kathy. Not that he offered up any information as to who he was or what he planned. He left that alone. Instead, he was inquisitive with an array of questions, mostly focused on Emma. Julia tried to ignore him, but his persistence, and Emma's taking the lead and giving a few answers, though oblique on specifics, seemed to quench his thirst for information. He would nod, shake his head, smile, even frown as the details spewed. He wasn't getting personal, not really.

More interested in Emma and the fact she was such an inspiration with her progress as someone with Down Syndrome.

Back on the trail, Emma walked in the front and San Carlos, taking Julia by the arm, pulled her aside.

"You are probably wondering why I ask so many questions of your daughter. My own daughter was like her, young and beautiful."

Julia saw a single tear roll past the scar on his cheek. Venturing a guess, she asked. "She passed away?"

San Carlos nodded. "Her heart. She had the holes. The doctors tried to save her, but God took my Little Angel."

A mother's intuition took it all together. "Down Syndrome?"

A slight pause.

"Yes."

Staring at the man, not sure what to make of everything, Julia leaned close. "Who are you and why are *you* here?"

San Carlos' face contorted as he tried to grasp the right words. Finding them, he let the letters sink in. "There is more at stake than you can imagine. People dying to control what Emma has inside of her. I'm not one of those, but I am part of a resistance seeking to help people like her, like my precious Maria, find a better life than what was forced upon us by evil men."

Guarded, Julia tried to gingerly gauge the statement. "How do you know about Emma?"

San Carlos sighed. "Honcho is my cousin, a few times removed."

The man wouldn't know who Honcho was or their relationship to him, unless he actually *was* Honcho's cousin. It might be a ploy, all a story contrived and pieced together from some droplet of intel sourced from the shadows. There were only a few ways to cut through it and find the truth.

"I don't recognize the name."

San Carlos caught the sentence, and realized Julia's lack of emotion meant business. "Ah, I understand. Proof of our family bond, right? Something only I would know."

Julia nodded.

Taking it for what it was, San Carlos offered up something Julia couldn't ignore. "There is a picture Honcho has, special to him. I'm sure you have seen it."

Julia was familiar with *lots* of photos Honcho had stashed. Still, she played dumb and shrugged.

San Carlos smiled. "Yes, well this photo has Honcho, Ryan, and a little girl and her brother. Taken at your house on the day you were able to bring them home from the hospital. A special day."

A good guess by anyone.

He continued. "Honcho brought two stuffed animals. Jaguars. They represent where his family, our family, comes from. But, special for the children, rare white spotted cubs that were twins, like Emma and David. Ciela and Guerrero."

That fact was only known by a select few of the inner circle.

San Carlos saw it register in Julia's eyes.

"I am here to help."

Tears formed at the corners of Julia's eyes, but she kept them at bay. Help and assistance from anyone was a moment to question their motives and how in the hell they came out of nowhere to materialize for the cause. Friends were never what they claimed, unless you knew them inside and out, and that still didn't mean shit.

Looking over at San Carlos, Julia pointed to BP. "Prove it."

Catching the attention of one of his men, San Carlos motioned him over, whispered something, and watched the soldier maneuver to BP, who was right behind Emma. A huge knife came out causing Julia to gasp, before it went up behind BP and with a quick lurch, released his bindings.

"A gift of trust," San Carlos smiled.

BP, free of his restraints, immediately turned and made his way back. San Carlos, still smiling, felt his grin fade as BP pulled back and punched the man hard in the nose. It caught San Carlos just right and sent him hurtling backwards to the dirt.

"That's for the last time, Asshole," BP spit out before outstretching his right hand to pull San Carlos up from the ground.

San Carlos took the offer and let BP pull him up.

"Good to see you too, Mi Amigo," San Carlos said as he wrapped BP in a friendly embrace. "Sorry for Nicaragua. My fingers were tied."

BP pushed back and gave San Carlos the eye. "Sure as hell left me high and dry. But, I managed to make my end. Water under the bridge, for now," he winked before hugging San Carlos again. "Good to see you too. Thought you were dead."

Julia, watching the encounter and not sure what to make of it, simply stood still.

"Oh, almost was taken in by mi familia in the other world. But, you cannot keep an old dog dead. More to do to save the world."

"You know him?" Julia dropped, her anger brewing at the hidden friendship.

Seeing she might be slightly pissed beyond belief, BP stepped close. "Hector here, well, he's a distant cousin from the other side of the family."

Julia didn't get it, and BP saw he had to explain.

"Right, you aren't all into our strange lingo. Hector here is ex-special forces for what used to be the Mexican marines. An elite group of commandos off the books who worked with us on occasion. He actually is a real cousin to Honcho, but to me and Ryan by extension, and serving together on some missions, he's family."

She was still fuming, so BP went on.

"Probably wondering why he and I didn't say anything before? Well, the last time I saw old Hector here, there were some issues. And these days, well, you get the idea."

Julia raised her hands up. "You trust him?"

BP nodded. "If he's here, then he's on our side. And the only one who could send him is Honcho. Hector went deep under after the last fiasco, especially if I thought he was dead. Mark wouldn't know a thing. Plus, I'd be the first to kill this guy if I thought otherwise," he grinned to San Carlos.

San Carlos grabbed his stomach and let out a hearty laugh. "Just like the olden times, my old friend."

CHAPTER 57

"Keep moving, Dad."

Reg dragged his feet as if he was three seconds from death. Not figuratively, but was damn sure taking his sweet ass time. Ryan popped him in the back for the hundredth time, a quick blow to convey who was boss and their need to quicken the pace.

It had been hours since the gunshots. Felt like forever. When Julia perked his earpiece, the trepidation that had consumed his body left like a vacuum sucking the emotion out into space. Hearing that San Carlos, better known in their tight-knit crew of ex-soldiers as Hector, was alive and kicking, didn't ease the feelings of dread in Ryan.

In reality, they pushed their way up from his bowels to compete with the rest of the garbage jostling his mind.

Hector was a good guy. Shit, he was Honcho's third cousin on his dad's side. Being blood didn't mean squat. Ryan knew that firsthand. It could be tainted, all dried up or oozing black, the bond shattered and thrust aside for some personal gain or demented demigod you believed was the savior of the planet.

Trust was still earned. Not gleefully retroactive without question to a time or lands so far removed from the storm of Hell brewing like a rancid cocktail of craft beer that would make even the most rock-hard stomach vomit blood.

You still had to prove your worth.

How Hector got all the way up north was the pressing question. Ryan could imagine the possible answers, all vague and lacking specifics, the kind of things that set off your radar wondering what the real answers were if they even existed. Honcho was full of surprises this time around, even getting BP to pack up and join their merry resistance effort. It was possible Honcho had more in the fire than he was willing to share, which was odd for him to keep so close to the vest. Ryan just had to trust one of his oldest friends.

It killed him to lay it all out there.

Reg suddenly stopped in his tracks, pointed with a motion of his head. They had reached the tree line and ahead lay a clearing with some type of structure. Tapping Reg, Ryan looked through his scope and panned the grounds. No movement, no sign that anyone was around. Pushing Reg forward, Ryan stepped back and kept his M4 up, ready to shoot.

"Getting a bit late. We plan on stopping for the night?"

Ryan used the muzzle of his rifle to prod Reg. "Keep moving until I say so."

"Yessir," Reg mocked.

It *was* getting late and they still had a lot of ground to cover. Ryan had hoped to reach the town of Blyn and find a working vehicle at the reservation casino. Fire it up and cruise along until they could get a boat and cross over to Seattle. With miles to go and darkness casting its shadow, hunkering down for the night after the last day's events was a better choice than trudging on.

Against his better judgement, Ryan went with the better choice.

"Over there," Ryan pointed with his barrel.

The house seemed abandoned. The whole property overgrown, the last inhabitants vacating long ago. Ryan approached cautiously, never-knowing if what appeared one way ended up a surprise ass kicking or meet and greet with Death. He preferred a careful and watchful eye, scanning for any disturbance that screamed recent intrusion. An indentation that hadn't washed out from the rain. A broken branch or kicked bottle or can. Even smells that didn't fit.

Be hypersensitive to strange whiffs to keep yourself above ground.

Not seeing anything that set off radar bells in his head, Ryan pushed Reg along and to the front door. The porch hadn't seen footsteps in years based on the collection of dirt blown atop it. Cognizant of leaving evidence, Ryan grabbed a board, threw it down, and had Reg walk the plank to the door. Reaching around, Ryan turned the knob which didn't resist, and using Reg's body as cover, maneuvered them inside.

Musty, with a hint of stale.

No decay of death and no telltale stink of sweat wafted Ryan's nostrils. Confident they were alone, he directed Reg to a chair to sit and then closed the door. A thorough clearing of the place to ensure they were alone, and Ryan sat down on the couch.

"Resting for the night, I take it?"

Ryan nodded.

"Seems homey enough."

Keeping his M4 across his lap at the ready, Ryan leaned back, eyes on his father. It must have made Reg uneasy, as he pivoted in his seat before bouncing from cheek to cheek and then deciding he'd rather turn all the way to the left.

"Problem?"

Reg shook his head. "Nope."

The barrel tapped Reg's right leg.

"Leave me alone."

Ryan found it comical. The sudden emergence of fragility of spirit. Reg had been a spitfire of an asshole, keeping his air of superiority front and center. Seemed all of a sudden, he had lost his vitriol of words to sling at his son.

"Why?" Ryan chuckled. "Don't like being on the other end of someone's ire?"

Reg flipped around, his eyes red as if he'd been crying, but Ryan knew otherwise. The red flowed from rage, the old man's face contorting and making his complexion washing over with various shades of color.

"You're going to die, Son."

Seemed a matter-of-fact statement void of sentiment.

"One day, sure," Ryan smiled. "But, not for a long, long time. I won't leave my babies defenseless against the evil you've wrought upon them. When you and your piece of shit friends are all crispy or feeling lightheaded from a bullet to the brain or my blade, then maybe, just maybe, my work is done."

The words looked like they hit a nerve.

"You still think you can win? You are the most arrogant son of a bitch if you believe little old you, Ryan David Carmichael, a misguided pissant who isn't a million miles close to being the badass he thinks, can defeat us."

Ryan leaned forward, the smile radiating a confidence that threw Reg into a fit.

"You're a dead man!"

Ryan shook his head. "No, not anything or anyone you think can take me on can kill this guy right here," he motioned to himself. "It's not bravado. Not even confidence. I *know* what I can do. Been doing it for a really long time. I get the job done and no one, not you or your little space nuts from above, can defeat me."

The mention of space caught Reg's attention and Ryan saw something register in his dad's eyes.

"Oh, you thought I didn't know about the little green men on the Moon?"

Reg shrugged. "No idea what you're talking about."

"Zulu Team?"

Reg's eyes widened.

Ryan laughed. "Yeah, that's what I thought. Nicknamed *Zombie* because of their penchant to wear war paint like old Viking marauders to scare the bejesus out of their targets. Not exactly the best moniker today given the state of world affairs with all of the other crazed Un-dead lunatics running around."

"How do you know about them?"

Ryan tapped his chest. "Who do you think trained those motherfuckers?"

Reg fidgeted in his seat. A bead of sweat formed, not from heat, but as Ryan surmised, likely his father beginning to see a bigger picture about his oldest son.

The question was more rhetorical and when Reg tried to respond, Ryan hushed him. "Be quiet."

Reg couldn't let it go. "So, you know about Zulu Team. So, what?"

A huge breath in and then out. "When are you going to get it through your tiny, blackened and decaying brain, that I am actually better than you? I'm not trying to kill the planet or force on people a dictatorship with rules that only mean death. I'm the one who is going to save them and get the world back on track. I've been doing it for decades. This is no different."

Reg's head cocked to the side. "No different? You were an errand boy for some power-hungry dictators and you didn't even know it! Did their bidding time and time again. No questions asked. This is beyond your comprehension. The world became a cancer that had to be irradiated. No other way to bring it back from the brink of collapse. We just were smart enough to carry it out."

The rifle butt smacked Reg hard in the chest.

"No, too stupid to do anything right. I'm left to clean up the mess once again."

Laughter filled the room. "You've been out of the real game for a long time. I'm sure the Zombies have some surprises. You'll see."

Ryan shrugged. "Just another day at the office for me."

Reg fumed before finding something to calm him down. "I can't wait to see you die, Son. Really, I can't. Hope it will be me doing it. You at least deserve to die by my hands."

The father got waved off.

"Sorry, you don't get the honor. You will be long dead before me. I can assure you of that."

A wicked smile washed over Reg's lips. "Keep believing the lie."

CHAPTER 58

"Care to explain?"

BP took this one, knowing that if Ryan was around, he'd be asking the hard question. Better he grill Honcho than Julia.

Honcho shrugged. "There's more at stake here than anyone knows."

Julia shot him the evil eye.

Recognizing the cloud wouldn't leave if he didn't offer something up, Honcho pointed at his cousin, three times removed. "Hector here, well, he's been assisting with survivor relocation. Back home his way, it's desolated. The virus did its work right. Up north here, with things so spread out with the forests and mountains, it is a perfect place away from all the crap going on in the big cities. Ryan mentioned his friend John doing the same thing, though we've had no connection with him. When everything went down, I managed to ping Hector through some intermediaries when the network was still jumping."

"So, you knew he was alive?" BP was angry.

Honcho nodded. "Rumors mostly. But, my aunt, the old nun, she had a last contact for him. I managed to get that before channels went dark. He came up about a year ago. Been coordinating ever since."

The information was hard to swallow. Why Honcho kept it hidden, he soon divulged.

"Listen, it's not that I was keeping anything from anyone. We all were focused on right now and the kids. Reg and Mark. Hector wasn't even a thought, until our backs got slammed against the wall."

Julia believed him. With adrenaline on super drive, there were cracks.

BP sighed. "Ryan would have liked to know that tidbit. Might have changed his plans going off all alone."

Honcho gritted his teeth. "Well, I can't argue that. All I can say is, I'm sorry."

A sudden beeping interrupted the mood.

Turning to his monitors, Honcho's normally brown complexion lost a few shades and his face betrayed the fear brewing deep in his belly. "We've got a serious problem."

Pointing to the top monitor, Honcho fiddled with the mouse and focused in on the scene playing out. A parade of armed men flashed for everyone to see.

"It's a shit show for sure."

Julia shook her head. BP nodded, and San Carlos shrugged. It was probably the worst possible predicament to be in.

And, no way out of it.

All of the ruckus on the mountain caught a lot of attention. The people Doris talked to who were coming for Emma. Mark's men.

Plus, Brainers.

Honcho had hoped to avoid the weirdos. Keep them ravaging away along the coastal towns where there wasn't much, but at least some distance since they weren't really the woodsy type to go for a hike or camp. Too complicated for their minds to try and survive off the land deep in the mountains.

Cities were better for their trade and way of life.

With all of the gunshots echoing around, sound caught the wind paths and traveled far enough to catch the watchful ears of those waiting to find some prey. Chuck in Mark's men not returning radio calls and the band of unknowns that Doris belonged to, and a recipe for trouble cooked up a mess.

The closest it seemed were a band of Brainers that hopped in their transports and decided to finally go for a hike in the forest. One of Honcho's remote cameras caught the delinquents leaving the highway and taking an old logging road until they had to dismount.

It wasn't hard to know who they were because of the human skull hood ornaments.

Tucked away in the safety of the silo, Honcho and his band of rag tag miscreants were fine. Buried deep underground and no visible way to know there was even a bunker around, he knew they could ride out the sadistic glory hounds for an eternity.

Ryan's ass was potentially in a pinch.

If the creeps caught wind of his trail, unlikely given his ability to cover tracks and misdirect, he was outnumbered by Honcho's count, fifty to one. It was possible they'd sniff him out since he had Reg in tow and keeping the bastard on point from digging in a heel to leave a fresh print or purposefully trip to break a branch was a constant battle. That scenario would leave Ryan exposed and significantly on the defensive. Keeping Reg quiet and contained while battling a bunch of psychotic killers aching to take some flesh off during a gleeful torture fest? The odds sucked.

For them, at least.

"Tell him," Julia begged.

BP touched her shoulder, but Julia pulled away. Reflexive, she couldn't handle any comfort in the heat of the moment.

Honcho sighed. "What do I tell him? 'Hey, you've got a mass of bad guys loose on the prowl? Sniffing down your back but at least a half day out?' We need to let him focus on what he's got to do in front of him and not what's happening on his six. Distractions aren't going to do him any good. The more we can alleviate the crap he's got to deal with, the better."

She wasn't sure how to take it. "How do we do that?"

Honcho's eyebrow raised, the message about to come, unexpected. "We blow 'em up."

BP spit out his lukewarm day-old coffee. "With what?"

Honcho threw out his arms. "This is an old missile silo. It's got some tricks up its sleeves."

"Decommissioned," Julia pointed out.

The eyebrow raised again. "It was, yes. Interesting how a few modifications here and there over the last three years has changed that."

San Carlos stepped around. "What do you mean, Primo?"

Honcho simply pointed towards the monitors on the wall. "This facility was built to send the big boys down range if Russia ever decided to cross the line. However, it also included in later years surface to air missile bays if any planes decided to fly on through. They're peppered all over and the tunnels get you to the trap doors."

BP was beginning to grasp the concept. "We talking like war crimes bouncing Bettys and old Claymore charges?"

Honcho grinned. "A friend of a friend had some old crates just lying around. We rig some surprises to throw them off the trail."

San Carlos smacked BP on the back. "That's my Primo!"

Julia stayed silent, her eyes brooding behind a darkness Honcho had never seen. Staring straight ahead, arms now crossed, it was ten minutes before she spoke. When she did, the others weren't sure they heard her right.

"No."

Honcho shook his head. "What do you mean, no?"

She slid into a chair and leaned back. "That might expose this place to them. We can't risk it as the safety of the kids come first. Ryan would agree. He's on his own."

BP started to protest before settling back down. "She's right, Honcho. Ryan wouldn't want that. He's got to deal with it. Let him be Ghost and do his shit the way he knows how."

Honcho threw his mug against the wall. "No! We can't just leave him to die. If it was the old Ryan, maybe, I might agree with you. This one is running on four cylinders out of a big block eight. He might have some horsepower, but no way in hell he can pull it off."

Julia got up and put her arms around the bigger than life man. She hugged him tight, and he felt the tears from her cheeks drip through his shirt. Pulling back, Honcho saw the red rimmed sockets and salt flakes on her skin. She nodded, and all he could do was nod back. He knew she and BP were right. A half functioning Ryan was still capable of dealing death like a fire storm from Hell.

It didn't mean he liked it.

"We have to at least do *something*."

Julia's eyes closed and her head lowered. "We do. Less overt and more covert. You said Liz has some surface to air missiles she's going to use for the shuttle. Can some be programmed to GPS a target?"

Honcho's eyes widened and the famous brow danced. "Maybe."

San Carlos poked the bear. "Get on it then, Primo!"

Focused with a deadline to act, the adults went to work. Honcho radioed Liz to see what could happen. It was a hope and a prayer it would work, but if it could, the playing field might soften a bit. Hector and his men, along with BP, set out to gather some supplies they might need that were located on the lower level of the bunker.

Julia left them to work and spend time with her children.

Emma was asleep on the couch, snoring away. The last days taking a toll on her little body. David was curled up with Pete. The boy's eyes half open, fighting his own battle with the Sandman. Taking a seat next to him, Julia rubbed his soft wavy hair.

"Hey, Mom."

"Hey, Son."

David turned to look at her. "I know something's wrong. I can feel it. Emma too."

Sighing, Julia patted his back. "You and your sister are getting too old. Can't hide too much from you anymore."

He produced a pained smile. "Teenagers, right?"

A slight chuckle. "Yup."

Rolling back, Pete now outstretched for a belly rub, David put his head in her lap. "Is Dad going to be, OK?"

Julia really didn't know.

Emma grunted, rolled to her side, and mumbled. Julia thought she'd wake, but the girl rolled back and kept snoring, the rhythmic sound bouncing softly off the concrete walls.

"Your dad is going to be fine. From what I've heard, this is all easy-peasy stuff for him. He's like a rock star super hero, remember?"

David smiled, a real one this time. "He is. Dad's my super hero."

"Your super hero," Julia whispered, as the boy's eyes went heavy and he soon fell asleep.

CHAPTER 59

"D-bags set to ruin the mosh pit."

The words came through the earpiece, waking Ryan from a much-needed slumber.

Wiping his shirt sleeve across his face to clear his eyes, Ryan clicked the mic. "Concert giving out refunds for a cancelled show?"

Honcho answered the question. "Too many attendees that are high as fuck. Hit the exits and go for a bite to eat, ASAP."

Ryan caught the warning, though it was sparse on details. He could guess the outcome. Liz failed to blow the shuttle and more players were joining the game. Reg was still asleep, so he kept the volume low. "Do I need to get my refund now or submit a request online?"

"Bite the loss, Amigo. Just bail."

Hearing that, Ryan knew he was in trouble. When you are friends long enough, it's the words not spoken that scream out.

"You have maybe a six-hour window. Less if the crowd surges towards the stage and catches you in the pit."

Ryan sighed. Catching a break at some point would be nice. Being behind the eight ball constantly was becoming a pain in the ass.

"Appreciate the news flash. What's my ticket loss?"

Some static before a reply. "You're out a hundred."

Shit. "I'll let you know when I'm home."

Sitting back, eyes closed, Ryan weighed his options. Honcho's message was grim. A hundred tangos within a six-hour distance. Not many foot traveling miles and a lot of bodies on the prowl. He did mention to get some food ASAP, so Honcho was throwing a bone to tell Ryan to get to Seattle as fast as possible. That at least meant the threat was behind him and not in front.

A tiny bit of good news.

Opening his lids, Ryan looked over at Reg. He was a liability, a thorn that wouldn't extract and kept digging in deep. If things were getting as bad as Honcho implied, and Ryan had no reason to believe otherwise, keeping Reg along was a distraction that could wind up a really bad mistake. If Reg knew the details, there wasn't any reason to think he wouldn't muck it up. The hatred he had for his son was cavernous and seeing Ryan dead a foregone conclusion the elder father hadn't kept hidden.

Reg relished in telling his flesh and blood he wanted Ryan dead.

With a bottomless pit of challenges staring him in the face, Ryan had to make some tough choices. On his feet, Ryan kicked Reg's boots. "Wake up, Sunshine. We're out of here."

Groggy and tired from all of the hiking, Reg rolled back over. "It's not even daylight."

Ryan kicked harder. "Sun will be here soon. On the road while it's cool and the wild animals are asleep."

Cold eyes staring back, Reg mumbled something unintelligible, before rolling to his butt so Ryan could pull him to his feet. "Fine."

Catching Palo Alto Road, the two men walked in silence. The sounds of early morning felt refreshing and kept them as entertained as much as it could, with the smaller forest animals scurrying across the road as the father and son duo marched along. An hour and a half later, after searching for reliable transportation along the way since cutting across to Blyn over the ridge would take too much time to hike, Ryan found an old pick-up in a barn. Battered from years of working the land, it was sturdy and built like a tank with American steel. Someone had smartly disconnected the battery to keep it from draining, and with a rusty wrench and some wiggling, Ryan got the posts hooked up.

Hopefully, the beast would turn over.

One crank, two cranks, and the engine chirped alive. A gas engine might be full of varnish as gas goes bad, but the old diesel fired up and blew out a stream of black smoke before idling like it had only been down a day. Hitting the junction of Highway 101, Ryan turned right and hit the pedal. They had distance to go and no time to encounter any obstacles.

The drive saw a pissed off Reg staring intently out the window with a gag ensuring it was a peaceful outing. Ryan contemplated letting Reg run his mouth. The serenity was a break from the storm coming and frankly, Ryan didn't relish in father and son chit chat that no longer had any sentiment attached. Three years and change ago, Ryan would have loved the time to spend with his dad. Diagnosed with cancer and time ticking away for Reg, the conversation would have been a great memory to have and for Ryan to share with David one day.

Not today.

The hateful anger inside and disappointment that Reg had forgone sanity and embraced the evil that coursed his bloodstream meant Ryan and his father no longer had a bond. It severed when Reg kidnapped his own grandchildren and used them for experiments. Chuck on top trying to kill Ryan, and Reg was no longer a beloved father or a grandfather.

Just another enemy to kill.

The hour went by faster than Ryan anticipated and smoother than he had hoped. Not a single distraction or signal in his mirrors they were followed or had a pursuit on their six. Reaching a place close to where he had landed the last trip from Seattle before turning the boat away, Ryan pulled into a driveway and followed the path to a house. Turning off the engine, he listened out the open window and hearing nothing, got out. Walking around to Reg, Ryan sidestepped the door as he didn't trust Reg not to ram it open, and pulled the handle.

Reg exited without a struggle.

Prodding his father towards the back of the house, Ryan suddenly stopped. Faint, but enough of a sound to catch a trained ear, he heard the whisper of the rotors.

A drone close by.

Pushing Reg into some bushes, Ryan forced his dad to the ground and then took a knee, panning the sky overhead. Small, yet visible, Ryan saw it flying in from the water. Not a commercial or military model, it was civilian and carrying something with it. Looking through his scope, Ryan focused on the object. Hitting the shoreline and coming about thirty yards in, just inside the tree line overhead, the drone dropped its cargo and then turned and left.

Waiting for it to be long gone and that no one else decided to investigate, Ryan checked his watch, figured it was time, and then with Reg on his feet, collected the goods.

A tiny cylinder about a foot long lay on the dirt. Ryan picked it up, retreated back towards the protection of the house, and popped the top. Pulling out the piece of paper, he read it, smiled, and then set it on fire. The ash disintegrated quickly, leaving no trace of the contents.

The grin felt great.

Reg tried to talk through the gag, but Ryan put his finger to his own chin, letting Reg know to be quiet. The old man obliged the request.

"We have a ride tonight. Time to rest and get ready."

<h1 style="text-align:center">CHAPTER 60</h1>

"Orders, Sir?"

Mark leaned over the table, the map of Seattle splayed out over the edges. He was deep in thought, roiling over something that focused his eyes on a specific point on the paper.

The soldier cleared his throat to get his superior's attention. "Sir? Orders?"

Mark glanced up, his eyes wide. "Orders? I want you to hunt down Ryan and eradicate him from this planet."

Hearing the name brought a sly grin across the soldier's face. "Carmichael?"

Mark nodded.

"Understood, Sir. Won't be an issue."

Stepping to the table, the soldier, the commander of Zulu Team, better known as Zombie Crew by its members and led by a prick of a leader named Zane Williams, focused on the spot Mark had circled in red. Glancing it over, he saw it was the Space Needle.

Mark pointed, his words low and direct. "Carmichael will inevitably go here. He's got a connection with these people and he is in desperate need of help. Good for us, we have people on the inside."

Feeling he had to ask, Williams broached it. "Carmichael was one of us. Trained my team. What has changed since we were last on world?"

The rage in Mark's eyes caused Williams to shrink back, but not leave the table.

"He's gone rogue. Has assets that are ours and we need them back, ASAP. The fate of the world rests on you and your team doing your job."

Williams knew Carmichael from before, knew he was the best of the best. It didn't faze him. Taking out the top dog would be a notch on his belt and bragging rights. Ever since the virus blew through and Zulu had been locked away on the Moon, the team had itched for a fight. With its fingers locked into their being and coursing their blood, what had been an elite group of commandos patriotic for country, had now diverged into a bloodthirsty band of killers with a singular focus.

Kill anyone they could without fear of reprisals.

"What about civilians? Are we confined by mission scope?"

Mark shook his head. "Kill anyone that gets in the way. There is no collateral damage."

Williams grinned. "Yes, Sir. You want a memento?"

The question caught Mark by surprise as he hadn't thought about it. Taking a minute, his head bobbing back and forth, he finally waved his hand. "Sure. Bring the whole head. After he tells you where his kids are located."

"Roger that."

Williams excused himself, leaving Mark standing over the map. He knew Ryan had to come back, there was no way he could manage to evade forever. The walls were closing in and every resource available out in search of him and his beloved children. The net thrown wide with resources watching every corner. The last call with a rogue group of the King's people Mark had made a deal with was promising, until the radio went dead.

That killed the vibe Mark had going believing the end was near.

The call did provide a location and search parameters. When boots on the ground found nothing but bodies, spent casings, and potential directions to Ryan and his brats a mystery, Mark simply decided to choke off both directions of traffic and collapse in the grid. Move in from the coast along the highway in case they were headed that way and go west from Port Angeles to block them and he hoped somewhere Ryan and his kids got trapped.

Like rats.

It all turned upside down when nothing came back definitive. The Ghost evaded capture like always, seemingly giving a finger to Mark with both hands. He was somewhere, it was just a matter of closing the loop. With Zulu brought in and boots physically itching for a fight, the prospects brightened. Ryan trained them, and if the teacher was the master, Zulu would take their lessons and turn them around.

Ryan didn't stand a chance in hell, and the Devil's dogs were coming to bite.

CHAPTER 61

The fate of the world.

In the right hands, what is could soon be what was, a blip on the radar of humanity.

To survive, there was no question there had to be a vaccine. The world was not going to make it without a serum as the virus morphed and strained itself to keep on living and bring about destruction to a sane human race. The shot had to be free for everyone and readily available. Not possessed by zealots bent on world domination being the fundamental dilemma that required a definitive answer.

Who controlled it was the key.

Ryan had mentioned someone in Seattle, a former acquaintance with access to a lab. Mary? Yes, Julia remembered the name. It seemed she might be the solution, *if*, she could even be found.

Ryan had been dead set on his plan. As the expert, it made perfect sense to let him run the show. Keep the kids hidden away and let him broker a deal, barter some kind of agreement, though everyone knew it wouldn't wash. At some point, the world needed help to rise from the ash. Not that having Emma and David part of the equation something Julia wanted or even dreamed being part of to see it all through. If more people had access to their blood, real doctors and researchers seeking to find a cure, there was a legitimate shot at success. Though by all accounts, there didn't seem to be a true end to the virus, if someone, anyone seeking to do the right thing could manage to produce a vaccine for all, then there was a chance the past could become a distant memory.

As the adults sat around the table, the strong tequila making its rounds, the trepidation evident on faces spoke without words.

"Julia, you realize this goes against everything we've been trying to do, right?" Honcho pointed out the obvious.

She nodded.

BP poured another shot and downed it. "It's dangerous for sure."

San Carlos paused mid thought. Started to speak and decided to pour a drink. Savoring the alcohol, he poured a second before he spoke. "Mi amigos, it is dangerous and goes right into the lion's den. They expect us to cower and hide. Not to take the initiative. While Ryan leads them astray, it provides to us an opportunity. If this Mary gets some of Emma and David's blood, quickly, then we can still follow Ryan's plan. Then, people can begin to find the right answer to what the world needs. No?"

Hector made some sense.

They were all fighting to protect the children. Live another day. If they controlled the outcome, allowed the right access to the blood supply to create the vaccine, then there was nothing Reg or Mark would be able to do.

"It could be a one-time event."

Julia wasn't sure she heard the statement. "What?"

BP's head was moving up and down. "One time. Enough of a blood draw and then be done with it. The kids wouldn't need to stick around. While my knowledge of modern medicine is woefully inadequate, and where it stands now totally unknown, my guess is if there's enough juice, we can go back to hiding them away until seeing daylight again."

Honcho smiled. "The bum is right."

BP smacked Honcho on the back. "Appreciate the support!"

Julia sighed. "How do we do this then? There's an army out there."

San Carlos filled their glasses. "They're on Ryan's heels at this moment. That leaves a window to sneak in."

Honcho's eyebrow raised. "Small, but doable. Liz missed the shuttle window and since she can't get the missiles she has left in position in time, it leaves taking out Ryan's pursuers, well, out."

"This feels like a betrayal." Julia was second-guessing herself.

BP offered some comfort. "Ryan has his hands full. He wouldn't have mentioned Mary by chance. My bet is his end game is eradicating the threat first and then with breathing room, get Emma and David to Mary. Three years Mark had the kids and didn't find the right equation. This isn't going away anytime soon. Get Mary started, maybe we get some positive stuff moving forward while Ryan does his thing."

"What if I'm wrong about this?" Julia knew it was possible.

San Carlos raised his glass. "Then my dear friends, we've lost the war."

BP decided to bring up the elephant in the room. "Ryan took the boat and sent it adrift last time, so that's out. Driving leaves us exposed. Time is against us, maybe. How do we plan on getting to Seattle in one piece and under the radar of every creep that's gunning for us?"

Honcho raised his hand. "Hector here has us covered. At least, part of the way. How do you all feel about horses?"

Julia raised her eyebrow. "Horses? The kids have never ridden and it's dangerous."

San Carlos muttered, then his voice provided the solution. "Horses part of the way to get to *my* boat. Nothing fancy, but she is fast and not flashy. Then it's a short ride to where we meet my other men. Caravan from there to the city."

BP had to ask. "How have you managed not to know then that Liz was alive? Seems if you had all *this* going on, someone would have spilled some details."

Honcho nervously sniffed. "I honestly didn't know. The King, or Liz, was not someone you wanted to deal with, so we kept our distance. Moved around her territory. We used the islands up north since they were far from cities and less contact with the crazies. Close to the coast and fish, so it worked out. Keeping a low profile for people trying to survive, ya know?"

BP wasn't sure he bought it all, but he'd never known Honcho to keep that kind of a jewel of a lie from the trio of friends.

Julia offered Honcho a gentle hand. "Look, what matters is right now. We've all had secrets to a degree, meant to protect those we care about or partition off what's relevant, a need to know. Jeez, my dear husband is the king for that! The past is irrelevant. Today and tomorrow, that's what matters the most. If we succeed, and Ryan does too, then we are all doing our tiny part to fix this mess. So, buckle up buttercups and do what matters most. Give people a chance again."

BP held up a hand. "You sure about this? We've been trying to lay low. Seems counterproductive to all that."

Julia smiled, until the tears began to fall. "They're never going to stop. Ryan said so and I believe him. Maybe, if we beat them to it, we end up winning and have the leverage. If they can't have a vaccine held over people's heads, then what *do* they have? I'm scared, terrified, but as this has unfolded and I've watched Ryan changing, there might be a chance we can save him too."

Honcho nodded and BP grimaced. She was right.

Ryan was their friend, a brother who no matter what, would die for any of them, twice over. Lost in it all was his greater sacrifice, the one unspoken, but hanging like a mushroom cloud on a windless day. Knowing their compadre, his mission was likely the last one to buy them time to go underground and get lost in the shuffle. The bigger play.

Die, for them all to live.

No one had really grasped the thought. Blinked, though it stared them in the face. The lone wolf he was, even on his worst day, was never one to call in his own chip. They never contemplated Ryan leaving with Reg as a one-way mission. It never crossed anyone's mind. They all figured it was Ryan being Ryan, the master operator and tactician, five steps ahead of his enemy.

Stepping back, the broader picture revealing its plethora of color, was dark and hazy.

"You really don't think he would, do you?" Julia asked.

Honcho sighed softly, his large frame rising and falling slowly with each breath. Glancing at BP, who looked at San Carlos, the room suddenly felt cold.

"I think Ryan will do whatever Ryan thinks will protect you and those rotten kids. Us? He could care less," Honcho gingerly smiled, trying to lessen the weight of the room.

BP agreed. "Sacrifice for the greater good."

Weeping at the words, Julia brushed her cheeks dry, and smiled. "Then, let's beat him to it so he doesn't have to leave us all."

Honcho paused, lost in thought. Staring at the wall, his fingers gesticulating with a quickness, he pushed his chair back and went to the far side of the room. Grabbing his tablet, he walked back, tapped and slid his finger, before an image came into view. Pressing a button on the screen, it emerged on one of the monitors behind BP.

"What is it?" Julia asked, not sure what he was pointing out.

Honcho blew out before answering her. "The airport is the only way in or out if you are looking at distance travel. Mark and his people came that way. The critters from outer space had to use it too to land. Control the field, control the game."

Julia didn't quite get it right away, but BP jumped in. San Carlos nodded frantically, and patted his cousin on the back.

"Primo! We all knew you had the brain in the familia. I can get men there to try and take it. I'll make a call."

Honcho grabbed San Carlos' arm. "Wait. I need to talk to Liz. My guess is she has people there too. Your men go unannounced, and it will be a gun fight among friends. Defeats the purpose."

San Carlos poked Honcho. "Good point. You call, I'll call, and we all will do what needs to be done."

CHAPTER 62

"Sit rep, Jones. Over."

It wasn't a question, but an order.

An immediate response, which was gratifying given the previous days' shit show. "Nothing yet, Sir. All eyes are on the area. No way he can get in or out without us knowing it. Over."

Mark didn't like the news as he expected immediate results. With time to kill, Mark decided to poke the bear. "Get my SUV and the raiders ready."

Mark was well aware of the territory King controlled. It stretched east to Issaquah and straight up north to Everett, and as far south as Tacoma. While there were additional pockets under King's protection as part of a larger conglomerate of loosely united communities, Olympia, Aberdeen, Duvall, Stillwater, and Carnation, the Brainer territories roamed free, just on the outskirts, biding their time to strike.

Mark wanted to incentivize some chaos.

He still found the term *Brainer* an interesting concept. Ryan used it in passing when they last met, almost casual, a term he must have come up with from his interactions. Mark could only believe it tied into the fact they still had some brain capacity working over the rest of the crazies. It didn't really matter what they were called, a label to define was all it was to Mark. Though he did find a sense of comedy in the description, and had used it ever since.

Over the years, fragile agreements with Brainers served a higher purpose as Mark pursued answers to his virus questions. *Work for me and do as I ask without question, and I'll provide weapons and essentials for you to do as you please. Cross me, and I will annihilate every one of your tribe.*

Tribe was the best description of the intimate band of nutjobs as Brainer groups didn't get along with other Brainers. They were competition for resources and sporting fun. The tribe mentality ruled the collective, though power struggles saw entire entities wiped out over petty disagreements. Their separate and strict delineation of loyalties suited Mark's purposes.

Play one group against another and reap the rewards.

As the days stretched to years, a metamorphosis materialized that was unexpected, yet fit with the parameters of evolution. Where they were once solely focused bloodthirsty primitives who rampaged the wastelands in search of people to kill for sport, a slow yet noticeable trait emerged.

Brainers developed personalities and learned to get along with others.

It came about at a snail's pace, yet with time, Brainers went from savages to regular folk sitting around a campfire roasting marshmallows and telling stories. Laughing, joking, even crying.

It was a researcher's gold mine to witness.

They were still cold-blooded killers. That never left their DNA. The change allowed for a more subtle relationship, still fraught with the occasional outburst that required a whole group to get burned to a crisp. On the whole, Mark could engage, converse, even begin to feel a bit of jealousy at their ability to create communities and live.

His feelings only lasted a moment before moving on.

Brainers still loathed anyone not of their kind. Especially survivors. Those not turned into one of the Un-dead factions or who failed to transform into a Brainer were the enemy. People who thought they were better and deserved to live over anyone else.

Their newly emerging personas could be used to an advantage. Throwing as much as practical to stick against the wall that might work, Mark wasn't above a bit of bartering for a desired result.

Finding a Brainer encampment wasn't difficult. They still cherished their traditions, though a bit less grandeur than before. Decapitated heads and rotting corpses were visible landmarks of a Brainer border, though the modern version of the psychotics dressed them up for wicked humor.

A funny bone only they understood.

Spotters on a previous pass through spied a large community near Seahurst Park, south of West Seattle. Known as No Man's Land, anyone with half a brain avoided it like the plague. Close to the water to provide fishing for the inhabitants, it also gave Brainers seafaring access for raids along the western outskirts of the King's territories. From the airport it was a short ride, less than ten miles and a good hour to navigate road debris and hazards. Warring factions at every turn?

Could take days.

Deciding to take a direct route, the caravan followed Glendale Way S to connect with Ambaum Blvd SW. The goal being get close and find a blockade to stop and request a meeting with the Brainer's leader.

Mark was surprised at the lack of obstacles encountered.

While the road obstacles diverted the SUV and Humvees around old cars and refrigerators, not a single Brainer obstructed their travel. An occasional sentry appeared, waved with what could only be categorized as a friendly smile, and pointed down the road. Turning right onto SW 144th Street, the muffled vibrations caught Mark's attention. Rolling down the window of his SUV he put his ear out, listened, and for the first time, a smile washed across his face.

"No shit."

The driver, caught off-guard, suddenly stopped the vehicle. "Sir?"

Mark glanced over, and pointed out the window. "Listen."

The driver confused, rolled his own window down. As the vibrations turned to sound carried by the wind, the perplexed look turned to curiosity as he put the SUV in park. "Is that what I think it is?"

A chuckle responded. "Seattle's finest are throwing a concert."

"Orders, Sir?"

Mark gestured out the window. "Follow the music."

The SUV crept along as one of the Humvees took lead. Heading through a neighborhood, the homes ransacked with their former contents littering the front yards, they reached a makeshift gate, complete with the required human skulls. Half a dozen guards appeared, smiles flashing, but their fingers wagging next to the triggers of their rifles. Barking in his radio, the lead Humvee stopped. Tapping his driver, Mark, said, "Stop."

Opening the door, Mark hopped out, a bounce in his step. He felt light, energetic for the first time in ages. Reaching the Humvee, he tapped the passenger door as it began to open and directed the soldiers to remain. Keeping pace, he stopped a dozen yards from the gate and waved.

"Good day, gentlemen! My name is Mark Simpson and I wish to speak with your glorious leader. I have something I'd like to discuss to our mutual benefit."

A burly man stepped forward. Standing close to six-six with visible sleeve tattoos peeking out from beneath the rolled-up cuffs of his red plaid shirt. His graying ponytail whipped in the breeze, landing on his shoulder with the intricate braiding ending in a kid's pink bow. The beard completed the ensemble with a twist and hair tie.

Taking in the massive size of the man, there was something familiar about him that Mark couldn't quite place. Then, it hit. "Excuse me, you know, you look a lot like-" before getting cut off.

"Not me. Get confused a lot. He's at the stage getting ready to play."

Mark could see that happening as the resemblance was uncanny.

"As for speaking to *him*," referring to the Brainer's leader, the burly man sighed, and waved Mark over.

Mark didn't move.

Seeing the response, the burly man grinned. "So, he's onstage playing now. When he wraps up, I'm sure he'd like a chat with you. Been expecting a visit given all the commotion going on around here."

"Appreciate the assistance. What now?"

The burly man motioned behind. "Drive on through and watch the show. Someone will get you when he's ready to talk."

Mark waved a thank you and headed back to his SUV. Grabbing the radio, he had a brief discussion with the raider team leader and soon the vehicles were on their way.

"Are you sure, Sir? These guys are bad news."

Mark simply raised a finger up. "Drones overhead that you can't miss on a low circle. Anything happens to us and this whole place goes kaboom."

The driver shook his head.

"Relax," Mark offered. "Seems the evolution of these lunatics is raging on. They're having an old-fashioned grunge fest. What's not to love about that?"

CHAPTER 63

If his own eyes weren't witnessing the scene, Mark would have thought he was hallucinating on some really wonderful 90s drug.

Maybe the proliferation of marijuana smoke cascading the air added to it.

Directed to a spot behind the crowd of patrons that looked like throwbacks to the era of grunge and metal from the old days, Mark had his driver park and got out. Working his way through the crowd to a place center of the stage, he passed side eyes wondering who the intruder in their midst was, until smiles and raised thumbs warmed to his presence.

The friendliness was surreal.

Brainers weren't known for letting anyone not part of their clan into the mix. They definitely didn't welcome strangers with warm greetings. A bullet or slash of a blade to remove a head was more in line with their MO. As he passed the sea of spectators, the wafting of weed through his nostrils, Mark couldn't help but wonder what brought on the emergence of what was transpiring before him. The evolution of the virus maybe, but adding a human element back to Brainers that seemed to have been eradicated at the onset when they turned from normal people into sadistic killing machines. Old Brainers had no regard for anything but their bloodlust. This was a phenom worth investigation. Reaching his destination, politely declining the joints offered, Mark panned the stage, felt his body nearly wretch, and stood frozen.

The stage was a who's who of famous grunge rock musicians.

Seattle and Washington were the epicenter of the grunge movement, spawned by local bands that bucked the system and played for the love of the music. Appearing more like homeless teens and young adults by the holey jeans and flannel shirts they seemed to love, grunge music took the world by storm. Starting in the late 80s and through the growth of the 90s, its expanse burst onto the scene, with most of the great bands being homegrown

Seattleites or transplants who migrated to the great city.

The planet would never be the same.

Staring from left to right, Mark saw the remnants of what were the biggest bands to emerge from the area. Platinum artists who sold millions and before the fall of society, still ruled the airwaves. Throw in the godfathers and godmothers who didn't stick it out or find their golden goose, these same musicians who's hits still rang true to millions decades later, were lining the stage and swaying to the beat.

Mark could not believe it.

Guitar amps crackled riffs and melodies. Bass guitars hit the lows, pounding vibrations that shook the ground. Drum skins resonated, cymbals clashed, and the beat vibrated his body. Focusing on one particular sound, a signature of one famous musician's catalog of hits, Mark thought his eyes were playing tricks on him. The distinctive beard and long brown hair, head bouncing up and down to the rhythm, Mark caught the eyes, the whole time never wavering from the gaze he felt penetrating his body.

There was no way the guy was still alive.

Watching and listening, Mark kept still, his emotions, or lack of them, never revealing themselves. He just stood, the eyes from behind the drum kit never leaving their focused stare aimed directly at Mark.

Anyone else seemingly throwing that much shade would find a bullet from Mark's sidearm blowing their brains out the back of their head.

Not this time.

Fifteen minutes of hard pounding grunge later, and the crowd erupted with applause. The drummer stepped forward to a mic and leaning in with his tall, slender frame, waved to the crowd and yelled, "Rock on!" Stepping back, someone else spoke into the microphone to let the crowd know there would be a short break. The crowd began to retreat towards what looked like food booths or beer taps, Mark couldn't quite make it out, before finding himself one of the few stragglers left behind. Before he knew it, he found himself face to face with one of rock's most famous grins.

"Enjoy the show?"

Mark nodded.

"Awesome, Man. Want a beer?"

Another nod.

"Great. Come with me."

Mark obliged, in awe, which felt unnervingly weird and out of place for someone used to being cold and full of hate. Walking beside the man, Mark wasn't sure what to expect, though he soon found out.

Handing Mark a beer after they reached their destination, Dennis Stohl downed his before getting a second, this time to sip as he pointed to some lawn chairs off to the side. Taking a seat, he offered Mark the second one and Mark sat down, feeling completely out of place and not in control for the first time.

"We don't get many visitors around these parts, you know what I mean? You caught us on concert night throwing a major rager. Usually, anyone wanders in by mistake or intentionally trying to take us out meets a bad end. Which are you?"

Mark took a sip, and turned. "The third kind."

"Third?"

"That's right. You mention two types that come around. Sometimes, you need to check before handing out your sense of fun."

Dennis let the words ramble around before he grinned. "Good point."

Mark tipped his beer. "Thanks."

"So, you have something to discuss I heard. What's the offer?" Dennis asked between mouthfuls of Washington's own take on an IPA.

Mark nervously coughed, before the virus took control and the Mark of old came racing back. "I have a problem that I need taken care of. A man who is a thorn in my side and needs to die this time."

Dennis took a sip, let it wash over his tastebuds, before replying back. "By the look on your face, this guy must have been a friend way back when. What'd he do to you?"

Mark managed a forced smile. "He's caused me more headaches than a drunken night out downtown after a concert at the Show."

Dennis grinned. "You been there?"

Mark nodded. "Came to see you guys play. I believe your first gig there."

A sigh. "I remember that night. Got to sign the back wall for the first time of many we played that place. Busted the skin on my snare at the end of the show. Good times for sure."

For the first time, Mark had a twinge of the old days percolate from the depths of his bowels. He wouldn't say it was *feelings* crashing through his hardened exterior. More an acknowledgement that at one time, he was part of the old normal scene and there were actually some good times.

Then, he shook it off.

Dennis leaned forward, elbows on his knees. "So, what's your *offer*? Better be good as I don't like my time wasted. Doesn't end well."

Mark nodded an acknowledgement, took a swig, and reclined all the way. "I assume you all still like to play with your toys?"

Dennis' eyes widened. "I'm listening."

Mark closed his eyes. "What if I assisted you to remove your biggest headache? No more of your people's heads adorning their walls as warnings to stay away?"

A long sip, the focus intense. "Interesting, but kind of busy here."

Mark's eyes opened, and he turned to face the Brainer. Searching the man's face for a hint, he saw it, and threw the bone. "I figured you would want to rule Seattle again and all the outlying areas. I have enough weapons and supplies for you to play for eternity."

Dennis took a drag on the bottle, playfully swished it around, and swallowed hard. "Solid proposition. I could always just kill you and take what I want."

Mark smiled and pointed up. "That's what I like, even with your metamorphosis back into partial humans, the love to kill is still there."

Dennis glanced up, saw the first drone circling overhead. Soon, five drones dropped altitude and did an elliptical around the Brainer encampment. "Just an observation. I like people of a similar mindset."

Mark reached over and clinked Dennis' bottle. "Same here. You scratch my problem away, and you no longer have any. Sound like a deal?"

Dennis' toothy grin said it all. "Let's party!"

CHAPTER 64

Horses.

The new luxury ride for the apocalypse.

The observation was sarcastic. While horseback was the quieter, and more maneuverable mode of transportation around the relics of the past that blocked the roads along their journey, the saddle-sore rear ends for those with delicate skin left a lasting impression.

Once they made the highway and took to a decent pace, the trip took less time than anyone anticipated. No impediments, no resistance encountered, it was sightseeing with all of the smells of nature you would expect. Fresh water caught on the breeze, the savory pine of so many varieties not found back home. Even the occasional wafting of a fire warming someone far off in the distance carried aromas to their nostrils.

Surreal with a hint of reality.

Julia managed Emma on her mount while BP took David astride his horse. Honcho had gear on his back and a radio to manipulate, which required a focus and no distractions from a boy on his first pony adventure. BP got peppered with a barrage of questions he vainly attempted to answer. Honcho was the better source as a Washington encyclopedia of information to provide details and explanations of the flora and fauna witnessed, so between clicks and quick discussions, he slowed his gait and offered up a tour of the area.

An occasional jaunt through the trees on a shortcut to a different road or path, San Carlos led the bunch until reaching their destination. "We're here, friends," he barked over his shoulder.

Coming up behind through the trees, Julia saw a beach and a boat, or at least, what was supposed to be one, washed ashore. Staring at San Carlos and shrugging, he laughed before pointing further out to sea. She squinted her eyes to block out the glare of the setting sun on the water, and caught sight of the craft.

It defied expectations.

"Seriously?" Julia muttered.

San Carlos wasn't joking when he said he had a fast ship. The old Coast Guard cutter, its former colorful markings painted over to appear subdued for better camouflage on the ocean, gingerly made its way towards the group. Reaching just offshore no more than a hundred yards, a boat appeared from behind it, a Marlin-type with a rubberized hull.

Two more appeared.

San Carlos held up his hand for everyone to stop, before yelling, "Take cover!"

Yanking the reins to the right, Julia headed towards the tree line. BP followed. From behind, they all heard the gunfire, a roar like nothing anyone had experienced in their lives. Covering her ears, Emma began to hum quietly to herself. Looking over her shoulder, Julia saw BP wince in pain, and realized he took a bullet. Slumping forward, he caught himself before potentially knocking David off. Glancing at Julia he motioned, and she immediately knew. Pulling to a stop, she turned as he stopped beside.

"You've got to keep going," BP coughed.

Fear shone through her eyes. "What are you going to do?"

BP tapped David. "He's a good rider and can manage if he holds tight. I'll hold the six here for you guys as long as I can. There's a town down the way according to Honcho. Don't know if it's safe, but at least you might be able to hide. We'll come find you when we can."

Julia dipped her head. "You sure you can't come?"

BP winked. "I'll hold you up right now. The pain is excruciating, even with the vest on. Hard to breathe, so best I catch my wind and do some damage for you to get away."

"Find us, please."

"You know it." Then, BP dismounted and handed the reins to David.

"I've got this, Uncle BP." David reached out his hand and pulled BP close for a hug.

"I know you do, David. Big man in charge, right?"

David nodded, "Right."

Slapping the horse, BP gave David a quick salute, and soon disappeared.

Catching David's gaze, Julia leaned forward to whisper in Emma's ear, before giving a swift heel in the stirrups, then her horse galloped away with David right behind. Weaving back and forth in the trees to avoid branches, the trio moved as a unit, much to Julia's surprise. She figured his first time on a horse would encumber David.

It didn't.

He seemed a natural born rider, easily keeping close while staying in the saddle as the beast stayed right behind the other. Gliding almost, David felt focused and determined as the sounds dissipated in the distance. Watching his mom closely to ensure he didn't miss a turn in the thickening woods, he suddenly yanked the reins and skidded to a stop.

Julia did the same.

Two dozen men, clad in an assortment of mis-matched clothing, betrayed their true identity. Julia reached behind and motioned her son closer, more for comfort than any protection it might offer. Panning the faces, Julia saw hate, anger, coupled with what could only be described as comical amusement, all in one. Even a morbid sense of humor as a few had on skinned pelts with glasses staring back. She wondered where the funny bone was coming from, then realized some of the stories Ryan told about his experiences with the infected framed a new image of what people were evolving into, including her own husband.

She hated with every ounce of her being the assholes who brought this scourge on humanity.

A man stepped forward, his brown shaggy beard adorned with colorful bows. His eyes, from what Julia could tell, were a light hazel, though they reflected a seething lust for a kill. She pulled her pistol from her hip, and aimed it at his head. She knew the children had a value beyond anything imaginable and wouldn't be harmed. She though had little value, and taking out as many as she could before they descended like rabid dogs to whisk the kids away a battle worth fighting for in her mind. The man simply grinned and raised his hands.

The rifles aimed in their direction meant the Carmichael's ride had ended.

CHAPTER 65

Ryan's heart nearly exploded.

Honcho had managed to radio a warning to Liz about the growing threats from all directions and the plans concocted counter to Ryan's. Bringing the children to Mary and San Carlos' men making an attempt to take back the airport.

Then, radio silence.

Liz met Ryan at the edge of the water with the news. "I am so sorry, Ryan. I have no idea where the kids are now."

His legs nearly collapsing from the weight of the news, he kept his cool and simply nodded. He could scream out, cry like a child, decide to completely tune it out like he hadn't heard a word. Or, solidify his focus and determination to wreak havoc like no one had ever witnessed.

The new Ryan turned off his emotions and kicked them to the curb.

Reg didn't hear the conversation, but must have felt a change in the air. His grimace at his predicament turned to the biggest grin you could paint on a human face from ear to ear. He managed a short jig dance before someone grabbed his bound hands and yanked him to a waiting truck.

"Thanks, Liz. Look, I can't predict the outcome of this and I'll be honest. As a collective, they have the firepower and men to make this a last stand. I can't see subjugation to evil and what they have in store for everyone a great future. All I can offer if you help is that it will end, one way or another."

Liz took Ryan's hand. "Long before you showed up, things were plugging along just fine. We all banded together when it all went south to protect ourselves from what's out there, knowing it was just a matter of time before the end would come knocking on our door. Now, shit has hit the fan. No one here wants a future where we are under the rule of some assholes who tell us what to do or preys on us. If it's a last stand, then, well, let's make it a good one."

Ryan smiled. He never liked to ask for help. Call it the pride racing in his blood at being capable all by himself to save the world. This time there wasn't an option to go it all alone. He had to have support, even if it meant the truth wasn't as black and white as what was thrown on the table for all to see.

"We'll make it one for the history books the kids can read. Promise."

"Great."

Taking a few more steps up the embankment to reach the path, Ryan sighed. He wasn't sure all what Honcho divulged as part of the group's betrayal to Ryan's plan, so he had to tread on eggshells. "Honcho say anything else?"

The color washed from Liz's face. "He also said the worst of the worst was coming since we missed the opportunity to blow that shuttle. Couldn't get positioned in time. What the hell was on that thing?"

The black and white answer was deserved. The gray area the path for the present.

"Mark has his own band of assassins he's called in from above. Long story there, but they're a bunch of old friends. They won't stop until they get what they want."

Liz stood, her face searching his for more. When she didn't find it, she blurted it out. "The only way they can leave is the airport. I can blow the runway."

The solution was practical. If, it worked. Mark would suspect any attack and plan ahead. Likely had a contingency in place long ago as a just in case. He'd see it coming from a mile away with the drones now lurking overhead. San Carlos attempting to take it was a bad move too. Something else, a diversion he wouldn't dream could possibly happen, was the key.

"As much as I'd go for that to hinder Mark and his goons, he's a tactician. He's thought about that and can counter it. We need a different approach and I think I know what to do."

Ryan stared off, deep in thought as he rummaged around in his brain for a file locked away in the basement of his mind. A minute, three passed, and Liz's impatience got to her.

"So, plan on telling me?"

Ryan's devilish grin was scary. "I'm going to call his bluff."

Liz choked, proceeded by a coughing fit. "What?"

"He probably believes I'm here begging for help. Thinks I have nothing to bargain. He's dead wrong."

She searched Ryan's green eyes, their former dull appearance awash in a brilliance Liz hadn't seen in another person in a very long time. As she gazed into them, a smile began to emerge, and she nodded. "Are you thinking what I think you're thinking?"

A nuclear bomb wouldn't remove the look on his face with the upturned corners of his mouth throwing out an excitement brewing below. "Damn straight. Mark brought the thunder, we have the boogeymen to rain on the parade."

Liz wrapped an arm around Ryan's and led him to a waiting truck. "I can't wait to hear the details."

Reaching the truck, Liz's right hand man ran over from behind and handed her a radio. Walking away for privacy, Ryan saw her face contort and frantically shake her head before whispering into the mic. She then chucked it back to her second in command before heading back.

"Something wrong?" Ryan asked, but knew the answer.

The pallor returned, this time with fear etched into her eyes. "Company's coming. A whole lot of company sooner than expected."

The intel wasn't that much of a surprise.

"How much time we talking?"

The sigh that escaped Liz didn't require an answer.

Ryan grimaced. "That soon, huh?"

"Yup."

Ryan touched her arm. "Which direction?"

Liz threw up her hands. "From the south up I5. We can stall a bit there. Others are coming south along the water. That chokes us up on two sides to defend."

The plan had to go now.

"Can we get them to come out and play this time of day?"

Liz shrugged. "We wake them without being prepared, it'll be a storm we might not be able to control."

It was a risk they had no choice but to take.

"Sound the alarm, quietly if you can. Get everyone to hunker down who isn't carrying a gun or have a purpose. Get the horde rockin' and let 'em loose. The rest of us will wing it the best we can."

Liz didn't know whether to laugh or smack Ryan at the bad joke.

"Company has come by water before. We have some tricks we can play there. Spotter says drones are inbound. Not sure what we can do about them."

Ryan let a breath out and inhaled quick. "Take my dad and secure him away. I need to get to a high point. See if I can take out some of the drones."

Liz pointed to an old beat up 4x4 with a young girl sitting in the driver's seat. "She'll take you wherever you need to get."

It felt like the last time he was going to see Liz, and not wanting to be sentimental or show what he thought, he didn't want to do it. He did anyway. Wrapping her in a hug, he gripped tight. "Honcho still loves you. You live through this, talk to him, for me, OK?"

Liz looked up, tears streaming down. "We *both* live, I promise."

Letting go, Ryan ran to the 4x4 and in seconds, was gone.

CHAPTER 66

Julia wanted to rip his eyes out for the smirk on his ugly face.

As the helicopter touched down and they were ushered off, her rage boiled over. Mark stood stoically, as if he was emperor and the world his to conquer.

The capture by the Brainers and transport to their base of operations to wait for the chopper to whisk them to Mark was a harrowing ordeal. Hours turned to the next day, waiting with thrill killers licking their lips, lusting to take just a small snip of her and being kept at bay by their leader didn't wash over well for the losers. Their conversations were violent and lewd, not the kind of words or images young children needed to hear. Julia fought back, in the only way she could, by singing songs to Emma and David to drown out the noise.

On the airport tarmac and heading into the clutches of a madman, Julia held Emma and David's hands tight, hoping for a miracle that wasn't going to come.

The ridiculous wave of Mark's hand set David off.

"You smelly butthead!" David yelled as he broke free of the grasp of the soldier's grip who was manhandling him and ran straight at Mark.

Still grinning from ear to ear, Mark reached out to stop the boy before finding himself rocked by a swift kick to the nut sack. The blow was harsh and found the target as Mark grabbed his crotch and doubled over. The soldiers stood by silently frozen, unsure what to do at the sudden display of anger coming from an eight-year-old. They came to when David began pummeling Mark with vicious blows that seemed to have the strength of an adult man as Mark winced and bellowed in pain at the onslaught.

"Get him!" Mark's second ordered.

David kept at it, before finding his right arm grasped tightly as he attempted to wrench himself free of his captor. Yanking away, David pivoted and threw a left into the shin of the soldier, which shattered under the weight of the blow. The man fell to the ground as his busted leg went the other direction. Realizing there was more to the boy than expected, a taser materialized and two prongs hit the boy in the middle of the back, sending voltage through his body that made him convulse, and in an instant, curl into a ball and foam at the mouth.

"Stop it!" Julia screamed as she too broke free and ran to her son.

Emma stood still, her focus aimed at Mark, still writhing on the tarmac.

Reaching David, Julia yanked out the probes and threw them aside. Pulling him into her arms she cradled her son, rocking back and forth as she wiped away the froth from his lips.

"What have you done?" she yelled.

Mark finally gathered himself up and rose to his feet. Pulling his pistol from its holster, he fired a single shot that hit the bullseye.

"You bastard!" Julia cried out.

Walking over to the body, Mark pumped two more into the chest. "This is what happens when you jump the gun."

A murmur floated among the group of soldiers before two moved around the mass of people and grabbing the arms, drug the body away.

Looking at Julia, Mark bent down, careful to keep his distance. "Problem dealt with. Can we move inside now, please?"

Emma's gaze began to make Mark uncomfortable. He *felt* an uneasiness, not sure where it came from, and searching her face and seeing the intent icy blue stare of her eyes, immediately turned away.

"Let's go."

Julia picked up the boy, still reeling from the taser, and carried him inside the hangar. Finding a cot, she gingerly placed him down and looking around, found a bottle of water. Using her shirt, she poured water on it and carefully wiped David's face. Unaccompanied and following on her own, Emma's eyes never left Mark. She suddenly stopped, and simply fixated on the man.

Taking a seat across from Julia and David, Mark pointed towards Emma. "Direct *her* to sit, please."

Julia, her attention on David's injuries like tunnel vision, suddenly realized Emma had not made it into the building. Nodding, Julia ran over to her daughter and led her to the chair.

Emma's eyes kept their focus.

The unease continued. "Get her to stop that or I'll pluck her eyes out."

Emma shook her head. "Try it."

The boldness the little girl exhibited was extraordinary. Mark liked her gumption, her sense of strength in the face of danger. Under different circumstances he'd appreciate her tactic.

Smiling, Mark held up his hand. "Let's get one thing perfectly straight and understood. No one will harm you, unless I say so. Behave, and things will be fine. Do anything like your brother did there or piss me off, and I *will* hurt you."

Emma held up her right index finger. "Make me mad, and *I'll* hurt you."

She was quite the firecracker of positive energy. Tired of the game, Mark motioned behind her, and Emma felt a hand grip her shoulder and squeeze. The pain hurt, but she didn't yell out. The grip tightened, an ache rising to the top, and nothing.

She simply smiled.

The direct display of disobedience hit a nerve. The soldier's hand dug in, each finger pushing into her flesh. Emma felt the muscle tissue separating beneath the violence. Turning her head, she caught his eyes.

Then, she giggled.

The wrath erupted, and there was no way to stop it. The virus' hold on the soldier, erasing his humanity and every ounce of positive emotions, lashed out with a vengeance. There was no way a child, one who wasn't even in his mind a whole kid because of her visible disabilities, was going to mock him. She'd pay the price, and suffer the consequences.

It didn't last long.

His grip tightened to the point where she should have screamed out in pain. Relentless as it dug into her flesh and pushed the muscles tissue deep into her body. He found himself high on adrenaline and hate, the mixture fueling a burgeoning rage that was about to break a little girl's shoulder and twist the damn thing off.

Emma kept giggling.

Feeling the snot in his nose, the soldier sniffed to hold it back. Failing miserably, he felt the first drop hit his right hand.

Then, another.

Seeing the bright red liquid, he paused. Wondered where it came from, before realizing the blood was his own. Confused, his grip loosened and his hand pulled back to a few inches in front of his face. Scrutinizing the fluid, he felt more find its way out. Solitary drips turned to consistent drops. Drops turned into a gushing stream, as if the vein had been severed and a river of blood let loose. Stepping away, the torrent erupted. Emma watched, still giggling as she took her right hand and simply raised her thumb.

Her childlike expression of a huge *screw you*.

Mark watched it all unfold. Mesmerized by what he was witnessing, fascinated by the sheer euphoria he felt seeing it all transgress. It wasn't some trick playing out. Magic didn't exist. The only explanation, a rational one, was his whole life's work crammed into this moment.

Science.

There was no other logical answer. The transformation of the Un-dead, the crazies finding joy in throwing a concert, of all things. Their massing into groups to party and have fun. It was evolution of the species, of the effect and hold the virus had on the human body for those it gripped tight under its autocratic hold.

Brainers.

Ryan had something there in creating the name. The brain was an intricate computer, capable of vast computations and memory storage. Only around ten percent of the mind, the gray spongy matter floating around inside of the bone shell helmet, was utilized. So, the old myth went. Some were able to tap into more to elevate their game to the next level. Twins had their own connection, an ability to speak with no words, to almost read each other's minds and communicate. Emma and David had a unique and powerful bond, but her disability hindered a full connection. At least, Mark assumed it did. Her disabilities had to set the phenomenon back a step or two. Instantly, the realization hit like an eighteen-wheeler going one-twenty.

The effects of the virus.

It had worked on the Brainers to up their cognitive abilities and morph into pseudo-society members. Maybe, with Emma, the virus and cocktails thrust into her tiny body had percolated, taken a ride in the blender, and concocted a drink that people would die to get just a sip of the tasty spirit. Imagine what someone would do to get a drop. What they would pay to sit at the bar.

How they would kneel at Mark's feet when he used Emma to force his will.

The thought electrified Mark to the point he got an involuntary erection. There was nothing sexual about it, just his body sending blood hurtling to his extremities, and his manhood happened to be a recipient. Even his fingers and toes got all tingly from the sudden rush. Grasping for the first time the last few minutes, a picture emerged. The kind of portrait worth billions.

David had shattered the leg of a man with his fist. An eight-year-old with the strength of a powerlifter. Not even a lucky shot. A hard-hitting punch that broke one of the toughest bones in the human body.

All with the fist of a child.

A soldier suddenly leaking his entire blood supply with no practical explanation. Mark had been so focused that he almost forgot about his man. Shaking his head back to reality, Mark looked over just as the soldier collapsed to the concrete in his own pool of blood.

Emma was staring directly at Mark.

"No one else will hurt you, Emma."

Her thumb turned.

Mark felt the pain behind his right eye. Had to be a migraine symptom from lack of sleep and stress. It radiated, growing more intense, a burning heat as if his head was on fire. He reached for a bottle of water and knocked it over as his legs buckled, his knees hitting the concrete with a thud. As the hurricane roared into a category five within his skull, his vision blurry with water from tears, he saw Emma standing in front of him. Reaching for his pistol, his arm failed to move. Frantically feeling his belt with his left hand, he attempted to yank his operator knife from its sheath.

His fingers failed.

Emma smiled, the grin beautiful and toothy. For the first time, Mark felt human again, a real person with feelings and emotions. The love he had for Emma was there, even for his old and dear friend, Ryan. Memories of past missions where they survived by the skin of their teeth and made it back to forward base of operations for a cold and well-deserved beer. Mark's heart felt, actually had a beat that had long been absent. He managed to touch his cheek and wipe away the salty tears as he quietly wept.

"I am not your pet. My Bubba isn't either. You've hurt my whole family and my dad. He better not die or I will crush your head like a grape."

Mark nodded.

"Mommy, can we leave now?" Emma shot over her shoulder.

Having been oblivious to a massive commotion that deafened the interior of the hangar, the little girl's focus on her prey had lasted minutes, all without a clue as to events transpiring all around her. Out of nowhere, as the sounds retreated and she began to come back to the present, a rifle butt smacked Mark in the face and he dropped the rest of the way to the ground.

"All set, Ice Pick," Honcho whispered. "You did great."

"Uncle Hon?" Emma turned, surprised to see him.

Seeing her confusion, Honcho pointed to the open hangar door, where San Carlos stood, a grin the size of Texas waving to Emma. Honcho walked over and knelt next to Emma, who had moved to be close to her mom.

"How? We figured you all were dead?" Julia managed above a whisper.

Honcho touched his chest. "Us? No. The worse for wear? Absolutely. BP got hit pretty hard protecting your rear-ends. He'll survive, so don't worry about him. We managed to fend them off, though by the time we did, your trail was cold and we realized the wackadoos had got ya. So, we got on that boat and hightailed here. Seems we beat the chopper, so we were able to get some things in place and wait for the right time to strike."

Julia held Emma close, not sure if it was a dream.

Seeing the look on her face, Honcho's trademark eyebrow raised up. "We're really here. Though it seems like the Carmichael children might not have required us to bail them out."

Julia managed to chuckle. "I don't know what to believe anymore."

Emma took their hands in hers, Honcho's in the left and her mom's in the right. "Nice to have the team back together," she double winked.

CHAPTER 67

Julia saw the bodies strewn about the airfield.

San Carlos' men had done their job. Done it so well that Mark's men didn't even hear Death approach and deliver the dreaded sickle to the head.

She hated going against Ryan. Under the circumstances, Julia felt she had little choice. Protecting the children was priority one. In the face of an evil that kept coming and would never go away until it either triumphed or was defeated in a roaring fire, Emma and David's survival was paramount.

Julia knew it, and Ryan did too.

Ryan was slipping into the abyss, his days numbered. Getting ahead of that curve and preventing the kids from being front row fans to the crash was a no-brainer. Her job was to sequester them to safety and go underground with the support of still trusted and loyal friends. Ensure that Emma and David grew up into old people if the world allowed. After, providing the world the answer to its disease.

Ryan's?

To do what he did best and kill the threat and bury the skeletons beneath his feet.

Honcho relaying to Liz that Julia and the kids were coming to Mary set events at play. It upped the stakes, and from what Honcho surmised, and probably hit the nail on the head, was Liz had a traitor in her camp. The band of traitors started with Honcho's old student that got eliminated along the highway and from there threw gas on the fire. Maybe not someone close to her, but within standing distance to hear or see things they could use.

For their personal benefit, or the reality of it, for Mark.

It all added up. Ryan had Reg and Julia now had Mark. It was a dream for the poker player. A royal flush if there ever was one. Except, she wasn't so sure the cards in hand carried enough weight to play a game with the powers behind the evil. Mark was expendable.

Reg, if what Honcho uncovered was true, worth his weight in gold.

Julia didn't believe her father-in-law, the man she had loved and watched wither before her eyes, was the bringer of death. His place in the cause, the unholy cabal of lunatics bent on world domination under a wicked regime that by all intents and purposes transcended the left or right of political beliefs, Reg was a king. Not the sole prophet of the psychopathic conglomerate of dystopian bringing assholes.

No, Reg was one of the ringleaders.

He was, as Honcho found out by chance rifling through a file of scanned documents marked beyond secret from a decade ago, Reg was a full-fledged member of the Council, though not the head of it. The Council being the round table advisers to the true mastermind behind the black mask that ran The Order. The man or woman who remained unseen.

There was only one head to this snake.

While Mark had his place, Reg was over fifty years deep in the deception and lies that were the foundation of The Order. The lone sentence, a castaway in an old scan that if you weren't paying close attention, the eyes would gloss over. Honcho happened to catch it, and add that to the information about Ryan's past, it made for a horror movie dreamt up by some crazy script writer steeped in the wildest stories imaginable. Reg let his son be used as the original test tube experiment.

While Ryan was the seed, the children were the end result of years of trials.

When Julia found out, she and Ryan hatched a plan. The children could never be taken. No matter what.

Then, she decided to change part of it.

Ryan was a losing cause if they were captured and a cure kept in the hands of madmen. His mind forever turned into a monster never to regain his humanity. As long as the children and Julia kept living in safety and somehow a cure by real doctors got created, The Order was screwed. If Ryan was taken, he could easily kill himself, though as a last resort. Contaminate his blood so it could never be harvested.

He had a method for that learned a long time ago from a CIA friend.

If Ryan did make the transition, then evil and its supporters were all hosed and destined to die. Even in an altered state, he'd stop at nothing to exact vengeance. The Order was the god of deception and deceit. Throwing shade their way with a ruse that defied logic, Ryan and Julia hoped to put an end to the madness.

Once and for all.

When Ryan's body was engulfed in adrenaline, he was a one-man killing machine. Virus and all coursing through his bloodstream. If he thought his precious babies were in danger, he wouldn't relax or shut down, which prevented the evil within him to be kept at bay. The calm, as he'd told Julia, was what brought about the tremors and terrors. When his body had time to recuperate, that's when he felt the devil ripping its way out of his chest. Stay a man on a mission amped up and no one was safe from his wrath.

Keep me on edge, and I'm their worst nightmare.

The lies all around, between the kids, Ryan, and even Honcho and BP, served a greater purpose. The truth was compartmentalized, all on a need-to-know basis. If someone was caught, tortured, or interrogated, they only knew their bit part. Ryan and Julia would take their knowledge to the grave if they had to sacrifice themselves.

No question.

BP had his own kids to get back home to and even Honcho, alone in the world when they found him days ago, still had Liz. Ryan had been trained for torture, hell, even had the scars to prove his metal at evading spilling secrets. BP and Honcho, as dear as friends as they were, still had something to lose. Julia could feign the lies as the ignorant and protective mother. Ryan masterfully keep up deception through the pain.

BP and Honcho had everything to lose.

When Ryan discussed his plan, quietly alone during a brief break from Emma and David, he mapped it out. Julia wasn't sold then, and still had doubts. If it failed, Ryan was dead. If any part succeeded, they still had a fight on their hands. By a miracle he managed to pull the whole damn thing off, the planet had the chance to set itself right and humanity to once again thrive and proliferate a species that didn't deserve a second chance.

Maybe this time, they would get it right.

<h1 style="text-align:center">CHAPTER 68</h1>

To sacrifice oneself for the greater good, is the epitome of love.

Ryan had heard it somewhere, an old philosophy book or spiritual saying as part of a proverb meant to open one's eyes to a greater purpose in life.

He didn't quite buy into the bullshit.

Sacrifice was usually finite. You die, and that's the end. No more living, breathing, enjoying the accouchements of being topside of the grave. Sacrifice on a lesser scale? That lent itself to a whole stream of different endings that meant you could keep on truckin' in this world and if you were really lucky, you got a nice pat on the back for doing a good deed.

He was setting up a sacrifice that he hoped showed The Order's cards and gave Ryan the intel he desperately needed to drive a stake through evil's heart.

Once and for all with everything he had left in the tank.

The constant hurdles made it all a mess worse than getting the squirts on a first date with your dream girl. Everything is going fine and you lean in for that anticipated kiss and without warning, your drawers explode with the brown goo of poo.

Date over.

Getting Reg to Liz was a big part of the plan to then draw Mark into a trap. When Liz's people got wind of the marauding army of Brainers heading north, the small wrench he could turn evolved into one that even the strongest man in the world had a difficult time rotating around. A small-scale assault Ryan could defeat with a number of different solutions and Liz's help. An onslaught of focused psychos who would decimate an entire town to get to their prey?

A game changer.

While he was used to winging it, this was one of those times that even for him, was where the light bulb was burned out and the back-up had a broken filament. Ryan had nothing to go on. The quick arrival of the Brainers meant action had to step up immediately and just see what transpired before beginning to ponder what came next. Deal with the first threat and then move on to the next one.

No way around it.

When the truck dumped him off at the stadium and was instructed to wait until he made it back if circumstances allowed, Ryan hustled to the top deck where it overlooked I5. From high atop the ground with an unobstructed view, he could take the sniper shot. The distance long, but within his comfort zone. How he was supposed to identify the Brainer leader? Not a clue.

He had some ideas though.

Make the shot and bug out. That was the grand scheme concocted in his flailing mind. If he could sow discord for even a brief few minutes, it gave Liz's people a chance to fight back and deflect the attack. Not a sure thing given the sudden appearance that for whatever reason, slipped through the watching eyes of Liz's scouts. If the caravan would have been caught on the radar sooner, then time was a friend. The boats on their way a quicker enemy to address, but at least they were waterborne and visible. Let bullets fly and sink them.

The massive flotilla jetting to Seattle proper, for any defensive crew, a difficult undertaking given any circumstances.

A two front battle was nothing new. History was chock full of those that popped up over and over for millennia. That was normally with one combative force in mind. Mark was the third wheel. His group of soldiers, now with a combat-trained death unit that Ryan was responsible for creating, added an element of chaos that widened the gates of Hell to release its worst demons. One known enemy's tactics was one thing to tackle. Brainers were consistent in their approach so you could anticipate to some degree their battle tactics.

Mark's men? Trained in the art of deception to make you second guess.

The realization of Zulu Team coming for him sent a shiver down Ryan's spine. He wasn't afraid of them and never would be for that lot. He knew each one, their strengths and weaknesses from years of training. That knowledge centered around the soldiers being in a specific state of mind.

They weren't in that headspace today.

Zulu was far different and getting inside their brains to figure out anything a shot in the dark. He hadn't been with them in over five years, the last time under the radar so Julia wouldn't know. After the incident with the government official and the threatened blackmail by said appointee, where Ryan showed up in the dead of night and was ready to hand the man his own balls for that transgression, Ryan got a few years of peace.

Until, Ryan did one last favor for a friend.

Pass the torch to the next generation and sign off on the leader of Zulu. Ensure a smooth transition and let a new man train and show the way. It was a quick space flight, three days, and then Ryan's days as a spook were done.

The weight lifted refreshing, the freedom the freshest air ever.

The cold shiver, as far as he could tell, wasn't fear or even hesitancy from any old loyalties. The reaction came with a growing glee for the battle ahead, one of those shakes when you're about to get into some serious shit and your body does a shake to ward off the cobwebs before jumping into the fight.

Ryan was thirsting for it, couldn't wait to get his kill on.

Confronting the truth for the first time for a man who didn't like to kill, actually loathed it but had done so out of a sense of duty for years, the feelings embracing his body and the sudden want to go all out and let the blood spray was like a warm cozy blanket.

Nice and soft and made you feel great.

He *wanted* to let the death dealer out. Yearned to take lives by the dozens. While he had over the last years and even the last month not hesitated to eliminate a threat, he had *felt* the desire under his skin. An itch building up, a passing scratch here and there. Growing into a rash that required attention, but the recipient ignored. All leading to the onset of a major oozing and festering infection that simply decided to let the fluids run amok.

No amount of antibiotics or sterile wrap was going to quell the spread.

Kneeling at the top of the stadium, positioning his sniper rifle on its bipod and resting the stock on the horizontal concrete wall, Ryan peered through the scope. The Brainer brigade was pushing through with heavy equipment. Two semis with massive front bumpers pushed vehicles aside while a front loader came behind and with its massive bucket, finished the job to create a path to travel. Brainers on foot cleared the final debris.

The sheer cooperative effort was fascinating to watch. Brainers didn't have a history of working that well together. The early days fraught with infighting to even get a fire started for a meal together. The grand scale of people working in unison and deliberately to remove obstacles was the kind of evolutionary evidence that in one breath was a researcher's dream and on the other a testament to the horror that was seeing strides as game changers to Brainers becoming intelligent. Less idiotic killers and a transformation into thinking psychopaths with purpose.

A scary proposition.

As he watched the event unfold, Ryan caught in his sights an old bus. The faded yellow exterior worse for wear, it was decorated with skulls and reinforced with sheets of steel. He panned its length and couldn't keep a snicker from escaping his lips. Pulled behind the old bus was a flatbed trailer with a sight that he didn't expect, but seemed as plausible today in the apocalypse as it would have been three, ten, even sixty years ago. That's when the sound caught his ears and he just laughed.

"If I didn't hear it, I wouldn't believe my eyes," Ryan mumbled.

Sitting atop the flatbed, in full regalia for the intent, was a band. And, not just any band. A supergroup of musicians who brought a talent that any concertgoer would dream to see live.

The who's who of original Seattle grunge and rock.

If it was any other century, Ryan would believe it was the war drums of a fierce African tribe. The marching beat of British Red Coats leading soldiers into battle against American colonists. Bag pipes of Highlanders cheering on the resistance to the British invasion of the north.

The cries of war as people stormed to their deaths.

Ryan recognized the members, the godfathers of Seattle's music scene that must have survived. Comprised from what he could tell from four astronomical bands of hard-hitting sound that in total, their former sales numbered in the hundreds of millions.

If he wasn't laser focused, Ryan would let himself get lost in the moment.

Instead, he searched for his target, and was surprised at the ease the man revealed himself. Ryan assumed that the leader of the Brainers would bring up the rear of the posse, protected and hidden away to emerge unscathed later.

Not be banging away on an old set of gold glitter-flaked Ludwig drums.

How did Ryan know? It wasn't that hard of a guess. The t-shirt emblazoned with the words *I Run this Shit* betrayed it a bit. The statement could have meant something else. The bass drum covers though, with *I Lead* on one and *You Better Follow* on the other seemed to telegraph a statement. It very well could have just been saying that the drummer is the heart and soul of a band and everyone plays off his or her beats.

Could have been true.

The ear whisperer though and the frantic pointing and directions Ryan lip read as the man responded to the words in his ear painted a different scene. Seeing who it was blew Ryan's mind on multiple levels. The man was a grunge and rock god. A member of two famous groups and success beyond measure. It all his experience since the world fell to crap, Brainer leaders were nobodies.

Nameless people who somehow rose to the top.

Never in his experience had he come across or heard of anyone with any kind of prominence or name recognition as a leader of one of the psychotic clans. No bankers, doctors, CEOs, sports figures, no one that in the old world led a team to victory or a successful business. Individuals you would think had the skills in the new environment to tap into their old selves. Those unfortunate souls seemed to have either died at the outset, at sometime during the last three years, or took their place beside the other minions, if they turned into a Brainer. Some were part of the Un-dead crowd, he knew. Most, if they managed to survive, took orders from someone more inclined for the current state of affairs.

Seeing Dennis Stohl leading a death squad was a chuckle.

Ryan found the revelation intriguing, a potential aspect to poke and prod. Mark would have had to offer the world to get Brainers to come as heavy-handed as they were making their way up I5. The guess?

Weapons and people to kill and torture.

It's what drove Brainers thirst. At least, it did before. Maybe Mark offered something different, though Ryan quickly chucked the thought out the window. Even in this new light, their DNA seemingly changing and morphing into a new kind of human killing machine with a funny bone, they were primal to the core.

He *knew* it.

His own transition revealed the secret. While his appetite to kill grew, and his emotions turned on and off like a malfunctioning light switch, Ryan still felt a silliness deep inside. Humor crusting around him. Even if he completely went ape shit insane and the journey into being the Devil true, as Honcho's intel suggested and Mark and his own father seemed to back up, somehow Ryan knew he'd still have the jokester lurking within.

In some form.

Could manifest in a number of ways. Finding pleasure in killing all kinds of humorous ways, or telling his old lame jokes that drove David crazy. Ryan didn't know with certainty, but with enough educated knowledge while he possessed his current brain power to deduce a few things, that he'd be funny and a cold-blooded killer all in one.

Dealing death, the greatest entertainment for a laugh.

CHAPTER 69

Emma shook her head.

She felt her father, and with her eight-year-old comprehension not up to snuff, couldn't place everything he was trying to hide.

Julia saw her daughter in the corner, struggling with something unseen, until it hit. "Excuse me, Honcho," she whispered, not wanting to interrupt the interrogation of Mark.

David must have caught wind too, as he was there before Julia managed to shuffle over. "Hey, Emma, I know."

She looked at her brother, the tears falling to the floor.

"What is it, Emma?" Julia asked as she tried to give a hug.

"No, Mommy!" Emma yelled. "It's not OK."

Confused, Julia tried again, only to be rebuffed. "Talk to me, please."

David frowned. "You lied to us."

Realizing the power of the twins, Julia pointed to some seats. "Let's talk."

David made his way, but Emma stood firm. Gently reaching for her hand, Julia took Emma's in hers and guided the girl next to her brother. Motioning for her to sit, Julia knelt in front of her children. Both glared. If looks could kill and they knew the finality of the deed, they might temper their anger just a bit.

Emma blurted it out. "Dad's going to let himself get caught to protect us?"

Julia turned white.

"Seriously? We can help him. We have powers!" David nearly fell jumping up from his seat.

Gathering herself, Julia touched their legs. "Keep your voices down. There's more to it than that. Your dad has a plan. It's a tricky one, but one I agree might work and ensure no one can get to you two."

Emma pushed the hand. "Go away!"

Julia sighed. Where to divulge and what to skirt seemed a lost cause if your kids had a sixth sense. She had hoped Ryan could keep a lock on it, put the kids at bay long enough to succeed. Seemed he had a crack in the forcefield.

"I won't go away. I'm your mother and love you both beyond this world. As you two have learned over the last three years and just the last month, the world is like a puzzle in a dark room. Some pieces easily fit, while others need light to snap together. At every turn, we have no clue as to what will happen next. Even with your uncles and friends helping us, there are some things we just have no idea what is around the corner or what we can do to protect us. Our enemy is smart, so we have to be smarter."

"But, Dad? Why is he doing *that*?" David desperately needed an answer.

There was no easy way to say it. "The people responsible for all of this will stop at nothing to find you two. And, I mean *nothing*. They will kill anyone and everyone they have to in order to get you and your sister back. Your father believes if we use Papa as a bargaining chip, we can get them to leave you alone."

Emma hadn't moved a muscle. Her icy blue star unnerving and uncomfortable.

Julia continued. "They have sent an army to track you down. We have Mark, but he's just a small piece of it. Stop him, and others step up in his shoes. Takes them back to the beginning, but if they have you, they can catch back up. Papa though, it seems he is part of a bigger picture. We use him and maybe we get some breathing room or get them to go away completely if the plan works."

The ice drove into Julia's flesh.

"Dad's plan is to be captured. Isn't it?" The look on David's face seared Julia's eyes.

She frowned.

"How does that solve anything?" Emma finally spoke up. "He gets captured, even with Papa, they have *him*. Dad's blood started all of this. They could recreate it and then nothing has changed!"

Julia didn't understand. Until, the bulb clicked. "Shit."

David pointed. "Language, Mom!"

The fractured glass began to take shape, the shards connecting and holding place. Color suddenly washed across, and for the first time, Julia saw the mosaic of the stained glass in all of its glory.

"Oh, no."

Emma slapped her leg. "That's right, Mom!"

Julia believed she was a partner in the scheme, a willing supplier of steps to follow. She hadn't fathomed her Ryan would play it five moves ahead to a ladder that went to a next level only he got to play.

The tears fell.

Ever the protector of their nucleus, Ryan was sacrificing his life for theirs. It was all there to dissect. He was falling into the deep dark recesses more each day, the signs he valiantly tried to hide, but if you paid attention, were in plain view. She should have known he'd bend the truth, lie even to make sure they were safe. Probably had a different deal going on with Honcho and BP.

Julia grabbed each leg and held. "Listen, Dad had a plan we were working on. The one you two *feel?* That wasn't part of it. He is supposed to use Papa to lure them in and then take them out."

"The Moon men?" Emma asked.

Julia looked at both kids. "What do you think you know?"

David looked at his sister, and decided to let her answer.

"Dad's going to let himself get captured. Get back to the leaders and try to destroy them. A one-way trip."

Julia glanced at David for confirmation. He nodded.

"How do you know that?" Julia prodded.

Emma touched her head. "As much as he tries to hide it, I see certain things and feel Daddy's pain. He doesn't want to do it, but feels he has no choice. He does have a choice. We can help," she sighed as she touched David's arm.

Julia didn't like the bigger lie than hers taking over. Ryan was running verticals side by side, which one the master and who knew what the key questions. She saw BP fussing with something by a stack of crates and quickly excusing herself, ran.

"What's Ryan's play, BP?"

He looked up and set the piece of electronic gear down. "What are you talking about, Julia?"

Stepping close, she huffed, "What is Ryan planning that I don't know about?"

BP sighed, and shook his head. "If you're asking me, then I think we're both in the dark."

Julia searched his face for a tell, and couldn't find one.

"Honcho," they said at the same time.

BP hurried to where San Carlos sat inside the hangar, his focus towards the freeway. Catching the sounds and smoke rising, BP leaned in, whispered, and then retreated. San Carlos motioned to one of his men to keep watch and then went to where Honcho was intently grilling Mark with questions.

"Hey, Primo?" San Carlos smiled. "Take a break. I'll talk to the man."

Aware of the sudden attention and BP and Julia huddled by, Honcho gave a thumbs up. Working his way to them, Honcho shrugged. "What?"

Julia started to tear into Honcho before BP poked her arm and she backed off.

"Bro? Ryan's got something brewing that the only one of us who would know is you. Spill.”

Honcho shot his eyes back and forth. “About what? All I know is what we have going on here.” Seeing their faces, he realized they all had been conned.

Julia saw it register and nodded. “He’s going to sacrifice himself, Honcho. Take out the group at the top.”

“How do you know?”

Julia pointed. “The wonder twins.”

His sigh echoed in the close confines and Honcho’s eyes closed. “That asshat. I probably told him too much and he’s going to go all *Ghost* on them.”

Julia didn’t get it, but BP did.

“You think so? Like Dresden ending?”

The reference was lost on Julia, but Honcho filled in the gap. “Total annihilation. Nothing left.”

She got lightheaded and swayed, and seeing she was about to lose it, Honcho reached out and wrapped her in his arms. “Hold on there, Julia. Keep it straight. If Ryan’s got an idea percolating in that warped mind of his, we have to give him some faith. Not that going solo and a one-way ticket to punch his forever clock I will support. He owes me money still for somethin’. But, we might be able to stave off that with some assistance. I do have some other friends still out there.”

Julia stopped moving and felt her body regain itself. Pulling back, she saw BP’s pursed lips and his eyes on Honcho.

“What can we do then, Big Guy?” BP tapped on a crate lid.

The eyebrow raised. “If my old security crew is holding down the fort in Seattle, we have an in.”

BP shook his head. “How are we supposed to tap into that?”

Honcho’s eyes narrowed as the eyebrow stayed put. “Channel 45.”

Julia looked at the man. “Channel 45?”

He nodded. “We used it for the clubs. It’s short range, but if those fools have any of what I taught them ingrained in their noggins, they’ve been monitoring that channel as a just in case to get what’s left of the crew together and safe. Someone close picks up and then puts the word out to others along the chain. Time for the boss man to call in his troops.”

BP’s lips pursed. He was beginning to sense a new plan brewing a dark roast that you drank black. “Is it secure and do you think it will work?”

Honcho’s grin from ear to ear answered.

Smacking his hands together, BP yanked off his pack. Pulling out a handheld radio and throwing some batteries inside, he shoved it at Honcho. Honcho hesitated, then saw BP was waiting for action.

BP frantically waved his arm. “Get to crackin’ then!”

CHAPTER 70

Options.

Too many to count on one hand.

Ryan had so many plays running it was beginning to strain his brain. What was left of it still working that is. Each had a part in a greater plan that only he knew the intricate details of and had to keep that way in case one part disintegrated.

Compartmentalized and siloed, hope for success.

If one piece failed, the others were unaffected. He had learned that concept long ago, on a battlefield in a country where the odds didn't favor you and success was measured in increments by some bureaucrat or pencil pushing dick who had never set foot inside the confines of a firefight. To be crystal clear, women could be dicks too and disengaged. Their own self-interest playing politics just as bad as a man.

Here though, the true limp pricks were all men as far as he could tell.

Taking stock of his bulleted list, Ryan wanted to check a few items off, cross them out and move on down to the next one. So far, his batting average was off, maybe hitting .250 if he was lucky. Not the .425 and home run king for the season he had hoped for coming into today.

His kids and wife venturing into the lion's den against better judgment before the haze was cleared. Major super dad and husband fail. His dearest friends radio silent, which meant things had gone south. Cooperative agreements with others for the cause teetering on the edge of a sharp blade. Ryan was skating by the seat of his urban camo BDUs. Any other sane person might call it a day and check out. Realize that sometimes, you just lose.

Not this guy.

With Dennis Stohl in his scope, finger on the trigger, ready to exhale and take the death shot, Ryan heard the squeal of a tire. From his perch high atop the stadium, he had a perfect view of the area. Taking his eye away from the scope, he looked on in horror as three SUVs pulled to hard stops outside the main gate and people barreled out the open doors. The truck that sat waiting for him suddenly engulfed in a storm of bullets. Satisfied with their onslaught, they advanced. Focusing in, Ryan saw what he had hoped to avoid.

Zulu Team.

There was no way they could have known Ryan would be here. There were no drones overhead as fortunately, Liz's people had managed to clear some space downing a few. That got checked off his list to tackle and no radio chatter betrayed his location. As he moved from face to face, counting the familiar looks he hadn't seen for some time and surprised at new ones staring back, the unit had grown from a twelve-man detachment into a nice two dozen death mongers.

"Shit."

That was all he could get out after setting eyes on Zane Williams. After hearing Zulu was still functional and heading home, Ryan had hoped Zane somehow got iced permanently in a fight when the virus ran amok on the Moon base or just died from its effects. There was no way it didn't reach outer space before supply missions halted. A pain in the ass ever since the denigrate made Zulu, he was the knife in your back kind of operator looking to advance up the food chain without a thought about who he betrayed getting to be top dog.

Shaking his head, Ryan took a breath. Held it, and then let loose.

In rapid succession, he got off five head shots, all on target, and watched as the heads exploded like watermelons smashed at a comedy show. Brain matter and blood sending a spray in all directions. Taken by surprise, Zulu Team went for cover. Three members too slow to react found powerful seven hundred and fifty grain projectiles penetrating out the back of their chests, their plate armor no match for the rounds. Crumbling to the concrete, the pools of red leeched down the stairs. Two more got nailed trying to drag bodies to safety.

Fourteen left.

Evening up the odds, Ryan managed a smile. Fourteen specially trained operators were still a group to reckon with under any promising circumstances. Sowing discord with a sudden rain of sniper fire and taking out members from the old regime and the newbies in Ryan's mind was a way to break them off into camps. The old guys huddled in one and the young crew another.

Loyalties to test.

With the high ground, Ryan had the advantage, if only for a short window. Zane, a missed mark in the first halo of fire, would eventually catch his breath and work the problem. Ryan had taught the bastard that. Zulu would regroup, filter off into two-man teams, and cover ground to find their prey. All Ryan had to do was pick them off, one by one.

Just, not from his current position.

Staying put was a quick ticket to Deadsville. Zane was a smart operator, top of his class from BUDS and years of SEAL deployments. When he burned bridges climbing his way up the ladder, and leadership not wanting to lose a still potentially malleable piece of soldier clay, he found his way to Ryan's old unit. The landing pad of the best of the best from all military branches. That led to his final deployment under the more exclusive and invitation-only point five percent club, where the true cream of the crop go to serve their country with less restrictions and more accountability to the President. Known unofficially as Alpha Canis.

Top Dogs to those in the sphere of knowledge.

Ryan had long left the Dogs and was in civilian life. Still an occasional trainer and until the kids, completing the darkest of dark missions. You never want to lose that kind of expertise. When Zane got picked up and Ryan read his file, the seasoned operator sought to get the thorn removed. Someone not a team player is a potential liability. The powers that be kept Zane afloat and Ryan managed to instill a sense of duty in the man.

Maybe, too good.

Ryan had taught Zane well and knew that knowledge was about to be utilized against the lone gunman high on the hill. Except, every intelligent special ops soldier keeps certain things close to the vest. You never divulge all your secrets, otherwise, you lose your tactical advantage and maybe your life if you're deemed expendable.

Keep the best tricks in case you need them down the road.

Figuring he had ten minutes tops for Zulu to sweep the building enough to figure out where the shots came from, Ryan went to work. Julia called him a packrat, keeping odds and ends of what she called *junk* and he knew were pieces of gold. When it came to his ruck, the essentials came along, and occasionally some of the tidbits and accrued stuff he figured might come in handy one future moment.

Today, that was the day.

Working his way to the top deck walkway that overlooked a railroad yard, Ryan pulled out his rappelling rope and fashioned a knot and carabiner to secure to one of the roof posts. This side of the stadium had a few balconies he could descend to and then work his way to the ground. The railroad tracks would conceal his escape as he wormed between cars and left the area long before he could be tracked.

That was the end game exit.

The immediate plan entailed getting to ground and coming up behind Zulu and take out the team one set at a time. At least, clear enough of them to throw some panic and get the mercenaries to hunker down to regroup while he bailed to safety. The quicker he moved as they meticulously worked up the stadium levels, the better his odds. While they would move at a steady pace, they'd still be slow-going as a safety measure.

The fast fox after the fumbling sheep.

He hit the ground with a light thump, a bit faster than anticipated which caused Ryan to stumble under the weight of his pack and heavy sniper rifle. Catching his footing, he let go of the rope, pulled the sling strap, then grabbed the handguard of his M4, yanking it up to eye level and ready to fire. All clear, he prepped for the show and found a place to hide the sniper rifle bag snugly in a crevice between some pallets to pick up later. Moving swiftly, he maneuvered carefully through the storage areas and delivery bays until he reached his destination. Panning left and right down the corridor, he spied a two-man patrol thirty yards to his left. Tiptoeing silently along the concrete flooring, Ryan got within twenty yards before he opened fire. Two quick and quiet shots to the back of the neck eliminated the threat.

Moving fast, he pulled out the radio from one body and from his ruck, a surprise he hoped did the trick.

Back to task and radio connected to his earpiece, Ryan listened to the chatter. Nothing much washed over the airwaves beyond quick words as each team cleared areas. As he caught snippets of their locations, he dissected each as compared to his current spot, and triangulating with his limited knowledge of the stadium from previous outings with Honcho for the occasional football game or soccer match, Ryan went to it.

Six teams remained.

Hustling to the nearest door that led to the concourse, Ryan carefully opened it, glanced around, and proceeded out. Finding the closest stairwell, he ascended the steps and reaching the top, stopped to listen.

The last radio check-in said a team was coming his way.

Kneeling against the wall, his M4 pulled snug across his chest and his Sig with suppressor ready to shoot, Ryan waited. Ten seconds turned to twenty. Thirty to forty. A minute passed before he caught a boot scuff, faint if you weren't paying close attention.

Maybe five feet away.

Knowing what was about to come next, Ryan shook his right hand to loosen it up. As the barrel came around the corner to clear the stairwell, he reached for the suppressor and pushed hard away from his body, keeping a firm grip to direct the weapon away. Coming around quickly, he pumped two into the abdomen of the first man and letting go, took a headshot that blew out the right eye of the second. Spinning on his heels, one more to the head of the first to end the misery of an eventual bleed out.

Two down. Ten to go.

Another quick placement of a goodie beneath one of the bodies and off Ryan went to prowl for more targets. When the two teams didn't check in, he heard the consternation in the previously silent Zane's voice come out.

"Dammit! We're down two teams, men. Carmichael's alone so someone else must have hit them."

"We keep going?" a team member asked.

"Affirmative. Could have been one of those psychos going off the reservation or maybe some of the King's people straggling around. Keep to task and shoot anything that moves. No way Carmichael got down from his perch that fast."

Ten men left to kill. The adrenaline coursing his body was on fire.

Ryan picked up another location and cut the distance. Single file down the walkway behind the seats of the next access point, the team disappeared inside the bowels of the stadium to be field side. They were exposed, but he would be too if he followed. Deciding to bypass them, he moved on and towards the next junction before suddenly stopping and deciding on a WTF moment. Grabbing the top of the hot dog warmer, he yanked hard and pushed it away, letting it fall and glass shattering into a million pieces as it echoed along the enclosed space. Stepping into a recess and concealed by shadows, he waited.

Ten seconds later from the opposite direction they emerged.

It wasn't the team that went out to the field side, but a different one. Realizing they were now attempting to lay a trap, Ryan weighed his options. Go head on and take the two out to lessen the fight or wait it out and possibly get more in the mix to focus his fire.

Time was his enemy.

M4 back to his chest, Ryan slid the suppressor out of his pocket and pulled the Sig out. A quick twist to secure the device and left arm forward, two shots left the barrel.

Missed the mark.

Shards of concrete began to fill the air as Ryan's position was now compromised. Keeping his wits, he pulled the trigger two more times. Immediate cries of pain as the men fell, a kneecap of each shot clean through. Stepping out of the dark recess, Ryan fired twice more, and the cries disappeared. Eight combatants left.

Fuck, Ryan thought to himself.

He had hoped to keep quiet, to make his kills and move on. This failure on his part, missing two shots, really? That left him open to discovery and pinpointing his whereabouts.

A Special Ops 101 "F" for the gradebook.

If Zane was closing in, how he didn't know, then Ryan was losing his advantage and had to turn the tide. Eight was better than more, and if he could peg it down further, a more palatable taste.

He *was* Ryan Carmichael, after all.

Brisk change of direction and down the darkened corridor, Ryan listened and the radio stayed silent. He kept moving, trying to anticipate an ambush, and came back empty. His movements were unimpeded, which left Ryan to wonder what Zane had in store.

Ryan didn't wait long.

Turning a corner to the south, a barrage of gunfire erupted, the pinging of rounds clinking off the concrete surfaces loud and deafening to his ears. Even with suppressors attached, the bullets making contact with the walls and floor made for a concert that was louder than a metal bash at a summer festival. Retreating back, Ryan chucked a smoke grenade around the bend, letting the white smoke fill the space as projectiles whizzed by his head. Checking his six for anyone sneaking up behind, a hand grabbed the back of his shirt and pulled back.

The pistol fell.

Reflexively, Ryan yanked the knife from the sheath on his vest and lashed behind as he put his right arm up to ward off a throat slit.

The blade caught something, he heard a yelp, and rotating on heels, he lunged forward. The knife hit the chest of his assailant and stopped, having made contact with the protective armor beneath the outer layer. Pulling back, he thrust again, this time aimed at the small area just above the top of the soldier's vest. Hitting the mark, the blade plunged deep just above the bone, slipping through the esophagus.

A hard jerk to the side, and out the neck the steel glistened red.

Blood spewed from the severed artery. Hand to the wound to attempt to staunch the flow, to no avail. The man crumbled to the ground, writhed in agony for a mere five seconds, and then stopped.

For good measure, his body excited at the coming act, Ryan brained him.

Back to his feet, a round hit Ryan square in the chest, the pain instant. His steel plate and trauma pad did the deed they were designed to perform, and swiftly finding the culprit, Ryan's knife flew.

It missed.

Reaching for his pistol, another round grazed his arm. Unfazed, his left arm came up and fired. Three quick shots reverberated inside the battle zone. The first caught Ryan's adversary in the right shoulder. The second, more to the right, went through the vest shoulder strap and shattered the clavicle.

The third found its center between the teeth.

The soldier fell dead, and with fire still coming from behind him, Ryan ran. Six men left, who they were the larger question. Some that he had tagged, Ryan recognized. The others, the newbies who failed to adhere to basic special operations practices and paid a steep cost. He didn't care who any of them were, didn't feel a twinge of regret or sadness for the ones he had shared a beer and conversation with before. They were enemies, nothing more, and any past relationships shredded when they decided to come for him.

Hell was going to be a fun reunion once Ryan made the trip.

With an unknown number behind him, Ryan hoped to do an end run and not meet any resistance. If he could get behind somehow, or even set his own trap, the smarter play, Ryan might catch them off-guard and whittle down even more of the threat. A trap could draw them in, but Zane would anticipate an overt approach. Something subtle could slip the radar, but even then, down to a half dozen operators, Zane would tread lightly and have his guard up.

Confuse, deceive, distract. Ryan always liked option three.

Zane knew some of Ryan's past history. It was the stuff of legend shared to greenies coming into the unit. Across special operations, The Ghost was a badge to strive for if you had the balls hanging below. Most, even the best of the best, were lacking that kind of sack to go totally all out. They held back, just a fraction.

Soldiers were still human beings with fears.

The present-day Ryan, the one Zane couldn't fathom the depths of his determination and grit, was the evolution of The Ghost. A new, more volatile version of the man. As the virus plagued his veins, ate away at his morality and gave way to the demon yearning for freedom to come out and play, there was no way anyone could guess at what Ryan would do, let alone think.

The decisions the old Ryan made, he never second-guessed. He decided and went about his mission. The new persona was different, though with a history, he was a new Ryan with force vengeance that would not fail.

Here cometh, *The Reaper.*

CHAPTER 71

"Let me go."

Liz ignored Reg. As a kind gesture, she had allowed the gag to be removed. She was beginning to regret the decision.

The chaos of the impending psycho horde looming had people running around everywhere to relay messages to those without radios and deliver supplies to fortify against the coming attack. It wasn't a white flag attempt at peace. The pyschos had never amassed so many of their followers to attempt a breech. With heavy trucks and a line of vehicles a mile long from the reports coming back, there was little time to reinforce the walls surrounding the fallback locations Liz would use in the event the enemy got through.

She hoped the preparations already in place and from the years of attempts and incursions, the defensive perimeters held tight.

Liz knew Dennis. Not from any sort of friendship they had previously, though a better description might be to classify it as a cordial acquaintance. Honcho was the one who had a better chance with the former rock god. From his days as a beefy security guard in the club scene, he had amassed quite the reputation and following among the musicians. A natural conversationalist with a huge personality, he put them at ease knowing he had their backs. They appreciated the protection against crazy fans and reciprocated the relationship with invites to parties and all kinds of goodies that if he sold them to their rabid followers, would bring a hefty penny.

Liz, as Honcho's wife, got to go along for the ride.

The more reserved part of the marriage, she wasn't someone to screw with either. In the early days, they both provided security and protection, him the familiar face and contact point while she relished in more behind the scenes anonymity out of the spotlight. She did her job well and cruised along, meeting a slew of soon to be famous that kept in touch with Honcho and by extension her, and bonds with the locals who didn't catch the breaks but kept the music scene alive and kicking for decades. Dennis fell into the former pile, rising from the club scene into one of the most famous musicians on the planet. After leaving Seattle for Los Angeles and touring the world, he kept loosely in touch with Honcho, especially when the band played the big arenas and free tickets at will call awaited.

How he managed to come back north and lead the crazy killers was a mind-blowing thought Liz couldn't grasp.

"If you and your people want to live, I can guarantee it. No one needs to die for my son and his brats. This is about the greater good. Protecting and helping people to live long lives. There can be a pleasant outcome for all. You just have to hand them over and it's done."

She glared at Reg, searched his eyes to gauge the bullshit he spit out. They seemed sincere, almost apologetic. She knew from experience that those affected by the virus were pathological. Words were ploys and tools to get what they wanted. Agreements or cooperation not worth the breath behind them.

"I heard the same thing from your friend, Mark. Worthless words as far as I'm concerned."

Reg's head titled to the side, a thought on the tip of his tongue. "What do you mean?"

Liz moved closer, but kept a six-foot distance. "Mark, you know? He came to visit, spouted off on similar stuff, and then proceeds to kill some of my people. And now? My bet is the psychos coming full force my way has something to do with him too."

Reg's eyes widened at the revelation. Mark had gone rogue, again. The venom welled within until it erupted like a volcano. "He doesn't have the authority to order that! I've been stranded with my wonderful son spending so much quality time I want to vomit. I have nothing to do with Mark's actions. I can send them away, if you allow me to speak with them. But first, we need an agreement."

Liz kept her poker face, trying not to let Reg read her. There were so many variables at play. Trust was in short supply, and Reg didn't come across as the type to keep his word. Her options weren't many either with a water assault close and ground force about to knock on her doorstep. Time wasn't a friend and quick decisions could mean breathing room, or sure death for the wrong one.

"Well?" Reg's impatience bubbled to the top.

"What guarantee do I have that you won't double cross me?"

Reg shrugged. "You don't really. What I can say is that I despise my son more than anyone or anything on the planet. Those heathen kids too. No one needs to pay for his sins. I just want them, and then I'll be on my merry way."

The sigh was hard to contain. "Not enough. I need some assurances."

He hated negotiations. Getting his way usually panned out given he had the upper hand the majority of the time. Reg lacked that tied up and in the dark on what Mark had planned. Giving an inch ripped at his black heart, but given the circumstances, he could play ball or do it the hard way. One was a quicker and surer thing.

Liz pointed. "Got something to give?"

Reg nodded. "I'll give you Mark. Seems he's been a thorn in your side. Do what you wish with him. I don't care."

It was an olive branch. Withered, but had one fruit hanging by a thread.

"A start," Liz replied.

He had to contain the anger. Deep breath and then a sigh to let it out. "Okay, I see you are a hard negotiator. What about this? No more psychos to ruin your day?"

Liz nearly spat hearing that. "You can do it?"

"Yes."

There were over ten thousand under her direct protection the last count. More on the periphery with fragile handshakes and nods to support one another. If she could simply deal with the crazy Un-dead lurking around, it was a one front war to get back to living without constantly looking over her back.

She smiled. "Let's figure it out then."

CHAPTER 72

In life, sometimes winging it is not the solution.

The best laid plans solidified in concrete or written in permanent ink the better play to ensure success or that your life will continue.

Throwing caution out the window an idiotic gesture that nine times out of ten, saw you standing in front of the real Reaper. Or, in Ryan's case, meeting the Devil and vying for who was the real top dog and going to rule Hell for the rest of eternity.

Zane was down to six men, which meant he had a smaller and now fractured force than what he'd arrive with only a short time ago. Ryan had made it a rather quick end for the others. If it was a contest, he was in the number one spot with a gold medal in reach. His adversary licking its wounds and regrouping to figure out what to do next.

Ryan knew Zane and what the ass kicking had done to his confidence and bravado. The man was second-guessing strategy and how to achieve his objective. Even altered by the virus' effects, Ryan knew the old parts of Zane had to be intact. They were some of the reasons Ryan tried to veto the soldier's addition to the team and subsequent rise to Zulu One status. Using the weaknesses to penetrate Zane's decision-making processes, Ryan hoped to come out on top with no scratches.

That outcome was wishful thinking on his part.

Even on his worst day, Zane was a competent special operator. He wasn't the best by a long shot, but could manage results palatable to the higher ups who demanded success. He didn't play by the book and went off course more than Ryan could count, which meant to a degree he was unpredictable. Even in unpredictability, there is still a pattern.

That, was what Ryan could exploit.

It didn't make any sense to a layperson. Barely added up for someone schooled on the factors or thought processes to line up the dots. For someone who mastered the art and chose to only follow through with the chaos when it served a greater purpose, Ryan was the prophet. He trained Zane to overcome hardships, think outside the proverbial cardboard box when mission critical success was paramount. Engrained in the man what to do and when to do it. Then, throw it out the window when the odds were stacked. Even in the moments that dictated a specific course of action, doing the opposite meant throwing your enemy into a frenzy. It was a checklist that every operator for decades ran through his or her mind. That process, even when it got ignored in the end and Zane went with whatever he could muster up, was what Ryan could counter.

He didn't teach Zane all the tricks on the cheat sheet.

People, even in their most unbelievable moments, have tells. You can hide them to your best ability, but in the end, a better player can figure you out. Dodge and weave, throw out breadcrumbs to lead the path astray for someone to follow and then sneak up from behind and slit their throat, there is still a glimmer, albeit a slight one, that reflects in the glass. If you pay attention, it shines briefly, and then you duck or turn and pounce. Miss it, and you're a goner.

See it, and you win the contest.

Up to the last skirmish with bullets blazing, Zane was directing his men close to the book. The last encounter, Ryan nearly getting his head lopped off from behind, a divergence from the script. Moving forward, Zane would chuck the pages and attempt a rewrite, though in a locked room that only he had the key.

Ryan had to pick the cylinder to sneak in.

Nearly to the far north side of the stadium after his Olympic sprint to reach it, his gait slowed to prevent accidentally slipping on the concrete floor. A fast walk to keep pace, Ryan listened for the tell, and hearing the echo from his left, he yanked the strap to his M4 and readied his aim.

Pffft, pffft, pffft. Pffft, pffft, pffft.

Two pulls of the trigger and three-shot bursts barreled towards their targets. The first halo found a mark, the cry of agony short-lived before an answer splintered concrete shards in the wall next to him. The second volley must have missed as Ryan found himself face to face with Zane, the sudden look of terror at coming feet away from Ryan catching them both by surprise. Ryan rolled with it, moving to his right as he fired off another short burst that got Zane to turn and run for cover. Missing again, he heard footsteps behind, pivoted on his heels, and dropping a knee, let loose.

Thud. Thud.

Three left to handle, giving Ryan a warm fuzzy feeling inside. Better odds, and less to worry about. Zane was in front without a partner, the last two-man team's whereabouts invisible. It was time to sweeten the deal and flush everyone out to the light.

"Long time no see, Zane," Ryan called out over the mic. "Should have called ahead. We could have gotten a beer or coffee for a nice chat."

Distract. Deceive. Divert.

Bullets flew by and missed.

"I thought we ended on good terms last time I was up there. I miss something?"

Another volley pinged past.

"Sorry about your guys. I would have thought in my absence you'd have trained them better. Guess I was wrong."

As he listened from his position, Ryan caught a whiff of what had to be sweat smell blow by. Coming from the right, he watched, waited, and saw his pursuers working their way meticulously toward the location of his voice. Figuring he'd bait them more, Ryan had to go there.

"Your guys really suck, Zane. Best of the best? More like bottom shit of my shoe."

Bingo.

Two bodies moved swiftly towards Ryan's voice. This time, automatic gunfire lit up the area where Ryan's words hid to broadcast their way to irritate the soldiers' nerves. The sudden groans of pain led the men to converge on the spot to finish off their prey.

Surprise!

The radio sat alone, hissing static as the call button on the other end stayed pushed in to add additional torment. Flipping around, two close quarter head shots ended the charade. Two more thumps to the ground.

Zane was now alone.

"You can't win, Carmichael. Too many of us to take out all at once."

Too smart to fall for the ploy.

Ryan cracked the mic. "By my count, twenty-four down to one. Just you and me."

Maniacal laughter reverberated in Ryan's earpiece.

"So, you think, Ryan. Those weren't all my men."

The statement caught Ryan off kilter. He was so engrossed in the thrill of the kill, did he make a mistake? Briefly closing his eyes, he went back to the snapshot when he first saw Zane bailing out in front of the stadium. It was Zane for sure. The others, as he scrutinized the men running for cover as he bagged them, did seem a bit off. The ones he nailed inside the corridors of the stadium were easy. The ones he knew from before? A fraction of Zane's unit. The picture began to paint itself.

Ryan had fucked up and he knew it.

The realization hit him head-on. Any other day, Ryan might have known, seen the small discrepancies in their walk, movements, even the gear. Today, his adrenaline amped up to a thousand and so many plans at play, plus throw in the advanced state of the virus racing through his bloodstream wreaking havoc like a drunk driver, and Ryan wasn't functioning with all his cards. The moment of truth bearing down felt like a ton of bricks weighing his chest down, barely able to breathe.

Super fail Mr. Carmichael, Ryan shrugged.

Zane spit gasoline onto the fire. "Tell you what, Ryan. Give up, and I'll make it a quick death. And, for old time's sake, I'll make sure my men don't hurt your kids. The wife? Well, she's gonna be a nice play thing. Been a long haul in space, you know?"

Ryan felt the rage seething below.

"March out to the fifty-yard line and lay your guns down. Hustle up, as my offer only stands for the next ten seconds."

Jet fuel for the flame. "That tiny pecker of yours will go great in my trophy case. Always had a problem getting it up with the ladies."

The words found their mark.

"You're gonna suffer, Carmichael! I'll make you watch as I cut your head off and in that brief moment of consciousness before death, I'll show you your dead body."

Advantage back to Ryan.

The infected didn't have brains firing on all cylinders. With rational thought having vacated the premises, their actions and responses were primal, even for those trained killers and soldiers who had had procedures and training burned into their beings. Rage fueled them at the core and directed their movements ninety-five percent of the time. The other five percent?

They were predicable.

Get them angry and focused on revenge, and you could work the problem. Get them talking and doing two things at once, and you divided their attention. That created gaps in their reasoning, what little was intact, and it opened the gate to exploit their weaknesses.

Ryan knew he had one shot to get out alive. Losing precious minutes locked in battles within the stadium, Zane's team had the opportunity to surround the complex and close off any escape routes. Overlap their fire, and any potential path out was covered. It could be a bluff, a lie to get Ryan out in the open and a clear shot for Zane to make a kill shot.

The possibility existed.

In Ryan's tortured state, his mind playing tricks on him, what he did on automatic with one hundred percent certainty now being second-guessed and questioned. The idea flew by. He glanced as it slowed, let himself read the flashing lights, and then sent it on its way. Even half functioning, he knew he let himself get conned.

The dilemma was how to crawl out of the pit he created.

Shaking off the disgust in himself for getting taken, Ryan sighed, took a breath, held it, and let it go. He had ninety-nine problems and this wasn't the one to make him wind up dead.

"Bring it on, Zane."

Turning off the radio as no traffic was going to cross the airwaves with Zane knowing it was compromised, the future looked dim, the colors drab and running together into a puddle of black. Living meant getting his head in the game and focused on what had to happen in order to see the next sunset and hold his kids tight in his arms. He had choices, go all out and fight like crazy with guns blazing a trail. Set more traps and try and draw Zane and his men into some messy situations. Even pretend to give up and see what magic and luck offered. Or, go with the plan that Zane wasn't going to expect since Ryan was not a quitter. He finished his missions, every time. With crap on the fan and uncertainty looming overhead, there was only one play.

Ryan set to getting the hell out.

CHAPTER 73

"Honcho!"

The voice that answered on the other end warmed the old bouncer's heart.

"Alive and still barely kickin', Joanna," Honcho acknowledged, memories of his old friend warping by inside his head.

"Where have you been? We all figured you would have made it this way," Joanna asked, the concern in her tone a welcomed act.

Honcho cleared his throat. "Here and there trying to stay alive. Got cut off and no way making it back home. Listen, no time to catch up as there's something a bit pressing, and I desperately need help with."

"You got that right. We've got some trouble here trying to bust through our gates."

Honcho didn't expect that remark. "Trouble? Are they soldiers?"

"No. Those crazy bastards that like to just maim and kill people are trying to storm their way up I5. A huge column of them, bigger than they've ever tried before."

A really bad development.

"Ah, crap," Honcho replied. "I know the ones."

"Yeah, King, I mean Liz, is looking to broker a deal with them. Some old guy."

Julia shook her head. It had to be Reg.

Honcho hit the mic. "Listen, that guy is bad news. He will sell you out in a heartbeat. He's my buddy's dad from hell. Worst of the worst. I might be able to fix that, but I need help if anyone is still breathing from the old crew."

Joanna laughed. "Some made it. What's brewing, Boss?"

Honcho laid it out. Brutally honest and straight to the point. When he was done, silence filled the air. Joanna didn't answer right away. When she did, it was not the saving grace Honcho required.

"I wish we could, Boss. We're locked down tighter than a hip hop show passing the blunt around."

Honcho, never one to beg, dropped the bomb. "Please, if we don't get to Ryan, and his dad talks his way with that horde of lunatics, it's show over. You all are dead and the rest of us with it."

The heavy sigh carried. "You're serious, aren't you? You really know these people?"

"Dead serious. I've got a history with these fools that goes way back and some inside scoop on the shit show playing the stage today. My friend is like the baddest of bad asses and if we can get him in front of this mess, we might live to see tomorrow."

Joanna coughed. "Um, your guy is at the stadium. Reports are there's a huge mess going on over there."

"You mean he's not with Liz?"

Another cough. "No. When word hit that the psychos were coming, he ran off to the stadium on some mission and left the old guy. Spotters caught a bunch of gunfire and then the place got surrounded."

Honcho nervously tapped the top of the crate. "Listen, if you have spotters watching the place, then you can loop me in? If he's trapped, he needs all the help the world can give him."

Dead air.

"Joanna?"

"Still here, Boss. Listen, we might be able to throw some help his way. Longshot, but if your boy can get away in the chaos, he might have a chance."

Honcho didn't like the tone of what she said. "What kind of help?"

"Creepers."

CHAPTER 74

"Knock, knock, King!"

The greeting, amplified through the loudspeaker system, could be heard for a mile. Leaning back on his seat, Dennis twirled his drum sticks waiting for King to appear. When no one showed, he slammed his foot on the pedal and hit a four/four beat of ear numbing bass.

"Oh, King! Come on out and play!"

Liz finally peeked over the wall and stood up on the milk crate to stare across.

Squinting his eyes, Dennis' face washed over in a huge toothy grin. "Oh, snap! Liz! The King, is that you?"

She nodded. "Hi, Dennis."

"Damn. If I would have known, maybe I'd have played nicer all these years and not crucified so many of your peeps. Oh well. Listen, there's this guy who really wants something you have and made me a killer deal. Hand them over, and I'll let *you* live."

The tone wasn't lost on her. "*Just* me?"

Dennis' shoulders dropped. "Better than nothing."

Reaching behind and below, Liz yanked Reg up by the collar and pushed him to her side. Whispering, she smacked the back of his head when he stood motionless.

Glaring to the side, Reg forced a smile and waved. "Dennis, is it? This deal you have, is it with a man named Mark?"

Dennis beamed. "Sure as shit."

Reg frowned.

Seeing the downturned corners, Dennis raised his arms. "Something wrong with that?"

Reg nodded. "See, Mark is, what would you comprehend it as, is nothing more than a groupie. He can offer up some small amounts of dope, but for the good stuff, I'm the only one who can deliver."

Dennis pointed a stick. "Don't do drugs anymore, Man."

Reg sighed. "Drugs, booze, women, first class accommodations, a Grammy. Take your pick. What the old world offered, imagine what the new one has that you can't remotely comprehend in your brain. Mark can't give you anything. I am the one who can make your wildest desires come true."

The famous musician paused his drum stick twirl mid spin. He looked deep in thought, pondering the words and hazy offer light on details. Soon, his head bounced up and down to some imaginary rhythm of a beat that must have been rocking, as within a minute he hit the skins, played a phenomenal solo, and then just stopped cold.

Reg waved. "Hello? Can we get back to business? The deal includes you leaving these absolutely fantastic people alone. At least, for a predetermined amount of time at which you two can handle your relationship however you want."

Liz glanced at her watch. It had been an hour since Ryan left for the stadium. Seeing her check it, Dennis' jubilant demeanor faded away.

"Got somewhere to be right now? Snap of my fingers and this," he motioned all around, "goes away and your people with it."

She shook her head and raised her voice. "Not at all. See, dirtbag here doesn't hold all the cards. Your offer to me is as weak as that last solo. My old dog played better."

The rage couldn't be contained.

"Listen you fuck! I'm going to enjoy slicing your flesh to the bone while you still live. Me and this guy here, we got a deal if he gives me *you*," Dennis ended, the sadistic grin radiating his engorged hate for Liz.

Liz raised her arms up and immediately brought them down. The fireworks went off like the Fourth of July.

Reg appreciated the ingenuity and cunning Liz possessed. He hadn't seen it coming, so focused on the conversation with Dennis, he really should have seen her people moving into position. When her arms fell, the explosions started, sending cars and debris high into the air and falling precariously the length of the freeway as far as he could see. Between blasts, elaborately camouflaged BBQ propane tanks spewed streams of fire horizontally from either side of the freeway. With the high ground, Liz's people opened fire, taking out the retreating pyschos seeking cover from the chaos.

The carnage gave Reg an unexpected smile.

The momentary excitement faded away as he realized Liz was occupied with directing fire and personnel. Stepping to the left side, he waited for her to grip his arm and yank him back. When she didn't and turned to yell into her radio over the volume of gunfire flying overhead, Reg simply stepped away. Thirty seconds later, he vanished inside a cloud of smoke.

"Let's find my boy and end this once and for all."

CHAPTER 75

The chatter about Ryan should have been contained.

Once he bailed his conversation with Liz, the murmurs on his destination floated around, a piss-poor effort at keeping it quiet. For some reason, they all thought Ryan making his way to the football stadium would give him some type of tactical advantage to take out Dennis and sow some type of discord among his ardent followers.

Reg knew better.

While chopping the head off the snake did wreak instability as being leaderless saw individuals vying for the top spot, Liz and her people failed to eliminate Dennis. Before escaping her grasp, he caught sight of the drummer hunkered behind the massive flatbed trailer, radio in hand, barking orders to his clan.

The elder Carmichael knew the wrath was going to rain down like a thunderstorm Seattle had never seen.

Catching snippets as he maneuvered away from the frontlines, Reg overheard talk concerning Ryan and the crap he was under at the stadium. Hearing the intel warmed his belly and produced a grin you couldn't knock off with a heavyweight uppercut.

His boy was about to get his card punched.

Not wanting it to happen without him, Reg found an old truck with the keys inside and commandeered a ride. Gently swerving past running people and forcing a wave of encouragement, he drove towards the location of the battle, hoping he arrived in time. Slowly pulling to a stop far away, he spied a camouflaged soldier by the looks of him, and taking stock of the old truck's contents, found an old dirty white rag. Stepping out, he broke off the radio antenna, fashioned the rag in a flag, and walked waving the makeshift peace offering from side to side. Catching the attention of one soldier, he nearly got shot as a bullet grazed the asphalt to his right.

"Seize fire!" Reg bellowed as he stepped towards the stadium.

Another bullet went to the left. Waving the flag frantically, Reg used a hand signal to display an upside-down OK symbol.

The shots stopped.

Continuing forward within thirty yards, the rifle trained on Reg's face and the soldier motionless on bent knee, Reg glanced around. Twenty yards still moving the flag, he caught sight of another soldier, this one a familiar face from past video relays. Flipping the bird, Reg stopped waving the flag. A hand signal from the face, and the rifle aimed at his head refocused on activity in the other direction.

The face hurried over and extended a hand. "Are you all right, Sir? Didn't expect you to be here," Zane Williams asked with genuine concern.

Reg gruffly accepted the handshake. "I'm fine. Was able to get away from all the chaos going on over there," he pointed towards I5, the commotion audible for miles. "Status here?"

Williams grinned. "We've got Ryan, um Carmichael, pinned down inside. He's got nowhere to run."

The blinding smile betrayed his joy. "Timeframe to elimination?"

"Sorry, Sir? I assumed with you here you would want him captured alive."

Reg shook his head. "The first three letters of assume are what?"

Wiiliams understood. "Yes, Sir. Do you want the honor?"

If time wasn't valuable, it would be different. "No. Execute and get back to base. Still need my grandchildren corralled, so we have too much to do." Reg took a step to leave before a sound caught his attention.

Williams put out his hand. "Sir? Mark has them. Got word some time ago."

Reg couldn't contain his giddiness. "Oh my! That is fantastic news. Use it on my boy."

"Affirmative. I'll let you know when we've wrapped it up."

Reg acknowledged the response with a curt flick of his hand. Figuring he had some time to kill unless Zane Williams managed the impossible, the elder Carmichael walked over to the parked SUVs and took a seat inside. A chill was beginning to blow through and without a jacket, his old bones felt the cold more than usual. Shutting the door, he decided to recline while he waited for confirmation. The interior warmth coupled with exhaustion took its toll.

Within minutes he was asleep.

Reg wasn't sure how long he had been out. Could have been minutes or hours. All he knew was he felt the soft up and down of the SUV as it moved, the shocks absorbing the bumps in the road.

Not even opening his eyes, Reg yawned, and barked an order. "I asked to be told when my son was killed. There a problem with your hearing?"

No response.

Irritated, Reg yelled out, "Asshole, I asked you a question!"

"Oh, sorry," came the reply. "I assumed the silence was an answer your bundle of joy is still kickin' it on this side of death."

His skin turned cold. Reg didn't anticipate hearing *that* voice. Cracking open his left eye, he turned and saw the trickle of blood running down the side of the face. Wishing he had a gun or a knife, he closed his eye and relaxed in the seat.

"Miss me?"

Rhetorically, Reg blurted, "Why can't you just *die* already?"

Ryan smacked his knee and it echoed. "Haven't you learned yet, Dad? I'm like a cockroach. You *can't* kill me."

Reg huffed and folded his arms across his chest. "Do I even want to know about Zane?"

The SUV took a hard right, sending Reg into the side window.

"Sorry. Road debris," Ryan mumbled.

"Well?" Patience wasn't in Reg's blood.

Tapping the steering wheel, Ryan hummed a few bars of a song, before he stopped both and answered. "Well, Zane and his goons are running around inside the stadium chasing a ghost. I relieved him of his man outside watching the vehicles. It'll be a while before they realize I'm gone."

A glimmer of hope. "So, he's still alive?"

Ryan saw the brief smile and watched it immediately vanish. "For a bit longer. He serves a purpose before he dies. Him and his crew need to survive a little surprise from some friends of my good friend first. A little on the bitey side, if you know what I mean."

"What now?"

He could toy with dear old dad, enjoy torturing him a bit, or be cold and transparent. Each had its positive attributes and choosing was hard.

"Sit back, relax, and enjoy breathing a few hours more."

CHAPTER 76

Complicated plans can suck.

They are ripe for pieces to fall through the cracks. A misstep, an ill-executed movement, even taking too long or not acting soon enough can throw it straight down the drain. Perform it perfectly to the letter?

You reap the pile of gold.

Ryan was used to running ops that carried the weight of the world on his shoulders. Those were all singular-focused, with a well-crafted and devised plan that didn't allow for any wiggle room, let alone the ability to wing it if required. You ticked off the list at each checkpoint and followed through to the end. Variants usually got you killed, though for Ryan, he'd had success when it all went to shit and he had to fly by the seat of his pants.

This though?

Running multiple ops all at once that crisscrossed each other and had so many players involved and dependencies that had to execute like clockwork or everything could fail? That was the masterpiece that every special operations soldier dreamed they'd complete once in their lives.

Maybe twice if they were lucky enough.

Taking stock of his predicament, since that was what he was smack dab inside of, one of a magnitude bigger than the Sun, Ryan rattled off the latest sit rep in his head. Liz's people were engaged with the Brainers to distract and thin out their herd. Honcho and crew occupied the airport and had Mark, according to the latest update. Reg was still alive with Ryan, good or bad depending on how you viewed the situation. Zane was still in play, though for how long depended on the next piece of the pie working its angle. Worst bit of news?

Julia was furious at Ryan for his deception.

He hated keeping her in the dark. It wasn't that he didn't totally trust her. He did, though there was still a nagging cloud hanging around since the rescue in California and life on the road the last month. It was a decision made to compartmentalize the mission. A need to know. In the event of capture, Julia wouldn't know enough beyond her part to give up critical pieces of the plan. Same for Honcho and BP. They knew enough to go about their roles, but not enough to divulge if it came down to it.

Hell, Ryan wasn't sure he even knew it from A to Z, and he made it up.

All he saw were checkpoints. Move from task A to B, get C to succeed, and so on. Each could fail and hinder a portion of the design. End result if even seventy-five percent found success?

Then it was possible they could win the battle and prep to end the war.

Ryan knew winning the war meant humanity survived. Lose this battle and game over. Evil wins and everyone better get comfortable subjugated to a life one step up the ring in the levels of Hell. Each battle wore down his enemy, forced them to second-guess and slip up. All tiny fractions of cracks in their consortium of false demi-gods who never fathomed that one man would stand up and give them the finger.

Two middle fingers with a smile.

Not that Ryan ever believed he could do it all himself. He was a realist. Even his old military missions and the ones performed post-special operations, there were teams of people who assisted, supported, and even came along for the ride. While he was the punisher who delivered the result, he could never be the best without someone in his corner.

This rag tag bunch of misfits was the best he could have hoped for.

Reaching the airfield by the backroads, Ryan parked and yanked a non-compliant Reg out of the passenger seat. The ride, circuitous to avoid any Brainers waiting behind to fill the void from the fight along I5, took an hour. The entire time Reg bitched and whined, spewed hatred and vicious jabs towards Ryan to try an illicit a response.

Reg's bloodied nose showed Ryan's answer.

Hearing all of the crap talking normally would have gone in one ear and out the other. Ryan knew his father's ploy, to try and get Ryan worked up to make a crack in his shell to exploit. The son wasn't buying the goods. He knew better and Reg should have too if his claims of being a former special operations soldier held truth. Based on Honcho's digging, there was a grain of reality to the background in some form, yet the extent remained unclear and cloudy, much like the future. As Reg raged on, snippets of information got divulged. Probably unintentionally and due to the elder Carmichael's inability to containerize fact over fiction in his current state of health. The virus was morphing and changing everyone else too.

To what degrees was the question of the century.

Reg revealed some intel he shouldn't, or that he failed to wrap in a layer of lies as his rage took control over deliberate thought. Snippets, nothing so linear it made sense individually, but when glued together with a lot of other pieces of the puzzle gathered from various sources of intel, and the old canvas' painting took shape. Any other time in the past and Ryan would call bullshit.

No way to discount the pixels taking shape today.

Dump what Reg coughed up and add to the soupy mix of Ryan's complicated plan, and the dark storm cloud overhead was about to dump a year's worth of rain in a day.

"Put him somewhere he can't bug anyone or talk," Ryan gestured to San Carlos.

San Carlos nodded, said something to one of his men in Spanish Ryan got a fraction of given the speed of words back and forth, and then San Carlos' soldier led Reg away to the back of the hangar.

Walking over to where Julia, Honcho, and BP were huddled around a small table deep in discussion, Ryan dropped his gear on a chair and leaned back against one of the crates. The glares spoke without words.

"I'll deal with you later," Julia hissed, not being able to contain her anger.

Taking the warning, Ryan sauntered over to where Emma and David reclined in a corner, deep in conversation.

"Hey guys. Everything OK here?" Ryan prodded.

Emma frowned and David shook his head.

"Seriously, Dad? Being a lone ranger keeping us in the dark. When are you going to let us help?" David's words were sharp and cut deep, even for an eight-year-old.

Taking a knee on the cold concrete, Ryan reached out, only to have his hands swiped away.

"No, Dad. Not this time," Emma sniffed, trying to hold back her tears. "We're supposed to be a team, right? That's what you always say," David added.

Ryan knew they were right. It was a family motto that Carmichaels took care of each other, no matter what. He'd broken that trust circle, all from years of conditioning where everything was on a need-to-know basis and you only shared the minimum, all to protect the "team" if they got compromised. It was hard letting his old world go completely, he'd been so used to being The Ghost that was now transformed into The Reaper and doing it his way that he'd lost sight of what mattered the most.

His children.

"Listen you two, you're right," Ryan began as he motioned them closer. Reaching out, he touched their hands, which didn't resist this time. "We are a team. Always and forever. But, sometimes the leader of the team *takes one* for the others to protect them from bad things. My job as your dad and the head of the Carmichael clan is to always make sure nothing happens to you or Mom. You two rotten kids are the future who have to lead the rest. I'm just one guy trying to do what I think is right. Definitely not perfect, but pretty close," he finished with a wink and his thumb and pointer finger scrunched close together.

"Not even close. Broken down old man," the kids chimed in unison.

Ryan nodded and touched his heart. "Feeling the love here, I get it. I've been trying so hard to be a superman and save everyone, I forgot that even a hero needs the help of all the super friends. Can't do it all alone anymore. Getting too old according to you wise guys. But, there are parts that only I can do, got it? That means, I say, you do it. Understand?"

Nods.

"Great. Now, I just have to convince those old people over there. Wish me luck."

Ryan wandered back over and pulled a chair around. Sitting with his arms on the backrest, he held out his hands in defeat. "I already got reamed by the wonder twins over there. I would say I'm sorry, but as you all know by now, there's a method to my increasing madness that goes back to being ingrained in me by the military. Sometimes, it's just autopilot. Sectioning off information protects people if they get caught. Keeps them focused on the task on not having to worry about the bigger picture sometimes I don't even know inside my mangled brain. I promised the terrors I'd be more of a team player, even if it kills me."

BP shook his head. "Dude, how long have we known each other? Got to trust us, man. We're all on the same side. Sacrifice to the end."

Honcho threw his pen. "Asshat," he mocked before a huge grin washed over. "Still love ya though."

Julia stared, her brown eyes burning his. He saw the anger, knew he was screwed later when they were alone.

"Don't do it again," Julia huffed.

Ryan looked around the table and bowed his head before looking up. "I was just trying to protect all the people I love, except you two assholes," he pointed with his fingers at Honcho and BP before getting up and hugging both men. Moving to Julia, he simply said, "I am sorry. It's my mess from the past it seems. Just trying to carry the load so no one else suffers."

She searched his green eyes, trying to see if it was the virus or her husband responding to them. Finding something, she sighed, and wrapped her arms around him. "I wish I knew what all was inside that head of yours. I'm trying to trust the man, but am worried about what is lurking within."

Kissing her forehead, Ryan leaned back. "Before it gets to that, you'll be the first to know. Even let you pull the trigger if you want."

She smacked his arm. "No. There's a line of people who want the honors," she winked.

Feeling they were back on track, Ryan kissed her cheek and went back to sit. A debriefing was in order to get everyone up to speed, and time was still their enemy. The battle for Seattle raged a war that awakened the Un-dead to an extent not seen in three years. While Liz's people were walled in, fighting Brainers and the dead on multiple fronts depleted sacred resources. If Zane Williams survived being eaten, then the potential for reinforcements grew with each minute that passed.

It was Hail Mary time.

"OK people, here's the master plan. Let's make it work."

CHAPTER 77

When Ryan finished, no one said a word.

Silence reigned for a good five minutes before anyone moved or made a sound. When they did, the electricity in the air vibrated with an intense energy.

"So, that's what you have in mind?" BP managed to get out. He was still processing the information and latest intel while trying to keep straight Ryan's plan.

"Hmm," Honcho murmured before the eyebrow raised and something clicked.

Julia was quiet, arms crossed. Head tilted to the right, lips pursed, she tapped her fingers. Ryan could tell she wanted to say something, but was holding back.

"Thoughts?" Ryan asked.

BP started to speak, held it, and then let it out. "Man, I'm not sure about this. It's divide and conquer to the extreme. We split up and we lose our advantage, in my opinion. We have Mark and Reg. We have major leverage, Bro."

Honcho mumbled to himself before motioning to BP. "He's right, to some degree. Mark and Reg give us a power play. We split and that puts us out of contact if something goes haywire. I get it. I just don't like it."

Julia shook her head. "No, Ryan's right. The kids are the target and we have to get them far away and underground. Work the cure to release to the world. If Ryan's going to turn, and trust me, it kills me to even think it," she said as tears dropped down her cheeks, "then we can't miss the chance to nail their asses to the wall."

BP shook his head. "That's assuming, and we know what that does, assuming the information Ryan gets is right and he can use it. Reg or Mark lie, and it's a sure death for our boy."

The love felt good. At the end of the day, his time was numbered with no indication when it would end. Better to go out guns blazing if that was what gave the world a chance versus turning into the psycho of all pyschos with an unquenchable thirst for blood and losing an opportunity to use his skills for good one last time.

"Kids won't go for it," Honcho threw out. "Probably will stop it given their newfound super powers."

The revelation caught Ryan by surprise. "Say, what now?"

The three faces opposite him glanced back and forth between them before Julia spilled.

"Ah, well, that. Guess we can't really be mad at you for keeping secrets given we have a few in the bag."

Ryan leaned back. "Really now."

Sheepish grins that attempted to go away.

"At least with the kids, we have some extra oomph to throw shade at them," BP offered up.

Honcho pointed at Ryan, shaking his finger. Words failed to materialize, just a look and a finger waving up and down. Must have been a minute before he said, "I believe I have an idea."

Ryan felt the life leave him. His adrenaline had been easing back to normal, and before he could stop it, the vomit hurled. He leaned to the side and let it all out. Wiping his mouth when he was done, he looked and saw the darkened blackness on his fingers.

There was no hiding it anymore.

The shock had Julia stare numbly his way. BP wasn't fully up to speed on Ryan's medical issues that were turning him into a full born walking dead man. BP knew the gist, just not the gory details.

"Ah shit, Man."

Honcho chucked over a towel. Of the three, he knew more and wanting to run a bit of cover for his old friend, spoke up. "One of the other reasons we need to stick together. The pinhead is sick and needs us to keep him straight. From what I've uncovered, I haven't even told him yet."

Ryan caught the look from Honcho, gave a slow unnoticeable nod to anyone who didn't know their *code*, and used the towel to clean up.

"How long, Ryan?" Julia had to know.

Shrugging his shoulders, Ryan was honest. "I have no idea. Could be hours, days, months even. Mark and my dad don't even know the extent, and trust me, if they did, they would have shoved my face in it."

Honcho touched the table. "From what I came across, and it's all pieced together with chewing gum and spit, and really more theoretical since from what I read, no one, and I mean no one, seems to be in our boy's class of coming wickedness. The people you call Brainers are distant cousins. Those off the wall jack slaps that do crazy shit to their bodies but look like they came of out a catalog modeling session? Those deranged piss heads are the closest thing I can think of. When it took and held, it was over months. Ryan's blood was dormant and something woke the beast. My educated guess based on what he's told me and I've gleaned? He's got days left."

The disclosure put a dark cloud over the room.

Ryan got up, cleaned the rest of the puke from the floor, and went to throw the towel away. The kids were far enough away to miss the show, but not so far away to not hear the aftermath of the sounds coming from their dad. Running diagonal to meet him, they grabbed his arms.

"Dad? Are you alright?" David asked.

Ryan was tired of the lies. He could only protect them so much, but as long as he could, he was going to suck it up. "Oh, I'm fine. Just a bad burrito last night."

Emma felt the lie, saw the twinkle of fear in her dad's eyes before it faded, and wanting to help, smiled. "He's fine, Bubba. You know how it is? Sometimes this world gives you the yucks and you hurl."

Ryan managed a smile. "That's right, Pumpkin. Daddy will be fine."

David wasn't so sure, but nodded. "OK."

Taking her brother's hand, Emma led them back and glancing over her shoulder, gave her double wink to Ryan.

Discarding the towel, Ryan went to the back-office area where Mark was tied up. Opening the door and walking past the front desks, he found Mark. Pulling up a chair, Ryan sat, placing his pistol on his left knee.

"I'm only going to ask this once. I think you are lying, and I will pull the trigger."

Mark spit to the side. "Ask. Doesn't mean I know."

The gun patted his knee. "Who runs this shit show? For real?"

Mark pursed his lips. "That's a bit complicated. According to your father, he does. I'm just a part of the wheel. A very important and crucial component that keeps it all together and not falling apart. But not the big cheese, so to speak."

Ryan felt his blood boil, but kept it in check. "Explain it then."

A shake of the head. "See? That's the hard part. There are many who serve on the Council here and others on theirs. Who they all answer to is a mystery."

Ryan leaned over and aimed the barrel at Mark's kneecap. Pushing it hard, he pulled back and the trigger clicked.

"What the hell?" Mark screamed out in anticipation of being shot before realizing nothing happened.

Ryan's right hand produced the magazine. He popped it in and pulled back to rack one in the chamber. "That was your freebie. Next lie and it goes right through your knee. You know what happens when a combat grain bullet rips through the knee, right?"

Mark frowned and nodded.

"Great. Let's try this again. Who is behind this madness?"

Mark fidgeted a bit before blurting, "I really don't know! There are rumors, but I'm way down the food chain. Your dad is higher up, connected. He knows more than me."

Ryan searched Mark's face. It could be bullshit, the virus' ability to mask the lies. It was hard to tell. Mark started bouncing, as if he had ADHD. Ryan realized it was a thought running through his old friend's brain. Tapping the knee, Mark felt the steel and returned to normal.

"Go on," Mark said.

"What are the rumors then?" Ryan saw what had to be fear, an emotion he hadn't seen before in Mark. Ryan knew there was an evolution happening to everyone infected and to varying degrees. Maybe he had something to exploit.

Mark must have seen Ryan's face register, as immediately Mark closed his eyes. "I tell you, and they kill me if it's true."

The steel pushed hard. "You are going to die anyway, Old Friend. For what you did to my wife and my babies, you don't get a pass. You can though choose whether it's quick and painless, or I wait until the monster in me gets fully out. We wait for that, and the things I will do to make you suffer haven't been invented yet. Lie again and it starts today and I let you ferment a bit."

Mark saw the truth in Ryan's eyes. It wasn't a bluff.

Clearing his throat, Mark stared at his former friend. "I can speak for our sect. Rumblings have been that it goes back to one of the great families in American history. The sons tried to leave the shadow of the father behind, and it cost them their lives. The father's support of the Nazis should have been a warning. Ideals that got convoluted by a madman who strayed from the cause and instead of working to make the world a better place, let his underlings do unspeakable things in the name of purification. The grandchildren of the American patriarch, at least some of them, decided to honor the past, though not for what it was, but for what it was meant to accomplish. Advocates on both sides to shade the true pursuit. All a cover for what really was at play since we have no party alignment. Both sides of the aisle are our brethren."

Ryan let the words seep into his brain. He didn't want to believe it.

"You have any proof to support it?"

Mark sighed. "Like I said, it's rumblings and gossip. I can say as far as a possible fact, the compound in Martha's Vineyard is vibrant these days."

There was no immediate way to validate and verify the intel. However, Ryan did know a guy who knew a guy that might be able to help out.

"Appreciate the information. It pans out, we have an understanding, right? It doesn't and you are so going to hate the shit I do to you," Ryan laughed, the dark tone so frightening that Mark cringed back in his seat.

"You can't win, Ryan. Destiny and righting the world's wrongs are coming to set it all straight."

The fist connected and sent Mark's head springing back. When it came full stop, Ryan's rage erupted.

"Listen, you royal piece of shit. Don't you then find it ironic, given all the bullshit you assholes believe, that my daughter, a beautiful soul and person who has a disability, is the savior of your demented ideology? Under Nazism, she was trash, a stain on the gene pool to be eradicated. For the future, she is the trillion-dollar prize to your sick and twisted scheme. Someone not fit to live then and looked down upon, now the only one who can deliver the goods for your reign of terror."

Mark spat out a mouthful of blood. "All an end to a means."

Ryan spit in his former friend's face. "Never. As long as I'm breathing, all *sane* Ryan or the demented devil that's coming, you will never get my daughter. I'm going to kill every last one of you and enjoy the torture I bring upon you."

Mark smiled, the evil leeching out the corner of his mouth. "You won't live long enough to do it."

CHAPTER 78

The rain.

Seattle decided to earn its reputation. Dark clouds that had cast an eerie shadow over the city descended with a vengeance. Coupled with the intense layer of smoke from the fires burgeoning along the battle lines near I5, the pallor of thick air hung overhead like sticky syrup you couldn't wash off.

Without a good northwesterly wind to clear it out, the day was doom and gloom.

Ryan watched from the protection of the hangar, just inside the doors. At first a simple sprinkle, it erupted into a storm with the sound of lightning cracking the sky a few miles away, the illumination almost catatonic to enjoy. Drawing closer, electricity filled the air and he swore he felt the electrons pulsing through his body. The onset drew a quiet sigh, one that wasn't quite dismay and not contained jubilation at the changing theater of war at his feet.

This is a mess, Ryan thought to himself. *Battle on multiple fronts and our resources are going to be outnumbered if reinforcements make it.*

The movie in his head played on repeat. The ending the same. Even with his confidence at getting the job done, there was still an uneasiness that a victory would stick. If Mark wasn't lying about the American sect, then it meant the tentacles into every corner of influence and allegiance was an uphill battle. America's darling family behind the leadership meant it really was a non-partisan coup of democracy and the future. Chuck into the pile the other sects and their leadership, whomever they might be, and it really was anyone's game. He could demolish the group stateside. It didn't mean the others wouldn't come to play.

He needed to find the head of the snake and send a message.

With his own clock ticking down, that reality kept just out of reach. Ryan knew he could only do so much with the limited time he had left. Try and do it all, and fail miserably across the board.

Focus his attention, and make the biggest bang for his buck.

Not that he couldn't set up others to keep the fight competitive and racing to victory. He just had to feed them the right intel to point them in the right direction. Without making his way back east again, investigating the Martha Vineyard's connection was moot. He required a faster approach, one that cut to the core and possibly spilled details long locked away.

Reg.

Hesitant to face his father, not from fear, but from the wrath he knew would burst the dam of his composure, Ryan made his way to the other set of offices in the hangar. In no hurry, the echo of his boots on the cold concrete reverberating in his ears. Reaching the door he paused, took a breath in and held it, before turning the knob and passing the threshold.

The door creaked closed behind him.

Reg sat in a comfortable leather office chair. Bound with rope and duct tape with no way to free himself, he sat stone-faced, brown eyes penetrating back with a venom Ryan had never seen.

"Come to face your death?" Reg snickered.

Ryan waved him off. "Mine? Your time is about over, Dad. You can live out the last bit redeeming your pathetic and miserable existence, or face a son who has no more conscience when it comes to killing you."

Reg tilted his head. "Empty threats. When will you realize you've already lost. I win, no matter the outcome."

The bravado beating within the old shell of a man was comical.

"Seriously, Dad? At every step I've beaten you. Me, just me, one lone person against an army and a handful of people poking the bear. You really think you have a chance in hell against me? Keep dreaming."

Reg thrust forward, his bindings catching hold. "You think it's simple coincidence you're all gathered here? Mark might have had his plan, but it was just a tiny blip on the map."

Ryan faked a yawn. "You bore me, Dad. All talk. No action."

Brown eyes lit with fire stared back. "Think about it, Son! Every action has a reaction. Every step a counter. You think you have been five steps ahead? I've been ten."

Bluster. It had to be as there was no way his father was better than him. Ryan was a professional, a master at the game. A man skilled at doing the impossible. His dad was just a truck driver who happened to sink into a life running with psychotics hellbent on world domination.

The old black and white photo Honcho found flashed by.

Reg had been military. The cover being he was stateside as a helicopter mechanic. The truth, according to Honcho's recovered documents, painted a different picture. Special operations during the Vietnam War, the missions blacked out and even Honcho hadn't deciphered them yet. Ryan always assumed his vigor for service was innate, something deep inside himself that had to be fed to ensure his thirst for preserving democracy was quenched. Maybe, it was all a façade.

The apple sometimes doesn't fall far from the tree.

When it hit, Ryan nearly puked his energy bar. Reg saw it, relished in the fear he caught in his son's green eyes. The elder Carmichael began to laugh, low at first before rising in magnitude. When he finally stopped, Reg was grinning from ear to ear.

"Something wrong, Son?"

Ryan shook, his head pounding hard. He stepped over to the wall and leaned, trying to corral his senses and gather his bearings. If Reg was the one ten steps ahead, Ryan was hosed.

"Not at all, Dad. Just felt a bit queasy. Not enough to eat today."

The lie didn't catch hold.

"No, I saw it. You're afraid. You realized something, something that spooked you to the bone. I can only imagine what it was."

Ryan rocked his head. "Sorry to disappoint you. Just hungry. Besides, the bullshit on being ten steps ahead of me makes me want to puke. You're nothing, Dad."

Reg leaned back and closed his eyes. "This is the only working airport around. A goldmine for anyone to possess. How in the world could your little band of misfits manage to take it so easily without a fight to the death of you all? I wonder?"

As the last word left Reg's lips, Ryan heard gunfire erupt outside. Turning to run, he glanced over his shoulder as Reg winked. Throwing open the door and slamming it shut behind, he saw San Carlos firing out the hangar door and BP and Honcho hustling the kids and Julia to the back. Making his way to them, Ryan stopped behind a stack of crates.

"What's going on?" he yelled over the noise.

Honcho tapped his head. "Seems our taking of the airport drew eyes. Brain dead filtering out of the cracks."

Ryan paused before following up. "How many?"

BP coughed, the pain his plate carrier took protecting him still reeling from the aftereffects. "Oh, I'd say a shitload."

Feeling the walls closing in as he knew their current situation was lean on guns and personnel, Ryan got a flash of a thought. "Leave them to me. You all stay tight."

Before anyone could protest, Ryan vanished into the gray of the day outside.

CHAPTER 79

The Reaper was in play.

Caution to the wind, Ryan had people to protect. He was still Ryan, the humanity beating wildly deep inside.

He just had the new version 2.0 as an asset.

The Un-dead were a ruthless bunch. Once they tasted blood, metaphorically speaking, they were blood hounds on the scent until a new fragrance caught their eye. Ryan didn't know which ones were lurking outside. It didn't matter much if it was Lurkers or Bolts. Either a recipe for disaster. If nature was letting evolution unfold, it could be a combination of the two, working hand-in-hand to stalk their future meals.

He'd seen it before, the cuddly coziness in the old train tunnels.

That cooperation might be their downfall. The present-day bond a fragile partnership that could be broken or damaged beyond repair. Their animal instinct, the one that controlled their brain function, the primal drive that was their being, Ryan could work with it to sow some chaos.

It was worth a shot with the rain taking a short break.

He had seen an old tanker truck parked just outside one of the hangars. From the looks of it, Mark's men had it up and running as the hoses had been unfurled to fuel the transport. If he could get to it, even in the light rain cascading down from above, hell fire could rage.

Grabbing a few grenades from his ruck and stuffing them into the leg pockets of his BDUs, Ryan went to work. Letting San Carlos' men engage the ruckus, he quietly snuck out to the truck. Checking the valves and gauges, the dials said it was still carrying some fuel. Flipping one of the old valve handles, Ryan ran to the hose and picking it up, quickly used the serrated side of his combat knife to saw just below the disconnect nipple before jet fuel began to spew out.

He barely made it.

Pointing the end towards the tarmac, he let the liquid fly, panning left and right to ensure a thick blanket collected over the top of pooled water. Satisfied with the result, he set the hose down to keep coughing out fuel and climbed on top of the rig. Taking a second to catch his breath, he stood, almost triumphantly with his hand on his hips, before he let loose.

"Assholes! Dinner time!"

San Carlos' men heard the shouting and paused their fire. The Un-dead, by the looks of them Ryan had figured right on the dot, were Lurkers and Bolts. Catching his words and changing their attention, he could see them what could only be a wild guess as *whispering* to one another, a chain of dialog moving among the mass of bodies. From one to the next, before they all focused their gaze singularly towards him.

The blood curdling horror of screams echoed in Ryan's ears.

Methodically, as a unit, the horde disconnected from the fight and moved towards Ryan. Stranglers closed in, until the mass of bodies became a sea, not quite shoulder to shoulder, but near enough you might think they were holding hands on a walk in the park. Never wavering, they almost glided in his direction, until Ryan lost count at the number of eyes staring back.

He'd never seen such show of force before.

Waving his arms, Ryan encouraged them over. "Hey, dipshits. Can you understand the words that are coming from my mouth?"

He didn't expect any response, was surprised when he heard it.

The hissing made his skin crawl. "Die."

Not letting the sudden awakening of speech slow his roll, Ryan flipped two birds. "Fuck you!"

The river of death kept flowing, as more emerged and joined the party. "Die."

Figuring what the hell, Ryan let go. "Naw, not me. But I tell ya, if you all are wanting a nice little meal, I know of a few nice bites around that will make your mouth water."

They kept on coming.

The new revelation hitting home, Ryan raised his right hand. "Is there one of you in charge I can speak to about something?"

It was a longshot.

The mass parted, and a lone figure materialized from the darkness. She would have been beautiful once. Her long hair, a shade of red almost coppery if it was clean and the curls magnificent if not ratted together with debris, parted to show her face. As she glanced up, the pale skin reminded him of Emma, though now the streaks of dirt added a hue to the woman that betrayed her past. She would have been radiant, a breath of fresh air with a smile that lit up the room. A delight naked above the sheets to love and cherish by the looks of her figure that swayed beneath the fading fabric of her paisley dress. The woman's eyes, an icy blue like his own daughter's.

The venom in them now burning brighter than the sun.

The former goddess he imagined was probably shy and unassuming, not one to grab her former sexuality and instead, was just a lovely soul, raised her arm and aimed it.

"Die."

Ryan waved her off. "Is there another word we can use here?"

This time, she gave him a real smile, revealing her pointed teeth and a flick of her black tongue. "You, die."

He couldn't help but laugh. Grabbing his stomach, he bent at the waist before coming back up. "Sorry. I was hoping for a bit more."

She titled her head, as if to think, before she smiled again. "You, and everyone not like us, die."

Ryan nodded. He had her attention and information from this small interaction that provided a wealth of data. "I get it. My kind kill you because you try to kill us. It's a vicious circle. The fact you understand me though says there's something inside of you that is changing. Maybe, we can help you change even more."

The woman stared, her head moving from side to side as if contemplating a response to Ryan's observation. Rhythmic, like a head dance. He'd seen Emma do it as a child. They always assumed it was part of her disability, a coping mechanism or fluid in her ears. He was trying to rationalize the unknown, hoping he made a connection, and it was not the time to do it.

When you assume, everyone knows what that means.

"We no change. We evolve. We like us," she growled.

Ryan held up his hands. "Got it. You all like the new you. To me though, at least on my travels, it's a bit rough living. What happens when there's no more food for you to eat? What then?"

She paused her head dance, and stopped cold, eyes glimmering bright. "Always food for us now with our changes."

It didn't make any sense what she said, until he thought about it. A bleak and gut-wrenching vision to comprehend. The bloated belly she pointed out was primal existence at its worst.

"I feel sorry for you."

The woman had kept slowly inching forward, her followers too. Maybe she figured Ryan would get lost in conversation, or the fact she had language and it rocked his brain so hard, he'd lose track. Get close enough that she would unleash her brethren and he was toast. Crispy sourdough black on all sides.

Off clicked *his* switch.

Hands to his leg pockets, in one motion Ryan's hands came up and with a flick of his thumbs, the pins on the grenades flung off. The woman stood perplexed, his actions so fluid and natural that she didn't, or her decayed brain couldn't, recognize what was about to hit the fan. A smile on his face and slight nod of his head, Ryan exhaled before he tossed the canisters in her direction. As the smoke leaked out and then the bright flames, somewhere deep inside of her, a fraction of human left over sensed what was coming and she froze. The primal scream of fear brewing in her gut raced from the bowels of her lungs in a vain attempt to get up and out her throat a millisecond too late.

She was standing before the new Death.

The fire engulfed the former beauty in an inferno of color. The jet fuel's octane on steroids compared to regular gasoline burned with an intensity that as it grew out, began to evaporate every ounce of flesh in its wake. The running hose had continued to leak liquid underfoot as the mass of flesh advanced on Ryan, something he prayed would happen. With an unsuspecting lake below their feet, the horde traipsed through, sloshing droplets on clothing and skin that once lit, was no match for a retreat.

Their frantic gesticulations from excruciating pain only fueled the flames.

Once he chucked the death dealers, Ryan bailed from the top of the truck. He knew once the flames caught, they would creep back to the source and soon the vehicle would explode. Getting as far away as possible was a necessity if he valued living another few hours. Looking over his shoulder as he fled, Ryan saw *her*, or what he figured was the fading remnants of her, still with eyes fixated on him. If he had any emotions left it would twinge his soul.

Those days were nearly gone.

Feeling he was far enough away from the destruction brewing behind, Ryan turned and watched as those on the outskirts of the group attempted to flee, only to be caught in the onslaught. For the ones not crumbling to the ground in heaps of melting flesh, San Carlos' men finished the job. Body after body fell, until nothing remained.

The roaring blaze the only movement.

Standing on the tarmac, the scene calming to his hardening new soul, Ryan smiled. Not from any sort of amusement or happiness. It was more a forced physical act from an epiphany at what occurred moments ago, a sudden game changer that meant a whole new dynamic to the game.

Evolution was about to find a whole different level of nasty unleashed.

CHAPTER 80

"Did you know?"

The question was vague. Details mattered in order to provide an explanation, if one was even available.

Mark rocked back in his chair to look up at Ryan. "Did I know what?"

Ryan stared back, his green eyes full of hate. "Did you know *they* can talk?"

The word didn't register at first. When they did, Ryan wasn't sure if the stunned expression was legitimate or another ruse.

"*They?* Are we talking the same language here as in the crazy brain-dead scavengers and killers running amok among the living?" Mark seemed like it was breaking news to him.

Ryan's eyes didn't need to respond.

"Oh, wow. That my friend, is incredible."

The shaking head said otherwise. "No, it's bad news. Seems they don't want us around. Prefer us all dead to living all peacefully together as one big happy family. I was told so a few minutes ago."

Mark let it sink in. "So, you actually *spoke* to one?"

An affirmative nod. "I did. A leader of a very large group that was about to rip this place a new one. Told me herself she wanted me, and all of us, dead."

"Given past history, not a surprising sentiment. Vocalizing it, a completely new discovery."

Ryan smacked the desktop. "No shit, Sherlock! Do you not fathom in what's left of that smart brain of yours that your little experiment has completely gone off the rails? The evil you bastards unleashed on the rest of us is evolving, and not the kind of opposable thumbs and using tools for crops kind that will make this a handy dandy planet to live on for much longer."

Mark nervously licked his lips.

"What were once separate groups of psychotic nutjobs have now joined forces. They don't just hang out in small gangs, corner thugs hitting the old bodega. They're amassed into small armies that think and speak. No more primal drive just driving the old bus. They've got leadership and ideas on who gets to be top dog moving forward. And, it ain't any of us, survivors or the likes of you and the other whack jobs. If you never noticed, our groups are in the tiny minority. They want to, they can eradicate us in no time at all. Your vaccine won't matter."

The picture Ryan drew registered.

Mark's eyes, earlier brilliant at what his old friend described, suddenly twinkled. Sitting, gazing up at Ryan, Mark shrugged. "Guess it was a great run. For all of you."

Nothing fazed Ryan anymore. "Us? I'm pretty sure your kind fall into the box too."

Mark shook his head. "See? That's where you're wrong. I'm guessing they despise any living soul that does not possess the altered state of being that they miraculously have achieved. My kind? Call us kindred spirits. Cousins even. We share the same purpose, in so many words. They want you all dead. We want you to fall in line. This opens a whole new avenue for a cooperative relationship. Resist us, and become fodder for them. I bet they'd like to not have to scavenge for food."

"Are you serious?"

A wicked grin. "Absolutely! This makes it so much easier for us to succeed. I can't wait to tell the Council and make your dad my errand boy."

He didn't see it. Failed to hear the hammer cock back. One second Ryan was scowling, envisioning what the future held, the demise of civilization in its entirety. A world where Emma and Davis had no chance at normalcy. Survivors nothing more than a food supply for the wicked if they fought for their lives against the dystopia that bared down on them with unrelenting force. It was the last lucid thought to enter his mind.

The next second, the bullet rang out.

He didn't even bother to put on the suppressor. Just pulled his Sig from its holster, cocked it and thumbed the safety off in one motion, and gently pulled the trigger. As the projectile existed the barrel, he released a breath. Felt the enormous sense of accomplishment at finally fulfilling the deed. As it struck the flesh, Mark felt the impact, jerked his head back, locked eyes on Ryan. A grin washed over his old mentor's face, and Ryan smiled back.

The blast echoed in the tiny room as Mark's brains splattered the back wall.

A decades long friendship suddenly lost to delusions of men. Ryan felt tears and anger, a confusing mix of emotions that simply let loose at once. Mark had meant the world to Ryan once. His mentor, protector, an evolution to dear friend. Mark had been the one to suggest consulting, to leave the life of an underpaid warrior and reap the financial security of hired gun employment. There was more to it than that, than just getting money for the gigs. There was the ability to say no, where as a soldier you didn't get the option. Even then, Mark advised when Ryan needed someone to bounce ideas off. The older brother who could make you think about a decision and bring you back to reality for a nut check if they had to make you grounded.

Mark was a loss he wasn't sure he'd ever recover.

As the tears flooded and the pain enveloped his body, Ryan grieved. He couldn't help it. He knew the time would come, the moment Mark would have to die for his sins against the Carmichael family. Pay for his cruelty that Ryan figured murdered millions in the process of experimentation. The finality of the act didn't bring the salvation he hoped would alleviate his inner rage. Didn't soothe his wounded heart. While the ending was carved in stone for Mark to perish, there was still no actual joy in blowing the brains out of one of your longtime confidantes. Sadness reigned supreme.

Mark's death another notch on Ryan's belt.

There was more to it. Mark wasn't just a number. Even in the face of a maddening world where the enemy looked just like you, Ryan knew more would face a wrath that couldn't be contained, more succumb to his agony over pulling the trigger and watching life slip from their eyes. Hell, his own father was going to get his at some point in the future. Justice would be served frozen for all who thought the life they thrust upon the world was theirs to dictate.

Ryan just had to kill them all one by one.

Wiping the water from his face, the quiet sobs ebbing away like the tide, Ryan felt weak, his body no longer capable of movement. Paralyzed was the feeling in his extremities. Standing there, he suddenly collapsed to a knee, his brain on fire with visions that couldn't be placed. Were they suppressed memories, his vivid imagination?

He wasn't sure reality was ringing a bell anymore.

Taking a deep breath, Ryan held it, counted to ten, and exhaled. His body tingly and his mind clouded. The past no longer believable to one hundred percent. Maybe it was all a dream, and this very moment a delusion. He wasn't sure about a damn thing being true or a lie. For all he knew, or thought he did, he might be the one responsible for the demise of the world. One of his missions the domino that set it all in motion. Shaking the thought or responsibility to the side, not able to face the idea, Ryan slammed the floor with his hand, and instantaneously, his emotions, every one of them, was gone.

Reaching out to Mark, Ryan touched the cool hand. "Goodbye, Old Friend. See you soon." Wiping the last tears away, he stood.

Time to finish what he started.

Walking out the door, Ryan saw shocked expressions all around. He shrugged, and kept walking towards the hangar door. Julia ran over from where Emma and David sat visibly shaken, catching up just as Ryan stepped outside.

"What happened, Ryan?"

He didn't want to talk, didn't want to explain. He turned his head, nodded, and walked away.

"Ryan?" Julia called after, before Honcho grabbed her arm.

"Don't. Let me talk to him," Honcho said as BP took Julia's other arm and led her back to the children.

Standing next to one of the SUVs, Ryan was watching the embers slowly dying out as the bodies fuel for the fire spent out. Arms crossed, leaning back against the hood, Honcho could see his old friend deep in thought. Finding a spot next to Ryan, Honcho blew out a gust of air.

"You can't just blow her off like that."

Ryan nodded.

"What the hell went on in there for you to do what I know you did if I went and checked, I'd see a dead man."

Ryan turned. His face emotionless.

"Are you even in there anymore?"

Ryan shrugged. "Barely, Honcho."

Patting his friend, Honcho leaned over. "Talk to me."

Ryan blew out, a huge sigh, and took a breath in before expelling again. "I just couldn't let it go on. I confronted Mark about what we all saw out here and what I told you about them having words and thoughts. At first, I could see he was scared shitless by the revelation. Hoped somewhere I could reason, come to some understanding that our two groups of humans are so outnumbered we need to work together. Then, it all went to pot. He went right to what he can do with them. Make us the food supply if we don't subjugate to his Council. Fear us into obedience. Threatened to tell them if he got away. Could not let that happen again. What he did to my babies, my wife, he had to die."

As much as Honcho believed it was the wrong decision, Mark was worth his weight in information that could help the cause of survivors, there was no way to second-guess the outcome. If Mark managed to relay the new state of the Un-dead, the future was all but over for humankind.

"What now?" Honcho asked as he wrapped an arm around his brother from another mother.

Ryan put his head against Honcho's chest. The attempt at comfort missing the mark as Ryan felt nothing, but knew he had to pretend to keep up appearances. "We get the kids to Mary."

Honcho kissed the top of Ryan's head. "OK. But first, make things right with Julia and the kids. Your recent string of actions has scared the crap out of them. They're worried and terrified their losing their dad."

Ryan's head bounced slowly, acknowledging the request. "Roger that."

He didn't want to have to explain. Didn't want to have to try and justify his actions. At the end of the day, he made decisions that kept them alive, whether anyone agreed or not. While keeping Mark around at first was meant to have the man used as a bargaining chip, it became clear his continued existence was a liability to everyone. Even in the face of hearing the latest evolution of the Un-dead having speech and thoughts, possessing an intellect and certain reasoning where they had a focus on what they wanted to do, Mark couldn't grasp the fragility of where that left the human race.

He saw the evil he could harness within them, not what their new being could do to end the world as people knew it.

With no redeeming quality left, and Ryan had hoped Mark might mysteriously gain some sanity and see how extreme the stakes were to life, there was nothing left of his old friend that Ryan felt was there. The mentor, the friend, the man he had looked up to for so long, was effectively erased.

Now, everything a void and only evil in the abyss, death was Mark's savior.

Julia sat huddled with Emma and David, her eyes locked on Ryan as he made his way to them. Pulling up a chair, he flipped it around and sat, his arms crossed over the backrest.

"Hey," Ryan managed to get out before Julia cut him off.

"I think it's time you go do your thing and let us go our way."

The statement hit to the core.

He searched David's face for understanding and only saw fear. Looking at Emma, tears drying at the corner of her eyes, she managed a double wink.

At least his girl still had his back.

"Listen, I am not going to sugar coat anything I am about to say. And please, do not interrupt. Mark is dead. Yup, I shot him. Do you know why?"

Julia glared. "I can only imagine."

Sighing, Ryan looked around the group. "I tried with everything I had to get one of my dearest friends, someone I looked up to for so many years who was my mentor, my confidante, a man who had my back so many times and lifted me up when I was down, tried to find a sliver of human left in him. Explained to him what happened outside with the Un-dead, how they were evolving, something I had witnessed on my travels that was terrifying to see. How we are the tiny fraction of the living left, and they outnumber us. It's only time before they totally run the show if they are smart enough to start hunting us and remove us from the planet. Tried to see if someway, somehow, he'd see that we need an alliance to save everyone. You know what he wanted? To use us as a food supply for them as a threat to keep us under the control of the madmen he obeys."

The words hung like a cloud.

"So, with no way of reaching the man inside I used to know, I made a decision. You all knew it was coming, so don't pretend to be shocked. That man threw me out the door of a helicopter to try and kill me. Took you all from me. Experimented on my children, abused them and allowed unspeakable things to happen. Left a body count so high of people used as test tubes and then discarded like trash you can't even fathom the death toll. In war, death happens. And family, if you haven't realized it yet, we are at war trying to save humanity before time runs out. I will not apologize for doing what had to happen. I just wish you all didn't have to be a part of it."

Julia relaxed her grip on the children, but kept them close. "Ryan? You incinerated an entire group of people without a second thought. Killed one of your oldest friends. What's to say that you won't do that to us?"

He felt anger brew at his wife even saying that, and then Emma jumped in.

"Really, Mom? Dad protected us. Those aren't people anymore. They have tried to eat us for a long time. And Uncle Mark? I'm glad he's dead. He hurt me and can't do it ever again."

David pulled away from his mom. He got up, fidgeted with his hands, before coming close to Ryan. "Dad? You're still you, right?"

Ryan reached out and stroked his son's cheek. "Big Man, I won't lie to you. I feel it inside me and I'm fighting it off. I'm still me, but it's getting harder each day. But, no matter what happens to me, I would never, ever, hurt any of the people I love who matter. Papa? Well, he's gonna kick rocks for what he's done to all of us."

The joke struck a chord.

David grinned. "As much as I think it's wrong, he deserves it."

"Yup," Emma smiled.

Julia sat, not sure what to say. Ryan had laid it bare. There was truth to his words, no matter how she tried to think of arguments to counter. It was war, a war that seemed like they were losing, but she held hope they could win. Ryan was the soldier, the warrior who she was just finding out had done things no one could imagine to save the world. He was still doing it, even if it was under darker and more sinister clouds that ate away at his very soul.

"Look, bad things are going to happen. I am trying to keep that away from all of you. Sometimes, there is no preventing it, no matter the circumstances. We need to move, and Mark was baggage that wasn't making the trip."

Julia turned her head towards the rear offices. "Reg?"

Ryan grimaced. "He still has some value. He's making a different trip."

Confused, Julia opened her mouth when Ryan connected the dots.

"You all can be protected here. Work on a vaccine that might do some good. I've got to do what I do best. Cut the head off the snake."

Emma *felt* his thoughts. Wanted to argue with her dad, but she knew. Felt it herself, deep inside her mind. David caught the unspoken words from his sister, and nodded. While losing his father once meant the end of the world, losing him again meant possibly saving it for good this time around.

Julia saw the contentment in the kids, knew that for whatever weird bond and transformation they had undergone, they knew more than she did. She didn't like being the odd one out, left on the perimeter of the inner circle while the three amigos shared some strange connection she could never begin to comprehend the meaning of, let alone understand how it worked.

"I thought we agreed we would not separate and stick together. That was the deal. You've been on a one-man mission since you left the silo. I need an honest answer, not bullshit."

"Mom! Language."

"Sorry, kids."

Ryan could lie. Could divert, misdirect, even ignore. He was tiring of the deceit, the need to keep his cards close to the vest. The truth wouldn't set him free, but it would make things as transparent as being naked in a room full of overdressed socialites.

"My days are becoming harder and harder to keep me the top dog. The *other* me is knocking on the door and keeps getting a toehold. He's going to kick it wide open and I'm not sure what will happen. The farther I am away when it does, you all might be safer. I'm afraid when he's unleashed, it's going to get really ugly for anyone in my way. I don't want my family as collateral damage to what I have to do to end this nightmare."

Julia touched his hand. "But why do you have to bring it to them? Seek them out? Make *them* earn it. Stay hidden while we find a cure or something to stave off what's happening to you. Then, when you're ready, eliminate with extreme prejudice. Isn't that what you special soldiers say?"

He caught the attempt at humor and appreciated the effort. She was right, to a degree. He could keep hiding, be around to protect the family and work the problem, see what Mary could do to find a solution. Have Honcho dig deeper for more intel that Ryan could utilize to strike back, and strike hard at the core of the issue. There was so much that could be done, and done in a way that didn't drop him right in the middle of a storm with no way home. She was right, like she was much of time. Unfortunately, that was the past. The present?

She was wrong on so many other levels.

CHAPTER 81

The precipice of sanity is a fine line.

You are either sane or not, so the saying goes. There are those that would argue that's not the case.

On the razor's edge, balancing precariously on the sharp metal, one side supposedly is what most consider normal. The other side? A free ride to the asylum. For those in the know, it's a fallacy. The top of the blade is actually flat if it's dull. You can step and look down one side and wander over and do the same on the other side. Even bend down and touch the cold steel, feel its smooth surface and rub it warm.

Standing atop the blade, you rule.

Possess the ability to partake either side without the need to jump off and fully envelope yourself. Have the best of both worlds, so to speak.

Ryan was standing on the dull path, awaiting his fate.

His mentor Mark was dead, a deed performed without any remorse. A war raged with the Brainers under Dennis Stohl's leadership. The Un-dead lurked in the shadows, word having spread like the wind of the man who must die to avenge their brothers and sisters. Zane Williams still remained a thorn to pluck out as recent intel validated.

Reg still lived.

Ryan knew the clock ticked on dear old dad. The elder Carmichael had a value. As a pawn in the game or simply for information, Ryan was undecided. He'd just as soon let the man ferment into a heaping pool of rot. Others had ideas, though their suggestions went in one ear and out the other.

Ryan was going to do what he felt best.

The airport was soon a beacon for every crazy in Seattle to bear down on when the fire raged and whispers floated along the ocean breeze. Retreat was a necessity, but not before getting the transport plane secured in a hangar for a *just in case* rainy day escape.

Or, a one-way ticket to Hell.

Ryan wasn't sure what to expect next. With Zane still alive, how many men at his disposal unknown, a threat existed. He had to be eliminated if the children and Julia were to stay safe and their whereabouts hidden. With the long-range radio in the transport disabled to prevent word getting back to base, Zane was limited to short range radio transmissions so for now, all was good on that front and put Ryan's mind at ease. The helicopter had a radio, but Ryan wasn't going to leave it around.

The big bird was their ride into the city.

Besides giving Ryan an aerial view of the war effort, it might reveal Zane. Not a sure thing, but Ryan hoped it might get the man to step into the open and allow Ryan a shot at seeing the commander of Zulu.

Figuratively, and literally, all in one.

Zane wouldn't expect Mark had failed, so Ryan had that in his favor. Lure his nemesis into a trap and take out the threat. With Zane gone it would give some breathing room until the next wave came.

When? Ryan didn't know.

The Blackhawk rose, with all essential personnel aboard with a caravan of SUVs and remaining military vehicles following below. Honcho had radioed Liz and she provided an update. The Brainers were isolated to skirmishes along I5 and firefights along the water just north of the city. She offered up a safe avenue for the vehicles if they kept to the west and managed to reach the old passenger water taxi routes. If they made it there, then her people could ferry them across.

The chopper could land anywhere near the Space Needle.

Ryan hoped Zane would appear. Think the movement of the aircraft with support vehicles in tow was an assault. Chock up the radio silence as a mission critical SOP in the works to avoid potential eavesdropping on comms.

Come out of hiding to want to participate and find his end.

Wishful thinking on Ryan's part. A possibility, given the mind that drove Zane. A want to always be in the fight and desire to add to his kill sheet. That bravado and blind ego were the traits to exploit. Ryan knew the old Zane well and with the effects of the virus sending those into overdrive, the solider couldn't resist the urge to jump into the fight. At least, Ryan wished the man would be dumb enough to forget a sane thought.

Never assume anything in a fight.

Running point in the helo, the trip took more than an hour. No resistance, no barricades to delay the journey. Caution was the culprit. Ryan could have had San Carlos' pilot, a former Mexican elite special forces officer Ryan had run a few outside ops with, simply put the stick down and drop off the cargo and then hustle back for cover overhead. It made sense. Get the critical packages safe and tucked away.

That defeated the purpose of exposing Zane.

Flying just above, it helped sell it was a mission, an incursion into enemy territory that was meant to sow carnage and get Zane to come and play. For all the man knew, Mark had multiple operations going and this was just one. Besides, Zane had his own mission to tackle, and if he bailed on it to come join another, for all he knew it was his own death sentence from Mark for failing to follow orders.

Deceive, misdirect, and manipulate.

Approaching their destination, Zane must have seen the helicopter in the sky and seeking to touch base and find out what was going on with all the radio silence, he peeked his head out.

Just a sliver, and Ryan had him dead to rights.

The caravan reached the parking lot for Terminal 5 and proceeded to park near the shoreline. All personnel tucked comfortably inside to prevent identification. Zane must have sought refuge on one of the Coast Guard ships in dry dock on Harbor Island. As the bird hovered a few hundred feet above the lot, Ryan caught a glint, and taking his binoculars, focused in. Standing on the flight deck of a Coast Guard cutter with a helipad, Ryan tapped the pilot and pointed.

Hitting the mic for his secured radio, he let Honcho know it was time. "Take care of my family."

"Always, Brother," came the reply before the radio went dead.

Adrenaline was something of a wonder. It coursed the body right before a fight, providing a rush to calm nerves and prepare for the battle ahead. Ryan felt nothing this time. His body wasn't amped up. His mind void of emotion.

He didn't feel anything except a desire to kill.

Strapped to the floor of the helicopter to prevent himself from flying out the door, Ryan prepared for what was coming next. His M4 was fine for closer quarters. His sniper rifle great for distance. He needed a gut punch, and nice for him, the M110 variant he possessed, the military version of the HK 417 chambered in 7.62mm, offered the fire power. Distance, accuracy, and selective rate of fire meant he could rain down on Zane and his men from above before they knew what hit their plate carriers. If Ryan got it right, their armor would fail within a single shot from his armor piercing bullets.

If he used the grenade launcher attachment, they were all dead.

The pilot crept close until Zane was in full view, his men around the walkway of the pad. Motioning for the bird to land, he stepped to the edge of the deck to give it room. Glancing at Ryan, the nod sent the plan into action. Flipping sideways, the helo glided in, dropping elevation as it descended. Thirty yards out on approach, the side door slid open.

Eyes locked on Zane, Ryan opened fire.

Shell casings flew all around. Finger on the trigger, the rounds flew to their targets. Sweeping left and right, Ryan let loose a barrage that caught everyone off-guard. Zane stood flatfooted, shocked to see Ryan so close, mowing down his former mates with ease. Some managed to return fire, only to fall. Magazine spent, Ryan popped in another and continued until it emptied. Zane's men dropped until he was the only one left in the crosshairs. Standing still, he glared, knowing his time was up and he had lost. The rage inside erupted, more for his own failures than being beaten by his old superior, a now middle-aged civilian who should have been dead long ago. Head bowed, when it came up, the devilish grin told a story older than time.

Ryan didn't see it coming.

Something landed next to him and instinctively, Ryan fired. As the projectile left the end of Ryan's barrel, his enemy's exposed forehead on target for the kill shot, Zane managed to flip Ryan two middle fingers, a last, *fuck you*. Eyes locked, Ryan waited for the head explosion to happen, the excitement letting a grin the size of Antarctica wash over his face. Then, from somewhere he heard a loud clank from above and lost eye contact, failing to see the body fall. The helicopter lurched left out over the water, dipped suddenly, and hit the surface before sinking below.

A few seconds later an explosion sent a massive plume of water skyward.

"No!" Julia screamed from the back of one of the SUVs. She reached for the door handle before BP threw himself back, his arm gripping hers.

"Julia, don't," BP said, his grip loosening as she crumbled into a heap. "We've got to get the kids clear."

Between sobs, Julia managed to say, "We have to find out."

BP kept his voice low. "There's nothing we can do. We have to keep to the plan."

Looking up, she nodded.

The moment Honcho saw Zane topple over and then the helicopter hit the water, Honcho had radioed Liz to send the boats. Time was still an enemy and getting the children to safety still priority one. Finished with the task, he got out of the SUV and pulled Emma and David close. Tearing up for the first time, Honcho let it go. He sobbed as he held them, feeling his own emotions intermixed with theirs as they sobbed uncontrollably with nothing to stop the sadness within. Honcho heard BP too, though quieter as he tried to comfort Julia. They had lost their brother. Julia her husband.

Emma and David, their beloved father.

A short horn blast interrupted the sorrow. Glancing towards the water, Honcho saw a small ferry approaching, guns panning the land behind him. Wanting to make it quick, he kissed the kids' foreheads and got back in the driver's seat to lead the way. The caravan fell behind and a crew ushered the vehicles aboard before quickly disembarking towards the Seattle skyline.

Stepping out, Honcho saw Liz for the first time. Red, tired eyes stared back. He could tell she had been crying, and when she saw him, they erupted. Walking over, he looked down, not sure what to do.

Liz closed the gap and wrapped her arms around Honcho. "I thought you were dead."

Putting his arms around her, he kissed the top of her head. "I thought you were too."

Pulling back, she glanced up into his eyes. "Ryan?"

Honcho began to sob. "The helicopter."

"What about Julia and the kids?"

He pointed over his shoulder. "All safe. Listen, there's a lot that's happened. We need to make this right. There's a hurricane coming and those kids are the only way we all make it out alive."

The words caught Liz's ear, and fear washed over her face. "What do you mean?"

The eyebrow found its way back. "The fleshy psychos are evolving into sub-human people. They told Ryan they want us all dead."

Liz's already pale skin lost a few shades. "Oh my god."

"Yup. If we don't' find a vaccine for all of us, as the virus is morphing in everyone, we might be next to turn."

Liz's heads bobbed up and down, the thought of a world totally void of actual normal people a scary proposition. She understood the ramifications, and knowing they were still threatened on all sides, knew it was on her to help or the world was lost. "Anything you need, just ask."

Leaning back, Honcho smiled. "Got any good beer?"

CHAPTER 82

Loss affects everyone to different degrees.

For Julia, it created a hole in her heart. Ryan was part of her world, her friend, companion, husband, and love of her life. Ryan was David's super hero. Dad was someone who David looked up to, and having finally gotten him back after three years to be close and feel his father's love and support, the loss crushed the boy's soul. Emma was shut off, not speaking, barely eating, a shell of a girl that had blossomed once again when her dad appeared.

Even Reg felt.

Not that Ryan's demise wasn't welcomed. His son had ruined the elder Carmichael's world and been a huge thorn in the side. Killed dozens of Reg and Mark's men. Reg had wanted his boy dead for so long, when it happened, a twinge of sadness popped its head out. The loss yanked Reg's heart strings, much to his udder dismay. He had hoped it was a truly exciting event to celebrate. For the first time, his emotions came back, though he kept it private.

Reg cried.

The tears a surprise, but he let them come. Mostly to get it out of the way so he could focus on his escape. He had to formulate a plan, and being lost in his former affection for his eldest son not conducive to planning his departure, hopefully with the children.

Honcho and BP dealt with Ryan's death in the only way they knew was a fitting tribute to their old friend. They got stinking drunk telling old stories and passed out at sunrise. Ryan would have done the same celebration of life for them if the tables were turned. Julia, after the kids were safely tucked in bed, joined the toasting to her husband. It felt awkward to participate when grieving was the appropriate emotion to wallow in, but Honcho and BP, who knew their deceased friend best, eased her in and allowed the sadness to quell, if only for a bit.

"To Ryan!" Honcho bellowed, his glass of Seattle's best homemade apocalypse whisky raised high.

BP's glass glinted as the warm firelight reflected on it. "To my oldest, and truly, best friend in the world. I will forever miss you."

Julia, too many ounces down her gullet, sloshed her glass back and forth. "To my Ryan. May your spirit be settled, and your wrath from Hell bring it on!"

As she swayed and nearly fell over, Liz caught the inebriated woman and excused herself to guide the drunken Julia to bed. Tucked next to Emma, Liz brushed the hair from Julia's face. "We *will* make this right."

Back with the celebrating men, Liz downed her glass and motioned for another. "What's next?"

Honcho glanced at BP, who snickered before leaning to the side and passing out. Smiling, Honcho filled their glasses and sat back in the chair.

"We get to work. Have Mary see what she can do to find a vaccine before it's too late. BP has to get back to his own kids so he'll be leaving as soon as things are settled here. Me? I've got to dig and find out more. There's something from the pie missing and it's been bugging the shit out of me."

Setting her drink down, Liz leaned back. "Like what?"

Honcho pursed his lips, not sure he had the words. "Everything is a lie within a lie. The truth so convoluted and layered that you could see it, and not realize what you are looking at even if it bit you in the ass. Fallacies we were told that somehow, were actually right. Facts we once believed, outright garbage. Sifting through it all a migraine on a scale to make your head explode."

"OK," Liz began, reaching over to touch Honcho's leg. "Got anything specific? Maybe talking through it with someone will help."

Honcho nodded. "Maybe. Here's the thing, I'm not sure there's even supposed to be a vaccine."

The statement caught Liz flat-footed. "Huh?"

"Julia said something to me days ago that I thought about, and then put it away. Think about it. Supposedly, this was all set in motion long ago. From what I've dug up and Ryan uncovered, what if everyone is supposed to turn now? The first round put trackers in the body. You see how it goes and then go to the next phase. When they realized they screwed up and couldn't fix it, the thinking changed. If you're bent on world order, why would you want to have to worry about resistance if you just had everyone in the same boat? I'm not talking about the Skinnies or as Ryan called them, Lurkers and Bolts. I mean, people like Reg and Mark, and Dennis' crazy followers. Those groups are pretty much the same, or close to it. Wouldn't it make sense to just let the people all become one miserable family to deal with the other threats?"

She had to let it sink in. Late to the game, Liz was playing catch-up to all of the information and experiences over the last years. Sitting there, from what she had gathered form the snippets of stories Honcho and BP told, Honcho might be onto something. "Say, that's the case. There's a sticking point as I see it. Seems to be competing goals among Mark and Reg. Mark was supposedly working a cure, right? All that research and body count he left in his wake. Reg and the one's behind all of this? I can see them wanting to do what you're thinking there. Why let Mark try to find a vaccine instead of stopping him? Why the hunt for the kids? Aren't they supposed to be valuable for a cure?"

As the words left her lips, Liz's horror at what raced through her mind emerged in vivid detail.

Honcho saw it, and frowned. "That's what I mean."

Deception on so many different levels and with such intricate details to pretend what was real, or even fake, could not be pasted together from the shards.

"I don't think it's ever been about a real cure for people. Mark's work a distraction, a side effect the nutjobs running the show didn't anticipate Mark would get traction on based on some of the old data I saw. Something to leak out and get people talking, to eventually submit and *obey*. I think it's been about preventing one, while trying to exploit the *powers* that are emerging from Emma and David. Julia mentioned an episode while they were captives and it seemed like scared mom talk, so I sort of went with it and then dismissed it. That had to have gotten run up the chain. You have your own little army of super kids at your disposal, you make anyone bow to you. Don't need a cure for that. I think that's when things divided on what the end game is supposed to be for us."

Liz held up a finger. "Didn't you say though that Mark was shocked to see what the kids did back at the airfield?"

Honcho took a sip. "I did. The extent of what the kids can do now probably has morphed into something bigger than what happened before. Given the loyalties and camps of supporters, it might have been kept from him. Julia did say that he wasn't always around with what was being done. Could have been him playing dumb, though it did seem to be a surprise."

"If it's all true, then why the ruse?"

The eternal answer to the fight between good and evil.

"Hope."

It made sense. Give people hope and they keep trying to persevere. If they learn there is none, they have nothing left to live for. Death knocks and they take the road.

"If you found out you were absolutely going to turn into one of the psychos, which one undetermined, would you want to keep living or decide to end it? You have nothing left to keep you going knowing that you will become a monster. People decide en masse to just forgo life, and it leaves you high and dry. No workers, no one to keep the machine running and oiled."

Liz's tears fell. "Do you really think so?"

Honcho sniffed from the cold air. "I can't peg it one hundred percent, but it seems logical, in a world where logic is in short supply."

Thinking it through, Liz wondered, "Pretend to give a shot, people gradually change into something if they're destined to, and if there is resistance from those with immunity, you have the twins, or worse, an army that makes sure no one gets in the way of *progress*?"

"That would be my take at this point in time."

"And if there was a cure?"

Honcho downed his whisky and poured another, this time two fingers worth. "Then, the whole charade comes crumbling down and the people have a chance to take the world back."

Getting up from her chair, Liz walked over and sat in Honcho's lap. He didn't resist. She touched his salt and pepper hair, feeling the texture she had longed missed. Caressed his cheeks and tugged on his gray goatee. Searching his brown eyes, she looked for the spark that once was there. It was faded, but she saw its embers stoked. "What do we do?"

The eyebrow was on full tilt. "We take those fuckers down."

CHAPTER 83

The needle pricks had lost their feeling.

Emma didn't move, just sat, as Mary took the last vile of blood she said she would need. David had provided his too and as a counter measure, Julia's blood as a comparison. Having Ryan's would have been a real treasure, but you take what good fortune you can and run with it.

"All done, kids. I should have enough to run my tests and see what I can do to help us change the world," Mary's forced grin offered to ease the tension in the room.

Emma had not spoken in days. David barely uttered three-word sentences, maybe added a fourth word if the response necessitated it. Julia was sick to her stomach watching her children lost in a depression that she couldn't remove. No matter what she tried, treats from the working bakery or stories about Ryan, nothing lifted the gloom from their spirits.

She hoped time would heal all of their wounds.

BP had left for home a day ago. He had been away for so long his beard scraggle was taking shape so he shaved before he left to look less disheveled than he felt inside. Promising to come back in a few weeks with his son and daughter to visit and take Emma and David for a mini-sub ride, he said his goodbyes and was gone.

Honcho had gone back to the Moose Lair to retrieve supplies and download information to sort through in Seattle while he kept tabs on Julia and the kids. Reg still had value, and peppering him with questions to connect more dots before chucking him in the Sound a pressing task. Back and trying to rekindle with Liz as the Brainer war ebbed and flowed, Honcho felt an unease. They hadn't even attempted to see if Ryan could have been saved from the helicopter, simply hopped ship and bailed. A patrol went later to check for bodies, but by the time they arrived, the helicopter lay deep enough in the cold water a cursory dive was out of the question without the right gear.

Maybe, the bastard has eleven lives. Could have a few on reserve. If he managed to survive, Ryan should have made his way already. Unless, he decided to go with the plan Z he was keeping hidden from Julia, Honcho thought before pushing the image away.

No one had that much luck.

Tucked in the corner of the upstairs apartment, the large window offering a view of the park below to distract when needed and a robust coffee on the small table to sip, Honcho worked the problem. When he came upon something requiring added explanation, he went to the basement and interrogated Reg. Sometimes, Reg confirmed a detail Honcho had five other pieces to help support. Other times, the elder Carmichael drifted into a delusion that could only be described as sorrow. He'd tell stories about Ryan that seemed genuine and full of love before he fueled his hate with obscenities and venom.

Then, the old man would sob.

On those occasions, Honcho wasn't sure it wasn't all an act, meant to ease the wall and potentially get too close to strike. Reg was a former soldier, just like his son, trained in specific arts to work his captors. When it felt real, Honcho listened and offered a nip of booze. When it was a ploy, the quick jolt of the cattle prod brought Reg back to reality.

The road to the whole truth a long, circuitous, journey ahead.

As he sat, sipping his coffee, Honcho caught sight of Emma and David, kicking a soccer ball in the park. Julia watched from a park bench, close, but not too close to make the kids feel she was being a helicopter mom. Honcho saw for the first time Emma smile, and David flashed a toothy grin. The moment passed, and they were back to running wild. The image seared Honcho's mind, a glimpse of the children possibly thawing out and finding a glimmer of life ebb inside their weary bones.

Wishful thinking, he knew.

Watching from his perch, Honcho should have noticed the sudden change. Should have caught the rigid movements below. Jumping up, he raced out of the room and out the apartment door, down the stairs and flinging the front door open, ran to the children. The fog in his brain didn't register what was happening, what he saw, his only aim to rescue Emma and David.

He was too late.

Emma stood, blood dripping from her nose before she collapsed. David was surrounded, the pile of bodies lying on the grass. Julia had managed to get within ten feet before she froze. As Honcho arrived, he caught more movement, and scooping up Emma, he yelled. "Follow me!"

Julia grabbed David and ran as Honcho led the way to the apartment. Letting Julia and David through first and with Emma over his shoulder, he slammed the door shut and hammered down the steel protective bar. Pointing to the stairs, David ran up with Julia and Honcho behind. At the next level, Honcho placed the barricade and this time, led them up to the third floor before hustling them inside.

The last set of bars lashed across the doorway.

Taking Emma to the bedroom, he gingerly placed her on top of the bed and ran for a wet rag. Coming back, he heard the sirens blaring and handing the rag to Julia so she could tend to her daughter, he joined David at the window.

"What happened, David?" Honcho barely got out.

David, his hands flexing open and closed, stared out. "They, they just came from nowhere. One minute, we're kicking the ball, the next, one is grabbing Emma and I, I just, I did what I had to do."

Honcho saw the blood on David's knuckles, and reaching to the small table, got a handful of tissues and wiped the blood away.

"What about Emma?"

David blew out a gust of air. "She saw them too. She looked at them, and they, they just started to *scream*. So loud, my ears hurt. Then, grabbed their heads, before, before, they just fell."

Honcho had missed the aftermath and came upon the end of the terror. He knew what had happened by the nature of the bodies and having witnessed what Emma and Davide had done at the airfield. The magnitude below was a far cry from before. There had to be a hundred bodies, some with their heads bleeding out from the ears and nostrils. Others, the ones David took out, were crumpled masses of flesh, their bones busted from punches to the face if he could reach that high first, the legs buckled in half for others before he pummeled them to death.

It was a massacre.

Honcho pulled David close, gave him a hug. "Are you, OK?"

David sniffed. "I'm fine. I'm not sure about Emma. I can't feel her thoughts. The last thing she said in her mind was her brain hurt from what she had to do to them."

Honcho looked over to Julia, who shook her head. Reaching for his radio, he stepped outside and came back a few minutes later. Behind him was Mary with a bag, and gently guiding Julia away and shooing them all out, she went to work.

Outside the room, Honcho handed out waters and waited. He had witnessed something miraculous, the words too much to speak. They all knew it, the powers Emma and David showcased against an onslaught of Skinnies, Un-dead, what Ryan called Bolts. Every single one of them now lifeless, the retreating horde that managed to live, screaming as they vanished back to their dens. Emma and David's evolution soon to be shared with an evil that would want them dead.

Or, worse.

When Mary walked out of the bedroom a half hour later and pulled the door shut, she tried to contain the grim expression. Julia jumped up immediately, and Mary eased her back in the recliner. A gentle hand rub to soothe a worried mother.

"Julia, she's not hurt. She looks fine. But," Mary sighed, "She's out."

Julia didn't understand. "Like, asleep?"

Honcho caught the inflection. "I think Mary means she's not conscious. My guess? Her body used up so much energy it's shut down to recharge. Sound about right?"

Mary nodded. "It's like she tired herself out. A deep sleep, one that she's not waking from anytime soon. Her body is spent, and has to get her strength back."

Julia sunk back in the recliner. "Can we do anything?"

Mary patted Julia's leg. "I'll get her on an IV for fluids and some kind of cocktail to give nutrients. She's zapped, but she'll come out of it. Promise."

David whispered, and realizing it was too low to hear, raised his voice. "Mom, Emma is going to be OK. I can hear her again. She's exhausted. She said not to worry. She just needs to rest."

It wasn't totally true, but he had to give Mom some hope.

Stepping to Honcho, Mary leaned in. "What the hell was that? Where did they come from without warning?"

Honcho motioned to the kitchen. When they got there, he kept his voice low. "I was watching the kids play one minute. The next? I see creepers all around. No warning, nothing. Like they just went poof from thin air."

Mary shook her head. "How?"

Honcho shrugged, and then the picture hit. "They're getting smart. Probably watching our defenses and found an opening. We've got to rethink how they act. They're *becoming*, and if we aren't careful, more of what's happened is on the way."

"What do you mean?"

Honcho leaned over to Mary's ear. "Those crazies that managed to flee saw what the kids did to their friends. They're going to tell the others. Emma and David are marked. Super big threats to those weirdos. They will probably come back with a vengeance."

Mary's eyes were wide. "Oh my. Shit. Can we do anything to stop them?"

Honcho frowned. "Get that vaccine done ASAP. And, test it on those bastards to see if it will change them. Long shot, but I'm all for the Hail Mary pass at this point."

She nodded. "I'll put in overtime. Let's keep this quiet. Close to only a few. It gets out, the panic might be too much."

Honcho agreed. Unless they had to spill, better to prepare and protect than create a commotion.

"I hope we survive this," Mary sighed.

Given all the intel and bits and pieces he managed to rummage from all the classified documents blacked out and the ones he ended up finding the original scans, the outcome looked grim. If the Un-dead were really on the path to transformation and their brains working even one percent of normal, the future was a black hole. Ready to suck life in and compress it until no more. Cooperation, thought, and the capacity to make *decisions* loomed large as a metamorphosis changed the enemy into a formidable opponent. With the numbers in their favor, if they really got their act together, survivors were odds on favorites to be wiped out.

Humanity needed a miracle.

A reassuring hand. "Find us the answer to our woes and we can win. Just have to have some faith."

Mary shifted and begged with her eyes for some reassurance. "You really think so?"

Honcho smiled. "Piece of cake."

CHAPTER 84

"Commander Williams?"

It had to be a dream. Not sure if the words were real.

A slight cough, muffled, to keep it contained. "Commander Williams? Are you awake?"

He caught the words in his ringing ears. Head full of fog and eyes glued shut, trying to focus hurt like hell.

"Commander Zane Williams? Are you awake?"

He pried open his left eye and made a vain attempt to track the voice.

"Commander, I'm over here. Don't struggle, you're lucky to be alive."

Eye back to closed, He took in a deep breath, held it, and exhaled. Trying to move his left arm, it didn't budge. Right arm free, it came across his chest, to find the left was held down with a restraint and from what he could feel, an IV line running down the length of his forearm with tape to hold it.

"Fluid and med line. Please leave it alone. We'll remove it when you're back to normal."

He huffed an acknowledgement.

"Commander, you are one lucky man. If we hadn't seen what happened with the helicopter, you would be dead. Managed to scoop you up and get you to safety before the head hunters came. Got that bullet out and set you to heal."

The words didn't make sense.

His body hurt like a son of a bitch. The aches and pains as if he had been back in high school playing tight end and linebacker. After a Friday night game doing double duty on offense blocking the pass rush and taking hits across the middle catching balls and then bashing running backs and quarterbacks while on D, the bumps and bruises requiring a hot soak to ease the muscles. Worse than the days avoiding bullets and thrashing the body around with a full seventy-pound pack and loaded with gear.

A hundred and twenty pounds when a full ruck required it.

Managing to pry both eyes open this time, he could see he was in the back of a vehicle. The smell familiar of old and stale military years of service. Catching the interior of what he recognized as an old Humvee, he was in the back on some type of gurney, this one configured with the box end instead of slant back. Looking up, he saw an unfamiliar face, young and not battle scarred. Blond crew cut, baby stubble that was probably a month's worth that barely popped the surface of the skin. Vibrant blue eyes that weren't hazed by failure or defeat.

A newbie to the fighting game.

"Ah, Commander, you're coming around. Jeez, Sir, I was worried for a minute. You've been out for a few months. Mumbling and fighting about so much we had to restrain you. Couldn't make any of it out, but it seemed like you were in the fight of your life."

The boy was amped up. Why? He didn't know.

"Sir? Sorry about your men. Someone took them all out. All we caught was the aftermath by the time we arrived. Got caught up in some war with the people walled up in Seattle and a group of head hunter mercs. Ugly battle going on there. Brought out of the woodwork the crazies to feast on the bodies and avoiding them choked us up."

He managed to slightly turn to face the young solider. The frown on his face registered.

"Oh my! Sorry, Sir. Apologies. Here I am rambling on and we've never met. Lieutenant Jamison, Sir. Part of Mr. Carmichael's detachment. We were on our way back to the airport when we saw you all leave. Couldn't catch you on the radio and because of the chaos, by the time we backtracked we missed the engagement. Wish we could have been there to assist."

The face softened a touch.

"Radios are still silent and haven't been able to get Mr. Carmichael for orders. Same with Mr. Simpson and his group. It's a bit unusual to not hear from anyone for this long."

He finally spoke. "How do you know who I am?"

Lieutenant Jamison looked sheepish, and his cheeks turned red. "Mr. Carmichael radioed before he went silent. Mentioned a backup plan to assist in finding the children if things his way at the sub base didn't pan out. Had us tasked getting transportation ready for our haul. Saw the shuttle come from above, so assumed the plan was in play."

Anger, tethered with restraint, responded. "No, I asked how do *you* know who I am?"

Lieutenant Jamison's face showed fear. "Sorry, Sir. Mr. Carmichael mentioned your patch on your plate carrier. Said I'd know it was you by it. The Reaper patch. Zombie Crew."

The Reaper.

Seemed that the hidden meaning behind the old patch was the lone identifying mark from his past. Co-opted for a different purpose. Just, not in the same way.

"Where are we headed?"

The Lieutenant cleared his throat. "You've been in a coma for three months, I think? Brought you back to base while we waited for Mr. Carmichael and Mr. Simpson to hopefully radio. Nothing from either of them, so I'm guessing whatever happened with you and your team got them too. With all the chaos around Seattle, we haven't been able to scout much. I received orders that when you started to wake, to get you prepped for transport. Was told to deliver you to a waiting transport at the Bremerton airport. Don't know who, but they'll take you East. They want to meet you."

They?

"Who are *they?*"

The question caught the Lieutenant by surprise? "They? You know, The Order. They want to meet you. Seems they have their own plans for the children. We have a detachment on the way that's to siege the city and wait for you to return."

"So, this transport? You have no idea who they are?"

Jamison shook his head. "Never met them before."

"Are they expecting us?"

The Lieutenant shook his head. "At some point. Haven't been in radio contact with them as things are a bit haywire with comms. We show when we show. You started waking up, so we got you prepped and here we are, heading there now."

The grin on his face would have been out of place if it was any other time. The Lieutenant probably thought it was there because the man was alive, excited about meeting the leaders of the cause, or that he was wanting to execute some secret plan that from the whispers Jamison had heard along the vine, was going to change the planet and humanity.

Laying back down as he ignored Jamison's comment, he closed his eyes again. The news was a surprise he didn't expect. It sent a chill down his spine, even a slight tremor that he caught and pushed deep down. Battered and worn, he needed his strength for what was coming his way. Less than one hundred percent meeting the ones running the show was not how an old special operator wanted to present himself to the glorious rulers of the new world. He had to be whole, his body refreshed and ready to go.

"Jamison, right? I'm feeling a bit queasy. Need to puke. Can we stop?"

Jamison reached over and tapped the back of the driver's seat. "Sure thing, Sir."

Three months was a long time to be incapacitated and off the grid. Jamison mentioned a war between the Seattleites and the psycho head hunters, with Reg Carmichael and Mark Simpson radio silent. That was news he could work with moving forward. Sitting up, he saw it was pitch black out and just the three of them, unless another vehicle was in support.

What were the odds?

He needed to handle the situation here to get back on his feet and get his bearings. His physical fitness at being down for so long was suspect. He hoped they filled his body up with enough nutrients and proteins to combat muscles loss and definitely hydration. Weakened muscles and cramping were enemies to what lay ahead. There was so much to do and so little time.

"Got some gauze and tape?"

Rummaging around, Jamison found some supplies.

Taking what Jamison handed over and closing the IV line, he unfastened the restraint holding down his arm. Ripping off some tape, he pulled the needle out, placed the gauze, and wrapped some tape. Opening and closing his fist, he felt feeling return to his fingers. Satisfied, he sat up and rotated his shoulders around. Sore, but they worked.

The Humvee came to a stop and Jamison moved from the jump seat and exited to let him out the door. Going around behind, he bent over and held his stomach, retching and coughing.

"Sir? Can I get you anything?"

He glanced up, wiping his mouth with his right hand, before standing upright. "You sure can," he groaned as his left arm shot out and caught Jamison in the throat.

As Jamison reactively put a hand to his crushed windpipe, he grabbed the Lieutenant and pulled out the soldier's knife from its sheath on his belt. Quick thrusts under the right armpit to severe the artery and a final to the right temple, and Jamison was gone. Wiping the blade clean, he walked around the side of the vehicle and caught the driver's attention. Bent over and looking up, he motioned for help. The driver popped open his door and stepped out.

The blade hit its mark.

Rushing over, he yanked the knife from the throat of the driver and gave him a final blow to the eye and twisted. The body slumped to the ground. Pulling the man away from the Humvee, he pillaged the bodies for clothes and gear. Smiling at the ease of the kills, he stepped into the Humvee and adjusted the seat. There was work to do, and he needed to put the plan into motion.

First, he needed to make a call.

CHAPTER 85

"I'm telling you, the data and results are what they are."

Honcho shook his head.

Mary pointed to the cages. "Look? Does that seem normal to you?"

He saw it, though given the three months of sleepless nights, war with the Skinnies and Dennis Stohl's horde of losers, and rifling through tons of old intel to try and decipher outstanding questions lingering and gnawing his brain, his eyes might be playing tricks on him.

"Seriously, this is not what I expected, at all."

Honcho walked over and tapped the glass. The sudden movement slamming into the side jolted the big man backwards. "Damn! That little beast is raging worse than a club kid on a bad Molly trip."

Mary frowned, the gloom in her voice heavy. "If it does this to a lab rat, imagine what it will do to a human?"

Honcho wasn't lost on the visual observation.

Sitting down, Mary reached for a bottle under her desk, and grabbing two glasses, poured drinks. "Sit, and take this. We need it."

Never one to turn down a drink, Honcho pulled up a chair. Picking up the glass, he asked, "So, what's the occasion?"

Mary reached over and clinked his glass. "To, the end of the world." She downed her booze in one gulp.

Surprised at the pessimism, Honcho took a sip and coughed. Harsh like gasoline, he'd been spoiled by the good stuff. This was the kind you gulped in one shot. So, he finished up.

"Another?"

Honcho nodded. Mary obliged with a bit extra. He titled the glass and swallowed hard.

"Thanks."

Mary smiled. "You're welcome."

Leaning back in the chair, Honcho began to sort intel in his head. There had been so much to cover and with Mary's work, connecting dots was a disaster. Truth so much a crapshoot and lies like sticky peanut butter. Which way was up or down a coin flip.

"I don't think we're at the end of the world, yet," Honcho offered. "We're still on top of the food chain and managing our way outside the gates."

Mary stared, her eyes dark and brooding. "Not sure I agree with you there. My tests don't lie."

"Then, walk me through it."

Mary sighed, poured another round, and decided the white board was the best approach.

A half hour later, the board color-coded with no room to write another word, Mary sat back down and poured more drinks. The writing, so to speak, was on the wall. If the calculations were right, and her data accurate, the tests run painted a bleak picture. As Honcho absorbed it all in, cataloged off and checked against lists, the eyebrow took on a life all its own.

"What is it?"

Honcho crossed his arms. "I should have seen this."

Mary downed another shot. "Speak."

A huge sigh. "What if we've been wrong this whole time?"

"Huh?"

Honcho motioned for another sip. "We have assumed that everything has had a specific purpose. Mark was working on a maintenance vaccine, one to curb the effects of the virus in people. You don't want to be miserable, puking your guts out every so often, the headaches and stomach problems, or potentially turning into one of the dead out there, you obey and they'll give you the shot. That was his work, right?"

Mary nodded. "From what I was familiar with and you've told me, yes."

Leaning back, Honcho continued. "Then, we have Reg, Ryan's dear old dad. He wanted the kids more than anything. Word got leaked about their abilities and what they could do. Ryan too, though it was one of those love/hate kind of relationships. Get Ryan to turn and be the enforcer of evil, then it morphed into just killing him. Mark though outright wanted him dead. Why? Seems to be two very different wants, right?"

Mary leaned on her elbows. "Go on."

The eyebrow flickered. "So, you get Emma and David's blood and start up on a serum to test. Three months later, here we sit. Those rats are feeling it, and it's not a pretty sight. Now, I'm stretching some logic here, but the ones based off your blood are passive, docile. Then, the ones with your blood and the kids? Same effect. The ones with just the kids? Violent is an understatement. Seem familiar?"

Mary's head titled to the side. Something registered, and she tapped the table. "Not everyone got the initial vaccine and turned into a crazy. In fact, there are survivors living inside of here and all over the place. If they got a maintenance shot, who's to say they don't end up on a killing spree?"

Honcho nodded. "You didn't get a shot then, you're not getting one now is my guess. If you want obedience, how do you corral the ones that won't follow along?"

The lightbulb went from dim to bright white. "You force it."

"How do you do that?"

Mary's face went white. "Airborne."

Honcho grimaced. "Exactly. I think that's why Ryan found Reg at the sub base. He was trying to get missiles. Use them to spread the vaccine. For those it wouldn't affect, no harm. Take away the ills and they fall in line. For those who buck the system and won't get a shot, you turn them and let the crazies go wild getting rid of the ones that won't bend the knee. Reduce the threat to your rule either way."

Seeing Honcho's eyes wide, Mary knew there was more to the story. "There's something else, isn't there?"

As the color faded from his brown skin, Honcho wiped the sweat on his forehead. "Reg told Ryan this all has been in play for a very long time. What if they knew all of this would happen, but there was a hiccup trying to contain it, and now they're trying to fix the problem? What if Ryan's blood was the seed tested and they knew, they knew what would happen to people?"

Mary was pale. "Like in, human trials for years that predicted this?"

Honcho nodded. "Yes. So, to avoid it, they worked the problem, only to royally screw up and miscalculate as their first vaccine when they decided to roll out their master plan failed and the boosters only made it worse. Throw in all the nasty home remedies and a cesspool leeched to the surface. The fluoride in the blood is the wicked step mom that started it all."

"My God."

"The ones that turned into monsters? Those nutjobs became population control while they put the brain trust together to figure out their mess. By that time, their brains all mush, the logical reasoning was gone. But, you can't have everyone turning into them? So, you now have to get the kids blood to remedy the fuck up. They can't have loose cannons around head hunting people when it's done. So, the ones that come back from psychotic mania, they keep. The rest who are resistant to the vaccine and the Un-dead out there, they eliminate. First, you up the game and rain down vengeance to get people begging to be saved."

The cloud of confusion began to dissipate.

"What about the powers the kids have?"

Honcho pursed his lips. "All else fails, you have the kids to get them to obey, or let the wonder twins kill them all."

CHAPTER 86

"What damn idiot is pinging me at this hour?"

Checking the nightstand clock, Honcho swore a few expletives before tossing his legs over the mattress' side. Shaking his head, the incessant beeping was about to give him a coronary when he ripped the person responsible for interrupting his sleep a new asshole.

Sluffing over to the dresser, he scanned the top, searching for the culprit. With a few radios to choose from, all set to specific channels and a few collected from Mark and Reg's dead soldiers, he had to wait a few seconds to find the right one.

"No."

Picking up the radio, he checked the channel. Hearing nothing, he figured the batteries were dying so he flipped it over, popped the back, and rummaging around, threw in another set. Setting it down and turning back to bed, the beeping started again.

"What the hell?"

Shuffling back, Honcho picked the radio up, and stared. He didn't like the joke and definitely hated being woken up in the pitch black of the night. Pissed off, he hit the mic and let loose.

"Fuck off asshole."

Static answered back.

Satisfied the jerk playing around would get the hint, Honcho took a step towards slumber before the radio chirped again. His anger raged and he nearly threw the things at the wall. The channel was a secure one and given the technology, hacking it was damn near impossible. Arm raised and about to slam it home, the beeps stopped him cold. A pattern, vaguely familiar.

Morse code.

Suddenly awake and focused, he listened, taking in the beeps and mentally trying to decode in his head. The fog and cobwebs winning out, he grabbed a pen and paper and frantically scribbled.

The words didn't make any sense.

Probably his memory wasn't translating correctly, so Honcho took a breath and listening again, this time writing down the pattern. Dots and dashes, until he had the brief breakdown visible. Staring and trying to remember the letters, he read the pattern.

.. / .- -- / .- .- .-.. .. ...- .

His eyes weren't sure if they were seeing it correctly, so he tried to decipher again in his head. Each time, the same three-word phrase appeared. Confused, he closed his eyes, took a breath, and did it again, only to come up with the same answer. Over and over.

I am alive.

Furtively glancing around the room, expecting a ghost to materialize, Honcho had to sit down on the bed. His energy was sapped, his heart racing a million beats. There was no way he wasn't dreaming. Closing his eyes, he knew if he opened them, he would be horizontal under the covers, woken up by a nightmare. Stress, sure, he knew that was screwing with him. The last days a blur and too much riding on the future.

Get it together Honcho.

A deep breath and letting it go, he slowly popped one eye open and then the other. The ceiling above a welcome sight as he awoke. Just a dream, a really bad one that he hoped would fade away.

No such luck.

He found himself sitting on the edge of the bed, perspiration beading down his forehead, the salty sweat burning his eyes. There was no way he wasn't imagining it. He was losing his mind, that was the answer. He knew the day would come when the marbles cracked and the old noggin' decided to let the yolk run out. Old age finally hitting and doing what it did best. Time was a bitch as it took the enjoyment of life and suddenly thrust you into a descent towards death. Arthritis, a bad hip, the gray hairs in all the wrong places. You had so many great years to shine and then in a blink, the decline when everything went to crap and the body decided to begin its rot.

More beeps.

Looking over, he held his breath so he wouldn't miss the words. Focused, he translated. As the last word hit, the radio went dead. Jumping to the dresser, Honcho picked up the radio and checked. He must have put in a bad set of batteries as the display was dead.

"What is it?" Liz yawned from behind.

Honcho sat, frozen in fear. He didn't know how to even begin to answer. Three months face down in muck trying to work a problem that had as its equation a set of variables that didn't begin to add up and pointed to a number that wasn't real, he felt the strain eating away his sanity. At every turn what got uncovered a potential storm if what was once true shattered into a million pieces and for every lie that was revealed false, a roadblock back to square one.

A jigsaw puzzle with so many thousands of pieces that were supposed to fit, yet even with the box cover as a cheat, the edges didn't line up and forcing the corners in simply didn't work.

Reaching over to rub his back, Liz asked, "What's going on?"

Honcho shuddered, and she felt it.

"Is it me?"

He shook his head.

"What then?"

Falling back, the huge breath scared Liz. She moved to him, cradling Honcho in her hands.

"Talk to me."

Looking into her eyes, the fear growing with each second, he finally managed to speak. A whisper that had no sound.

"What?"

Clearing his throat, the words came. "The Ghost Reaper is alive and Hell is about to get a new god to rule them."

ABOUT THE AUTHOR

Jason McDonald is an American author who writes suspense and psychological thrillers steeped in twists and turns that keep you guessing and make you think. Stepping outside the typical writer's box, he bases his books in current events, historical references and personal experience, and then turns it all into a fictionalized world for your entertainment.

His debut novel, Pandemic-19, created a storm as it grows in readership across the globe as one of the best original works of fiction to tackle what happens when the world we thought we knew collapses and a new one emerges from the ash.

With multiple novels waiting in the wings, he is now devoting his time to publishing his library of works for his readers and followers to thoroughly enjoy an escape with new stories.

Away from writing, Jason loves to spend quality time with his family, enjoying the outdoors, travel, and watching his imaginative twins grow. They inspire, support, and provide the drive to pay it forward.

For more information visit: jason-mcdonald.com
Follow on X: JasonMcD_Writer

www.ingramcontent.com/pod-product-compliance
Lightning Source LLC
Chambersburg PA
CBHW021214220726
48287CB00014B/226